Anna Browne Jenner was born in Egypt and raised in Britain during World War II. She was active in British theatre before she immigrated to the Finger Lakes, New York, with her husband, a U.S. Air Force officer, and had a family. Jenner has written plays for stage and radio.

To Edward Jenner Sr., my late husband, whose discussions about Sir Algernon started his story.

Anna Jenner

SIR ALGERNON

AUSTIN MACAULEY PUBLISHERS™
LONDON • CAMBRIDGE • NEW YORK • SHARJAH

A CIP catalogue record for this title is available from the British Library.

ISBN 9781788785693 (Paperback)
ISBN 9781788785709 (Hardback)
ISBN 9781528955690 (ePub e-book)

www.austinmacauley.com

First Published (2019)
Austin Macauley Publishers Ltd.
25 Canada Square
Canary Wharf
London
E14 5LQ

My deepest thanks to Gail Jenner for patiently and professionally setting up my 'real-writers' computer. Also prior to Gail, David Burt who helpfully supported my writing. Top of the list too is Ed Jenner Jr. who brought in Jack Myers for magically righting this screen whenever I met with technical blocks. A big thanks to Peter Jenner, who thoughtfully straightened out my finances, so that they work. Susan Jenner's generous support and uplift have been dependable and constant, and Maddie Jenner's too from faraway Virginia. To Ron Mc Dougal, my deepest gratitude for valiantly digging into the 'Algernon legend' and making enticing sense of it. Big thanks also for support from friends Craig Horning, the late Dawn Henderson Brown, and Dawn's daughter Lydia. Also Angela Bailey's alike-thinking impassioned explosions when 'the book, the book' became too much. Long ago thanks are due Professors Griffiths and Kolpacoff of Hobart and William Smith Colleges for their kindness and expertise in guiding my literary craft. To all of these many contributing people, my relentless gratitude for helping 'Sir Algernon' to have life while not forgetting the supreme encouragement and peace due the serene, rippling waters of 'Lake Seneca'.

Synopsis of 'Sir Algernon'

Sir Algernon Cholmondley-Rute had never cared for his 'Downtown Abbey' cousins, though both were from old family wealth that had helped build the British Empire. Avoiding an 'Abbey' family reunion, Algernon celebrates his retirement from the Foreign Service by going off to tour the Finger Lakes, New York State, U.S.A. Being a Cholmondley-Rute, Algernon is expected to raise his aristocratic hyphenated name. Not easy when Eton's prestigious name also taught him to respect buggery which sent him towards divorcing his wife. Fortunately, the influence of his morally radiant mother had also sunk into Algernon; though as she died when he was adolescent, his mother's better traits did not quickly emerge.

Exploring Western New York State, U.S.A., Algernon stops for the night. The inn's owner and her 'live-in' admire Algernon's Lamborghini and arrange for him to meet their good friend needing a pedigree buyer for his mansion and winery. Reluctantly, Algernon joins them; though confronting the mansion, he is extremely shocked! To the last carved Victorian corbel, this mansion was the exact materialization of sketches he'd made during unspeakably boring Moscow Foreign Service meetings!

Purchasing this enchanted house, Algernon meets Laburnum, a 'Great Civilizations' scholar and a clairvoyant, who sometimes gets it right. Algernon's winery employees are bewildered when he refers to himself as 'One' instead of 'I', but Laburnum sees he is adjusting from high-flown international diplomacy and helps him understand rural Americans. Algernon's respect for Laburnum as a woman friend is unprecedented as he'd vowed to avoid another legal debacle after his father Lord Cholmondley-Rute's arranged marriage for him to a faithless blueblood notoriously failed. Contingent on that union, His Lordship lost a considerable packet and land for the manor. Enraged, he made sure that the Foreign Service posted Algernon a good, long-distance from England.

Internationally awarded for his brilliant diplomacy, Algernon is delighted that here in the Finger Lakes, U.S.A., Laburnum understands his career frustrations. Platonically, he and she research 'golden ages' together, till one black night their restrained desires exploded in a night of exquisite sex-love. Present was Laburnum's dog, one of three estate dogs that are secretly not surprised that nuclear arms treaties fail as they condemn the terrifying world mess human beings have made in getting along with each other. These brilliant dogs debate what they see and hear from their human owners and determine to keep a strict watch on Algernon and Laburnum's researching.

Foreword

I first met Anna Jenner when she was preparing several of her short plays to be performed on radio. Having participated in a few of these, I came to know her to be a superb writer and a wonderful person. I am, therefore, honored to be asked to provide a brief foreword to her latest work.

'Sir Algernon' chronicles the journey—both physical and emotional—taken by a recently retired, high-level British diplomat. Restricted for his whole life to date by his status as a member of the English ruling class, he decides to escape his dysfunctional family, and the narrowness of his profession, with a trip to the United States.

There he finds—either by serendipity or fate—a near replica of the 'Supreme Habitat' about which he has fantasized and sketched during his inattentiveness in the dull meetings at the end of his postings. In addition to this property, a coteries of locals alternately befuddle and enchant him as examples of the 'lowliness', from which he has been excluded due to his position in the British upper class.

One person in particular—the 'witch-woman'—who resides on his property as a tenant, confuses and exhilarates him. The development of their relationship parallels his battle between a fear of becoming 'provincial' and his growing enjoyment of his newly formed outlook.

All the characters (including three very erudite canines) are so skillfully drawn that a reader will feel he knows them very well, very quickly. The same is true of the descriptions of upstate New York where most of the story takes place.

Good fiction can leave a reader wondering what happened next for its cast of characters. Barring an official sequel, the future will require of the reader a little of the imaginative musing which Algernon applied to his idealized 'Supreme-Habitat' fantasy. Such an undertaking could be well-worth the effort.

My advice: Have at it! Enjoy this very fascinating tale. Employ your own creative faculties to expand the narrative as you best see fit.

R.E. McDougal – 'Supreme Generalist'

Chapter 1
The Cholmondley-Rutes

What in all Hades was happening to me?

I'm not a man to ever ask such a question. Though modesty aside, Lord, how did I have the wits to successfully soar through all those decades of my highest-level diplomatic career? Tell me that!

Gazing the wall of white cloud through the plane window, I must—*though I just can't*—begin to understand—what I don't understand, is—how in all sweet-smelling Arcadia has all this happened???

Look, Algernon, pull yourself together! You've got the home you wanted, so should it matter how you got it? For all the petrified saints, just let go of it. Accept the glass of wine from the nice stewardess and relax! Let recent events emerge, naturally—till fully and comprehensively getting a grip on it all—mastering it?

Very well. *All right!* Best to start with what I do know. This trip back to the Cholmondley-Rute Manor, U.K., is strictly to settle purchasing the Runditz Estate in the Finger Lakes, New York State, U.S.A. – just that! I'll also select from Mother's fine antiques what's suitable for my beloved 'Supreme Habitat'—as I call my extraordinary property find!

I suppose that this trip should also be to inform my family I was buying property over in America and intending to live there; though I wouldn't use the word 'immigrating' yet, no need to feed their cynicism.

My 'Supreme Habitat' had become a far more expansive purchase than I could have ever expected; because apart from the mystery of how its existence came about, I will be running its winery. *Algernon, won't I?*

Once into Gatwick, I rented a dull little airport car and expediently drove out to the Cholmondley-Rute Manor. Straightening my body walking through its Great Hall with its suits of dusty armor showing off its black eye-holes, and all its tarnished dangling weaponry, one was reminded afresh of my family's brittle pride in their anachronistic capitalism. Regardless of having been bred here among centuries of this historically outstanding manor et cetera, my fondness for the old place is noticeably more strained. Everyone now in the whole wide world knows that equality is beneficial, not only for equalizing gender and incomes but for contrasting the manor's ambiance with the quaint status quo. I found it all so impossibly cloying, one wondered why my ancestors had fought for the Magna Carta? Monarchical as Britain still is, it had been plentifully slashed with secular coups necessitating political and religious openness.

The following morning—having made sure I was off to the city early—Brother Gillie was using his limo, so I had to take that rum little Austin Healey Cornwall Classic I'd rented at the airport. Admittedly, it did dodge vehicles neatly—double-deckers too—and got one where one wanted to go. Being nimble it could cut through beloved old London's alleyways, even those with traffic-prohibiting steel posts if one cunningly slid between them—wrong-headed anyway despite the ever-increasing traffic. Though I have to admit, this bourgeois little vehicle got one where one needed to be.

Ollie, the family solicitor, was of the generation whose professional disinterest, in my request, for a large sum of money to be sent over to America, was assumed with a loaded smile of nearly stationary dentures. The elderly here often insist on private dentistry for keeping themselves well-distanced from the National Health or for fear of looking like the hordes disporting gleaming, snow-white smiles! Such a mistake! As Ollie had no need to ask questions of the son of his ancestrally related Lord Cholmondley-Rute, we'd seemed to be on our way, with his rather unsanitary smile accompanied by umpteen, dithery head-nods.

Pulling over a Jacobean chair to sit opposite the bent old fellow, Ollie set his eyes on the dusty chandelier to sing-song, "So C.R.'s to give up running the manor, hmmm?" His hum was appropriately forlorn as the grim smile sustained. One informed him that Father had given up manor management over a year ago. "Only the tomb will keep that old warrior from his, ahem, work." Once again, one sternly look straightened him out that Father was already retired, but Ollie's absent smiles and rocked head showed no further comprehension, and one recalled that Gillie had joked about Ollie not being much of a listener. It was imperative I caught a quick return flight back to where I most dearly wanted to be, so I again pressed my request. But Ollie's vacant nods continued under his waxen smile turned caustic, because his attention had wandered to fumble some yellowing forms. Reaching across his massive desk, he displayed graying armpits to his once-black suit; then he dropped a page or two on the carpet, also two paperclips, and even his fountain pen. Buzzing in some anxious-looking young clerk, who retrieved each, I wondered how on this pleasant planet Brother Gillie ever got any manor business accomplished! Father, 'the old warrior', had undoubtedly dished out threatened jabs galore if Ollie didn't keep it moving; and Brother Gilmore, one presumed, would have done a fair job of emulating Father.

When this old duffer finally produced some outdated form for one's business transaction, one's heart sank. Neither he nor his clerk could find this year's, making one resentfully have to have a second appointment. This inefficiency was abominably maddening because except for this financing, my American property purchase was well on its way. *What on this earth had led me to believe that all it would take was this appointment made faster by one's family solicitor to get the 'Runditz Property', legally and morally, my own? For Gillie's sake, one strained to not histrionically fling up my hands and leave for a properly functioning solicitor, as—more of Ollie's smile, smile, numerous spastic head nods et cetera*—having flown all this way, I was profoundly put out that one's undertaking could not be simply concluded; and before leaving that musty outdated office, I gave the clerk my fiercest wealthy old family grimace, along with a venomous phrase or two to make sure he'd compensate for Ollie's selfish refusal to retire.

With images of my 'Supreme Habitat' keeping me passionately desiring it; and because without doubt, age had made Father yet more intolerable, this trip back to the family would have to be brief. Coming in on this atmosphere was not improved by Father's constant demands. Jasmine, one's sister-in-law, had written how loathsome his demanding had become; and after my arrival had received its usual tepid welcome, if one's patriarch got into one of his white-faced ravings, one did what I'd always done since boyhood and held one's breath, as if awaiting the dispersal of that despised odor filling a train in a tunnel. Though Father had developed more antisocial peculiarities, and it had to be faced that since giving up the manor's management, our parent's personal demands needed far stronger handling. How Gilmore, Jasmine, one's sister-in-law, or their children put up with—what they referred to as—his 'occurrences' challenged one's imagination! One couldn't blame their children for having rushed off to boarding school or university, as it relieved their bed-wetting, or so Jasmine, let on.

Jasmine also shamefully told about the day before when a kitchen maid had been bending to clean the main drawing-room's fireplace, and Father whipped his walking stick up from his wheel chair and royally goosed her. Jasmine and their doctor had sat all afternoon talking the despondent young maid out of overdosing, till finally she refused to work around Father's unpredictable behavior anyway, making rehiring more of a constant problem for Jasmine. One certainly felt sorrow for Jasmine, who tried most with Father, because Gilmore persistently denied that Father had problems.

One hadn't been sitting at the Cholmondley-Rute dinner table for two minutes before I took in what being over-90 can do to certain men. Making the most of his ludicrously childish voice, Father insisted Jasmine summon their cook. Gillie, one noticed, bordered on objecting; but before he did so, the cook came in as Father stood from his wheelchair; and with Jasmine and I rousing to what he was up to, took up his plate and tipped the steaming plateful of stew over the cook's chest, legs, shoes and the Persian carpet as she stood screaming and retching into Jasmine's instantly offered serviette. This as Father screeched on about the food being 'sewerage' between his thrilled, nocturnal animal noises.

"Really! Oh really!" Jasmine was aghast.

Remaining seated, Gilmore shouted, "Can't you clean her up in the kitchen? Won't anyone pay attention to me-e? My stew is cold!"

"Forget yourself for once, Gillie!" Jasmine curtly reminded him. "You could have watched what shenanigans your father was up to."

"Your job!" Gilmore censured, "I've far too much to do to spend time on…" and beneath his breath, "…that, belly-aching basket-case."

Huge and too stolid to resist, Maudie came in to stand before Father and iron-grip him by the wrists for dumping him back in his wheel chair. Militantly, she pushed him off to his study, as kitchen staff swarmed in to clean the messed up insulted cook and the carpet.

Jasmine let on that part of the trouble with Father's 'debilitation' was that he could pick a time the household was into various pursuits to slip out of his wheelchair and creep about in his socks. Recently, he had crept beside Gilmore and next to his ear had loudly blown his old safari horn. Delighted he'd nearly caused Gillie cardiac arrest, Father's insanely shrill laughter filled that wing of the manor—or he'd hold his breath between devilishly exhaled snorts. On another legendary occasion, this creeping away of Father's had even fooled Maudie, his personal aide, who did a superb job of 'maintaining Father's dignity', as Gilmore directed. When Maudie discovered Father's wheelchair empty, after an all-out search, Horace the factotum discovered Father with his trousers down squatted behind a Great Hall pillar. Only Horace's covering for his defecating the marble floors saved the 'old warrior' from Jasmine's insistence they institutionalize him.

Lord, how quickly can one get out of here?

Father's previously tyrannical nature should have warned the family that with age he would embrace this malevolent jester's role. Nothing new here, his life-long spite had just grossly increased, which sorrowfully one was catching up with one's return to the fold. Listening to Father's high-pitched expletives, observing this, one saw how hopeless it was that Father might have gained a spot of wisdom for softening his dotage.

Jasmine put it pathetically, “We really cannot put up with more of his ridicule, Algernon; it’s too much responsibility!”

“You have a nurse?”

“Four very good ones have done their utmost, but each one of them came down with nervous disorders. Who can blame them? And raising their salaries was unrealistic; no amount of money compensates.”

When Father had begun to need more care, Gilmore and Jasmine had him and Maudie move from their west-wing apartment to be with them in the manor’s central receiving section. Surely, they regretted this move, because he was present every minute of the day. One’s filial duty on a visit was to try with the despised old rogue, though trying wasn’t easy when Father took an unholy pride in his empowered ‘debilitation’. Couldn’t this have been expected, and quite honestly, one was finding his despicable behavior too maddening to deal with? My own financing transaction, and the susurrus of those utterly peaceful boughs over that Finger Lake’s rippling waters, U.S.A., agitated in me as I awaited testing my wonderfully opportune winery management skills. I was bloody well not going to let my enchanted ‘habitat’ slip through my fingers because of father.

Gathered in Gillie’s office after lunch, Father sat like a wild boar stricken with untreatable constipation as he awaited the least inspiration for inventing some misconduct. Suddenly, he loudly gagged; and scarcely breathing, he alarmed old Horace, who rushed to help him, only to receive Father’s walking stick jabbed between his ankles tipping the poor old fellow flat on his face. Luckily, Horace had been a parachutist during World War II and knew how to fall unhurt, as Jasmine and oneself ran to help Horace up. Father’s response was to heave great snorts of obscene hilarity. Little of any of this appeared to be unexpected.

Even if attachment to one’s parent was mainly obligatory, the Cholmondley-Rute line had given impressively to one’s country in the past, which Father and I, as Old Etonians, appreciated. Still retaining some vain hope that my career accomplishments might put a stop to the old scoundrel’s belligerence, after dinner we’d all settled comfortably, with a completing demi-tasse, in the drawing room when out came Father’s coloratura. “Never inherited a gram of my I.Q., did you—Backside of an East African mandrill? Due your stupidity, your wimp mother used to shut herself up to bawl—ha-wk, ha ha!”

This derogatory reference to one’s dearest deceased mother truly pained. “You’re referring to your having Dobbin shot, Father?”

“Didn’t need that over-eating pony. Cholmondley-Rutes do not spoil children!” Came Father’s falsetto shriek at me.

“Fa-ther, that wasn’t.” But NO—instead, one counted to the proverbial ten. “You know very well that that was not the reason!” But in taking him on, I was falling for his bait, and I didn’t need more of his disgusting lack of control.

Up rose Father's wounded wolf's howl, "D'you think you'd have made it into the Foreign Service if I hadn't bought that Normandy villa from stinky-toes Hobney? Hadn't thought that one out, had you? Couldn't. Too much privileged rearing. Can't stand gloomy-jocks! You didn't know how to crack a smile. Lazing around you couldn't even decorate this place. Had to get rid of you." Which in fairness, one saw might have had some truth to it. And after all, though being shoved out of sight of my family had been painful, it had saved the smidgen of one's character influenced by one's brilliant beloved mother. "All you were good at", Father blew on, "was making spectacular mistakes for the press that were about as legit as a Hollywood docu-drama! You turned out to be a worse simpleton than your mother!" And more of those fabrications he wallowed in. For Gillie and Jasmine's sake, I cooled my offense and played out the role of the degraded son while doing all one could not to listen to his doggedly stressed fairy stories until, "Listen, Excrement, what's all this puke about purchasing land out in that colony?"

"Father, you know perfectly well it's been the 'United States' for 200 years." But as I was still being blasted, I gave up and hastily excused myself to leave the living-room. Walking away a good deal more than ruffled, I was determined to keep my discovery of 'Runditz's Estate' well away from Father's psychedelic destruction. One's family would only disparage my settling in America, turning it into comic relief without a thought for the 'Cholmondley-Rute Wine' one was to give their precious name to, so why tell them more? Though one's compassion did make me admit sympathy for Gilmore and Jasmine not bearing to institutionalize this once-astute though recklessly corrupt and greatly feared business man. Putting parents away was the lousiest of jobs, but having chosen to have Father living with them, their socially maladjusted lives had to be theirs. For myself, I hastily reprehended myself for not making a resolute priority of getting out of here and back to the States sooner, with all I had to learn about the winery. Striding off to go to Gilmore's office, I'd make that second appointment with Ollie.

Through the Great Hall one's footsteps echoed, as one saw how useless it was to expect Father to understand. How could he… it hadn't been his experience to sit in broiling desert outposts through dull ideational meetings across from muckety-mucks unversed in which hand to shake. Was it so surprising that bucolic visions of one's finger-nails clotted with earth had been the image that had held one together? It was one's testosterone that strode along the west lawn for clearing one's angered pain, passing its absurd new statuary and fountain as one went up into the woods. Uppermost was getting back to Runditz's peaceful sanctuary, though, *was I getting anywhere with digging out my recent events and all that had utterly kept one in a mystifying dark? Having refused logic?* Not making headway with all this, I kept straight on walking right through the woods and on to the consoling village meadow I'd much loved as a boy. Here scatterings of sunlight illuminated harebells and primroses, so the breezy place took on a look of a traditional, marveled-at English spring-time. Even touched by this pastoral scene before me, I still couldn't comprehend so much that had recently happened, that had over-filled my mind. After all, when had those mystery events got started? *Get at it, Algernon, narrow it!*

Then out of the heating sun and the chirping skylarks emerged AN EPISODE!

Hooray!

I had been feeling it coming! Felt sure I was about to have a vital 'episode' that could show me why one is moving around in this thunder cloud of deepest mystification. But through this 'episode', one could be about to at last get some understanding of all that had most profoundly happened this last couple of weeks. This flashed episode must have all my purest attention! It could throw great beams of light on all that is obscure and incredible.

All right, this episode now… *For God's sake, Algernon, don't lose it! Hang onto it and give it every chance! A 'Eureka' kind of exposé! Right, I will, I will!*

Moscow!

Moscow?! This piercing flash was from back when I'd been stuck in such unforgivable Moscow cold, it had frozen the inside of my nose and more than my bones, and hadn't I been studying my precious sketch on the back of one's *charge d'affaires* discarded envelopes? Fine! The sketch had looked very much the way I'd remembered its detail on one of those admirable Victorian houses driving north out of Washington D.C., U.S.A. My doodle had exactly caught it—professionally! Decorative struts supported the horizontal porch arches with panache! Apparently, I have an unusual affinity for that intriguing Victoriana. But oh—one had to worry—what had just been said? It had been up to charges d'affaires Cadney to run this meeting now, even though he kept looking at me to bail him out. *Mustn't say a word, Algernon. It was all his now!*

Finally, Cadney got some apathetic rummaging going on this simple agenda item, which let me shade in areas of my fine house's porch and bring back those delightful sunlit decorative shapes on the porch pillars. Someday Cadney would catch on to what was just another memo sent down by commission. There was little point to fussing about this stipend business item that could've been decided in minutes. *Figure it, Cadney, and stay out of it, Algernon!* My job now was to give the man room to find out how he can move items along.

Unfortunately, very little of my instructing him had been taken to heart as his mundane, barely audible voice still came over 'bleat-bleat'. I'd done my utmost to show him how to develop some curiosity—dig in, ask questions, activate the item, wake everyone up with a touch of humor! Giving up, I tried subtler suggestions; pointing to the wall clock, I crossed my eyes and voluptuously sighed. Though that didn't seem to click with him either. Cadney had bragged about the department's despairing need for clerical enlightenment! Which I supposed was why he obsessively dug at every least polemic—for filling reports? Or so he and his cohorts could upstage one another idling time away, but even doing this as a pretext for eventual more urgent communication, this 'bleat-bleat' of his was a damnable abuse of officers' time.

Darkening more of my porch decoration shadows, my house's sketch suddenly took on a truly realistic depth I really liked! It's strange what can electrify one even in preposterous times! The more I studied what I'd sketched, the more voltage it bestowed on one—absolutely corking! It even brought a new classification to the entire house, hinting at other details I'd add, as Cadney kept thumbing through his notes, warning that there was a lot more to get through this. He hadn't called it 'trivia', but listen to them! Was I wrong? Wasn't professional morbidity settling in around the table?

My ankles were as frozen as cast-iron gate handles. Weren't everyone's? Slouching down in my chair, I viewed beneath the table. Stellin's foot was pushing off his other Gucci loafer, so his socked foot could give friction to his other frozen ankle. Couldn't Cadney see that also there were two other nodding fellows around this table that could very well get expensively hurt falling off their chairs? I don't mean to be hard on the man just because I got such a clumsy ass dumped on one as my side-kick, but as he lapsed again into more pompous little haggles, we were all realizing that this meeting shouldn't be expecting much. *Get used to it, Cadney; my hands are full adjusting to my coming retirement.*

Two more weeks of this Moscow mission housed up here in Santa's Arctic workshop, and it would be over! All of it would be over, including my entire 30-plus years with the Foreign Service, come the day. At least old Thaddeus and I are down to days that can be counted now, as I renewed my wonder at that ringed date staring down at us from the wall calendar. Thinking beyond these last few weeks, as one always did when one's cerebellum, I think it was, began to ache; but then, hip-hip, et cetera! No more unexpected urgencies from Chancery, no sudden packing a bag to jaunt off and act being Fagan, cursing out representatives reneging on their all but signed agreements. And no more of these dragging afternoons priming the demoralizing Cadney takeover! That ringed date up on the calendar meant utter abandonment to entire days of one's own! *Absolute Fre-eeedom!*

Titillating at my mind's edge came hints of how I would relish my retirement paradise! Virtually supine driving my superb Lamborghini in fast neat little accelerations, straight or winding, as magnificent scenery begged one to drop one's speed, to stop, get out, savor! Scenic images that calmed one's rattled and aching mind!

Sketching in a hooded, tall Victorian window shadowed under the porch, I can't adequately describe how much I'd really begun to love this house! Which was after all, my own built sketch! Yet, was I inordinately loving it? Loving this house, I'd been conceptually building from all I had known or admired of fine American Victorian houses, I could no longer call it a doodle—it was indeed an architectural sketch! Almost a blueprint, deserving a name, like 'My Habitat'. On the roof and on its captivating cupola, that would have huge overhanging eaves to protect it from all weathers; and as you walked through the house's unforgettable main entrance, you would be smothered with such historical solace, it would give new meaning to what I would call 'Home'! Oh-oh, damnation, with everyone yawning, I didn't catch what was being said.

Huh, still on this unresolved stipend! Quibbles lobbing back and forth, like sopping wet tennis balls as Cadney prepared for his own eventual big show. Pressured considerations, I supposed, because it had been commission's high office that had sent down this item. Officialdom like that could be counted on for inspiring Cadney to latch onto what didn't matter and get going one of his torturous 'diatribes'—diatribes being his métier. He hadn't got it in him to managerially evaluate whether an item was important.

Most of all, I must keep reminding myself that, hallelujah, I was daily sliding nearer the retirement fray! I say this because my disappointment with our abysmal achievements here at this Moscow mission were only outdone by our outrageous lack of anything of worth being accomplished by most of our Foreign Service! Pride in past brilliant attainments had eroded—gone! My own thoroughly bored, wrenched mind, and its attached soggy soul, could not keep putting up with these dangerous symptoms of abject disillusionment; though—thank 'All That's Everlasting'—one was on one's way out.

There had been a time of powerfully persuading sovereign states—of convincing and shaming them—creatively caressing and seducing them with 'x' and 'y' advantages if they'd just get with it and blasted well making it to the table. Admirable work was achieved then—technically, politically psychologically and historically admirable—with brilliant colleagues, like Thaddeus, patiently primed to persuade. None of these staffers' frivolities about insignificant stipends; when nations threatened with near destruction were holding their breaths, we'd at the very least secure a promise or two.

It was no wonder my house's sketch kept becoming more vivid. With details to enhance with recalled from an American Victoriana houses magazine, I was amazed how much I had truly fallen for this 'Habitat' of mine. No, better call it my 'Supreme Habitat', as it was to radiate architectural perfection! My shading needed to be denser to the right, suggesting an intriguing depth going far along under my porch's roof. Looking long and critically at my porch, I tried extending its struts' decoration to see what this did, but still it needed—I tried a low-keyed

Dorian capital topping a porch pillar—this moved my sketch onto other stimulating details I'd seen in America that one couldn't try out quickly enough! Inside this house too, with its fine high ceilings—essential for a tall man—and its well-appointed rooms with tall, narrow windows for adventurous sky-to-lawn views.

This last hour I'd been aching to walk off the Moscow cold and reclaim my mortared feet, but now quite honestly, I was past it, too frozen to bother; and anyway, this meeting had to be about through. How does one instruct someone that there was nothing on his agenda list that couldn't be dashed off quickly, and we could all spend much needed extra time back at our desks? I realized that Cadney and company were rehearsing for their big show of 'new policies for galvanizing every department of the Foreign Service in Russia'. I'd done my best not to laugh! But oh, wasn't that the door? God help us—we couldn't only be at tea-trolley time???

Holding our boiling cups, Cadney busily warned, "I won't dismiss this meeting when there's so much more to go over." Thadd's unrestrained yawn had a domino effect!

Bracing myself for this only being tiffin-time, seriously, with Cadney about to step into one's shoes 'designate', wasn't it most fortunate that our mission was not in a crisis? With the clink and crunch of tea cups and digestive biscuits—I let mine cool as—I studied the validity of my Victorian house's shadowed new details, letting them draw me into their original romancing of me with their percussive viewing experiences! *Or I was doing so quite contentedly until, without a word, Cadney reached across the table and snatched his used envelope from me! His unbelievable rudeness left me staring at the heavy Johnson's waxing the table had been given.* Thaddeus couldn't stop snickering before he, and I too, sat up to sip tea and nibble digestives.

Oh, those fabulous 19th century houses in America!

How elating it would be to walk into my own picturesque little property, my own 'Supreme Habitat', in some outlandishly peaceful spot! Well, why shouldn't there be? England might have a house like it hidden away somewhere, awaiting one's limitless free days for devoting to it? Victoriana though wasn't high-styled in England. It took American builders using the stunning pliability of wood to create that thrilling Victorian flamboyance that they'd made their own! With my house, wherever it would be, one mandatory requirement would be, *at least a continent away from my God-awful father—a requirement that automatically ruled out England!*

Father was out! Brother Gilmore too—OUT!

Not so different from my Foreign Service decades, when by mutual consent I'd been out of my family's sight. Handily, my life's work had posted me a good distance from them, the manor, and all that went with them. Yes, because for this

‘Habitat’, ‘my home’, all family was *out!* I wouldn’t even see them, except for minimal obligations for maintaining one’s Cholmondley-Rute allowance.

But keeping with it—once freedom was attained—it would be that squarely built Victorian design of rock-solid construction I’d be after, because that era’s best quality materials had been selected for those distinguishing overhanging roofs and crisply spiraled corbels. Its lid-like eaves would be upheld by Grecian-influenced cornices, the supports done in thin, thicker and thickest laminated construction. Whew, I felt quite weak with all that magnificence, because the cupola’s echoed square proportions, with its own vast overhanging roof, would match it to perfection! Marvelous all those great eaves snugly protecting the house’s inner riches! Distinguishing it too would be the vertical narrowness of all windows and doors to selectively sluice the lovely light. Yes, there were the doors—especially the main entrance—I’ll stick to double-doors with its windows ingeniously protected by brilliantly carved local wooden decoration.

As with any house that one was to at last call ‘Home’, I’d be living in just that one place. Envision it! No more moves to yet another embassy! One had traveled intensely all these decades to so many extraordinary sights and one’s share of risks, and had been thrust into environments of appalling indelicacy as well as every other kind. *Which was one’s incentive, wasn’t it, Algernon, old chap?* No more being sent off anywhere! Time now to settle into a comfy wing chair among Mother’s selected fine antiques in exquisitely decorated rooms that guaranteed that one’s toes could root around into the floorboards!

Even without my despised sketch, I’d brought its image back in the table’s highly buffed Johnson’s wax as the clinks and snacking of tea-time ended. Teacup in hand, Cadney was still holding forth. Replacing his cup with a pencil, he twizzled in the air; its point just missing his clubbed ear as in that didactic rough-edged voice of his—that at least now he’d made louder—he recited some reason. Shamefully, this made me understand why the means of being educated needed to vary so enormously... unkind? Yes, from one’s Cambridge conditioning, it certainly was. Cruel, actually, no one could help what background they’d been raised in. But sitting here during these protracted weekly afternoons, knowing there was no possibility of a scintillating little quote, or a devastatingly nuanced insight, not to mention the chance of a spark of humor, how couldn’t one be critical? Sighing, I checked the wall calendar again, and its comfortingly emphasized date behind Basil’s pompadour—it still solidly spelled out the promise of days soon to become all-personal.

That same afternoon a week later was our last.

Each of us were handed a slim manual and expected to follow Cadney reading from it aloud. Slowly, on the off chance we couldn’t read, I imagine, as he punctuated it with obvious comments. Once Cadney’s voice had got into its drone, I didn’t waste any more minutes. Images of my cozy Victorian habitat broke into one's mind full force with its wonderfully high ceilings, and I started to add in other details, particularly a southward-facing wrap-around porch. Though Cadney had so rudely discarded my drawing, I supposed that the poor sop had been using me as an example of the inane pifflings that one of 'The Demented Dead-Woods' had come up with! If so, then at least it proved that my 'designate' could once in a while make a clear, authoritative move!

Abruptly, Cadney's voice became so overused, he had to soothe it with horehound pastilles; and making sure I'd stay awake, he demanded I took over reading. Stellin unobtrusively raised his page so I made out where we'd got to, and I deeply regretted not getting to my house's shutters—and I'd had some thrilling visions of its interior. Instead though, full-voiced—as reading aloud was what I was known to excel in—I read, so at least this ridiculousness got us up to tea-trolley time—thank all the 'angels in the heavens abiding'.

Downing this mission's black-and-orange pekoe with one's inevitable digestive biscuit helped fill the minutes Cadney summarized this meeting's measly achievements. Then theatrically, he pushed his papers away and holding his entwined hands on the table in front of him, he made an effort to acquire sincerity in a look that reminded me of Anthony Hopkins in *Silence of the Lambs* as he confidentially spoke for the tableful wishing Thaddeus and myself, "All the best at playing ninepins and bowls! Enjoy your honoring in London next week. We'll all be thinking of you!" To various 'Hear hears' and other pleasantries.

On that final afternoon's staff meeting, with Thadd and myself about to take off into our much envied 'freedom', there was general malaise as our colleagues were perplexed with these oncoming personnel rearrangements. Across from me, Thadd too sat souring as we all did, because Diatribe Number Six was bleating on—Cadney's subject? Of all the choices! 'Dressing for the eight o'clock black tie'... so sad really as Cadney hadn't picked up a smidgen on what suiting to take to his tailor. He never could understand that any old shiny serge just wouldn't do.

Thadd and I met younger chaps over late night brandy, who eagerly let us know how greatly they admired our systems for efficiently running departments and meetings; and before retiring that night, Thadd and I had one last tipple because—I'd seen it coming—Thadd had begun to get droopy during Cadney's afternoon well-wishing. With our Moscow-London plane taking off at 8:00 a.m., I slapped old Thadd's shoulder to buck him up, as by then Thadd's melancholia had truly set in. I shook his shoulder again as he complained, "Not sure how one's to manage this one after we've had our big 'Do', old man. It's been a bloody good life! Entrancing capital cities! You and I, our damned good 'explorations'! Oy-yap, oy-yap." Thadd's lurid old boy's laughter, "It won't be the same y'know, old plug! No more fantastic dinners with those acrobats and

Egypt's jolly king. Politically, the old bore's feet were in cement, but he knew how to make a feast spectacular, plenty of pomp, busty women, ear-splitting brass bands. Nothing left to chance. In the Far East, too! And Algie, that's not beginning to get to the Shah! Heads of states go for the best of the best when they're out to impress. Oh Algernon, my good old chum, you do understand it's all *en-n-d*ing?" He found someone's napkin to dab up the wetness dropping onto his tie from his trickled jaw.

With my arm keeping him upright, he still fell into a drinks trolley as I sympathized, "Listen, old cock, I know you've been longing to do other things."

"No, you don't understand, Algie. I'm not even wanting a woman."

"That'll pass, Thaddeus, old reprobate. You've money, you're in good health; you've kept yourself trim and well-turned-out. You'll soon have the world's most gorgeous women competing to rip your trousers off again. You can travel now, anywhere you want. Maybe meet some Fiji islander with gyrating hips? There'll be all the time you've ever wanted for reading up on the hottest casinos and nudist beaches. Then there's your family, Thadd; you know they'll set you up with a juicy financial scheme or two. They'll have to… they won't want you hanging around them."

"You're not seeing that our best days are over, Algie! They're GONE! Oops, give me a hand, Algie, old bird," sloshing over a filled punch bowl. "By God, though you'll hear what I'm saying when you're sitting around for 12 long empty hours each day." Thadd begged me to stay for 'just another teensy lickle one of this damned good stuff'.

Conditioning it to 'our very last drinky-poo', I gave several yawns in succession—rather crudely, I'm afraid.

After getting him upstairs to his bed, sitting on it beside Thadd, we worked on this last snort, gruffly toasting old recollections, "To secretaries with boobs below their hemlines."

"I'll settle for curves like Aristide Maillol's."

"D'you think there'll be any willing good-lookers at our honoring, old sock? Here's t'our old 'recommendations'!" Swigging, Thadd's reminiscing got more of his 'Oy-ap, oy-ap' going as the lust in him began to look forward to London. Though it was when he recalled his little Algerian-French soubrette that his words slurred most badly; then his body started to slide too further into recline. Finally, he let go of me and out came a muffled snore as I yanked his legs up on the bed, slithered off his shoes, covered him against his last bitter Moscow night and seeing him looking peaceful at last, took off to my room.

Huh, so much for looking forward to some quiet reviewing of all I'd got 'built' of my fabulous Victorian habitat! Ideas embedding in such a moving orchestral coda that even while listening to old Thadd, I was surrounding my house with an arbor and long rolling lawns. Then on my own last night in

Moscow, I fell asleep screeching country corners, driving one's chic Lamborghini on and on as I sung my lungs hoarse, gloriously headed for stupendous new adventuring. Was it just at this moment that I wondered if I'd heard a shout?

My vivid recollecting of the rest of that outlandish event would have to stop… damn it—a crying shame when I was so hot onto the whole pathology—the shout again?

Turning to look, oh hell, Jasmine was hurrying towards me!

Blasted sister-in-law! She called again, then getting close, "Ah, thank goodness, Algernon!" Getting her breath, "Ollie's called! And listen, brother-in-law, you know how Father and Gillie need dinner on the dot?"

Ollie! It had only been Ollie's brazened incompetence that had kept me from having happily returned to my supreme habitat and its wonderfully fulfilled inhabitants!

This gross interruption of Jasmine made one's laugh come out, as if from a horse in heat. Still, as always, one naturally roused, stood, and jovially took Jasmine's arm. We returned through the woods back to my aggravated brother and father, who both sat reproachfully thumping rhythmic fists to the table. Only little bits of terse conversation helped pass this annoying meal, though Father's newest contribution was that one had, "Gleefully given family obligation the finger."

This might be deserved, though he'd been the one who had sent one away—to school, to camps, and to the Foreign Service. Replying I said, "I may have done my share of shunning filial duties, Father, and I am truly regretful if they added to Gilmore or Jasmine's burdens." This new agreeing tactic quite put the old devil off, and for once, he simply sat still and got more food into his mouth.

Later that evening, standing with Jasmine in Mother's antiques storage room, one knew exactly what to select for the 'Supreme Habitat' that would remind one of my beloved mother. Jasmine held onto a couple of her favorites, and I must say as we talked, I began to feel sorry for this shoddily treated relative. It was Jasmine who was suffering the brunt of Father's perverted aging, as she had done all she could, having got in two geriatric specialists for him on the national honors list; though each had declared that with Father's volcanic tantrums, an effective enough strait-jacket had yet to be invented. Other than institutionalizing him, each had done their damndest to evade giving further advice.

The following morning, Ollie's shrewd clerk had made sure one's financial statements were prepared, and one readily signed where needed while putting in a minimum of more idiotic family talk with doddery old smile-smile Ollie. Which included yet again promising this family solicitor one would strongly advise Father 'not to retire!' Gillie, I hope you appreciate your brother's thoughtfulness! One left clutching one's precious envelope as one shared a grin with the clerk and headed for the Austin Healey.

One was free to make arrangements for returning at last! Hip-Hip Hooray, hip hip… All was happiness!

With this fiscal proof of owning one's beguiling 'Supreme Habitat' safely under my arm, one fairly skipped to the car, singing a wonderfully full-voiced sampling of Verdi's Requiem, and 'hearing' its perfectly attuned chorus so joyous behind one's solo. I sung it over again while triumphantly dodging the mid-day traffic.

Driving in through the wrought iron gates, my gaze remained on the stately double-winged manor with its original central ramparts choked with Elizabeth the first's tall chimneys. Now I was to leave, two family facts stood out all along the long driveway. Fact – with one's superb lineage, like it or not, one should never forget that Father was my blood-related parent. And second – however inhumane Father was, he was not yet immortal! One needed to digest these facts because one's success at the solicitors had flooded one with so many joyful prospects, it could get missed that there was little hope for the inmates here ever being happy beneath all those chimneys of Lizzie the first. With everyone at the manor cowering before Father's 'quixotisms', as Gillie referred to them, how could these poor wayward souls begin to re-stabilize?

To help them along, one needed to apply one's innate patronage to one's pitiable family and get it over with. Bred to gentleness and being superbly trained in justice, one was well thought of for spreading kindness as well as fair-mindedness. I should certainly be altruistic when one's own future looked so ticky-poo, as I geared up to be generous with one's cosmopolitan advantages. After all, what must it be like to be Father with eyes so dim one bit the air because one often didn't see the food on one's fork? Offers to feed Father recalled Jasmine's attempt ending when Father threw the cut-glass vinegar bottle at her. Still, when one studied one's antediluvian parent and saw that he was little more than skin and bone, this surely meant he was not getting enough nourishment? It could be too, that just as he complained, his legs truly did give him pain, and though it was hard for any of us to believe his insistence that his pancreas kept 'popping'; as the second son of even this miserable blood-sucker, how heartless could one be?

These rudimentary facts pressed me to think up some treat for brightening the old whiner's days. The following morning at the breakfast of toast fingers for dipping in eggs-in-the-pot, one suggested to Father that Horace, in the role of Gilmore's chauffeur, run us over to Corfe Castle. Horace agreed that getting Father breathing some fresh sea air might knock better sense into him, "It would be a change and make a right good ride in the limo, sir," he persuaded.

Jasmine could not believe that Father would agree to go, because she had often described possible limo excursions to him, but the thought of a couple of hours break from the decrepit old gas-bag quite transformed her into a lovely, far younger-looking woman, and she did her utmost to talk Father into going, "Enjoy the castle, Father, and come back to your favorite broccoli soufflé."

We were both pleased with our success getting Father to agree, until he knocked his orange juice onto that poor, abused Persian carpet while giving that well-known clarion call—his irate shriek of "Maud-DIE-IE-EE!" On he caterwauled, "Gil-mo-O-ORE! Dock Maudie's wages! She's still NOT got me dressed!" This sent Maudie, this pillar of much density and size and indescribable strength, who deafened herself to the blather of this disintegrating Cholmondley-Rute figure-head, "You lousy mute, speak so I hear!" To this noble soul, who in this case accepted Jasmine's raises and like a massive chunk of diamond flint, simply stood inanimate before Father, awaiting her frothing employer drying up. Such an impervious attitude brought on another slew of his insults; while glassy-eyed she stared through him, as if he was a cobweb.

According to Jasmine, Maudie had taught herself to withstand abuse having been brought up with delinquent drunkard brothers. To Jasmine and Gilmore, Maudie was not just a model aide but a self-effacing archangel in every meaning of the phrase 'enormous proportions'. One did one's best to persuade Maudie to join Father and I on our Corfe Castle trip, but the priceless angel shook her head and stayed as impervious to one's persuasion as she was to Father's abuse.

Nothing for it, one had got oneself into this. I had Gilmore's limo brought 'round to the only step-less entrance, and with Father bathed, respectably dressed, wheel-chaired, and lifted into the farthest back seat, one wrapped his safari lion's fur around his legs; while Horace, in his chauffeur's uniform, collapsed the wheelchair and packed it. Armed with a picnic basket and given joyful waves from Gilmore, Jasmine, and Maudie, we set off.

It could be an Elysian journey to Corfe through some of the finest English countryside, and to one's continual amazement, Father quite fixed to the passing landscape and didn't say a word! One wondered if his pitiful memory had gone blank on the beauty of this trip, because it turned out to be an unexpectedly pleasant hour in the company of one's father, and the pleasure of Gilmore's Rolls' superb engineering driven by Horace.

Arriving at a parking place with a frightfully fine view of the Corfe ruin, one got out. As one did so, a distinctive drawing sensation ensnared me, because this was the spot one's dearest mother brought one as a boy for getting to know Corfe's rapturous mystique. After taking a good stretch and elating with the taste of salt on one's lips while hearing the distant thunderous drumming of the sea, as Father remained quiet, one had Horace set up his wheelchair, so he too could experience this exhilaration. Though it wasn't till Horace lifted Father's unusual submissiveness into the wheelchair that one became more impressed by his placidity and was even concerned as one looked questioningly at Horace.

"It's all right, Sir Algernon, His Lordship's reactions have just gone turbid these days."

Nodding one's affirmation as one was sure that a retainer of as long-standing as Horace would be well aware of his 90-year-old employer's idiosyncrasies.

With Father entrusted to Horace, one yielded to this immense draw from the castle's ruins and the long ago magical trips here, as one took off down the slope and up the other side in a good hard stride until the lugubrious stonework was close; and, here it was, roofless for centuries, Sargasso fragrance mixing the muskiness of time-rent dilapidation! All hitting exactly as one recalled it! Fixated, one wandered within the fortress' truncated walls with a few ravens, noting the same ambiguous crevices, its dark holes, or this *one* hole.

This particular configuration of sun-bright sandstone bang next to a depth of a black un-mortared nothing positively struck one, as having been a corner one had hallucinated at back more than 50 years ago! Pulsing sensations as these distinctive odors from my earlier self-seeped in to enclose one as elation and head melodies vied. Though there was no proof that this corner had been the actual one—naturally one had not been brought up to leave one's desecrating carved initials—though these walls and their owners' bloody mediaeval history were most certainly what had drenched one's boyhood imagination, until Mother had explained away the family's murders to prevent one from dwelling on morbid past evil. All so frightfully spiffing! Though one mustn't get too waylaid, this was Father's outing, and one was here to give him a pleasant hour or so along with the pleasure of Gilmore's splendid Rolls.

Using one's burning hormones in long-legged strides of voluptuously renewed well-being, I quickly got back up the hill to Horace. Though in his wheelchair, Father's head still remained unnaturally skewed and slumped to his body. "Hor-ace!" One attracted his attention. "Look at him! Is this normal?" As one completed one's question, one heard a resounding slap, and one had to sternly reprimand, "NO, Horace!"

Horace gruffly explained, "His Lordship has these foibles, Sir Algernon," and drawing from his pocket a folded paper, handed it to me. "Here, he's written out his preference for being brought too."

"By slogging him? You can't be right!" I asked giving a glance at the familiar scrawled signature on this paper while Horace's next slap sent Father's bullet head into an alternately cocked tilt. "Surely, by now he should be coming around?"

"Two usually does it! But for safety's sake."

Before one could stop him, Father's jaw had received Horace's solid left fist. "No MORE, Horace! Positively not! Three such remedies must be given their chance!" As Horace had at one time boxed in the East End, one was truly concerned; but Horace only shrugged looking disappointed as Father wasn't showing any change, other than having his head flung from side to side. It could be that this aspect of Horace's job gave a balance to Father's personal abuse of him, but going to stand before Father, one bent to take his pulse, that, despite his comatose state, was bouncing along cheerfully. Placing a hand on either side of Father's head, I righted its strange tilt, yet barely a flicker to his eyelids. "Horace, doesn't he have medicine?"

"You mean his nitro, sir? The glove compartment. Should I get it?"

One thought Horace might have tried the nitro before socking his old employer, but returning with a phial, he removed its cap, took out a tiny pill; and standing with a sturdy leg on either side of Father's lion's-fur-wrapped knees, Horace yanked down his lower jaw, grabbed his lumpy white tongue and stuffed the tiny pill beneath it. Clamping Father's jaws together again, he held them. Continuing his iron grip on Father's jaw, one reminded, "That should do it, Horace!"

One had gone to sit down the hill on the grass to await the pill's effect, and Horace came and sat companionably close. "You see the castle here good as any place," Horace observed looking wearily wrinkled after driving. Horace wasn't young; and one had to agree that as there were hardly any cars here, it was sensible to stay with this splendid angle of the castle.

Studying the castle's shapely mass of worn stones, how easy it was to ignore one's own evolving as the various stages of one's bestowed years might even throw light on the elusive 'why' one had anthropologically done what one had. Admittedly, this might be 'blindly burrowing the past, like an ignorant mole', as one's former charge d'affaires Cadney would disparagingly phrase it. Though since retiring one was learning to look a good deal harder at Cadney's lauded sayings.

This castle, stunningly dramatic in compositional chiaroscuro, though dampened by the disappointment that Father wasn't showing any movement, other than his head being flung from side to side. Placing a hand on either side of Father's head, one righted its strange tilt affecting barely a flicker to his eyelids.

Horace had taken off for the picnic basket. Not that one disagreed with Horace, but in taking this initiative, he was being pushy. One surmised that driving must have made him hungry; then besides being tired, he was surely soured by a life of Father's overbearing shrieks and indecipherable mumblings that Horace probably didn't always hear as he once had. Looking at Horace back up at the limousine, one watched him returning down with the basket; as one also noticed that the Rolls needed re-parking, so that another car trying to pass it didn't have to honk. Back down beside one with his head already inside the basket, Horace was not going to be bothered by any annoying honks. However, Horace's dismissal of the other car should matter now one was expected to share public places.

Waving one's smiled thanks to the other driver for patiently waiting with his family, one strode back up to the lengthy limo; but, oh dear, one hadn't the ignition key and had to return down to Horace. By the time one was back up again ready to re-park, the other driver was outside his car; his brute face borscht-hued as he crassly waved his fist and shouted. One should have sent for Horace at once because his well-developed muscles would have cooled this crude man who had started to menacingly walk towards me. "You've ruddy well held us up!" One caught this vulgar, over-reacting man's comment. "We didn't come all this pissing way to just stew in a scalding car!"

"Won't be a jiff." One gave him my most charming smile as one waved the car keys at him.

"Damn, well won't be if you don't want those keys re-shaping your rectum!"

One laughed at his capriciousness, sure that this patriarch's behavior would become more exemplary once he'd given a thought to his watching wife and children. But the beetroot driver had got quite near before one gave up on his better parenting and yelled, "Hor-a-ACE!" Luckily, one's chauffeur heard and quickly loped up the hill with his mouth filled and half a sandwich in his hand. Horace did not appreciate his lunch being interrupted, but sizing-up one's situation, his square muscular appearance in his trim black coat and cap looked appropriately underworld to make this impatient driver turn and amble back to his car.

Having re-parked the limo, one looked back at one's Father and—oh dear Lord!—neither Horace nor I had remembered the wheelchair brakes! Father was rolling off down the hill and gathering speed. "THE BRAKES, FATHER! GRIP THE BRAKES!" one yelled through cupped hands.

Uncannily, Father's mental workings returned, and his skewed head righted as he yanked at the brakes. But so hard that the chair, with him in it, double-somersaulted. Loose-bowelled with guilt, Horace and I sprinted down to see what pieces Father was in, and we hastily turned him over; which wasn't difficult, his being near to anorexic. Horace upturned his wheelchair and helped get Father into it again and dust him off. He and I each took a side to push this dazed 90-year-old back up the hill, as amazingly, Father's coloratura recovered to screech a litany of tortures and more such nonsense that Horace and I were in for once we were back at the manor. Astounding! Having rescued him, and both Horace and I being breathless with this uphill push, how could anyone take Father's lack of gratitude seriously? One remarked to Horace, "It's dumbfounding what range of moods Father's venerable constitution still produces, isn't it, Horace?" Horace grunted giving a wild-eyed variety of expressions while Father's tirade kept on. Neither of us could accuse the old reptile of not bearing Cholmondley-Rute blue-blooded toughness.

Horace used lemonade and a serviette to get the mud off Father's forehead. He was concerned that Father's 'pancreas popping' might be fatal this time, as Horace as well as I were responsible. We finished our sandwiches with Horace breaking off chunks of a banana sandwich to stuff in Father's mouth and effectively silence him. Having finished the picnic with Father more settled, I had a suggestion. "You look as if you've had enough, Horace. Best you ride in the far back seat and lean your weight against Father to keep him sitting upright. Take a nap, and one will drive us back to the manor."

Stifling a yawn, Horace replied, "Decent of you, Sir Algernon, though you might want to swop places before getting to the manor's drive."

"Ingenious, Horace, one will!"

This was how we drove, returning through the luscious countryside with more than its share of bluebells and blossoms. On village curves, one gave a warning honk to oncoming motorists that the limousine would take extra room as I reveled in swinging the great car's length into the opposite lane.

Jasmine must have been nervous about Father because handkerchief to mouth, she was waiting outside for us. Sighting us, she signaled Maudie, and in no time Horace and Maudie had Father in bed and resting from his unusually tiring day. All it took was a couple of hours' rest for Father to be down with us for dinner. Over the fish course, Gilmore asked Father the conventional post-outing pleasantries, and one worried that Father's memory could serve him too efficiently and include his tumble down the hill. I fervently hoped that knocked out as he had been, Father wouldn't remember. In appearance he didn't look too bad, other than his forehead being a bit red that no one remarked on. Possibly because Father had been stimulated by the sea air, but thankfully, his answers remained mercifully mild.

Jasmine, as expected, diplomatically befriended her father-in-law. "It was very different without you here, Father! We worried you'd had a rotten sea mist covering the castle."

"Saw all I needed to!" Father's brows rose almost appreciatively. This was so uncharacteristic, we all stared at him. He had answered politely, despite the broccoli soufflé aimed at his mouth dropping either side of his jaw. Then suddenly, Father said something that astonished us even more. "That car's all right, Gilmore! Not a bad drive!" One took in Gilmore's ogled disbelief, and our eyes met in a blaze of concerned amazement that Father could genuinely like anything!

Unfortunately, though Jasmine had taken offense. "Really, Father? You remember how Horace and I begged you? Made careful plans for us all to go to Po'tland Bill?" But Father sat there mostly missing his food and biting the air as he waved his forked soufflé at her. Much of Father's soufflé had gone on the floor, as the new cook, innocent of Father's ways, dished out more for him.

Low-voiced, one consoled one's sister-in-law. "Most likely he chose to come because of the rarity of my visit, Jasmine."

"Any change from these abominably boring days!" Father's high-pitched insistence continued, amazing us all.

One continued to soothe Jasmine, "After all, when was one last here?"

"Awarding yourself medals, Snotbottom? As a son, your inadequacies are grossly disorientating." With this diversion from the wheelchair brakes fiasco, one tensely accepted that this was all.

Stiff with offense, Jasmine asked, "Father, would you come if Horace and I set up a lovely trip to Lyme Regis?"

"Don't like women."

Jasmine was shocked. "Right, but I am your daughter-in-law." Steeped in old-world wifeliness, Jasmine geared up to give him her list of all the sights she and Horace would tempt him with, but while Jasmine persevered, Father trigger-fingered his soufflé-loaded fork at her, landing it in her hair and nose silent-movie-style as he broke into his African wilderness snorts.

Gilmore abruptly stood and quite affectingly took his serviette to his wife's face. Putting his arm around her shoulders, he guided his deeply disappointed lady off to the washroom; and one was left with Father's tormenting guffaws, and one's barest concern he might fatally choke. Having heard his hysterical laughter, despite her size, phantom-like Maudie appeared, holding the anticipated wet face flannel and towel. Cleaning him and the table up, she had neatly removed his thrown and dropped food before Gilmore and Jasmine returned.

After Father's malevolent laughter exhausted, the four of us, including Father, settled down to the cook's special welcome-home dessert—strawberries with clotted cream on home-made meringues. This delicious 'pudding' calmed us down despite the manor's meal time tensions, as we all returned to our pretending mode that the days here never changed from being affable and serene!

It wasn't until getting up in the stratosphere again that I was able to continue my 'episode' that had thrown some light on what the hell I'd been up to. This had all come out densely and been welcomed as one's means of obtaining insights into this cloud of mystery still enveloping me. Continuing with it—as expected—oh, where had I got to? Yes, all the stops had been pulled out for the London retirement dinner honoring Thaddeus and myself.

In this spectacularly flamboyant 'do', one was charmed that with other past and present renowned men feted for their diplomatic distinction, Thadd and I received flattering and witty speeches. Anecdotes with a perception or two and plenty of enjoyable comradery that made me believe our careers may truly have been appreciated! The celebrity speaker was Prince Charles, who gave his graceful appreciation of the two of us and the Foreign Service generally, using his typical drollery. Later, the prince delighted me by recalling my investiture presented by his mother in the palace ballroom—a very amiable chap when you got to know him—and so this fine celebrity retirement evening bumbled along.

Thadd admirably held off getting overwrought, and I caught up with old chums from various stages of my venerable career, though I carefully hid any plans needing to protect one's coming independent 'freedom'; even as one vowed to keep in touch and so on, you know how one does. It had been one of those evenings when the best part of each of us locked on to one another in this uniqueness of being about to no longer be seeing their familiar mugs, which quite made these special hours enjoyable. Thadd's commendable demeanor won him a word or two with the prince too, and by the time we all held hands and sung 'Auld Lang Syne', we had been made amply replete with splendid foods et cetera; and for myself, I was perfectly happy to be sent off believing that my personal attributes were as viable as ever for whatever they were to be applied to.

Accepting this highest public approval fanned one's self-esteem more than I could want, and it certainly didn't do Thaddeus any harm. His face became cheerier and more youthful as the night wore on, and his eyes resisted dwelling too vulgarly on the serving maids' vaudevillian necklines, and even those of certain female administrators. I judiciously remained sober, having learned that losing control could cause one horrendous setbacks, which put me a jump ahead of Thaddeus. Before going over to our hotel and leaving our department chaps virtually forever, I expressed my gratitude to Montrose and also Franklin—my reliable old booster from Chancery. It was good to meet-up with old pal Gus again too, here to write us all up for *The Telegraph*. I'd be dishonest to say that farewells to special colleagues, kindly ancient mentors, and others I'd admired didn't affect me, because being a man of dissembled passion, each type of handshake, shoulder grab, and even the odd masculine hug, had its percentage of distress. As with relinquishing all that had once long ago been profoundly meaningful for me of the Foreign Service's serious objectives, but—as they say in America——'that's how the cookie crumbles'.

Being quite honest though, all this leave-taking wore me down. I'd experienced this kind of allover deadness and knew one wasn't likely to restore my inner dynamics with one night's rest. Removing my shoes up in my room, while needing to revive one's 'Habitat' thoughts, I fought the fog of oncoming skull-rattlings as I attached the 'Do Not Disturb' sign to my outside door handle and locking it, off came one's evening jacket rhythmically, sleeve, sleeve, trousers, leg, leg… removed before there could be no stopping oneself from falling onto the quilted counterpane, where I had just enough bodily strength to get it over my ears and roll up in it. Though, Lord. I was beyond tiredness! Not even time to review my Victorian house's new additions with the counterpane clutching me to its bosom and sleep-sand dashing one's eyes for carrying one off singing and supine, bucketed and belted in my incomparable Lamborghini.

The following morning, rather than going over last night with old buddies, I phoned the manor's factotum, good old Horace. By 9:00, he was here for me in London, and the dear, blessed old soul chauffeured me as he reeled off his 'retirement advice' as he called it, driving me out to the manor and my own superlative four-wheels. Like a dear old uncle, Horace's East-Ender's concern asked, "Had all the tiddledywinks you wanted, sir? It's torture keeping off the good gay and friskiness on a night like that, isn't it?"

"I behaved, Horace."

Horace gave me that glance that implied 'you certainly wouldn't have once', but he only said, "It pays, sir. There's another thing it's best you know, sir. Y'father isn't any better," which I'd guessed as Horace needlessly pointed to his forehead. "Engine is out of oil. His pistons aren't in too good shape either."

Minding Horace's information, I decided on just one night's stay at the manor, enough to finally accept a few praises from one's family. "I'll take the car over to drive Central and Southern France," I told Horace, "It'll cool me down."

"If anything'll do it, sir," he replied doubtfully.

"And I can think myself through."

I repeated these plans to Brother Gillie and Jasmine, who were in the dining room worshipfully devouring platefuls of grilled bacon, potatoes, mushrooms, tomatoes, eggs, sausages, and crisply fried bread. As my announcement hadn't pierced their plans for me to stay, I announced this again at lunch, while they were eating their cold meats, chutney, and rolls. I settled for a café au lait. Father neither looked up nor mentioned last night's Foreign Service honoring; and I wouldn't have noticed any change in him, except that he had become enchanted with dropping one utensil at a time on that poor, old Persian carpet while loudly making its would-be sound, "BO-YNG-G-G!" Using up his cutlery, he reached for Jasmine's fork, "BO-YNG-G-G!" Then her full water glass, and had just got a grip on it when Maudie's hand came around from behind him. Maudie—that marvel of an aide especially assigned to Father—had once again saved a situation.

Gillie's only acknowledgment of my retired status was to shoot his rolled-up *Telegraph* across the table with its creased photo of oneself with the prince. I could tell by all that was not being said that Father was being problematic again; but not being up to dealing with their problems when my own immediate adjustments had me in thrall, I decided to push-up my planned French holiday by taking off this morning.

That part of my brain that rattled, the cerebellum I'm sure it was, wasn't such a horrendous ache, but nor was it the kind to fade away easily. Undoubtedly, it was waiting for me to muster some new incentive for ignoring it, so driving away this morning should help. Seeing me off, Horace whispered his concerned aside, "Sir, you'll cool down right fast if you'll say no to rich food and drink!" I appreciated Horace's avuncular advice, and his admittance that I'd been somewhere last night that was over-saturating the newspaper's second page. Though unlike old Thadd, thankfully even though it had been an ultimate occasion, Horace will take pride in me when he finds out that I was truly careful about over-indulging. Having learned how to appear over-indulged but in actuality steering clear of it, or most of it, I recalled my megaton marriage break-up only too well when one's psychological damage was at its highest calibration. As Horace recalled, that had taken much time, humiliation, and endless mending of one's mind and money. Last night I'd vowed to stay virtually ascetic, and as I watched old Thadd and others, I was glad to be thoroughly through with overdoing it. Think of it? After all those decades of work, why would I ruin my hard-earned 'free-eedom'?

Damn good sense, Algernon!

No longer at Whitehall's beck and call, I drove off the boat in Boulogne with my faculties nicely intact. Freedom certainly felt pleasant driving away in the world's most-adored automobile accelerating along familiar roads deep into the center of sunny France. I'd decided to start off my retirement by sightseeing a couple of my favorite chateaux, but strangely as I drove, even in the world's most delectable sporty automobile, I couldn't put my finger on why; but my headache worsened, and I just wasn't enticed into what I was doing! Was it possible that I was personally a mite up in the air? Though this didn't come clear till one took a long sit on a bench with that driest of French sunlight penetrating one's garments and saw that, overall, coming down from my decades of fraught Service work, even though I'd so congenitally looked forward to this 'freedom'; still, I shouldn't be expecting, *what?* Some up-churning inner tune-up?

Sitting there though what I soon understood was, I was not doing what I really wanted to do!

Into a protracted consideration of this, as I downed my modest freedom reward of a lager or two at a typical French outdoor café, I saw that touring the Europe I knew well may not be enough to celebrate this retirement milestone. Because—although this may sound ludicrous—I was still very much hung-up on making additions to my drastically conceived Victorian house! So much so that did it really have me enslaved? Did I, Algernon Cholmondley-Rute, from my fantastic lineage, really mean this? Yet, a dire need of that American mansion flashed details with its considerable intricacies at me, so compellingly, with its wonderfully historic atmosphere, that I needed to attempt some new rationale.

Because of that house I'd sketched? What an iron-y!

It was even more ironic when I realized that creating one's house during those boring staff meetings in Moscow hadn't really been so bad! At least one's need to construct a noteworthy home had been mentally titillating!

Spinning 'Lamborghini' around stylishly, one drove back to Boulogne and noticed that immediately my cerebellum-rattle improved. Replacing it a lovely chirpy tune greeted me that I recognized as that bright, little 'Anitra's Dance' of Grieg's, which I hummed, then gave it my solid tenor. While into the Grieg, I passed those regimented, fabulous French roadside trees for a good many miles, then those ultra-cared-for lollipop trees in front of enormous blasts of sunshine-yellow sunflower fields! How wonderful they all looked, how cheerily transcendental!

Because I had a more significant purpose?

Listen, old fellow, 'You are your own man', as they say now, so why not fulfill that dream of yours? Go on, say it.

Okay, Algernon, take off and tour America?

Particularly, the Great Lakes and lesser-known northern parts!

Sighing with improved affection for myself, I still zestfully sang, struck by what a lot there was to know about one's predilections and disinterests! One was now into a heavenly new prospect that I'd rarely ever glimpsed from within the bulwark of one's Foreign Service postings, as I saw how the entire handling of my predilections was up to me! As long as I kept them well away from Father.

Back on British soil later that day, 'Lamborghini' and I cruised to Southampton, and I watched my cherished car being swung up onto a freight carrier's deck. Actually, it had been given the care a noble automobile was owed; but now I had more exciting plans, I couldn't wait to see my phenomenal car coming off the boat at a New York City dock! First though, I hired a cab and returned to the manor to pack all weights of clothing, shoes, boxed-up books, Guerlain Homme astringent, binoculars, basic office needs, et cetera. I did my bit taking Jasmine and Gillie to dinner at some favorite flatulence-producing restaurant of theirs; then early the next morning, Horace ran me to Heathrow. "Watch it with those tricky Yanks, sir, smart as hell at bargaining," he warned sending me off. Once in America, I'd send Horace a P.C. and would really do some touring, and not just to get North of Washington D.C., U.S.A.

Chapter 2
Ah, America!

One would like to think that with that 'episode', and all that had been bewilderingly buried for recent days, that new resolves were pushing through these unknown curtains of mysterious darkness, but truthfully, one has to wonder if one could clinically be an amnesiac? *Although Algernon old scout, that can't be! One's unparalleled upbringing and all that sort of thing? Though quite honestly, one does keep having a problem or two with recent recollectings.*

Instinct assures me that one's episodes of quite scintillating memory were headed for a denouement. Forcing this belief I must continue to delve that intriguing momentum of my 'episode'. *Yes, reputed as an outstanding humanitarian, of course, you must, Algernon!*

Through the Delaware Water Gap and on into the verdant undulating spring countryside, U.S.A, 'Lamborghini' whisked one along the fine broad roads in a swinging motion that perfectly suited one's better mood. One was quickly into the fragrant Ichabod Crane country, I'd heard about; then I dropped down to smaller highways to examine Dutch hillside farms and mills. Getting used to there being all the time I ever needed now for whatever I wished to do, I satiated my curiosity by orientating myself at little local museums. Western New York State wasn't as bland as my road map indicated, because coming to the first Great Lake—surprise!—it was so vast, it looked as wild as the Atlantic! New York State shared this Great Lake with Canada, though it was too misty to glimpse their mounted police on the Canadian side! Sorry, old chap, one couldn't resist that little joke! One's new solitariness, one supposed.

Heading south from this Great Lake, as the sun became hotter and lost its humidity, urban sights became pictorially clear, and then one came to smaller lakes. According to a local museum, these lakes had anciently been made by glaciers. Five parallel glaciers had pushed longitudinally through Western and Central New York State, making attractive smaller 'Finger Lakes'. 'Smaller' is relative, as thrilled; 'Lamborghini' and I climbed the steeper inclines concertinaed between these picture lakes, rising and descending with their hills and gorges. Up high I could look down on a panorama of one smooth lake punctuated with waterfalls and the odd marina that made me want to drive this lake's entire circumference—which I did. This lent wonderful viewing and took 75 miles to ring this Finger Lake with its Indian name and an Indian ambiance; and it was all lovely and exciting except that I was getting aggravatingly tired. Not so surprising, I'd been driving since meeting-up with my shipped, world's most outstanding car early this morning at the New York City dock.

Everything scenic attracted me or was soothingly pleasant, but tiredness came on in growing surges. Probably due to undergoing one's retirement adjustment and the resplendent London-shindig, but fatigue wafted at me in muscular waves—one was 60 after all! Sighting an uplifting little inn nestled ahead among trees, I made for it and gracefully swung into its parkway. Once out of the car, I stretched lengthily; then reaching backwards, stretched out my considerable stiffness again. Going in this inn, an attractive woman behind the bar had seen my car and greeted me, knowing how a Lamborghini owner should be treated, and we quickly became friends.

Settling one's bag in an attractive country bedroom, though actually one's height made one have to stoop for lintels and even ceilings; but it took no time for 'Sylvia'—I'd heard this woman's name being called—to get me tasting some of the best local Chardonnay west of the Azores. Truly, one had to remark on its rosemary dashed with Brussels sprouts, I think it was, similarly with the laudable body and pungencies of her other viniferas. Quaffing away after sitting all day, I'd been so driving-tired, I let my bones loosen all I could on a bar stool, too fatigued to more than pretend to listen to Sylvia's conversational efforts. But when Sylvia determined to convince me that some local property attached to a winery was aesthetically in need of an epicurean's taste, such as one's own, one had to laugh. She kept on about this again to this handsome fellow coming in. One phonetically recreates this fellow's speech because it was so remote from one's prep school English, as he said, "That properdy is the Creador's gift to a man o' discriminading tastes!" What could one to do but curb one's mirth?

Not that this entertainment stopped either this chap or Sylvia from insisting that this 'gem of a lucrative little winery' was the perfect place for a sophisticated retiree! "All it needs is a buyer with your kind of finesse!" She blatantly complimented.

Dear, oh dear!

Then, weren't most bars amusing little places?

This couple suspected that one might be expansively versed in European wines, and in this they were right! Many a holiday had been spent testing the fine German and French cellars. Celestial heavens, don't get me going on the Chateau de Beaune estate! The rarity of their '39 Montrachet—unimpeachable! As with the '46 Meursault Charmes' fine aggressive aroma! Ah those rarest of vintages! All so extraordinary, words are never enough! Indeed, few connoisseurs relished the nuances of those superb extra sec as one had! Though sadly, this also recalled the misery inflicted by one's ex-wife's incorrigible self-centeredness that must have had as blinding an effect on me as an opera's love-potion! Those French and German cellar owners were related to one's double-dealing abomination of a spouse; and consequently, as I made it clear to Sylvia, those most glorious wines had to be relegated to the past. This said, no more of that!

Sylvia and 'Reb', as she called him, continued to smother me with their amusing wayside hospitality, even though one had not been introduced, which didn't matter as I was only staying for one night. Having simply gathered that her chap's name was just 'Reb', I wondered where a twit name like 'Reb' came from? Reb! Reb-el? A Reb-herring? Inwardly laughing, as living alone one needed to liven up one's thoughts with intellectual little puns. Though one found they were best kept to myself—spoken aloud they received such sour-faces!

Sylvia was Reb's comely bartending paramour, and it came out that she owned this inn. At this point, Sylvia gave me a 'Be-back' wag of her forefinger as she left me with 'Reb' to take a tray of drinks to a table. She was certainly an attractive country soul, shapely calves, 45-ish.

Alone with 'Reb', still without being introduced, he said, "Can't beat that property! Hans Runditz owns it, and I know for a fact he's been looking for the right man. Never out to steal y' blind, not Hans! That place is made for an English gentleman, like you! You're retired? A Brit, aren't you?" I nodded to both his questions noticing that Reb's smile had a twinkle to it, as in a summarizing tone he informed, "Have to see it to get at what I'm saying… 90 acres of real good Seyval, Niagaras, and grapes of all kinds, and as cool as an antique farm house." And as no words were adequate, he gave an over-awed turn or two to his handsomely sculpted head, "And get this – licensed for a historical sign! All kept repaired and done up with a tasting room to beat any overlooking the 30 miles of Seneca. Seneca is a lake." And as one looked at him quizzically, he went on, "Good-sized barns in the coolest shape, one's a rental. Bonus there, you'd make extra off that." As he rubbed his palms together, "And, shh!" Holding up a tanned finger, he lowered his voice, "Here's what no one knows. It's all about to go on multiple listings!"

One has to confess one was mentally busier replicating Reb's rural-American dialect than absorbing his context. Though with Sylvia back, one became aware that this couple were succeeding in getting one slightly stoked up if you will. She telling about the flowing lawns and the 'jewel of an oak deck overlooking the humungous view', as Reb handed me a titillating little local *Gewürztraminer*. Yet pleasant as this coddling was, one really didn't want to listen to more as all this real estate talk was getting too close to having to explain one's personal life, and that one was divorced—oh so messily.

"You've got to see it, it's so-ome place!" Sylvia elaborated. "And you couldn't meet a more awesome guy than Hans Runditz."

They kept this up till one realized that with such genuinely kind people, one had better come clean; and one applied one's finely practiced diplomacy for letting them believe that though all their persuasion may have struck a chord, one was British after all and had no intention of becoming 'a prospective buyer'. I went on, "In all honesty, one's singleness has been indescribably sportive since one's divorce." This received a mix of glad and sad exclamations as they awaited one's elaborating, but one had not been brought up to go on exposing one's dirty underwear in public—though this really was an exceptional *Gewürztraminer*—and as gorgeous Sylvia pressed one further, one's explanation suddenly came out, and shamefully, far too loudly. "Once freed from that virago." A name that stumped Reb, though Sylvia's nodded understanding carried him as beneath my collar heat intensified. "One finally found people that gave one more consideration, and one's newly divorced status moved into remarkably free days."

I omitted the weeks of languishing in hospital drying out among far more white-coated concern than was necessary till being assured that my divorce was finalized. Then as expected with ancient blue blood, like mine, plodding along in one's veins, self-respect quickly re-emerged, and one's vitality renewed. "As you're observing, Reb, now I can appreciate a modest glass or two of wine, which led me to discover that one's wine sophistication was certainly intact, along with one's admiration for grape growing, and all that stomping around in bins on certain harvests till the juice fetches up a cunning little extra brut champagne!"

"You're better off now you're divorced, then?" Sylvia asked charmingly.

One was taken by her personal directness as much as her good curves as I felt free to say what I wished to over here with these friendly curious people, that anyway after tonight on my tour I would never see again. "It might be hard for you good people to understand, but that man-eating temptress."

"Your wife?"

"Francesca, my wife, yes. She managed to make those fine Continental wines devilishly fraught with desire—not sexual, one hastens to explain; but fraught with the desire to escape her, Francesca, as she'd wanted one to succumb to a more desperate need for wine! But what could one do when one's appreciation was being skillfully maneuvered by a venomous spouse who knew full well how destructive intoxication was to one's public profile as a Cholmondley-Rute, not forgetting one's position in the Foreign Service."

"The FOREIGN SERVICE!" Sylvia was loudly awed. "Oh, are you? Oh, that's sad! Can't one – excuse me, I mean, can't *you* put all that behind you and start over?"

"That's what I'm determined to do, Sylvia. My name is Algernon, by the way, Algernon Cholmondley-Rute. Cholmondley spelled 'C-h-o-l-m-o-n-d-ley', pronounced 'Chumley'. Chumley-Rute."

"Alg'non," Reb repeated.

Returning to the gluey tentacles of one's former marriage, "Being a man of principles, it took umpteen years for one to recognize I was legally no longer enslaved to that effete slut."

"Slut, yeah…" Reb preferred this description.

"I do my best to obliterate those days of Francesca's brandishing the whip," and to the dropping jaws of Sylvia's customers along her bar, because to these Americans, one's staccato English might sound too much. "Well, whip is a mite illusory! But, oh did she de-mAND!" Catching one's reddening face between bottles before the bar mirror, where I saw that my mounting intolerance was a smidgen inappropriate for these kindly country souls. Modifying, "I will just say this. That woman showed a greater respect for her diamond-collared pet anteater than her loyal spouse. Lord, she made me run in and out loading her car with suitcases, Channel carrier bags, glossy Vogues, emergency Wellingtons, douche bag, zipped bags of her moistened prunes; and only a higher order knew what else while she made 'adjustments' before her boudoir mirror. I paced, like an unfed platypus, for a half hour beside that idling antique Armstrong Siddeley Sapphire of hers—dear heavens, how that woman could fume! It's little exaggeration to say that one's burden due to that gross slut could outweigh quite a tricky problem at the Security Council."

"The SECURITY COUNCIL!" Sylvia and her customers awed astonishment.

"But your parents?" Reb gently probed.

"Yes. One should explain that I didn't hang around the family manor, as one had been trained from infancy to know that it was not in a second son's future to run the Cholmondley-Rute estate. Older brother Gilmore had been amply conditioned for that. Because I was not to take over the manor—I needed to—pardon! Rather one should say, *one* needed to… huh!" Pulling a self-reproachful face , "One tries not to resort to the subjective 'I'. One mustn't lose one's worldliness just because one is retired!"

Sylvia had turned to quaintly repeat to Reb that because of one's worldliness, sometimes one called oneself 'One' instead of 'I'.

Companionable as these pleasant people were, it wasn't apropos to tell them too much about myself as there was no proof that these charming country chaps—'folk', as they like to be called here—were genuinely out to aid their community by luring one's European influence to it. Less charitably it struck me that they could be talking up this bogus property purely as an evening's bar-time amusement. One couldn't blame them—who doesn't like to be entertained?

However, as I'd put in a heavy driving day, and one's vitality was running down, one let in the pleasantness of this friendly inn with its moon-glow lamps and its unobtrusive jingle of voices. But much as I appreciated the appealing owner and her 'live-in's' information, I did wish they would get off this wretched real estate topic! With the spring's clear air wafting through an open window into this agreeable non-smokiness, just about any other conversation would make a frightfully gratifying conclusion to one's touring day. Without the energy to initiate some subject, I finally resorted to the only alternative of getting them off one's back. "Oh, righty-ho then!" And I feebly made an 'appointment' to go to this mansion winery with 'Reb' and Sylvia, making sure they understood that much as it was frightfully kind of Sylvia and all that, one reserved the right to cancel and continue one's tour. We left it that, and ostensibly in the morning they were to drive me to this mind-anesthetizing place!

Having devoured a plate of 'burger n' fries', Reb handed me a magazine with its dog-eared page corners turned to an article he recommended on local wines. Bidding them goodnight, I watched for bumping my head as I took the stairs and got ready for bed and reading Reb's information on Pinot Noir in New York State. I must have slept soundly after all the talking and quaffing; although awaking the following morning, one's breathing was worryingly stertorous till one removed the wine magazine smothering my face, and more regular breathing quickly resumed. Checking my watch, a couple of hours before the so-called 'appointment' with Reb and Sylvia, an 'appointment' one didn't take seriously, so no need to rush waking. One's habit was to always skip any sleep-disrupting early morning food.

On every waking retirement day, including this morning, I was refreshingly greeted by my abundance of each of my days being holidays. This may have been why I felt a mite lightheaded. My good mood could most certainly be put down to one's freedom for indulging in the pleasantness of a country morning lie-in in America. Flat on one's back, I stretched out my legs, feet dangling between the bed's brass end-struts; and feeling the full length of one's able-body, I put a second pillow to raise one's head and look about. Outside on the window's sill, a gray squirrel neatly revolved an acorn between his nimble little fingers. Some splendidly shaped young 'Squirrel Nutkin' with the friendliest disposition as he looked in at one luxuriating in this new full day of one's own in Western New York State. His companionable nibbling lent such serenity and enchantment to this morning, I was whisked back to my childhood—not so unusual with fine mornings, as one's earliest childhood years were the criteria for perfect mornings!

One's childhood days had been enchanting because Mother saw to it I'd been rapturously carefree! Or she did until Nanny, tutors, and schools used their insidious rules to swill my magic hours down the sewer. Believe me, with rules for eating, sitting, walking, breathing, speaking, learning, and, not to mention, reforming one's digestive system both up and down, one quickly comprehended that one was being ground-up like a chunk of rump meat to be slipped into an intestinal membrane and made into a societal bratwurst if you please! One was lashed, scorned, and shamed into understanding that these rules were to obtain what all growing persons were supposed to desire, which was… form! Not 'my' form, mind, but 'their' form. Especially Father's, who reiterated that 'the least of human existence receive excruciating punishment if he or she didn't develop 'form!' To Father, 'form' meant everyone else's behavior, though never his. Sadly, once 'rules' had been applied, my valuable young spirit never returned again. Never! Form eclipsed all!

I'd been fully awaking on that U.S.A. morning with one's inquisitive white-bellied squirrel still gnawing as he regarded one through the window, and slanted sun blocks brightened the ivory ceiling and wall. One could only wonder at this sudden affinity to one's charmed childhood back at the Cholmondley-Rute estate, as Mother—that most precious of all angels—made sure I'd only had my own carefree self to amuse during those unforgettable days before Father banished one off to boarding school for having the nerve to be alive. Even more of a pain than Eton though was one's inheriting older brother. One has to say that during the war years with all the sheltering, dodging of bombs, and machine gun bullets, there hadn't been a speck of adult encouragement for getting to know one's brother and even less from Gilmore himself. Not even when I'd nabbed Nanny's bird crust to share with him in the family air-raid shelter.

Marriage, after a good many years of freely working for the Foreign Service and the refreshment of being well away from Father, had to be just another challenge to one's status that had to be braved, though why hadn't I insisted on my freedom during Father's evil arrangements?

Because, one knew astutely that when Father made a major demand I'd be naïve not to watch out! Father surrounded himself with tough handymen on probation. "Murderers," Nanny had whispered. Behind him too were uncles, threatened cousins, and others with well-paid off perverted pride in Father and the legendary Lord Godfrey Cholmondley-Rute, whose bloody swashbuckling crusade had been alongside merry old Lionheart Richard. One's revered family line was quickly rubbed in one's face when it was convenient.

One has to say that one's living standards would have been tighter without one's private Cholmondley-Rute income, which Father had a phobia for constantly threatening. But having embraced singleness till middle-age, it was horrendous too to find oneself being fed, like a mouse to a cobra, to this fanged daughter of a land owner—absolutely terrifying—all to satisfy a business whim of one's beastly tyrannical parent. Father had even rigged one's 'emergency leave' with some dotty peer, who ordered me home where I'd awaited my doom addled with fright as Father's merciless 'probationers' hid behind the Great Hall pillars for making sure I stayed put.

One had been forced into marrying that vicious Francesca on that much-trumpeted day, and it wasn't to matter that I had only once met one's wife to be. Virtually dragging along what felt like at least the Rosetta Stone, one had to legally and publicly commit to this adulterous scheming female of Father's in, of all places, St Paul's Cathedral! To this day, one can only get that virago's name out of one's mouth by recalling that one's ex is now safely off in Capri, posing on the wall of her Corbusier cliff-dwelling overlooking the Med as she thrusts out her pointy little breasts for *Daily Mirror* photographers!

Yet is it credible that a father could conspire to do this to his own flesh and blood?

As expected that whole marital disaster, along with one's famously relieved new bachelorhood, was over-sensationalized by the tabloids. Proving to this pitifully squeezed-out husband that the institution of matrimony must be avoided at all costs! Cambridge was right—women were not the movers and shakers in this world of even dwindling empires, and one had observed enough of one's parents to know the truth of this. Francesca though mocked marriage by flaunting her faithlessness till Father actually lost the land deal! Though it was with me his anger erupted so lethally that he pulled all kinds of strings to get one sent to the most distant of exotic Foreign Service outposts in Mau-mau country. One has to say that one had only survived by intensely involving with one's new nation's 'consuming' interests! Please excuse one's awful joke.

That inflated marriage debacle proved that despite centuries of splendid old Cholmondley-Rute stock, one's father's conjugal arrangement had been horrendously wrong-headed! Oh, for heaven's sake—here one is all churned up with one's parental crime again—*shouldn't I forget it now I'm retired?* Ha! A knock at one's door?!

One had needed to slow one's over-working breathing after all that unpleasant reviewing of Father's despotism. "Come in!" The distraction of one's pleasantly replying helped.

Thankfully, Sylvia entered carrying a cup and saucer, and my hostess looked scrumptious this morning, adorned in an artful little off-bartending summer frock, which completely stopped one from re-living any more of that disastrous parental crime.

"Coffee, to get you going?" she urged placing the deliciously aromatic cup on one's side table. "Donuts and cereal are downstairs." though as one's head was going from side to side, she didn't bother finishing. "The wine gave you a good sleep?" she asked noticing one's feet stuck between the brass bedposts, "Oh, you are tall!" She turned toward the windows, "Tst, Reb didn't pull?" Sylvia certainly had excellent legs.

“One prefers the curtains not pulled, and yes, one did sleep well, as one usually has of late.” One checked one’s watch.

Sylvia noticed my check. “Reb will be here in half an hour. We’ll take our car,” stated with nurse-like brusqueness.

“One would prefer following you and Reb in one’s own vehicle.” One stated making sure she understood that one’s hormones were as well activated as hers.

“Whatever!” Using that trendy, Cadney-type word, which one accepted as reluctant agreement before she smiled and left the room, closing the door.

Showered and in fresh, well-pressed trousers and shirt, due to one’s travel habit of ‘subbing’ for oneself on urgent international journeys. I was known for packing ingeniously, and having combed one’s admired crowning glory, one splashed one’s defined cleanly shaved jaw with Guerlain Homme astringent. Adjusting the swing to the floor-length standing mirror, one’s lithe handsomeness had certainly long since established full recovery from that abomination of a marriage to the succubus. Reflected, one stood tall, left knee slightly bent, right hand on the hilt of one’s feigned sword, and deciding to trot this fine image down for the benefit of other guests at this inn, one descended the stairs as steadily as a well-trained colt.

Looking to the left in the sunny courtyard on this serenely fresh day, my stream-lined Lamborghini awaited my tour continuing. Politeness though made one check to the right on the off-chance, Sylvia’s hot persuasion had not been flippant. Surprisingly, there were Reb and Sylvia deep in discussion, their heads close as both leaned elbows to the bonnet, or ‘hood’ over here, of a surprisingly decent-looking Lincoln Town car that I would not have expected American country persons to own! Their heads rose on hearing the gravel crunch beneath my Swedish walking shoes, though they continued what secrets they were about. Nothing amiss here, because as any diplomat knows, the human mind is fraught with pockets for secreting away the most classified of information. All one had to watch was that these two weren’t concocting some strung-out joke—but no—plentiful mutual smiles, hands put out cordially for shaking, and lots of small affable nothings about the fineness of today’s weather considered apropos for one’s native islands believed to be under a continuum of monsoon.

Driving my soigné sports car, I followed Reb’s gray-green sedan, still wondering at his owning that tastefully well-kept Lincoln! More extraordinary as I really didn’t know these two. Last evening, one had observed that lack of introduction was usual in rural New York State, even when one had given one’s name. Instead, Reb and Sylvia simply moved in on my least-given information and added their own embellishments. Not that I really minded when new acquaintanceships reaped such entertainment.

Getting this ‘appointment’ over with, so ‘Lamborghini’ and I could continue our tour, one kept the rear of Reb’s Lincoln in sight though—pay attention, old chum! We were turning down a lane lined with fine French-styled 40-foot or so tall trees. Reducing speed, I could see vine rows between these tree trunks diagonally that as one drove swiveled to end on, and all without a weed! Again, European-styled with commendably symmetrical planting! I had to admit my interest was perking up.

Much as I love driving one's most stupendous of all sports cars, here I am at last retired, which was also to be when I was to make room for another serious long-term objective of mine—throughout my illustrious career, I had secretly always longed to become '*lowly*'. I'm not joking. I believed I could learn how to appreciate lowlier living if I studied loosening one's decorousness and allowing oneself to become more plebeian. As I was currently renouncing the glamor of the upper crust and the high-profile living that had so heavily directed my professional life, my curiosity had increased for that 'lowlier' life. I'd envied in young salesmen, or when grabbing a coffee at an airport kiosk, or observing men with women in a hotel bar, how they talked, their relaxed vocabulary, the way they checked one another out, their crisp endearments. This captivated me and made me dearly aware of this walloping great side of humanity I'd barely known. Good grief, such a void! When here I was, a professional humanitarian! Oh-oh… Reb's Lincoln was slowing to a graceful crawl. *Watch it, Algernon!* More of all that another time.

One wondered if we could be passing Reb's 'converted barn'.

This was confirmed when my friend's brown hand extended from his Lincoln's window to point to this barn and give an Italian-type rub of the finger-tips that over here in America must mean money too. One's Lamborghini dragged past the cheerful yellow trim to this barn's windows and doors that I deduced to be Reb's 'rental bonus'. Beyond this, as the drive bent around, there was another large mansard-roofed red barn, typical of this region, and again it appeared to have excellent construction and be beautifully maintained; and by the activities of two men seen through its sunlit doorway, this barn was being used as a wine-production center. Reb may have said it was. Coming out from between the trees lining the graveled road—I'd call it an avenue—I had lowered Lamborghini to less than a crawl around these barns and was into a small parking area looking across the flowing lawns, Sylvia had described last evening, that went straight down to a fringe of trees and this Finger Lake's tranquil great breadth. One had been aware of this splendid lake off in the distance, driving here behind Reb's Lincoln Town car; and now, as one's celebrated car followed, looming on one's left—oh my God, yes! That's how it had been! I'd FOOTED THE BRAKES!

DEAR LORD! Reb had said an 'antique farm house', but this—this was VICTORIAN! And oh no! It was MY Victorian house! With MY recessed door, my grapevine relief! Though how can this be? It doesn't!

I'd stirred up more sensational reactions as I looked all this than I'd ever known! I'd followed Reb, and—but I must be wrong—this isn't making sense! Though there it was again; no doubt about it, I was gazing at MY mansion as scalding chills ran up and down my chest—my back!

MY hooded, tall windows, and my deep wrap-around porch, with steps coming down to the lawn just as I'd designed them! My house-wide front porch!

Even in this super recollecting, how was it possible to accept that I was actually in front of my own conceived mansion reverie?

Well, one has to admit that…

Here I was at last re-living this outrageously mind-dislocating scene again! Dammit all one had been amnesic! Truly I was! And I'm still drowned in bewilderment! Though. I recall that one had bitten right through one's lip, which my tongue found now as a healed hard lump, because studying every incredible detail, I must have been into this confrontation unlike any I'd known the world over! Though here one was looking at the incredible materialization of one's own original sketch! There was no doubting that this was indeed one's most carefully constructed and beloved 'SUPREME HABITAT'! Conceived thousands of miles from here in a freezing Moscow meeting! Yet, HOW?

One's spirit, mind, and entire bodily temple were suspended. And again, ignominious gawking was all I could manage! Because, this house before one could only have risen from—but hell, reality? Science? How was this possible?

Oh, come on now, Algernon, you had to have seen it once, buck yourself up; be rational.

Though there it was festooned with those outsized, Victorian, fluted moldings; its gigantic overhanging eaves—that I'd thought up! Towering before me was the materialization of my own most secretly constructed superlative mansion! Touchable, dimensional, wryly communing, authoritative, and dramatically adorned with all one's admired enrichments! Cornices conceived—yes, oh yes! Conceived right out of those insufferable Moscow meetings!

Will one ever really accept that this was so?

So, there it was, that was it! *Here it was!*

I had successfully recalled this epic traumatic supernatural event! That had given one amnesia?

Chapter 3
Hans

From refining my doodles in that Moscow meeting, till confronting my 'Supreme Habitat' here in the Finger Lakes, New York, U.S.A., I'd been caught into the pathology of what had happened to me. Assessing this metaphysical event as coolly as one could, it was no wonder my mind had been drowned by that mystery knocked into that refusing to clarify cloud hanging over me! In recalling what had happened, I felt quite limp. Yet it had needed recollecting with fanatic exactness—no understanding of its enchantment, sadly, but chronologically certainly that's much of what had happened—and I had recalled it! Though no recollections of it had returned—Had Reb and Sylvia previously known me?

Its enchantment still stretches far beyond my acceptance of normal seeing, hearing, and feeling as I sit here in Lamborghini holding my head in my hands—For how long? For far longer that I knew.

Had I glimpsed that this would be the end of my story? That my more competent, capable, and wiser self would now move into it with greater understanding, and my bewilderment would fade?

After all, this had all been before returning to the Cholmondley-Rute Manor to get the money from Ollie. But before that, hadn't I also met the owner of this super-terrestrial mansion? Hans Runditz—not so unforgettably.

Fixated to this illustrious architectural accomplishment, trying to force a smattering of calm before Reb and Sylvia came over to me, I was incidentally aided that moment by a flash of this region's history, from one of those quaint little museums that informed me that this type of fine Victorian showpiece was historically very much North American, having been built during the height of that lake's booming barges era—that time those fine steam boats towed scores of freight-filled barges, and all that sort of thing—information that quite braced one's dilapidated faculties.

Reb's country voice came through the open car window, "Wanna get out an' take a peek? Give me a minute to say hi to Hans." The elderly man Reb went up to meet the actual owner of this property, who was hung onto a cane and needed Reb's arm. An elegant elderly figure, lean and dignified in white shirt and chinos, speaking to Reb up on the porch—my porch of this building's outrageous mystique—just as he might meet someone anywhere! While down by the steps, Sylvia studied her foot idly toeing the grass.

Whatever force one had inadvertently touched off during those dullest Moscow staff meetings, I was being shown that my reveries had had a far greater power than I'd a hope of understanding, making one think could this have anything to do with my secretly wishing to become 'lowly'? Because in one's most fair-minded, deepest, self-comprehending state, one had experienced so many instances when 'lowliness' had eluded me. Could this house be going to show me if 'lowliness' really is that blissful state of forever being away from all the formalities of decorum and glamor? From all that pomp and God-awful smiling small talk loaded with blatant white lies that one's former position had necessitated?

Though to purchase this reverie mansion, as I would have to, dear heavens, Reb was beckoning me from up there still next to this 'Hans'! *Then, Algernon—brace yourself!* Crudeness of non-mastered feelings could dash one's renowned reputation for well-practiced negotiating. As this mansion was going to be mine and was not in one's own country, to purchase this enigmatic place, one would have to use every bit of one's admirable rearing and shrewdness.

It felt strange realizing that this had just been another greatly changed day of my retirement holiday in the Finger Lakes, intended as a touring holiday. Though one had simply come across this seductive wonder-house, and 'life', as I'd known it, had stopped. Instead, now I was being asked to join this owner of *my* house!

To become this surreal mansion's owner—to walk in and out of it as anyone might their own beloved home—one had to ditch any further touring plans and prepare instead to simply push through the meanderings of purchase. Oh! Over by the porch steps Sylvia was beckoning me. *Fullest attention, Algernon!* One got out and went to her. I must be doing better at taking in what I'd always believed was real, because as I bent to Sylvia, she cupped her hands around my right ear, which was the closest I'd come to one's once-known 'reality'. "Thought you might want to know, Algernon," cozily using my first name as she whispered, "the woman renting the apartment in that second barn we drove past is a witch!"

Not needing to hear this, I tossed off her concern with one's bon-vivant laugh and didn't bother with what else she had to say because coming across my miracle of a Victorian villa was enough. Though retrieving my voice, one assured Sylvia, "Righty-ho, yes, one takes your point." That happened to come out in a maddeningly juvenile voice, though it was conveniently saying nothing. One must be restraining my euphoria, because by Sylvia's anxious look at me, I could tell she knew I hadn't paid attention.

Instinctively, one's upbringing kicked in, "If you and your partner would be good enough," endeavoring to pitch my voice to B-minor, "to be my guests for lunch later? You say where?" Sylvia's nod was enough. Which was probably because one's inane smile refused to stop.

Calming down continued to be an effort, particularly now when there was a 'witch' on the premises! *Extra control on this one, Algernon, no offensive laughter! As a buyer, it would not be good business to have to explain one's hysterics.*

Certain areas were striking of this extraordinary meeting with this mansion's elderly owner! Having tapped my foot on the wood, though I knew, the house was certainly real as I also studied my most satisfactory details as I walked along my villa's sturdy porch—the scalloping surrounding the porch arches, the perfectly integrated moldings—right out of one's excellent sketch before that arsehole Cadney had so blunderingly dumped it.

'Hans' was all smiles and attractive charm! Reb actually introduced us, and 'Hans' clasped his free hand so hard around mine, my fingers were scrunched. This was one's first formal introduction in New York State! Reb apparently had known enough of Hans to put himself out for two Europeans, and when we were through hand-gripping—happily relieving one's digital pain—Hans lavished on his accented warm welcome. His German background came through unmistakably as he swung his expressive arm back in his bountiful manner, which unsteadied him; so Reb and oneself rushed to rebalance him before he could lead us inside his sublime, metaphysical mansion!

Hans Runditz was a sinewy man with parchment skin and an impressive heavy brow that prominently ran down the bridge of his nose, fish-like, making his viewing difficult, which was undoubtedly why he turned his complete head to each of us as he spoke. Yet there was a wealth of experience in those wall-eyes, and he had been handsome, was still in his piscine way. He struck me as a man whose endless former vitality was now sadly reduced to his vibrancy of speech and his wide arm-gesturing. Following him through the massive double doors that had my carved window protection of magnificently designed acanthus leaves, Hans nodded to my constant appreciation! I noticed too that Reb revered Hans, like a father, having held one of the double doors wide for him; then he caught him on each waver inside too, as we both tried to.

In continuing his welcome with another of his expressively high-arm swings, we were to sit where we wished or reverting to his accented-English, 'Vere ve vished'. One chose an armchair, ignoring its little footstool as one's lengthy legs stretched out well above it in this tastefully appointed parlor that, in keeping with the mansion's magnificent exterior, continued its exquisitely fine interior restoration. One couldn't find an overlap in the wallpaper or a chip in the paint, and complementing its former era, it contained quite valuable vintage furnishings. "Please feel free to wander all of rooms," was Hans's response to one's devoting to this tall room with tall doorways. One's usual concern for a man of height, and as one looked about, whatever one saw only endorsed the house's titillating need to become mine! Or very nearly it did, I'd replace that maple tallboy with Mother's regency, mirror-backed chiffonier.

Hans Runditz's manner of swinging his free hand high till he over-swayed as Reb rushed to steady him toward a chair, where he continued this arm-gesturing to the gracefully curved stairway going up around this parlor's side and back walls. Looking up at this too, one asked, "Three bedrooms?"

"Four bedrooms up. Four!" Hans held up four long fingers in that rather irritating Germanic habit of making sure he had pierced one's denseness. "A convertible study, he is down. One bath, he is up," the forefinger pointed, "The washroom, he is between study and kitchen."

After explaining more about the house's layout, Hans excused himself and asked Reb and Sylvia to follow him into the next room, where one could just hear the three of them making arrangements to entertain one out on the deck. As it was not one's business to know about 'the yellow closet's wine glasses', et cetera, one sat back to take in that one was truly and actually sitting inside my supernatural house! Looking around this unreal room, wafts of the Rienzi throbbed its noble wrenching tune all through me in electro-magnetic gusts, filling this formal yet hearteningly fine parlor with its bounteous all-absolving stately emotion as my eyes lingered on the muted, lyre-patterned wallpaper. *Great Deities, could one's heart bear much more?*

Though I disciplined my heart as despite the luscious music, there *was* a lot more.

I caught Sylvia's distanced phrase from another room, "Yes, Hans, he's retired from the Foreign Service." One assumed that Runditz had been needing to know all he could about one as a buyer. His probing of Sylvia and Reb was perfectly sensible, as according to Sylvia, Hans had been on the lookout for a connoisseur buyer for his valuable mansion winery for some time. I couldn't hear more of my new friends' conversation, as it slid into a hum mingling one's head music and dominated by Hans' voice.

Listening to Hans, one wondered how he had come across this wonderful house, and whether he knew anything about its origin. I sat in stately ease inside this unbelievable 'Supreme Habitat', one savored one's obstinacy that it was to be mine! It was incredulous to be sitting here in this splendid little parlor with nothing but topping good feelings rolling out of one! I could not be anything but grateful to be retired, in perfect health, with one's share of good-looks, single, and free. And how trivial it all seemed now that on the other side of the Atlantic, one's father and brother believed one slimy and slithering, beneath contempt!

Sitting here I was even receiving flashes of being my old sophisticated and scintillating pre-amnesic self again!

While growing up, Father staunchly believed it mandatory that any future Cholmondley-Rute wife not only needed to be good-looking and gentry only; needless to say—as I continued entertaining myself while waiting—an especially good-looker for Gilmore, who was to become the next lord of the manor ,et cetera. Gillie, in Father's words, was 'God Almighty's divine catch for a woman!' One had inwardly chortled! One supposed this was why Father drilled away at making the best of Gilmore's disproportionately sloping shoulders and his pigeon-toed 'turkey strut', as Father termed it. Gilmore's sole noblesse obligation was to trap some beauty worthy of bearing consummate Cholmondley-Rute offspring for keeping up the line. Though, as expected, due to Father's asinine conditioning, Gilmore developed an unbearable overconfidence for ensnaring this woman, who would be sure to know if there was a split-pea under 30 mattresses.

Gilmore had certainly not been what even charitable persons could call handsome. One had heard that Father had considered Swiss facial surgery for his first son's gilded leadership, or so Mother had consoled me. Believable when Gilmore's braying laugh disclosed broad gappy teeth, that even as extravagantly tooled as money could render them, were set in a blare of pink gums that pitifully affiliated him with a beast of burden. Mother, being the epitome of discretion—from whom else had I inherited my diplomatic tact?—did her utmost to downplay her eldest son's unattractive smile, turned in feet and that bow-legged look of having just alighted from an overfed nag. Worst of all for Gilmore, however much fencing, martial arts and private posture-training were bestowed on him; the pitiful man simply lacked grace. No instinct. Apart from this, Brother Gilmore wasn't really such a snotty old bleeder—if you ignored his gooney-bird's hopelessness at making decisions.

It certainly was a delightfully restful parlor Hans had left me in! The lyre-patterned wallpaper was in the gentlest-misted Monet hues—though back to Gilmore—I could not say in all objectivity it was Gilmore's fault he'd sprung from the womb without a single one of Mother's famed patrician features. A masculine edition of Mother's remarkable beauty had awaited its reappearance in oneself. You've only to view Mother's dead-straight lengthy nose and her chiseled looks hanging in the National Portrait Gallery to be assured of one's compensating second son's heritage. No snarling nostrils of Father and Gilmore's ragged snouts noticed as our high-profile family was persistently photographed for the public's perversion. Many a tender-hearted paparazzi had cunningly redirected the reader's attention to Gilmore's 'ancestral fascination'.

Amazingly, Father paired Gilmore off with a quite beautiful woman—'Jasmine,'—though sometimes her 'r's' had the misfortune to come out as 'w's.'

Jasmine presented Father and Gilmore with five girls before; in an understandably hysterical speech lapse, she finally bore a 'weal wobust male heir'. For oneself during this, having been sent to various foreign capitals for polishing one's skills, I was aligning with other nation's foibles. These cultures, particularly the more cannibalistic, disclosed that all this hoopla about family heritage and being blue-blooded was shockingly myopic. An anachronistic burlesque, if you will. In his maturity now, Gilmore might agree—while contrasting poor Gilmore's enslavement with what could be bliss for oneself 'down the pike', as the trendy Cadney term goes, Hans Runditz hobbled back.

My good host broke one's rambling thoughts, declaring, "My legs, they are not good. I wish it not so, but no longer can I take you over house." His swung, nearly self-injuring arm generally indicating his priceless mansion. Over one's sympathy, Hans continued, "Reb is very good touring guide. He knows all house, carpenter much times with me, and he lives here through harvest. Know everything! Everything! But what I will tell you is, all things work excellent. Eva, my wife, would not tolerate faucet who go drip-drip, or window who rattle with wind." Hans gestured as he pulled a complicated facial expression at his wife's sensible intolerance. "I was good carpenter, plumber too, Reb will tell, till these dummkopf legs!" On this, Hans sunk onto a love-seat to put both hands to his left leg, as if it had no auto-lifting power, and raised it onto a car rug. Getting comfortable, he sighed and waved to Reb, "Feel free!"

With Reb given his cue, one arose and was directed through to the house's north side. Its attractive dining-room's delightful broad bay of windows, its convenient narrow corner doorway through to the kitchen—such good sense! Beyond the kitchen, unequivocally, would be my study with its paned outside door overlooking vineyards and a vista view of the lake. I paused here, seeing it piled with Faulkner novels on the desk within an arm's reach of the single little upholstered chair; and instead of the George Grosz over on the paneling, a more pleasing later Cezanne. Certainly, nothing horsey.

Reb nudged one on to be ushered up the invitingly curved staircase with its opulent chestnut hand rail contrasting its glistening white banisters—optimal maintenance! One was greeted at the top by a tall set of lancet windows looking out onto another spread of endless geometric vineyards. East of these, trees edged Lake Seneca's quartz-like glinting under the higher sun's brightness; and fishing boats dotted it, like mirrored fly droppings, all before the Ruysdael-hued hills several miles across on the opposite shore. These arched windows before one were actually paired and of decreasing heights. The tallest central pair being double French doors that opened onto a narrow balcony with two chairs—an ideal spot for savoring one's morning Turkish coffee.

Following Reb again along a short passage, we were into a huge white-tiled bathroom with glass faucet handles—such an original touch, just what I would have used. A stuffed chair with chintz irises covering it was beside an ancient wooden table that lent a pleasant hominess to this spacious room. It may once have been a fifth bedroom.

Everything Reb showed me seemed as if it was flowing from my own choices. Even a stream of childhood sensations accompanied each familiar room, restoratively papered by Hans's wife, Eva Runditz, as if I had thought them up! "All most beautifully kept up, Reb," I muttered as greatly pleased, as one was amazed. These interiors couldn't have been more fundamentally Victorian, though Eva's taste, and one's own agreeably uplifted; and again owed to Eva, each room was equipped with a wash basin, European-style. Everything my eyes took in endorsed that one was in one's very own home! "Despite Hans's miserable legs, it's been masterfully maintained," I said smiling, as Reb thumped thumb to chest, letting one know a good deal more about the skills of Sylvia's good 'live-in'. "You've known Hans well?"

Reb nodded, but turned, unwilling to talk about him. "This way, Alg'non."

This same tasteful precision had been lavished back along the landing, where Reb turned to open one of several closet doors; and astonishingly, one of them revealed a narrow staircase that spiraled up into what must have been the cupola! An ingeniously secreted stairway! "I say, how absolutely corking!"

"Corkin'? Nah. Bottlings…" Yanking a fist to the production center.

"One is in awe!"

Reb's look was unreadable as he pulled a light cord on inside, and I followed him in. One had to watch for one's head on the low lintel; and bending to ascend, I clonked my skull anyway as one admired an area of Reb's 'original wood pan'ling', which even up here on this unseen stairway had a French finish rubbed to a luster beneath one's pressuring hand that took in its sturdiness, as it too had to have been given the best of skills. The stairs too were sturdy as one's weight rose on the turning solid treads. Every nook and corner of this dwelling demonstrated Hans's willful concern, his endlessly loving care. High up in this cupola room, Reb explained that the bed and dresser were his. Furniture heights thoughtfully below all four window levels on all sides that gave him a special little look-out nest up here among tree tops and crows! From this height, Reb pointed to where Hans' property boundaries lay, and one studied these before looking beyond them again at this Finger Lake's long glittering spread, which I now knew as Lake Seneca.

Returning downstairs, Sylvia and Hans were at a table out on an oak deck. This deck itself was glossily finished to a mirroring shine that extended the breadth of the house's east side. The wrap-around porch we'd first come in through was around the southern front's impressive double-door entrance. In a delightfully private roofed area here, Hans and Sylvia were away from the small tasting bar south of it where a few visitors still finished up, and this was next to a discreet-little porch wine shop.

One was particularly impressed by the floor we were standing on; and as Reb perpetually smiled, one was sure he'd been responsible for its indestructible finish. Quite a conversation piece with its many layers of varnish hard-worked to plate-glass protection; and walking on its perfect surface, one was again looking out at more long vineyards. "Seyvals," Reb had seen where one looked. I noted the kind of grape as I followed the vineyard's ideal slope down to the lake. Two men were working down there in the high sun's brightness, one in a cap, and I could just tell that the vines were promisingly loaded with tiniest butterfly leaves of palest celery.

"Admirable!" One breathed out more of one's private feelings than one had meant to in response to Hans' glinting pride, as one nodded to include Reb in one's head-shaking veneration. Accepting the chair Reb pulled out for me at their more secluded porch-end's table, just outside the window door to 'one's cozy study', my passion for the place kept on, "I can't compliment you enough, Hans!" Consciously restraining one's exuberance until having to relent. "More truthfully, one is swept off one's feet by the professionalism of every area of your extraordinary restoration!" One's straight-forwardness won out as Sylvia sat looking pleased; her earthy attributes healthy-looking under her protecting sun-brightened rose umbrella that she'd needed beyond this unroofed porch's extension.

One's joyous mood expostulated, "Coming here, what an adventure it must have been finding this ruined historic house, Hans?"

"Coming here? An adventure, you say?" Hans repeated, peculiarly pausing, fumbling. "Aah, 'FINDING' the house—her winery too?" His flustered voice squeaking to an eerily loud interrogative.

Had the mere thought of 'finding' this house hit a nerve with Hans? Had one unintentionally touched on his German trauma? "Hans?" One sought to renege.

Reb and Sylvia's concern also fixed to Hans, "It an ad-VENTURE you say, coming here!" He got out in scary blurts; surely, he wasn't being facetious. Had I any idea what I'd got going?

With more speechless single arm waves, Hans gave a turn of his head to eye the bottle and four glasses, "Sylvia, you pour." As she did so, one's host transformed this finest of atmospheres into a prospective dark, because he launched into a fervently jumbled explanation about his wife Eva, and him buying what had been such a relic of a house it had been listed for fire-burning practice. Waving a hand as he caught at himself for a moment, then explaining in a nervous but slightly more offhanded manner that during their first two years here, Eva and he had replanted three vineyards! "Three-ee!" holding up three fingers. “With very little help. This because Reb, he two years old only!” As Hans laughed too, this broke us up, and our worrying about him at least lessened.

The Runditzes and Fritz, their German winemaker, had replaced whole vineyards of native vines to make much finer wine blends. Turning his fish-like profile to me, Hans’ forefinger was held high for us to await him recalling the early days on this property. Then he sat forward on his specially cushioned chair in this shadowed sun’s warmth, and in stridently mocked awe repeated one’s too casual first question, “It an ad-venture, you say, coming here?”

Concerning with his apparent difficulty, one objected. “Hans, one hadn’t meant…”

But his dead-straight forefinger waggled yet higher for one’s patience, and he righted an irritating cough. “Where to start?” Or ‘vere’.

“Hans, there’s no need.”

But my host’s prerogative was bold with his retrieved voice, and as if bestowing a gift, he stated, “Newly married to Eva, I built first home in Schwarz Vald.” Launching into what had apparently been bottling him, between little throat clearings, Hans’ voice continued, making one wonder if he had prepared this talk—and if Reb and Sylvia had expected it. One’s chest tightened.

Sylvia too, queried him, “Ha-ans?”

“Hans, don’t let this be too much,” one insisted. Needing Sylvia though, as my purchasing plan was immovable—one was going to own this house—“Sylvia?”

Damn the woman, Sylvia shook her head at me, though she kept our glasses filled. Not having heard me, Hans barreled on telling how Eva and he had heard about the persecutions as he, Eva, and their families fled. Hans and Eva dodged a group execution and other horrific incidents before meeting up with other desperate-to-get-clear of Nazi madmen. Hans’ hatred of Hitler halted his cheerfully wafting arm that now lay leaden across his lap, having sharply changed all our moods. Re-living his and Eva’s epic journey with its grossest terrors, instead of gesturing, now he went into sudden isolated stares that forced one to pick up on his mind’s insane imagery. Sitting on this one’s Supreme Habitat’s front porch, I felt I owed him listening to his trauma, so we all heard how he and Eva eventually escaped through northern Italian ambushes to an overloaded ship that took them to dear old London, which coincided with Hitler’s blitzing of one’s homeland’s capital.

My host’s momentum was too powered-up and had locked both of us into the razor chills of mass killing’s grimness. One had to listen to Hans’ terrible saga and understand as he did that the Almighty had forced he and Eva to get out, leaving family members behind. Listening to Hans tell about getting over here to America, and their struggle to offset their profound despondence for those they’d had left behind and the Germany they had once loved; and having purchased the ruined house over here to cover their debts, he and Eva threw themselves into working the fields from dawn till dusk.

Almost horribly tragic, *but why in hell was this property-owner telling me all this? I desperately needed ownership of his mansion, and that was all! One was here to get this man to sell his property, because gripping me, overwhelming me, was his establishment of this heavenly spot of my 'Habitat's' creation.* But as Hans insistently kept on, how could one not feel the passion this owner had for all that his house had meant to him?

I was about to push more aggressively for what I was here for, but *hold it, Algernon—get wise! Has any building in all one's travels ever clonked me into the next century the way this one has? Sitting in this mythic home, this enigmatic mystery-mansion that at last now I could just begin to understand.*

Patience, Algernon!

Fact – the radical enchantment of this place can't be meant for anyone but me! This house has to be purchased! So, for God's sake, only blockbuster patience! Think.

Though Hans still had more to tell.

To keep up with him, I forced myself to listen by reluctantly looking back at the past too, though I hadn't wanted to.

It had been London for me at that time with all that frenzied organizing of escaped, displaced persons, such as Hans and Eva, in with its ineffable terror-ridden days. One's throat still pained just recalling that continual mania for dodging bombs, the black arm-banded mass of grief, while one's blasted comprehension plunged one into a dungeon of empathy for that poor escaping German couple.

One had known enough about all that, and one's imagination winced with what it must have meant to the Runditzes as barely surviving refugees.

Tilting his turned head, Hans muttered, "The house you'd said, *ja*, I know what it is you ask!"

He was not forgetting one's question?

Filling us in, it wasn't till long after the war that he and Eva made it over here to the States. A German winemaker they met up with knew of wine growing in the Finger Lakes hill country; and when the threesome made it here looking for vineyards, it was incidental that peeking out from under fallen trees they found decayed construction materials entwined by throngs of wild vine overgrowth. Then, details of the ruin of this former show-piece. Aware the details were of that former Victorian era, it had been through smashed hearts and paining muscles that with worker-bee sorcery, the Runditzes and Fritz transformed their ruin into its incredible present magnificence!

Trying not to think back to those gruesome years of Hans', of that massive war effort, for oneself too, as a child and young adult. One's impressionable young mind had known little else other than desperate men crouching the curbs eyes on their dice as they muttered their overburdened dirges—struggling, always struggling for food, medicine, shelter, clothing, and transportation—especially terrible if they were returned to barely surviving wives and children too. Frustrating under Parliament's astronomical debt and its decidedly new non-colonial outlook; borrowing prohibitively for what had to be done for the vast under-doctored, under-sheltered, underfed, and the vast still-smoking sections of flattened burned-damp cities—most notably and most excruciatingly, London. If one really did look back at all this, as one was reluctantly having to now, it returned with such breathlessly suffocating bouts, one needed to force stability as it couldn't be too unlike being buried alive.

Hans's gesturing caught at one's attention as one was needing to think more about all he'd been saying. Then the more I thought, his influence made me soften till… yes, Hans, you are right! This being an enchanted edifice, I'd better know anything that could throw light on its extraordinary powers. As a buyer of your unworldly house, I had better know of all the extraordinariness that has gone into it!

After dark when the snows came, with little money, the Runditzes worked at what was least ruined to reconstruct a room or two for themselves and Fritz. It took many hard-restoring years for the winery to produce, and more still for Hans to hire help and concentrate on the authenticity of his house's massive restoration. "Getting it rebuilt," he explained, "Reb's mutter over here, she do much with Eva all through, room by room. When Laburnum she arrive—she who rent barn apartment, and who helped much too." *Laburnum? The witch,* one wondered checking over at Sylvia. But engrossed in Hans' saga too, Sylvia wasn't showing any response. "Repairing walls, Eva and Laburnum studied much reproducing wall-paper and precise apply. Clever, the women, they digged out much."

The Runditzes' high standard wasn't only set by their winemaker for wine. If Hans built a doorway that was less than professional, Eva made him tear it down! Avidly, she inspected for whatever wasn't well-carpentered. Hans quickly saw the advantages of working to Eva's demanding standard, which both Runditzes insisted on when they hired workers too, for plumbing, heating, electricity, re-plastering, and papering; and more slowly and even more immaculately, for crafting the wooden exterior restoration. Eva also urged on extensive museum research and got it well-digested before getting in any help. But gradually, emerging from the terrible energy, triggering their slave-driving work, so antidotal to their tormenting grief and forced exile, slowly the mirage of what had once been splendiferously Victorian began to re-emerge; and over time, they returned the condemned old ruin to this present show-place in its fullest historic glory.

"Without doubt you've created a paradise!" I inadequately praised still on edge from all that tragedy. Reb too had sat listening to Hans's epic drama, as if hearing each phase of this house's renovating for the first time; though he did nod and add in murmurings he had undoubtedly known from his mother.

"We scythed that mud tractor lane you drove car in," Hans described the straight overgrown 'track' or 'avenue' from the highway to the barns, pointing out that as this present tree-lined road was a good distance from the highway, their estate stayed tranquil. He and Eva had planted the trees their first years; and recalling the gravel road one had driven in and its rows of fine trees, one certainly agreed that they had succeeded in keeping the house and barns serene. Hopefully, this was to be a selling point.

For all this detouring into Hans' tragic story, I was also seeing how unusually privileged I was to be given this history of the house I was to own. This was because while Hans told of its recreating, one had become aware that his wondrous mansion had never stopped claiming me. Actively! Arcane as this sounds. And this may have spilled through to Hans too, as he had so vigorously needed me to know the long years of his arduous and laborious work.

One had to keep reminding oneself that only an hour ago, one hadn't met this man!

This house's unusual story wasn't one Hans told easily, and in the buoyant spring air, still the question of why he'd insisted on telling it hung suspended between us. Desperate as Hans must be for his Shangri-La with winery to continue, one felt sure this shrewd property-owner knew only too well that one was already obsessed with purchasing his towering adult life's work.

One saw this wine drinking with him as an introduction to the transference of his property's ownership.

Needing a breather, Hans suggested Reb walked one around the vineyards or down to the lake. However, as Reb was needed by an employee from the production center just then, one assured him, "Please don't concern yourself, I'll enjoy a walk." With this agreed to, one left Sylvia and Hans exchanging what they knew about me.

After the surprisingly intense upheaval of this morning, one strode heartily around a lower vineyard that didn't have a tendril out of place. Glad to be alone after Hans's unexpected catharsis, I admired the precise 'H' tied vines with their immaculately tilled rows between them, the fragrance of the well-churned earth, before diverting down an inviting dirt track to the lake. I kept turning back to check up on the hill for every view I could get of 'my' extraordinary 'Habitat', formed from Hans and Eva's limitlessly learned skills for reconstructing, learned too from their incinerating tragedy.

By the lake one found a wooden dock, Hans', one presumed, and looked out across the peacefully rippling breadth of water. It brightened unbearably on one's sight toward its center, then diminished to muffle the far shore in soothing honeyed colors a couple of miles away. One had only seen this view with Reb from the mansion's upstairs, but needing to sort one's unsettled emotions, one listened to the water's musical lapping. A convenient silvery driftwood log made a smooth seat; and as one sat beside this lake's tunefulness, it became clear that having identified only too penetratingly with certain sections of Hans' traumatic saga, I too had been feeling some inner biffs.

From one's recently retired perspective, one saw that immediately after that world war, that like Hans, I too had survived, granted on opposing sides, that along with most youth one had determinedly whacked at those cosmically destroyed images, as everyone had. One had rarely looked back at this, though one had known an affinity with Hans when I'd worked with committees for transforming less damaged loved old sights to restored wonders. An endlessness of that restoration—often stuck in dire under-funding, or by intellectual impasses—should they be noble new quality ideals, or cheap, plentiful shelter for all? All that eternal debating. It had taken decades of aggressive politicians, city planners, brilliant engineers, architects, and craftsmen to cut through it all to replace with what everyone had been dreaming of pre-war London!

Not everyone cooperated. For example, shamefully, one's Father. Unless it served him commercially, Father hadn't shown one ounce of forbearance as he shouted around that he'd done 'more than his charitable share on a battleship'; and once out of uniform, he lost no time strong-arming vulnerable war widows to under-sell their land plots for increasing the manor's estate. Never having been an altruistic man, Father could not be called a model of post-war magnanimity.

In the Foreign Service too, one had been swept into the awesome experiences of other ruined countries' desperate return to a norm. Making sure I had the country's language down expertly, I'd found I had a proclivity for selecting compatible people and organizing the kind of meetings that usually made much needed progress for creating material consequences in all that brilliant bureaucratic, artistic, and muscled rebuilding that had one's humble efforts in with them. Today, far from this sparkling New York State Finger Lake, their proof can be sight-seen.

In telling this, Hans and I were different. Immersed in Europe's rebuilding, my pals or colleagues, like Hockney or Thaddeus, were filled to the gills with 'belief' in some clean surreal future that could become so strident that outwardly I believed it too. Even when it became obvious that belief, however re-charged with fresh possibility, only brought back fragments of that overwhelmingly longed-for image—pre-war London! Britain's capital! That matrix everyone had met family in, ventured, or grown up in, having wandered absorbing forever its wide variety of smoke-flattened wet smells, its brave new infusions, its wholesome ethnic atmospheres. Though was anyone noticing that even pre-war longed-for halcyon days could no longer be as dreamed about?

One wondered whether one would ever want to tell one's personal war story as Hans had. Quite a number of living years after all, and back when, incredibly, all nations had been unanimously rejecting war! Though in one's younger days, all one could see then was the next day's doped up struggle to rebuild; and just as paper remains on top of a rushing stream, doing all one could only floated one above the fathoms of governmental struggle hurtling youth along.

But why all this now?? I had long ago finished with all that!

It was that cunning old German rascal up there who had got me going with all this! Even so, as the fair-minded man one was reputed to be, I had a glimmer of why Hans had insisted on giving his house's story. Profoundly he needed his mansion's rarity to be sold with it. He was conveying its deeper meaning, and this was to be kept understood, always—through the ages. Because his priceless mansion had been built out of that world war hysteria and.

Could not otherwise have been restored to such magnificence?

Was I right?

Taking some deep breaths... Surroundings, environments—damn them! Nature's lovely material surroundings are supposed to clear one's head! Clean out my restricting bewilderment to make sense of it and lessen my wearying efforts!

Looking harder at this fascinating Finger Lake—'One of five fingers formed by an ancient glacier', one museum stop had said. This crystalline water, and ornamenting its lake bed its surreal stones, as if Fitz Hugh Lane had painted them. All sizes and rubbed sensual shapes. Though one's attention distracted with the tinsel flash of an occasional minnow, as pulling from that overloaded past, one was immensely glad of this minor underwater diversion. Hans Runditz's magnificent work had needed this serene estate here on this peaceful American continent, and now... mustn't I be needing it too?

Just then a fishing boat came silently by floating on the current, the nearly silhouetted fisherman in it giving a wave. Still caught into differences in personal fates, one absently returned his friendliness as sunlight bounced, sparkling myriads on the water all around his boat.

Back up on the porch again Hans cleared his throat. "Now though, it is time to give up all I make here and go live in town! Sad, *ja*, *ja*, but that how it is! Eva and I not have children for to take this over, but I am worn down and expiring, Sylvia, she know it," wafting his arm again. "It is the time that this", a swing of his arm indicating all his property, "keeps on." His last phrase resigned to the lamentable business of the years having torn at his overused body. I have to say I am both admiring and already fond of this feisty old vintner. Adjusting his torso more comfortably, Hans turned his trout-like head to me and said, "My cousin, she has big room on ground floor I make mine." Making himself smile, he shrugged off time's callousness. "Understand this, Mr. All-of-your-name."

"Algernon. Please call one Algernon."

"Now, Algernon. House has much value here with winery, and you see I will always love him. Which is why I need you to understand I must be, 'reasonable'." On this extra-stressed word, Hans hit fist to palm, and one amply understood what his 'reasonable' meant. Though one did not know what Reb and Sylvia had told him about one's prospects as a buyer. But it soon turned out that this stressed statement was to be the seed for negotiating this enchanted house between the masterful Hans Runditz and oneself.

After Hans' epic 'finding of this mansion', the elderly owner looked used-up, frail, and it was Sylvia who stated that one's remarkable new friend needed rest; which I could tell, he certainly did. I finally took leave of this legendary man, after I had agreed to stay on at Sylvia's inn and meet with him out here again the following day. Worn as he was, through his tiredness, a piercing little spark of satisfaction and expectation lit those widely spaced eyes. Badly needing his own time though, one suggested Hans keep the following morning for a good long sleep-in before setting up our first appointment.

The next day as the sun sank behind the western hills and lost its washed energy across the vineyards, becoming admiring of this wily old estate owner, we once again heartily shook hands. We got into our first business meeting, sitting out at that same porch table that Sylvia had spread with what his property consisted of—the house, with certain antique furnishings he no longer wanted, the rental barn's two apartments, the winery, all the vineyards, the production center with its offices and various outbuildings. Then there was a woods and a large amount of valuable lake front, and some miles of unused adjacent acreage that had grown wild or was used for farming rental. We discussed these until Hans grew tired again, and one left him to return to Sylvia's country bedroom with paper, pen, and the local newspapers to consider what a fair price would be.

On the second day's meeting, one put forward a tentative offer; and as it was generous by local real estate prices, one was shaken realizing that with Hans Runditz one may have met one's negotiating match! It was a good thing I was growing fond of this old rascal, because along with this mansion's relentless claim on one, I was being pressured to dig deeper into one's pockets.

Re-stating and amending Hans' 'reasonable' estate price, he kept our numbers going back and forth, jotting figures on a notepad as he turned his complete head to me in a newly developed foxiness. With his sprawled eyes conniving, they began to slant upwards as each of us scribbled numbers and showed them, testing the other's 'dissatisfactions' – with the winery's price, then with the barn and its apartments, together, then separately. The lakeshore was simpler as we agreed on a flat rate per foot, but for oneself, buying in another country, one knew that this transaction could be a liability as a considerable percentage of one's honorably labored earnings had been shamelessly nabbed by one's virago ex-wife. Any man with as much of his wealth absconded needed to make absolutely sure he kept his wits.

Again, amending Hans' totaled amount for the house, barns, lake front, vineyards, and acreage, one chiseled at his marketing concern that one 'didn't appreciate' the quality of his construction materials till one had this soundly laid to rest! An area of our complete agreement was Hans' strong opinion that the winery employees receive equal percentages of the profits. Not only was this equitable, but in one's own profit-sharing experiences, individual responsibility and satisfaction for the product increased.

During these haggled 'thinking-throughs' and 'meeting-ups', Hans informed one that his present wine-maker, Sigmund, had returned to Germany as his father was ailing. Hans' original refugee wine-maker, Fritz, had succumbed to heart failure years ago. Sigmund, though, was to return here soon, and though one was disappointed not to have a wine-maker on the premises now, this had to be accepted as the humanitarian side of wine-making's personnel problems. One had immensely enjoyed all this interaction with Hans, the scuffles too, because one was also getting to know the full range of his highly respectable 'special' wines.

Whatever Hans had warned in needing to be 'reasonable', one had no doubt as he'd pause to give me a quick droll glance, even as the irises of his angled eyes kept his unaltered sternness. Even as the creases beyond his eyes deepened—which may have been one-upmanship—but I was sure that those intriguing eyes also had another meaning—an obscure but very potent meaning. Both Hans and I were possessed by this grand, outrageously enchanted edifice! In this, Hans Runditz and I were soul-mates!

Not that this got articulated, but there was no doubt that both of us were responding to this building's highest level of communication! Even during disagreements, each of us yielded to a stronger negotiating undertow coming from this splendidly bullying building! A communication that secretly assured Hans and myself that ultimately, we would have success! During spells of good fellowship, the certainty of this uncanny knowledge even allowed Hans and oneself some cautious teasing!

Though it wasn't until divvying up the wine cellars that our negotiations came to a mutually satisfying close, and one could pay attention to what else one's major move over here would entail. Like returning to the Cholmondley-Rute Manor to dig up some money lying in British coffers and shipping choice items from Mother's stored antiques—which would take some arranging.

Though one's thoughts were being diverted, in high expectation, Reb and Sylvia had just joined us out at the porch.

Hans' head turned to Reb and Sylvia to announce, "Now that this house, he will be yours, Algernon." Making them both clap their hands, hug Hans, then Algernon, and all but jump for joy! With everyone much relieved and happy, as they quietened, Hans turned back to myself. "You would not mind, Mister Algernon, if Laburnum, she continues to rent her apartment here?"

"Laburnum? One hasn't met this woman renter." Euphoric with one's ownership settled, one playfully hesitated. After all, one didn't need to acquiesce to everything Hans wanted.

"You could not find more model tenant. Many length years she good friend to Eva and me." He pleaded as Sylvia and Reb nodded or agreed.

Though according to Sylvia, 'Laburnum' was a 'witch' who lived in the estate's lower barn apartment. One noticed too that at Hans' mention of the name 'Laburnum', my new friends exchanged amused glances!

One didn't find out more about this witch-renter till that evening, celebrating one's conspicuous local purchase by footing drinks for the regulars at Sylvia's inn. People either side of one at the bar festively raised their glasses in congratulations and a readiness to carouse; which as Sylvia gave me a head-turned wide grin, I knew she appreciated. Good, healthy country faces, and as one answered questions of these new acquaintances, one was merry with the similarity to one's homeland's pub chumminess. Though one did have to act contemptuous of some youth's shushed unworldliness when he mockingly referred to my formal use of 'one'.

The negotiation of the Runditz property had been satisfactorily completed to both past and new owners, as one expansively laughed and quaffed. What extraordinary things were happening! With one's trip home to finance Hans' sublime property, now it was spiritually, legally, and morally one's own, my only concern was this Laburnum lady, whom I intended to find out more about from Sylvia when she was through serving some fellow. Finally feeling proficiently oneself again, one nailed her, "Sylvia?" Catching her by the elbow, "Now let's talk about this Laburnum woman."

One's downright question had a slow effect on Sylvia, who hesitated, then said, "Laburnum? Oh wow, Algernon, just you wait, she is so-ome-thing!" Setting up other customers with a couple of lite beers, she went on, "She once ran a dance hall out in central city!" Sylvia's expression mischievously insinuated what more Laburnum's job might have entailed. "Guess she had to get tough keeping riled pan-handlers from wrecking the place, though she saved up a nice nest egg; and when she got sick of sorting all the brain-splatter, she moved up here. She's never had much family, orphaned pretty much, but she'd always had this weird..." Handing some fellow his lager, "...she often knows what's going to happen! Good thing. She got out of that dance hall two nights before it burned to the ground. Back east here, she's got to know more about her psychic stuff, meets other mediums." Sylvia gave a little grimace.

"A coven? Surely, that's harmless?"

Nodding, Sylvia drew a dark beer for a customer. "Besides the full moon, there are nights she likes to roam."

"Around here?"

"Other vineyards too. The woods are what she likes. They have 'meets', she calls them, gets together with psychic friends to work on some hunch—great witchy stuff! They zero in on a haunting kind of image, I guess. Not sacrifices or anything that gross, Algernon, if that's what you're thinking. Never, not Laburnum!" Sylvia turned from me, "Here, Mr. Movie-star, you're Guinness." She touched a frothing glassful to the arm of a young guy talking to his friend, then turned back. "Laburnum goes nuts over dogs. You'll always see her big red setter with her."

"You and Reb have known her how long?"

"Since I've had this place."

"How did Laburnum meet Hans and Eva?"

"I'm not sure."

"Oh, you've some idea?"

One wanted to know more about this lady, but Reb had come in and was putting his arms around Sylvia's shoulders to romantically nuzzle her hair.

"Reb, you tell? Come on now, hon, tell Algernon how Hans got to know Laburnum."

But spring had got into this handsome countryman, and he couldn't stop his cuddly kisses deep under Sylvia's collar. One couldn't blame him, she looked luscious tonight—shiny golden skin and all in yellow—as pressing her to him, her lover kept making her bartending tricky. Belatedly hearing Sylvia's question, Reb turned to look straight at me. Not answering Sylvia, Reb smiled as he got his hand under the waist of her shirt, his gamin liveliness letting one appreciate how sculpturally handsome Reb's fine face was. Finally leaving his lover alone, he held his head back to skeptically inform me, "Y'see, Alg'non, that's for you to ask Hans!" with an annoying chuckle.

"Now listen!" one acted tough, though I lapsed into a grin, remindful that after all we were now the best of old friends. "This Laburnum lady will be virtually living under one's roof, and all I know is that she roams around nights, has a dog, and foretells what's going to happen! Come on now, one of you, out with it." But all one received were giggled outbursts.

"Want me to tell her you'll be over to meet her tomorrow?" Reb asked; his hilarity lighting him up at each mention of this renter woman.

"Uh-uh better not, Algernon, there's the deed," Sylvia sensibly remembered. "The lawyer's tomorrow."

"There's the afternoon? One will take this lady a fine bottle—"

"'One'? Is 'one' what you people call yourselves across the Atlantic?" One overlooked Reb's rudeness.

"No, Algernon, no bottle!" Sylvia more loudly informed. "Flowers would be great for Laburnum!" And again, as their eyes flashed, I saw that she and Reb had this amusement going on between them. Most likely, they were just celebrating that Hans' winery that would continue; and that happily they too were about to have interestingly changed lives. The winery, with all its grape growing at the Runditz's Estate, and Reb's carpentry, must have certainly been a large part of their routines, or was this exchange of amusement just an end of the day larking?

"Look, you two, is there anything important about this woman one should know?" Each gave the other more of their pre-connected glances before Sylvia burst into another peal of laughter, and a comical little neighing "He he he," spluttered from Reb! One still wondered whether their amusement was all to do with this 'Laburnum', or could it be to do with oneself? One had been used to alienation out in foreign parts and knew a good deal about body language's outright dislikes, though that wasn't the behavior of this wholesome loving pair. Better to push aside one's paranoia and in Cadney's lingo, 'lighten up!' "Have a heart, Sylvia, does this woman tenant flaunt a long, scaly tail?"

"No-o!" she said disdainfully, though she still laughed.

"Jes'a single eye in her forehead!"

Reb was not the one to be helpful!

Sylvia was one's best hope as one pleaded with her. "Does she prowl around one's windows at night? Scare people with her phosphorescent green eyes? I'd better know what I've got oneself into." But each time I spoke, Reb got such a laughing jag going, one was giving up! Though one had the strongest feeling that there was something here one should know. "Look, one understands that you two have done me an exceptional favor bringing me here to this house and to meet Hans Runditz, and one will certainly do all I can to show you my boundless gratitude."

Nothing one said got me any further as Reb only kept up his surprising high-noted 'He he he!' He poured more of the Riesling one admired. Handing it me, Reb's face straightened; finally, he had the grace to refrain from laughing. "You've nothing to worry about, Alg'non, just remember that. When you meet Laburnum tomorrow, you'll see!"

"One sincerely hopes so!" One also hoped that their amusement hadn't anything to do with one's being British. *Though come on, Algernon old lad, there's no xenophobia here! Too many people adore the German Hans Runditz!*

One will just put their amusement down to one's new good friends overdoing some private joke.

Chapter 4
Welcome Home

Longing to get back to my most 'Supreme' of 'Habitats' in the Finger Lakes, U.S.A., I greeted dear old Lamborghini with a few fraternal pats as I stashed my suitcase in the trunk. Oh, damnation! Dear Lord! One remembered old pal Thaddeus who would flay me alive if he got wind of my being in Toronto. One hadn't bothered with old colleagues since the Foreign Service's splendiferous London disgorgement, but as long as one was in this city, it would be best to get Thadd done. Though as my precious proof of legal purchase was singing away in my briefcase, this visit to old Thadd would have to be brief.

Very well. Then up through all this urbanity of underground parking, and the sterility of Toronto's corridors... Augh, Kafka nightmares!

And, listen, Algernon, in purchasing one's dream house, no hint about the supernatural, just remember that! Bleary old Thadd is unlikely to be up to extrasensory comprehension, so simply find out what the old sinner's up to—and keep it brief!

Rum old bonhomie Thaddeus had landed up permanently in, of all places, Toronto's 'Royal York'! This hotel of gold and scarlet grandiosity used to so impress high-level conferees it was a joke, though joke or not, few of one's profession protested if meetings were arranged in this luxurious palace, which included oneself. Even that deplorable time one's virago ex-wife had accompanied me and loudly hit the management with a comment or two for updating their interior décor worthy of her spastic elegance—which one tried not to recall more of now as one waited for an up-arrow elevator.

Currently smitten with a Canadian skiing champion, one pressed the elevator's button again. Thaddeus may have been favoring his latest idol by retiring to permanent residency in this glory-hole—one recalled Thadd's attachment to ambassadorial splendor—which made one prostrate with wonder that as a retiree he hadn't been aching to get away from all this orbiting pomposity. I might be eccentric, but I couldn't understand not wishing to use one's years of earned freedom for distancing oneself from the stress of international empathy-building, not to mention the over-aspiring Cadneys.

Lord, all those rat-race days!

Whitehall's demands on one's field of policy eternally waiting in the depository! Unrealistic new orders summoning one's erudition in the constantly refilling ditty bag! Our High Commission offices continually shrieking 'live by compromise and measure', don't you know? Hellish migraines and sore throats persuading non-proliferation nuclear treaty reps to appreciate their prerogative and ruddy well get there for St. Ignatius' sake! Plus, the whole range of other crucial concerns right down to those endlessly tiresome fish in international waters and their wretched net sizes. *Augh!*

Oh, when was that elevator coming? One pulled a shared look of frustrated hotelier disgust with others awaiting this elevator and returned to one's nobler thoughts.

Being from a family of awesome lineage, one's vocation had been fraught with one's peers' unrealistic high expectations, though by birth naturally, no Cholmondley-Rute had the right to be ordinary. One had been bred to take whatever went with one's familial requirements, by dearest Mother too, all that was assumed in with one's obligatory birthright. Currently though, retirement really was meaning true liberation from all of that! Gloria in Excelsis! *Lord, how one's fettered spirits soar from the strain of those endless duties!* No more lavish banquets certainly—tough on old Thadd—then also no more escorting the ambassador's wobbly great-aunt to multi-lateral treaty celebrations! One soared too from the dusty webs of over-bejeweled chatty wives balancing exotic cocktails, their eye-removing Turkish cigarettes extended by lengthy decorated holders; and most devastating, one was finally released from Father's deranged phone calls demanding one applied his idea of an international quick fix to a tensely sensitive ongoing international conflict! *A-ah, the elevator!* I jumped in before the slow old lady and her fancy walking cane! Father's solutions typically included extensive bloodshed—of other nationalities, needless to say. Now though no more such noblesse obligations, retirement had already become one's very own marvelously expansive adventure!

Getting out I pressed Thadd's buzzer. How greatly one longed to soil one's finger-nails weeding grape vines with the sun burning the shoulders of one's obsolete oxford shirt as one got enlightened with all that one had personally missed of a 'lowlier' lower-level of humanity. Oh-oh, the handle of old Thadd's elegant suite door creaked! *Okay, Algernon, let's get back to one's old chum!*

Decorating the doorway was Thaddeus's partner, the skier? Had to be! Nice-looking enough, 30ish, introducing himself as 'Omar, Thaddeus' verr good frien'. Not what society columns would call a 'hunk' in Cadney's lingo, too narrow-boned, and having such rugs of black hair, it made most of his shaved-face ultramarine. Explaining who one was, this chap welcomed one as he took me in to where—*oh, oh!* Whichever way one looked, wall-sized mirrors reflected one in place of fine art! Making one aware of my classic good looks being variously reflected from these silvered walls and even the ceilings! Certain angled double-mirrors showed oneself in profile too. Reminding one of Cagney's vicious reference to one as 'Mr. Punch'—grossly unfair—one's nose might be long and fine, but it did not turn down!

Thaddeus' 'verr good frien' was quite personable as he ushered one in to where Thaddeus in white ducks and azure shirt was already pouring whiskeys. One didn't drink that beverage anymore, so after a noisy bear-hug, one let one's drink sit as the two of us got through the expected blaze of curiosity for what each of one's selves and one's sporty old pals had been up to since the London blow-out whoopee. As Omar couldn't participate in this exchange, one ignored his appearance of censoring what was being said, while he sat precariously on the edge of his upright chair observing us with notepad and pen. Realizing that Omar was aggressively staring at each of our mouths, and was... *wasn't he muttering what Thadd and I were saying?*

"Take no notice, old buck," Thaddeus' head tilted at his partner, "Omar is studying our uses of English." Thadd's gruff, warm voice expanded, "Tell one, Algernon, that abomination of a father of yours! Has he finally let our planet have some peace?" Drawing a large handkerchief from his trouser pocket, Thadd dabbed at his watery eyes beneath his glasses—*sad, this inevitability of aging.*

"Not a bit, Thaddeus old cock, though one did one's best urging him to! One left him in his wheelchair on a hill at Corfe where the old orangutan went rumbling off full-tilt till having to brake so hard he double somersaulted, wheelchair and all, landing arse skywards, his forehead in the mud! Nothing finishes him off!"

Crackling lusty hoots from Thaddeus, as despite his watery eyes, he looked fiddle-fit flaunting a tan from a recent trip to southern waters that complemented his silk Ascot. A trip to relieve Omar's painful language learning, one gathered. On cue, Omar passed me a glossy photo of his bikinied muscular magnificence surfing a large wave. One duly scanned it, catching old Thadd's sidelong smirk; then returned it to Omar so he could continue with his notepad and pen.

"My old man did pop off incidentally, Algie, wouldn't you know," Thaddeus stated inconspicuously. One's afforded sympathy was ignored. "You recall that for years his doctor pronounced his mind equated that of a seven-year-old? Though faced with being put to pasture, he roused and raised it a year or two. The solicitors left his name topping their headings as clients prefer imagining Pater still having the wherewithal to make miraculous financial decisions, oy-ap oy-ap!" Thadd's ridiculing wayward mirth. "It amazes how loyal clients will take off if they don't have some semblance of that dotty old man keeping an eye on their investments—oy-ap! Much had to be done in private, as you'd expect. Even giving it his best concentration, the gov' took half a day signing a release and whatnot." Old Thadd suddenly threw his head upwards, marking the awesome passing of years. "Holiest of Lambs, Algie, what *are* we putting up with?"

"One takes your point—" *Although one didn't.*

Thaddeus also spoke of his elderly mother, whose mind, unlike his father's, was remarkably agile at 94. "Keeps frightfully lively with each new beau, always did, y'know. How else to pass the time Pater was ostensibly off doubling our fortunes? She still has a couple of cousins and a brother of the same vintage. One may as well look forward to many long well-cared for years!" Thadd tittered, "No news of Hockney, by the way, and nothing but travel postcards from other old chums."

Eventually, amusing as this exchange was, one was no longer drawn into questionable tidbits about old colleagues, or Thadd's annoyance with an ambassador's solution for another Mid-East crisis that struck one in retrospect as all being far too ineffectual. One had quickly had enough of everything to do with our former formulaic careers and all its clichés and closed mindedness. Still, Thadd kept enthusing about hackneyed High Commission's efforts, and as one was no longer steeped in them to the gullet, they didn't mean anything to me. Listening to him, one had the sensation that one was single-handedly yanking along a cart full of rocks, only to find it kept dragging one several steps backwards. Making one see that unlike Thadd, I was more than content now to let the Cadneys be the ones beating out their brains. *Which was fine anyway, because one's 'Supreme Habitat' was drastically demanding I attend only it!*

As Thadd fed on our old times, he didn't want me to leave, but quite enough time had been spent wallowing in these bearded office associations, so one decisively stood to go. Steadfastly I refused a meal downstairs with one's lecherous old friend and his Omar, even though Thadd kept persisting. Thadd couldn't have understood my longing to get back to that hauntingly bejeweled 'home of one's reveries' in its fine setting among the Finger Lakes, nor all of its hammering at one with its powerful images. Sad for Thadd, but this was how it was. Though as Thaddeus wandered with me to his suite's front door still pleading, "I say, don't go, old chap." Omar followed just as passionately documenting each of us fine diplomatic old fellows on his notepad. Giving one's shoulder an affectionate punch, Thadd enticed, "That was when we were at our best, Algie, old fiend!" Then at his door, Thadd desperately returned us to our sporty old chums' favorite leave-taking finale! "Hell of a colonic irrigation, old man!"

"Oh Lord, Thadd, don't—do-on't!" As one's laughter at his colorful recollection turned us so brutally speechless, one's sides hurt!

"Though nothing beat the New Delhi's palaces, y'know, that two-day spree? Beneath the full moon, out on the silvery dunes? You were there, old Pip!" *Oh, and hadn't I been there!* Legendary debauchery that prompted more of our erotic eruptions as each of our words got precisely recorded by Omar.

"Not to mention, those voluptuous offers from one's frightfully lonesome Asian prince!"

Thadd countered. "'Scheherazade, yours!'" *Oh yes, those flabbergasting recollections!* One could only grab Thadd's door handle, and opening it, leaned one's forehead to its jamb. "Not that any of that outdid the signor's hospitality! You're puzzled, Algie? Contortionist women? Over-endowed chamber maids sent up sans their 'smalls'! Tops, when you're going in for women."

"Explorations of old Morocco's purple parts, Thadd!"

Thadd's eyes slid sideways for reminding me where Omar might be from. Though not even this new love of Thaddeus' could halt our gushes of laughter, because at the same time both of us got the beat and sung out, "Oh down in the dregs of old Casablanca!"

Mythic!

On one of those outings with Chum Thaddeus, having donned ingenious disguises, we'd been trotting off on an *'exploration'* only to come face-to-face with old stinky-toes Hobney, powdered and be-wigged in a taffeta party dress! Hobney was teetering about on stiletto heels pretending not to see us, but Thadd's shamefully heartfelt greeting stopped him. Some scruffy actor awaited Hobney as he turned to beg us, "Shhh! Appearances highly classified! Our fine families and all that rot, there's good lads-!" *Uproarious!*

Sordid districts or not, one's career had certainly known its share of erotic levity.

"Wonder days, Algie! Luxurious living! We were lucky—nothing like those anymore."

"Privileged, indeed!"

"You really have to go? There's a guest room here any time." And to my shaken head. "Then come again soon, you lewd old libertine!"

One had got out of his door and quickly jumped an open-door elevator.

Our leave-taking had brought on questions to oneself about our good Omar's gender. With Omar taken into Thadd's fold; naturally, one's cardinal rule was to never let loose with personal information about old reprobate Thaddeus or any other colleague. Insinuations so easily get misinterpreted, and just as one would wish for oneself, the best of friends' personal intimacies must remain exclusively their own. Though one hastens to add just one exception, one hadn't cared what the society columns trumped up after one had walked in on Francesca with that bovine, naked tennis player romping and other hi-jinxing on one's bed! In that instance, seeing his leathery buttocks and biceps and more gold in his teeth than on St. Peter's Basilica, one threw 'privacy' to the wind.

One felt justified in confiding one's society-bride's infidelity to a paparazzo that became incontinent with gratitude despite Father's anger after losing the manor's adjacent territory. Because Francesca had been bribed with everything! Trousseau by Chanel, precious antique jewelry of one's dearest mother, a personal maid, that ludicrous grand wedding with choir in St. Paul's! Her ill-bred cheap betrayal deserved the scummiest of tabloids! *Succubus* is too kind a description for that cuckolding whore, *though—yes, just as Sylvia had reminded—all that's long since over with.*

Having taken one's final leave of Thaddeus, speeding along the QEW once more, one had the sublime enjoyment of one's finest of cars, zipping past incompetent vehicles to smoothly cross the border, et cetera, as one's envisioning was taken over by the 'Habitat's' upstairs bedrooms. Recollections of basins styled with glass bathroom knobs stirred my craving for the sumptuous place—that I thought about room by room—all pleasingly smooth driving till coming nearer 'home', when due to travel tiredness one supposed, one segued into some strangely dubious thoughts—*because of old Thadd's elegant retirement?*

It occurred to one, I didn't have family or people one knew here in this country that one was so enthusiastically making this audacious move into. Some distant kin of one's same culture for giving one a boost or two. Settling into this winery of Hans', would one's applied knowledge of departmental management be workable? And even in that splendiferous abode, could a rainy day's spell of loneliness attack one, dig out one's unperceived winery inadequacies? Bloody Hades, what had I been up to purchasing property on another continent, not knowing anyone north of Pennsylvania Avenue?—and other such soul-injuring worries. Doubts that stabbed at one even as one kept up one's driving pace. Then finally, and oh so inevitably—great joy! That wondrous 'Habitat' was really coming!

That much imagined avenue of trees was about to come into sight—just in time!

And dear God, what a truly sanctified avenue it was!

Bringing to mind again that day Sylvia and Reb had led one here. But with all its imagery pulling at me, as I was about to confront one's superlative Supreme Habitat again, one became quite choked up! Though because one could never stop admiring Hans and Eva's 'avenue' of uniform and well-spaced trees, spinning my steering wheel to turn into it and thread the healthy beauty of these trees jolted one out of one's doldrums! Such lithe yet robust maples, now splashed with the rufous-gold of the late sun angling across the western hills to reanimate this blissful spot's heaven-sent peace!

Even fatigued as one was, all doubts were vanishing! Vamoosed! A-ah, the miraculous 'Supreme Habitat' was having its fantastic effect! It had done it! One was becoming truly euphoric again!

Dropping one's speed to a low cruise, one instinctively bellowed out that Italian symphony's first sprightly tune of Mendelssohn's as one did an opulent job of replicating all its cheerful instruments! One let it soar nightingale-style, due to my true home's possessiveness as one coasted towards Lake Seneca's dusty-looking waters after the rains; and one viewed once again one's very own vineyards! As expected, stirring up more groin-chilling, the barns blocked viewing one's now legally and financially owned habitat mansion. Rolling down one's car window to let in this better late spring evening for cooling one's boiling forehead, 'Lamborghini' and I crawled around both barns' curves noticing that the shadows on the lawn reached like lengthy tendrils, and then... Oh dearest of greatest communicators! Here it was, utterly undisturbed! One's own enchanted Supreme Habitat nest in all its vibrant reality! Touchable! Formidable! Ready to clasp one to its bosom! One's manifested dream had awaited one's return without changing one smidgen of an iota!

Late amber reflections on the cupola windows burned brilliantly to crown one's dozy habitat as it prepared to recede into the restfulness of oncoming dark, and a more finely crafted late day beauty would be hard to find; though *was that a movement up in one's cupola?* With the windows ablaze with sun's last effulgence, I could have been mistaken; but then—oh coincidence! Coming out on the porch below, wasn't that dearest good friend Sylvia?

Though Sylvia? Why was she here? How really friendly and wonderful as she waved merrily, as if—expecting me?

Though one hadn't been in touch!

Looking appreciatively at Sylvia, radiant moments piling radiant moments! Slipping out of the car, one's happiness waved back at her before leaning into the back to grab one's grip.

"Hey, great timing!" she called coming down the steps to take one's free arm and hang on to it. Leaning, she gave one's cheek a cuddlesome, good old friend's kiss—a knock-out contrast to steamy old Thadd's current physical connecting! Sylvia kept hold of one's arm quite naturally, and one went up the steps with her and strode back into one's superb domain. "Supper's just about ready!"

"Supper? How did? You guessed at one's arrival?"

"With help from Laburnum."

I looked at her questioningly, "You know one hasn't met this Laburnum?"

"Didn't matter, you'd left your glasses."

"Ah, one did leave them? One had another pair, though it occurred to me that I might have left a pair here."

"Oh, look, Algernon, there she *is*!" One turned to look where Sylvia did, eager to see this mystic that caused them so much amusement! Going to the fine double-entrance doors, one screwed up one's eyes to see all one could of this lady in the dusky late sun, but could only catch the back of an unremarkable woman, of I'd say at least middle-age, in a long dark coat, was it? She was headed up toward the highroad with her large dog at her knee. "That's Laburnum!" Sylvia enlightened.

"The witch, Sylvia?"

One hid one's disappointment. Out on a stroll one could have passed this locally reputed woman, though one continued to watch her marching across the lawn in this crepuscular hour; and as one did, so this Laburnum lady happened to raise her head as if recognizing someone ahead of her. Moments later, a man came out from the wilderness of that untamed land—one's untamed land—beyond the lawn. In this light, this man had little distinction beyond his flamboyance in greeting Laburnum. Laburnum though did not respond similarly.

About to remark on this remotely viewed little incident to Sylvia, though as she was returning to the kitchen… *why tell about this clandestine little meeting simply because this lady rented a barn apartment?* What one had happened to witness of those moments belonged to Laburnum, and like each person one was getting to know here, one would rather let any first knowledge take its course free of interpretation.

One was looking appreciatively again at the sharpness to the carved wooden vines protecting the main doors glass in this faltering nostalgic light. Brimming with curiosity, one called, "Syl-via? How did you know I'd be back on this day, and at supper time?"

Coming to the doorway, Sylvia answered, "Laburnum can hold someone's possession in her hands and tell you all about its owner."

"No-o-o! You're saying that holding one's glasses?" One couldn't entirely believe that this renter-lady could, though one had known of extraordinary Romany prophecies through held objects! "Laburnum?! You must have trusted that this lady had the right day her *landlord*—if you will—was to fly back!"

Entering the kitchen Sylvia said, "Laburnum thought you'd need to catch up with Reb and me. Hans too. He'll be here anytime, by the way. He wants in on welcoming you back!"

"Hans?! Perfect! How's he getting here?" One asked still looking at where those two distanced figures had disappeared along a path where the lawn turned into underbrush hiding them. Following Sylvia back through to the kitchen.

"He'll drive short distances, groceries or a library book, that type of run. Anything else his cousin or I drive him."

"To the doctor?"

"No-o-o, no doctor! Hans won't go to one! Laburnum does all that with herbs." Standing beside Sylvia in the kitchen, one watched her stirring the gleaming saucepan poised on a shiny glass-topped burner. "Hope you didn't mind my going ahead with your welcome home supper, Algernon?"

"Mi-ind? It's exceedingly good of you, and thank you! One's astounded, this place is full of thrilling surprises!" Which living alone one truly felt, unused as one was to such enveloping kindness. A novelty that was vastly different from former Foreign Service living. "Is Reb taking care of the inn?"

"No, Nollie takes over when Reb and I are out. You've met Nollie; he's real responsible. A happy guy, people come in for him. Nollie knows plenty about this place too, Algernon, ask him sometime. He grew up around here and helped Hans out, like Reb." *Was I hearing footsteps? On the stairs?* "Reb," Sylvia murmured in explanation.

At that moment as one turned, a loud welcome expostulated. "We-e-ell, look who's wing'd it back! If it isn't the brand-new owner of Runditz's Winery!" Beaming, Reb shook one's hand with true old friend voracity, "Welcome back, Alg'nun, we've been waiting for you!"

"One appreciates both of you being here!" As one certainly did appreciate them; after all, Reb and Sylvia were the reason I'd discovered one's magnificent habitat, and it was a particularly pleasant surprise to have their company now, "Very glad!" One persisted retrieving one's well-shaken hand.

"An idea," Reb started though he interrupted himself to go over to the saucepan Sylvia was stirring and inhaling what was in it; he gasped with delight. "A thought, Alg'nun. You'll be needing me 'round here for settling furniture it looks like. It might be better if I stayed up in the 'look-out'."

"As you do at harvest time?"

Reb nodded. "Early morning will get us a better start."

"You wouldn't prefer a bedroom?"

"Naw, it's better higher up. Get woken with the crows."

"Fine! Glad to have you. Were you up in the cupola when I drove in?"

"Waving at you like a dog's tail!"

"I thought I saw someone."

"At harvesting, Sylvie will be with me some nights. Not tonight though, eh Sylvie?"

"Glad you'll both be around."

"That bed you ordered came, Alg'nun. We put it under the roof in the tasting room. You'll be needing Nollie an' me for lifting that." One recalled having selected a fine sleigh-bed at an antiques barn, as Hans had taken the bed he liked with him.

"The mattresses are with it?"

Reb nodded, "Both came from Malley's. Listen, what do you think? If one moved the bed from the south bedroom into an empty one, the sunny south room would be free for one's new bed?"

"Better room, my opinion! It gets good light, and you see the lake. Sylvie was saying she'd guess you'd want a view of the lake. Hans restored that empty room first because Eva liked looking out at the vines." Talking of Hans, the sound of a car's engine refusing to stop made a scary jump. Alarmed, Reb rushed out as one quickly followed.

Thankfully, Hans was all smiles safely sitting in his car! As we hurried over, he gave a quick head shake, meaning that the car's racket was nothing! He certainly looked all right as Reb opened his car door and reached for Hans's elbow to ease him out. Hans sheepishly pointed down, "Foot he slip brake-driving!" He excused his bad stop, grinning at us. Giving a nod, he turned his head fully to me for seeing around that dominant nose bridge and said, "Very good, you make it safe back, Algernon. Wel-come to your new home!" Handing Reb his cane, Hans swung his hand out stylishly and brought it down on my arm. "You accomplished all that you had wanted. Your lawyer, he say that too! Yes, he phoned here that it all okay! And you see your family?"

"It's all settled Hans, thanks!" I was amazed that Ollie had had enough good sense to phone Hans. "And yes, they are all the same as ever back there –" seeing Hans wobbling one got on his other side.

"Not mind planes—car driving?"

"Enjoy both. But one's ready to stay put here now to learn all one can about the winery and for really settling into this finest of all fine houses. One needs time here now, plenty of time."

"That a good conviction, that way you will make time!" And looking at one intensely, "I very much relieve that this place has your appreciating, Algernon! We talked, so I know you are like me and will not over-commercialize the winery. That a worry! We must not put off loyal customers coming here for the tranquility. You will see, many good people return for some Runditz quiet when they stock up on cases."

"No, rest assured. I will always hold on to this quiet that you and Eva worked for so hard. My preference would be to always keep it just like this."

"Reb and Sylvia, they had good insights to bring you here, Algernon, I could tell—you a natural!" Hans turned to Sylvie and Reb, "Laburnum, she said so too." This exchange had got us up on this legendary porch, where Reb continued helping Hans back inside the house. In the parlor, Hans stood leaning on his cane that Reb handed him, as he airily swung his good arm so wide it threatened his balance again. "Now, Algernon, let me give your hand a good shake and welcome you here to your own American home!" One was moved by this continuation of warm greetings as our completing 'Habitat' transference kept up happy smiles in our genuine rolling enjoyment, till still smiling, Hans said bashfully, "Well and good, well and good! Now, more serious. For Algernon, he just travel; Sylvia, you saved that Riesling?"

"Mel and Garrett brought them over, Hans. Come on in to your chair," she got us all moved into the dining-room, pulling out the well-cushioned chair for Hans.

How impressed one was again by this dining-room's long bay window looking out onto the darkening. And there was this room's quaint corner door that so usefully went through to the kitchen. Sylvia had set the oval table off with spring colors, table-cloth, candles, flowers, and napkins. Four buff plates flaunted a single, painted blue hyacinth, making it all stunningly appealing and cozy! *How utterly Utopian!*

"Sylvia, this is a very fine surprise, I can't thank you enough! Driving here I'd wondered which way I'd cook myself an egg."

Reb pushed Hans' chair in getting him comfortable and headed for his own chair laid for him to carve. Sylvia indicated she would sit opposite Reb, which left me the chair across from Hans. The candles were lit, and a couple of amber lamps brightened the interior from the breadth of windows' dimming light, and a bottle of wine was handed me for opening. Sylvia placed a wonderfully fragrant golden roasted chicken before Reb, with crisp bacon strips across it, as smiling she asked, "Did the bacon make the chicken 'English style', Algernon?"

How right she was! Pausing Reb's carving, one's good friends raised their glasses to one's homecoming as we relaxed amid the actuality of one another's renewed affections. "It's been a very long time since one tasted any better chicken, Sylvia."

"It's from Hans' farmer buddy. Great, isn't it?"

"Henderson's, Algernon, don't go anywhere else," Hans informed. "He lets them run, keeps place spotless, and feeds them well. When Sylvia, she roasts them, you know they're delicious."

"I hope you don't have to pluck them too?"

Sylvia shook her head. "Henderson's machine does that."

"They're Mennonite!" Hans finished for her, back to running the show again all right! "You've seen their horse and carriages?" One nodded, as one's mouth was too filled with delectably roasted chicken and Sylvia's cheesy broccoli. "They came from Pennsylvania. 'Invaders' some call them. Bought up land. Good carpenters, you'll see. They have well-managed farms and make good strong barns." There was much about the Mennonites that impressed him; he appreciated their crafts, especially the women's elaborate quilting designs. Sylvia too liked their washing yanked high up to their barn roofs with clotheslines on pulleys; so the clothes waved around so high, they dried in even a slight breeze. "Can't say they are not an asset," Hans went on. "Though don't get caught in all the bikes and carriages headed for Sunday church!"

"Who farmed here before the Mennonites?" I asked.

"Danes and Swedes. Many are still around. Nollie's family are Johannsens." Then that swinging arm of Hans' reached across through the candles to land his hand on my arm. "Algernon, it pity the wineglasses they go dry." Reb passed me another bottle of this fine white Runditz dinner wine, and one replenished the glasses.

"Who do you stay with when you're back to your family in England, Algernon?"

Sylvia's personal question came as one neatly maneuvered a dollop of her scrumptious herb stuffing with one's knife European style onto one's convex fork. I was particularly pleased one had saved one's appetite by refusing Thaddeus' invitation; as finally, rather reluctantly, I replied, "One's 90-year-old father still keeps on breathing, Sylvia. Brother Gilmore runs the manor estate now." One didn't have to elaborate, but in the ensuing silence, one felt it polite to continue with all the unexpected pleasantness of this fine dinner and their warm affection; and also, I was to live here now, wasn't it natural my friends would want to know more about me? Making one kick all former thoughts of loneliness off into Lake Seneca! Without much thinking about it, as the central guest, I rambled on, "Gilmore has the most miserable job as Father vetoes anything the poor twit decides."

"Twit?" Reb asked and was shushed by Sylvie's 'tell you later' look.

Fatigued from one's trip, one had not intended to blurt on about one's family, yet any awareness of one's lack of demeanor couldn't slow me down. "Being truthful, one has to say, that Father has become really unbearable—outrageously! In his old age he even plays foolish pranks." And to their polite disbelieving expressions, "No, truthfully! He's much more belligerent these days and impossibly rude! He loudly criticizes anyone, which makes it hard for people to stay around him. You're all so pleasant, but you wouldn't believe how he shrieks at one's brother!" These words came out so heatedly, I too was surprised; and the more one got going, I was amazed to find that the words oddly seemed to stick in one's throat and make one cough.

One coughed them away anyway, or tried to, though this didn't stop my having this miserable jabbing ache across my throat, and *had Sylvia muttered 'oh dear'?* Not being sure, one rashly became more intent on giving one's new good friends this honest impression of one's trip. "Father is frightfully horrid to Maudie. Maudie is such a loyal aide, she should be in line for sainthood," one raspingly got out to the mute tableful. "She's the only person that'll just stand there and let Father yell at her all he wants." Was one using strained cadences? Whenever one had spoken at public events, one had received politically flattering responses or shrewd encouragements, which could be what I'd become too used to. Weird! And one's friends' lack of intrigue suggested that one shouldn't be telling about my wretched family at all. Well! So, why did I feel this compulsion to spill? A better way? To let it naturally come up? From incidents, home news? What was the matter with me? As such a man of the world, was one too overqualified?? Finally, I decided to get out of it altogether and tempered. "Probably if Father had worked with his hands like you, Hans, or gone off with pals to play—to play—huh, golf." *Oh Lord, one had never been a stumblebum!*

Unforgivable! What a clot! Come on, Algernon!

Damnation, as a diplomat of some standing, one had given talks to every breed and level of humankind—for all the animals loving St. Francis! But wasn't this being 'lowly'? Yet here one was undergoing some sort of gross 'discomfort', was it? Come on, in how many capitals had one's speeches steamrolled over even the most damnably rude or obscenely rowdy opposition? But for lord's sake, in simply telling these few generous souls about one's kin, I was making unforgivable flummoxes!

Thinking more about this 'discomfort', one observed that I flurried most whenever I mentioned the word 'Father'. Decidedly, I must ease off him. After all, talking about one's parent was unquestionably subjective – not the sort of thing one should do. It made sense that speaking so personally, I'd become inhibited. Driveling on about one's trip like this! After all, talking about oneself was well-known to be undiplomatic as well as unsophisticated, and one hadn't been retired that long after all, I might not be ready to forget former societal rules.

Apparently, it was hard for a former Foreign Service diplomat to push aside what everyone in higher cosmopolitan circles had always known – that speaking of oneself personally was both inefficient and pitifully unworldly—which one most certainly was NOT! *Think about it, Algernon, diplomatic service conditioning hadn't been entirely wrong deeming personal palaver superfluous?* Which made one wonder, *was one's diffidence 'stupefying', more accurately, because there might be more between Father and oneself that one didn't perceive?* One couldn't believe this likely, but opportune as it had been with these good friends asking about me, one was most decidedly being shown it w*as best to keep off 'Father'.*

"Sa-ad," Sylvia sympathized, and as Reb and Hans exclaimed similarly, one saw that if on some other occasion one really wanted to give these good friends even a brief impression of Father's tyranny, one would have to give it to them as a far more in-depth report. Though it was piss having to hold back when one felt all this warmth of unusual friendship and kindness with each person at this table. Particularly irksome now that retirement had ostensibly given one 'lowliness' and set one free!

As one still had these good people's attention, instead of going on about 'Father', one grabbed at other manor occupants and described Horace and Maudie's uniqueness, as one amused my friends with Father's talented special aides.

"I'd want to be well-paid if I was Maudie," Sylvia's empathizing helpfully moved one further off Father.

"One's sister-in-law sees to it she is, Sylvia. She has little choice; the family would all be on couches spewing to shrinks if they didn't have Maudie." One was relieved when Hans and Reb chortled.

"You used to live with them?"

"Only as a child, since then one's kept well away." One neglected to say was 'ordered' away.

"Foreign Service, you said?" Hans politely kept it going, though one felt sure one's story was becoming tiresome.

One nodded. "Yes, and it worked well when one was posted to other fine far-off countries!"

"Your wife and children went with you?" Sylvia asked tentatively, "Francesca, wasn't it?"

"That didn't work out, Sylvia. No, Francesca's far away now, basking by the Med, thank God."

"Oh right, you said you'd split! I bet she couldn't take the traveling? I'm sure I couldn't have either."

"Yes, that too." One passed the Francesca abomination off with a forced smile, but as nothing more was asked, one brought this scrutinizing of one's dirty underwear to a close. "Ha! One can truly say that one didn't know what happiness could be till living without that—that wretched woman," one groaned with restraint.

"The slut?" Reb helped one out.

One could tell that speaking ones out-loud thoughts to such direct and commendably fulfilled good people, I was disclosing more of one's rearing differences than I had anticipated, and as one's travel-tiredness had crept up one's limbs to tingle them toward numbness, this lighter mode was very much what was needed. One looked at Hans, the eldest here, who was keeping a knowing nod going with a wicked Germanic gleam that from time to time he darted at me from his creased wall-eyes. Having fled his homeland with the love of his life and one or two family, he had undoubtedly known the full range of family antagonisms.

I was discovering that there was much more to this *lowliness* experience in my unpredictable retirement-adventure!

"Shame, just a shame!" With all her goodness and true kindness, Sylvia's empathy was heartfelt. Gratefully I looked at Sylvia, as I accepted another helping of chicken.

Sylvia, by nature, was a domesticated, straight-forward, voluptuous, and personable woman who demonstrated her business acumen running her popular inn. One could tell she had discovered as sound a means of fully living out her years as she could wish for! Reb, her masculine counterpart, was wholly in line with Sylvia's sincerity with his agreeing groans and expostulations making him a most suitable mate. Though I'd noticed that on his own, he wasn't willing to lose a second if he was expected to make a decision.

"Algernon!" Hans loudly got one's attention. "What it is you need is quiet for watching the grapes how they grow!" Hans, as wise as ever, had gone right to the best of remedies! "That's what I finded. It marvel what restore happen when you go inside his growing cycle, watch him return each spring. Most dependable he is! You cannot stay aloof from helping out the vines—the vines it is, what I talk about." Hans was off with plenty to say about his vines; and with much gratitude to his beloved Eva, he even admitted that she had been the one to persuade him not to use chemical fertilizer! "For visitors I pretend it my genius, but truly, it not so! Eva it was, Reb remembers it so. She beg we not pollutify beautiful Seneca's water with chemicals! But you know, the old countries! Manure and composting! Yuk—not good!" Giving a hypocritical grimace as his hand did a thumbs-down, not-wanted sign! Though as this hand moved on into a hearty slap to the table, he laughed sardonically.

As a wine connoisseur, I believed too that organic grape growing was environmentally best and raised better grapes, making one wish to know much more about Hans' organic experience. Thankfully, this turn in the conversation quite took the onus off one's peculiar inability to speak about one's father.

Later though in the kitchen, Reb was scrubbing baking dishes, and in with the pitching-in custom, here I got out a fresh dish cloth. As I rubbed the dish's repellent surface, my annoyance persisted that I had not felt free to comfortably speak out about Father or anything I'd liked. Which reminded me that in the Foreign Service, talking up personal experience categorized them as gauche or depraved. One recalled colleagues, and oneself particularly, wincing at embassy gatherings if a guest became embarrassingly impassioned by talking only about himself. To diplomats, this was tasteless and *unsociable,* and such a repugnant lack of breeding needed to be dealt with. One was often beckoned over to surmount some guest's ignorance by moving him to one side and blathering with him about some banality, such as the obvious equatorial heat! Or one used one's knack for professionally questioning him while soundly maneuvering whomever needed to be returned to more 'sophisticated' conversation. Often at those gossipy embassy festivities, gin and orange in hand, one successfully manipulated a guest's turn-around just through changing the subject matter to anything mundane, because one was depended on for keeping the occasion above 'personal turpitude'.

In retirement though, one's *'lowliness'* was to set one free! But this was 'then', which in retirement was to have completely changed. One's inner everything was to have been released from *rules!* Yet as one thought about this, it had only been earlier today with Thaddeus that I too had eagerly distanced his and my own fathers by casting them as elderly and uncouth—or too embarrassing to talk about. Old men were past it, jokesters! More honest observations might have got us seeing what physical difficulties each father had been suffering. I saw this now next to genuine people like Reb and Sylvia here. Saw that one's old colleagues like Thaddeus and myself seemed pitifully outmoded, overly concerned with maintaining only 'tasteful' conversation. One must never again be sought for remedying 'lack of taste', I vowed. Lineage and background must never stop anyone on this diverse planet from expressing what he or she wanted to say.

It disappointed me that with all one's recent excavating of what had really happened to me that I'd recently dug out in the UK, it had not given me more confidence in my 'lowliness'. Seeing that one had a good deal more to contemplate about all this when one's wasn't so travel-tired, I looked forward to being guided by one's 'Supreme Habitat's' insightful humanitarianism for acquiring more lucid enlightenment.

Chapter 5
Runditz Winery Persons

While in the UK, back in my 'Supreme Habitat', my persistent imagining was sleeping in the bedroom overlooking Lake Seneca. Though one's bed was not set up yet, so instead, I slept in a spare bed in a guest room. This anticlimax disappointed, and was why I tossed and sprawled? Till through the window I glimpsed—*what was it?* Could it be a mild aurora borealis? I hadn't expected it could be seen from this region. Letting one's tired eyes follow its willowy movements, I finally wavered around with it till quietening down. It wasn't as spectacular as observing it nearer the arctic, but lovely luminous wraiths hovered the sky, reminding one that there was more to explore here of nature's endless fascination. Finally, at last given in to the affection and beauty of my fantastic home, I drifted into a deeper sleep.

Awaking well refreshed, I lazed into realizing that I was. The early sun gathered onto this ceiling's unblemished whiteness—odd what interior décor one observes with ownership. The new day brought an immensity of new sensations—aurora borealis influenced? Immense, like the gases buffeting our planet, making sensations that spurred numerous good feelings, despite yesterday's aggravating self-doubts driving back here. Using the sensible wash basin Eva Runditz had insisted on, I got up energetically and washed any tiredness away as one sang Tchaikovsky's 'Where 'ere you-ou walk' to this thrilling new day, pulled on one's shirt, some ancient favorite Austin Reed shorts, shoes et cetera, combed one's hair, that was already sun-lightening, and went downstairs and out through the intriguing side entrance of one's splendiferous domain.

Ah, here was all the voluptuousness of another day's 'Supreme Habitat's' environment, back here waiting to be lived!

One was to seek out Mr. Mel and Mr. Garrett at the production center, which had the look of having been active for some time. Reb had said that both chaps were early-risers. Introducing oneself Finger-Lakes-style by simply starting to talk as one let the men show me around each area of Hans' wine-making, or rather Mel did. I hadn't met Mel, but he also worked here, and one listened to his eager swingy style as he laid out Hans' directions for the production of this most splendid of biblical beverages.

Eagerly explaining each section of the commendable Germanic orderliness, Mel included the well-kept cellars with their addictive fragrance of aged wine in the ceiling-high redwood vats. "Hans' great pride," he said smiling. The cement floors had been swept to a shine wherever we went, and all was in excellent working order. Reb had shown me all this prior to purchase, though at that time one's head had been too overloaded in shocked wonder of one's Supreme Habitat's materialization! With all that as understood now as it ever would be, I supposed, I was free to assimilate Mel's detailed information.

Mel certainly was the livelier one for doing this explaining. A narrowly built fellow, a bit of a sport with his thin-ending lips intriguingly expressive as they slowly curved to display a dazzling whiteness of tall teeth, impressively contrasting his near black skin. With that loose gait, typical of a Caribbean islander, he was of good height and posture—if one ignored his too forwardly held shoulders. Hans said he'd been brought up in the Dominican Republic, and as the informer of processes, Mel answered any question delightfully, miming out Hans' method in fluid double-jointed gestures so one easily saw Hans' instructing. Showing one around, he apparently enjoyed managing this center and what else Garrett and he were responsible for, as he proudly ran off the advantages of two newer machines that he compared to ones in 'award-winning wineries'.

Garrett was less expressive. Pleasant, but the type with little weight on his limbs though he sported a decided belly—*he enjoyed his beer?* One noticed too that his walk was lopsided, and as he moved to another machine, he could well have been some chap who'd spent most of his life at sea. With his sparse comment or two, he partnered Mel compatibly, though one's needing to know about this production center may have intruded on his pinpointed oiling the undersides of his well-rubbed-up machine. Completing the chore, he wiped his oiler and hands on a rag and attentively stood by, ready to join in with what was being said.

Finishing this initial lesson, one watched the gleaming bottling machine at work; and when he turned it off, I'd wanted to know these men better, I paused with them at the sunlit doorway and asked, "Do you ache to see Runditz wines at the top of the publicity pamphlets, Mel?"

"Me-e?" An incredulous leap to his voice. "Having to give trumped up talks to bus loads! Not on your crappin' life! Hope you don't mind me saying this, but Garrett and I just like to work here as Hans trained us." An emphatic agreement from Garrett. Then having mentioned his former owner, Mel re-thought, "Why do you ask?"

“It’s good to know you have one’s same way of thinking,” one reassured him.

“*One’s,* er?” Mel’s curvy-ended smile hesitated until we each moved along in the cultures we’d been brought up in; as he flashed that mass of near transparent blue-white teeth again, his cheeks widening yet further for all their width and brightness.

Garrett continued to nod heartily with a, “Guess that’s right,” or two, happy to let Mel do the talking, but his definite affirmative every so often demonstrated his thorough agreement.

“Hans says you’re to keep our profit sharing?” Mel asked diffidently.

“Because that’s worked well, yes.”

“Me and Garrett like it here a lot for that,” both men grinned.

“It keeps more interest in the wines’ quality too.” One’s agreeable comment was met with enthusiasm.

Talking more casually, one found out that Garrett had a wife and two children and owned a house in town. Mel was single and had the apartment over Laburnum, or as I knew her—‘the witch!’ It wouldn’t hurt to have the odd employee Hans had trained living right here on the premises since my plans were to follow Hans’ admirable management, and one was becoming less surprised at what had come with one’s property purchase!

Later that morning, I was out estimating the estate’s boundary lines along the vineyards north track. Inhaling the delicate pungency of the Chardonnay vines with their glorious preview of American summer weather, I saw that this renter-Laburnum-witch-woman with her fine red-setter happened to be walking towards me. As we got close as I realized that in keeping with Finger Lakes etiquette, once again one may *not* be formally introduced—and I’d guessed right! Each of us were happy to meet at last et cetera, as she and I got going such outbursts of simultaneous explanations—who each of us were, names, the fine weather—till we both laughed, stopped, and more conventionally shook hands!

“You’re my landlord. I’m Laburnum.” She re-organized our meeting.

“Algernon.”

Laburnum affably welcomed one as she smothered this intro with profuse thanks for letting her remain in her barn apartment. Dark-haired, or mainly darkened, or whatever this elusive renter did to her hair, which she tossed back and smoothed with a movie-star like gesture, implying how luxurious her locks were—actually, they were nice enough but not as impressive as her gesture led one to believe they were. Laburnum continued her appreciation, “Wonderful living here on this estate; so many great walks,” as one was taking in that she wasn’t too petite beneath her loose clothing—large patterned shirt, jumbled necklaces, a pendant or some such trinket in with them, ankle-length skirt. Not as unattractive as last evening's distant first impression led one to believe when in manly fashion she'd marched off across the lawn. A black mole spoiled; *no,* more correctly emphasized, her smooth tawny complexion; otherwise, one couldn't say that Laburnum was as extraordinary looking as her 'gift of prescience' might have stereotyped her. No Capricorn bandeaus, animal teeth or paws, fringed shawls, or dangling mythological emblems. Though her dark-rimmed prescription glasses were on crooked, then anyone can make an amusing little mistake!

One's renter spoke leisurely about enjoying living here at 'Runditz's', and one was impressed by her tapestried voice and its plentiful self-mastery. Not arrogant self-mastery, not at all the Cadney type of inflated ego, one hastily adds—one would be vastly inexact to imply that—but her sultry voice had bemused Lauren Bacall intonations to it as she called, "Pa-ay-cock!"—*The dog?*—to fondly remind him that he was expected to sit if she stopped to talk with someone. Dog 'Paycock' had been too consumed with a rabbit hole and growled at it—or was it at me? Smiling, Laburnum explained that although one may not realize it, her handsome red-setter really wasn't adequately well-trained yet! Then, in fear of offending the dog, she called him over and caressed his head with this same droll-earthy manner while continuing to affect one with her unusual vocal variances. Laburnum was an intriguing woman, though it irked me she wouldn't just straighten her glasses. In fact, her attire, generally though attractive, had a carelessness about it.

Answering about where she had been walking, she used a low poignancy or some other such ineffable quality, some other timbre, was it? One was at a loss to define! Whatever it was, one had only met it once, and that was in a reclusive distant cousin who had experienced a voice change from its lack of use—*'reclusive', as Laburnum might be too?* Laburnum spoke about Paycock cleverly tricking her, and while looking straight at one, she caught into some further thought till turning away to gaze into it. It could be that Laburnum's most helpful company was her own.

Turning back to me, she asked, "No unpleasantness returning from England?"

It was hard to believe that this playful psychic didn't know very well that one had been perfectly all right. I smirked at the needlessness of her question before playing out her game, "No unpleasantness, no, none whatsoever!"

"A trip that needed to be made?" She dug at one, a smile catching about her woodlands brown eyes.

One laughed as one didn't know what Sylvia might have passed on about her 'landlord'. Though having made the acquaintance of this curious Laburnum lady out here in this growing warmth of the mid-day's sun, one ushered one's hand in the direction she had been going to suggest we keep walking. Laburnum took a few steps, but having got her dog to finally sit, dog Paycock was not at all keen to get up. Unexpectedly, this splendid dog looked directly up at me and revealing the full length of his incisors, gave a sharp growling bark! Having been brought up with hounds, I didn't fear angry dogs, but Laburnum bent to explain to Paycock that because I was "a very kind man who was letting us continue to live here Paycock, you should sit and lift a friendship paw." Paycock gave me a dubious look, and I was obliged to make him doggie compliments, but the setter wasn't in a receiving mood and out came two other strident yaps. "Please excuse him, he's over-protective of me."

"Natural enough."

"A case of a 'barking dog being worth— *no, no*—I don't think it's two in the bush."

One had to laugh, "No, that's not how that old proverb goes!"

"Though isn't it some kind of bush?" She'd continued till one's amused statement reflexively caught her up. "O-oh? Why not? Isn't it sequential?"

"One understands what you're saying."

"Sylvie says I muddle my proverbs, but I'll look it up, because I do admire them." Making a mental note to herself, one heard her mutter '*important'*. We walked on in this finest of weather, till she reminded, "Weren't you checking your property boundary?" Though one hadn't mentioned what one had been doing.

Feeling especially virile, one looked at her askance saying, "One sees one shall have to watch what one even thinks around you, Laburnum!"

"Not to worry, they're only good guesses," given tautly, as if to protect her precious independence?

"It was far more than guessing when you'd held one's reading glasses and announced to Reb and Sylvia what day I would return."

"They couldn't wait to greet you with a Martin's chicken dinner! It would've been shameful not to give them a hand."

"You didn't join us?"

"I needed to see a friend—a previous arrangement."

"Not the right time to bring your friend?"

"He's not too sociable like that. With certain people, it pays to know them on their own terms for a while, doesn't it?" Hoping she would say more about this friend, one waited. *Would she identify the man one had seen her meeting last evening?* Then answering my thought, she said, "Rafferty loves poetry. He gets deep into it visually, using gestures. Occasionally, he tries a few lines of his own, but his best talent is learning pages of verse and dramatically rendering them. Ballads mainly, though he rarely recites to more than one friend; or at the most, two. He was excellent last night. I'm sure I could get him to include you if you'd be interested?"

“Kind of you.” Laburnum was not like any of the female office staff one had known—one’s criteria when it came to the other gender. Instead, one was discovering that my renter was an entirely different breed of woman, making one quite interested in her. It was a left-over diplomat’s social addiction to be curious about people, certain habits don’t fade; and with her witchery, one became interested in her as a personality. More so as walking one was following her and noticed that her ground-length skirt was comically tucked up into, what? Her knickers? Due to careless dressing or using the bathroom? The upshot was that it disclosed her ‘scandalous’ bare brown calf, its heel, and her ankle in an attractive little sandal. Surprisingly, she was too concerned with making notes to herself about her silly proverb to notice this comic rear view, and one decided that drawing attention to it might embarrass her.

“Yes, Laburnum, one should like to hear him. ‘Rafferty’ is his name, you say?” She nodded. “With this marvelous quiet here, one was intending to get further into literary interests. This was partly what had induced one to settle in this peaceful American lake country.” One had stretched this point, though Laburnum eyed one more seriously, while keeping her thoughts to herself. Then her look changed, and one quite distinctly sensed that back when she had held my reading glasses in her hands, she may have learned more about me than I knew myself. For example, did she know what had deep down caused me to leave my own country and settle over here in this Finger Lakes estate? And of a larger concern, could her witchery be chiming in with my Supreme Habitat’s most secret enchantment? An abstruse thought, though as one was quite liking this woman, the thought pleased more than trouble her. After all, having been ‘selected’ to create this ‘Supreme Habitat’ here—magnificent and all, opulent as it was—it had also drawn me into a lonely adventure—the Foreign Service having rarely encouraged one’s being solitary.

We were standing in front of her apartment. “It only takes a few minutes to make coffee in the cafetière, Algernon. Will you come in?”

Coughing, I looked around. What was the etiquette over here? One didn’t want to repeat more of last evening’s diffidence with another ‘Supreme Habitat’ person. One said, “One’s afraid it was remiss of me not to have invited you over to breakfast, Laburnum.”

“Oh, you eat breakfast? You keep up a cooked morning meal? Foreign Service, weren’t you? You’ll find you can relax over here with that—no expectations of boiled eggs in fancy pots in this rural wine country! Though you could ask me over some other time!” She smiled, and curling her beckoning forefinger at one, one was reminded that after all, at heart she was a *witch!* Paycock trundled in exactly beside her with his tail in full sway, and I, having first noticed some heavily constructed stairs going up to—*Wasn’t the upper apartment, Mel’s?*—followed them into the barn’s entrance.

“Mel’s, yes,” she answered my unasked question.

“Would it suit you to come over some evening with Reb, Sylvia, and Hans, Laburnum?” I asked.

The witch was keen on this idea. “It’s hard to believe you cook.” Which made one admit that I had very little skillfulness for making meals. Laughing, she said, “Not to worry, Sylvie and I are good at whipping up tasty entrées. Or Sylvie is. Thank you, yes, let’s do that! Don’t we all adore Hans? One of the best of men, as you know, Algernon. And Reb and Sylvie have been my closest friends for many years. As we all get to know you better, we could be in for some congenial summer evenings.”

“Mel too if he wants.”

“You’d better ask him. Mel meets friends in town most nights.”

“We’ll help it along with a couple of the winery’s finest bottles.”

“For you four, it’ll be grape juice for me!”

“No-oo! You’ve managed to remain TT living at a winery?” In lieu of an explanation, she nodded smiling.

Laburnum though had turned right; and following her through her apartment’s cheerful yellow door, one was into a light, airy, attractive country room. Unlike one’s main house, there wasn’t the strongly reproduced former era here. Instead, a colorful modern muddle of coziness that Hans and she must have concocted for her small but adequate living quarters. Not a high ceiling, I noticed, as she hurried off to a handy little kitchen around a corner to deal with the coffee—still with the back of her skirt hilariously caught up! Among this well-ordered smaller spaciousness, there had to be a bedroom and bathroom. “Here, Algernon, I’ll show them to you.” She non-verbally accommodated. One smiled at her mind-reading as one was led through a door to the neatest little apricot-enameled bathroom containing a free-standing footed white bath.

“Hans’s wife had some say in that separate toilet?” One supposed noticing that the lavatory was a smaller room on its own, old European style.

“Isn’t it sensible? It beats having human odors ruining a good soak, doesn’t it?” One mildly agreed, while being surprised at this somewhat intimate comment from a woman I scarcely knew, but caught by a room around the corner that had one of my favorite De Stael paintings over her bed; one admired her selection of the painter’s colors for the counterpane, which was still roughened where she’d lain. “Yes, this is where I sleep,” we both looked in at the chestnut wooden headboard and books piled on a little bedside table that she had apparently been studying as a voluminous one was open under her lit reading lamp.

When Laburnum turned to one again without any self-consciousness, she suddenly yanked up her long skirt, and one averted one’s gaze as she freed her hem from her underwear’s grip, saying, “No wonder my left leg felt cooler!”

Laughing, she shook her long skirt to get it to fall straight. "Please excuse my mishap," giving a nod to back at the living-room, where we were to return, "Most of my living's done in here, Algernon. Eating is over here," pointing to the set-out mat and cloth napkin. "The table's other side is my desk that gets that nice window light."

"Concise designing!" one complimented noticing that one living-room wall was almost entirely of built-in closets and drawers, often labeled. "Every space has been carefully thought out." Her coffee smelled delectable. "Nothing wasted, yet everything you need is at hand. Is that how you'd envisioned it?"

"Without much housekeeping!" One kept looking at this much lived in room, all fairly orderly. The only concession to her clairvoyance was a dream-catcher in the sunlight back above the sink window; otherwise, just the odd sketches or photos of buildings of famed historic importance that competed with framed photos of dog Paycock. "With Paycock though, there's always some cleaning." At the mention of his name, Paycock padded over to rub his back against her knees till she drew a treat from her pocket to hold over him. "No barking ever again if Algernon is with me, Paycock. Promise?" The dog cocked his head at her quite sweetly, which earned him his reward.

Laburnum poured the coffee as one browsed her books, taking care to avoid changing any opened for current reference. One didn't know why one was surprised, but there were various heavy history volumes, and a single notepad lay open on which she had been making notes in a stilted sharp-edged hand, from 'The Ancient Persians', a title one muttered aloud. In this pleasant quiet, my new friend came over to see what I'd found interesting and lowered her head to read certain words she'd written. Remaining myopically bent there for some moments, her written phrases had to have sent her into some expansion of their meaning, because her head gave a quick shake or two as if she was alone making a mental note. Rousing from her page, she attended to myself again and paced back to the kitchen while off-handedly explaining, "Civilizations of pre-Christian values." While wanting me to make myself comfortable on the sofa or chair, both of bright red leather or faux leather—as one sat, one couldn't tell.

"Pre-Christian, yes, so I see," one affirmed her information.

For a tall man, Laburnum's furnishings were attractive but on the small side, though she was fairly tall herself as well as quite buxom. In the frequent need to sip from one's large cup of excellent coffee, one swung it between one's knees and intrigued with Laburnum's interests one was not a bit unhappy diverting to this unexpected aspect of one's retirement adventure. Though actually, having so heavily re-lived what had led up to one's mansion these last two weeks, all that cerebral activity had muddled my poor head, and I was needing to find this witch less of an intrusion. *More to think about there, Algernon? We'll see.*

“There’s much to know about outstanding civilizations before Christ’s ideals, as you know, Algernon.” Giving me a fierce little checking look from a sudden flame in her dark eyes—*for my response?*—she continued, “Christ’s ideals were pure and beautiful in themselves, except that they paved the way for interpretations by fanatic followers determined to outdo one another.” Another of those quick inquiring demon glances at me. “My interest is in what other ancient values or creeds were inspired by exceptional civilizations before that, with it philosophically being a blossoming time.” Listening to my new friend getting deeper into this surprisingly serious discourse on this early history, as she went on, I realized that her syntaxes kept gaining in height, as if she was needing to convince me of civilizing’s extraordinariness in these regions many centuries before what she referred to as our ‘Science Era’. One kept nodding one’s agreement until her information came out in such swaths of well-researched intensity that one empathized with her afforded effort. One’s education had not been remiss about those remarkable earliest civilizations on this world’s various continents, both on land and under the sea—she didn’t need to work at me so hard. One wondered if one seemed formidable to her with all one had come from?

“Laburnum,” one cautiously intervened to slow her down, “Certainly science has overwhelmingly dominated recent history, all so different from say the Renaissance; or when the arts, crafts, and guilds were livelihoods besides being esthetically inspiring. Comparatively, one cannot doubt that as you’re saying, at present we’re into a far more massively combustible age.”

“‘Combustible’, yes!” Laburnum picked this up, liking this description as her brown eyes glinted again at last. I welcomed her relieved sigh and her less tense, more amused expression. Though this more pleasant, quieter dimension of her persona wasn’t here to stay, because quick-voiced, she went at it again. “While we quaver before warheads and chemical excesses that could extinguish nations at the press of a button, even living in all this God-awful fear, our instinct is still to become better human beings, isn’t it? There’s this ever-pressing need to try.” And more hotly, “Yet how is it possible for the humanitarian side of civilizing to make worthwhile changes if we aren’t free of *fear?* Fear takes a precedence and reduces benevolent capability, doesn’t it, Algernon???” Using one’s name so pleadingly, with such quirkily fierce little looks at one, that ignoring one’s filled head, I hastily half-nodded my agreement. “We’re at a point in our evolution”, she was just as forceful, “when decisions made by nations have never been at a greater international cost. I heard that you know more about this than any of us, but—oh—it’s all so monopolizing.” Given with that funny quick shake of her head and shoulder-length hair, again using that specious gesture of her hair’s unusual glamor. My guess was that this heated opining was not manna to Laburnum, and one kept being moved by that sporadic fierce little glance of hers, as she kept concerning—*she might offend me?* Or *that her thinking may not be in line enough with mine, her landlord?* Then abruptly, she attempted to relax, and her bent head twisted up to look at me with far gentler directness as she said, "Sorry, Algernon, I should have asked; having retired from the Foreign Service, this subject could be one you'd far rather keep off?"

"No, no, be assured!" One's auto-politeness hastened to put this right, because I was being most pleasantly surprised, even if her feelings were headstrong, and I certainly didn't want to do anything to dull them; *after all, I'd spontaneously walked in on her assumption that I'd like to hear what she had to say, hadn't I? Also by the jerky way they'd come out, she could be in bad need of airing them.* "Laburnum," I started ultra-calmly, "you may have heard that I'm very glad to be retired and away from the Foreign Service." Indeed, it surely was one's turn. "One would like to explain that this is not because of what one should be doing to help remove weapons and organized evilness. The amount to accomplish there is endless. Though, should you be wondering; no, it's just that I haven't missed the societal framework that was also a good part of my vocation."

"Oh!" she exclaimed—*disappointed*?

"The droning on of wives' interminable teas, for example, or the 8:15, protracted, black-tie state dinner."

"Ha, yes, I'm sure you're glad to be done with those!"

One nodded emphatically. "This intriguing research of yours though," More slowed I kept her at it, "These early civilizations studies? Are they to give you a historic perspective on our 20th century impasse with the Cold War?" She became aglow with halted alertness as I continued to ask, "Is this why you're contrasting today's advantages and faults with those of outstanding earlier civilizations?"

Glad of one's excellent coffee, one dawdled with it as she answered, "Even with all we've developed, it's hard to believe we could ever lead as a great modern peace power, Algernon. We haven't civilized enough to become a morally beneficial civilization—a new 'golden age'. How can we while protecting our stockpiles of nukes if we don't understand how accomplished former great ages were?"

"'Golden ages' that endured?" one agreed with her. "Laburnum, as you may know, the terror you're talking about, those increasing weapons on everyone's worried minds were what kept one's career at boiling point. And I must say, you know, having just been introduced to you, this is an extraordinary first conversation!" Both of us chuckled as one couldn't stop being aware that our rapport had again slipped into yet greater seriousness—making one wonder if this enchanted place was again up to something as one displayed one's more public smile and added, "Yes, naturally, it's certainly sensible to talk about it.

Talking is our best means of keeping abreast of whatever the next mind-boggling international event might be."

"A-a-ah!" She sighed pleased and relieved as she more elegantly raised both her fine hands.

"One empathizes with your excitingly studious quest, Laburnum, and admires your perspective—to a point! And one must say it's remarkably pleasant to find someone living next door that has a penchant for all that's happening worldwide."

"Not the renter you'd expected?"

One let one's brows rise and fall at this intimation that Laburnum had more of an idea of oneself than one did of her! "Though in filling out your view; oh, but one must say, this is frightfully good coffee!" Leaning to her tray, she poured us each more from her prized cafetière. "Lovely, thank you! Filling out this view you know so much about, we must remember that incredible as 'golden ages' were, for one reason or another, each did come to an end. I have to say that with your fears and your current agonizing over of all that's 'combustible', one can't see how you can be anything but 'fatalistic'." No reaction from Laburnum. "Also, do keep in mind that the number of old and newly independent states grinding away at reversing the spread of international weapons often do succumb to debate, as they discover how much it's in their best interest. What's more, occasionally, these debates finish up as agreements or even treaties! Much as one is fully behind your concern that nuke threats do their damndest to dehumanize us, although one's sure, you kno-ow," giving the extrasensory meaning to this word with one's most sardonically amused glance, "that as one who was in on extraordinary levels during these debates, one has to defend what *was* achieved! Do understand that their weaknesses do get re-appraised vigorously re-worked."

Laburnum was looking at one attentively—as was her dog. During this more blending moment, both she and Paycock sat regarding one with alert tall brown-eyed interest! Paycock's interest was so profuse that his ear roots all but knotted up on his head as he appeared to be taking in our discussion!

Just then her dog's head turned back more curiously to her as she spoke. "It takes exceptional nerve to come away from your years of unimaginable responsibility and still sustain strong hopes for what can be done, as you have, Algernon!" Her kinder, more extracting look at one had amusement in with her commending, and aware of one's already filled head, one began to wonder, *how in blazes have I allowed myself to get lured into this loose use of one's many decades of infinitely crucial work? Better watch out that this is what you want, Algernon, tired, ridiculous old world-traveler!!* And another thought pressed, *according to Cadney, women now must never be spoken down to, had this been what I'd unintentionally been doing?* This must naturally be a collective concern for women! *For me, it had been dearest Mother who decades ago had defined this unforgivable inequity in women.*

"Unfortunately, though," Laburnum continued, "treaties do fail, Algernon, and promises *do* get revoked."

"*Credence*, you know, Laburnum!" Using one's often stressed conviction for dousing argument, as in good conscience most people were obliged to sustain hope for the continuation of the human race—one had to admit I was enjoying regaining a touch of one's former interests here with this witch! And Paycock, *he didn't nod just then, did he?! "Credence!"* one soothed with again. "One has to believe that accumulated efforts will help produce improved international understanding."

"*Believing it*, though! Despite all those huge cultural differences and all the distracting national interests? I must say that's pure courage, Algernon."

"Any littlest bite could be a chance of reinforcement. An opportunity for getting a foot in on the improvement of our mind sets."

"Though with our future so stacked against us, that's such a mightily hopeful view! It makes you a very special diplomat, Algernon." One's acceptingly raised brows listening to more of Laburnum's well-versed thinking as she poured one a third cup of her delicious coffee—one was glad of her guess at one's amount of cream—one's neighbor and oneself were into a similar pause as we needed to accept that she and I were on opposite sides of this futuristic question. This brought a hint of a smile around the witch's feverishly sparkling eyes, as again one was sure she had long awaited this sort of discussion. Think, who would she have talked over this very serious work of hers with? It was unlikely to be Reb, Mel, or even Sylvia—*although the poet friend?* One wondered this as one stirred one's cup, and she dropped her ample body onto her chair again to plunge head on hand in Rodin's 'think' position. After I'd put down my cup, unselfconsciously, this was the same position I dropped into too, being amazed that this conversation with this brightly informed good soul—whom one barely knew—had aggressively reached into the heady classified preparations one used when representing one's country. Inwardly, I had to chuckle, recalling how just weeks before retiring I'd so voraciously shoved foreign policy into a closet and locked and bolted it—one was not going to spoil one's retirement!

It was sad but perfectly true, just as Laburnum stated, that there could certainly be setbacks to conflict-negotiations because of re-issued orders from headquarters or from dull-witted Intelligence. Collations depressingly sent out by the War Office that didn't permit the slightest of headways to those of us precariously poised ready to activate them out in the missions. Yet as Laburnum was making clear, here one was, having finished one's part in those headiest of international games yet, still believing that even the tiniest of concessions could generate hope—*naïvely?*

“As you say, I’m not as hopeful as you are, Algernon. Maybe it’s best we start off with what we do agree on? Like what you’ve so aptly described, as ‘combustible’, and that this fabulous world is riddled with over-complexity.”

Given with this sporadic warmth and an easier friendliness, along with the subtle good coffee, one was getting the oddest impression that one had once known this female clairvoyant! Though one had scarcely ever talked like this—anthropologically, if you will, outside of one’s embassy work. Why? Because one had always made it a point to find some other subject, particularly to a civilian! Yet, here one was compressing some of one’s critical ambassadorial work into a coffee-hour discussion! Ha! And one must admit, with her keen responses, I was becoming surprisingly quite eager to do so!

“Poor, old, abused planet!” Laburnum lamented in summation while laughing ironically. “It demonstrates that old aphorism, ‘A camel is a horse designed by a committee’; or they used to say that in one of the old countries, I forget which one, but I can prove to you that this maxim’s correct!” Turning in her armchair, she reached up behind her to grab a large book off a shelf. “I’ll make us more than one dinner if I haven’t got this one right!” As she twisted to yank her large proverb book down on her lap, her reaching made her long skirt rise above her shin and disclose an ankle and her lower leg’s fullness—not a greatly attractive leg, but certainly with no physical defect. Though this unintentional leg show was more of an invasion of her intellectual dignity, her impressive bouts of piercing inquisitiveness.

As Laburnum leafed through her book to find her confirming page, one said, “Laburnum, one would say that you were correct about the camel and horse proverb as an undesirable metaphor for the threats to our planet. Though it would be lacking as an overall view of governments,” as one bestowed on her one’s most beguiling smile.

“No? Then a more accurate saying might be that our poor suicidal planet is ‘like a chain that is no stronger than its weakest link’? Or—oh Lord—is it ‘the chain that hangs longest’?”

One’s mirth came out in bellows! This witch-woman with her arc-bright intensity for world affairs gave such importance to these old-fashioned proverbs—yet they just didn’t stick! One sobered from this entertainment to help her. “You’d had it right! It’s the chain that has the weakest ‘link’, and it’s the ‘creaking door’ that hangs longest!”

“Ah-h-h, thanks! How great that you admire these loaded nutshell wisdoms too!” One hadn’t said one admired them, but it did relieve me that Laburnum’s gift of prescience didn’t always hand her everything she wanted!

One reluctantly took leave of this formidably alluring witch-renter with a handshake after Laburnum had walked one to her door. Turning, one smiled as one left her and her aroused dog and this unexpectedly memorable interlude.

Quivering from her excellent coffee, one was glad of the vineyard's fresher air caressing one's hot forehead as I went back around her barn to return to checking one's boundaries. Passing the Riesling vineyard, one observed that the leaves greenness looked strikingly a deeper green, as was there a noticeably more stressed spring to one's step? Because one now knew that this Laburnum witch—one's newest woman friend and neighbor—was on a quest here for philosophic-sociological ideals.

What a frightfully transcending coincidence!

One kept up one's stride, aware that Laburnum was a whole different breed of womanhood for me. Though naturally, one would continue to maintain a lid on any sudden burst of unfamiliar feelings. The only women to have worked alongside one back in those far-off foreign offices were business-like and 'stand-offish'—which was the only description that came to mind. Though, in fairness, after the Francesca marriage disillusionment, they could have been respecting one's preference for relentless bachelorhood. Other than that Succubus Francesca and quite apart from one's unique and extraordinarily beloved mother, I've rarely been persuaded that women could be of much helpful importance—procreating aside. One's father's generation must have been eternally ecstatic that women couldn't vote. Lord knows what women leaders would've desecrated given political power—not meaning to intimate that women were only 'playthings'. Cadney as a younger 'modern man' used to have a lot to say about all that, though one's private life had proved that they could be! Though, Algernon, overall, which was the gender that had added so expansively to each of the empires? Unless Laburnum could change my thinking, my God, think how quickly Laburnum would have come up against her limitations back then if she'd professionally been into foreign affairs!

Back to this morning's session with the witch-woman's delicious coffee.

One had to admit Laburnum had surprisingly evoked one's stubbornly shelved career! Being completely honest, it amazed that with her, one had quite enthusiastically dipped into one's former Foreign Service experiences, and—surprise!—they hadn't produced any of those nauseating associations of what could be awaiting one in the ditty bag, et cetera. Nor had it renewed the utter tedium of escorting the ambassador's elderly family to another formal 'do' in scorching formal rig. Inevitably, this was because of one's effort to 'move on' from one's vocation, which wasn't likely to happen in a snap. Settling into this fine lake-side wine country, what better friend than Laburnum could one wish for to touch on one's opulent past with, now and then?

How absolutely ticky-poo!

Chapter 6
The Dogs

Outside in what had once been a lush spot behind the barn apartments, Laburnum gave her dog Paycock a deeply approving scratch on that responsive stiffer part behind his ear. This scratching added to Paycock's saturated happiness because he was expecting a good meet-up with his best dog friends Rowley and Bruno. If they came by, he planned to get this nuke treaty topic of Laburnum and Algernon's going and with them get it settled once and for all! He knew it would warm the cockles of his friends' occiputs, and that they would drool pints to get in on a topic of that much substance. Paycock planned all this busily as Laburnum snapped him onto the dog cable attached to the catalpa tree—bright dogs needed the neuron-exercise of a well-chomped-over discussion.

On his own, Paycock had done some heavy mulling over of Algernon and Laburnum's nuclear thought levels; though most honestly with this day's magically fondling breezes, he was entirely engrossing in their spectrum of delights; and as Laburnum left him, he frisked around his breezes-feelings in this splendid sunlight made for letting everything release as he gave a joyful messaging bark or two. Although with such a lot to think about, he soon slumped to the ground to spread his limbs about exuberantly. Finding this damp flattened long grass oozing his belly fur so ticklish, it made him giggle; it became even more of a priority than his owner's nuke debate, and all that he knew that would sooner or later have to be drastically contemplated. Fascinated with the freshly messed up acrid odor of dewy grass, he began to think harder of Bruno—Mel's old basset hound—and he messaged another bark to get that lazy short-legged friend over here from the production center, so he too would see how fragrant this spring time long grass could be. Bruno would give him an inspiring sniffing up; and if Rowley got away on a rove from Henderson's, he'd give him a sniffing up too. Rowley was an admirable mutt, a respectable collie-sheltie mix—though Rowley didn't admit to 'mix'.

The results of Paycock's messaging on this fine day was that his two best dog friends happened along; and just as on any meet-up, they couldn't wait to playfully greet one another! Pawing each other's chests or withers, and seriously reviewing any changes to each other's rectums, before rolling on their backs to rub the grass down for more of the cool grimy earth. Or to just rid their energies, they would act annoyed with one another—though it was only acting; they were never truly upset—till Rowley, being the one to have come some distance, got tired and flopped down; his pert ears cocked to listen to his trusty friends. Rowley's fatigue influenced Bruno and Paycock's frisking time, as they politely finished up too. Panting, they dropped down heavily on either side of Rowley, their long fat tongues dripping and swaying pendulum-like as they moved into the dozy elation of each other's wondrously audible vibrations. Though—as Paycock worried—with all this beautiful weather, any intellectual challenges they should be being responsible for could be wafting away merrily on addictive breeze melodies.

Paycock was the only one who knew about Laburnum and her landlord's talk during yesterday's intriguing coffee-time discussion, which had kept him wrestling his synapses around bits of it ever since. Once he'd announced this nuke-talk to his best dog friends, they would all have far more on their agendas than they could possibly want, but right now this spring's abundance of eagerly bursting buds and seasonal new odors was causing delicious longings for touching and deeply inhaling into their lungs this renovating freshness, and these completely pre-emptied even their most urgent attentions! Every moist aromatic whiff cried out for a separate exacting intra-analysis, each ramification demanded a specialized drift appreciation—what meteorology!

Fortunately, besides being occasionally excitable, Paycock had plenty of typical Irish-setter patience. As an extra smart Canidae, he knew that once he'd diligently distilled all he'd overheard of Algernon and Laburnum's lofty talk, he would easily sell his best friends on this captivating, sinister, provocative, elusive, and most likely highly classified nuclear arms question that Algernon and Laburnum had barely got a start on. Being a setter who aspired to baffling his best friends with wisdom, he knew how to store it for gaining independent perception. That discussion of Laburnum and Algernon's had wound Paycock up tight all right; and much as he resented another male coming in on his and Laburnum's intimacy, he would look forward to testing Algernon's optimistic conclusions on his brilliant dog friends.

"Paycock?" Rowley though needed more mundane information first. "*She* didn't bring you over?" Both dogs knew that *'she'* was Laburnum.

What humans or sapiens don't comprehend is that once out of *their* earshot, dogs have immensely proficient vocal communication. This secret is so sacred to them, they instinctively keep it ultra-protected.

Also referring to Laburnum, Paycock replied, "She wasn't supposed to go for the chickens, you know?"

"You're right, Paycock. Reb drove over for them," Bruno informed from that even more pathetically wrinkled, droopy-eyed look Rowley and Paycock found so painfully hilarious.

"Does *she* still have you in training?" Rowley asked snickering at Paycock.

Paycock's laugh went out of orbit! This moment he was back being an easily excitable setter. "I let *her* think *she* is!" He said as he forced calm for keeping up his reputation for being unusually perspicacious. "The key to being a happy dog is to keep *her* thinking there're more commands and cute tricks a pet can learn—ha ha ha!" Laughing because he loved his own wit! "Trust me, it gets you treat after treat till you're sick of them!"

"Don't be too sure, Paycock. A wrong move can land you up overnights at dog school. You can't imagine what a racket a bunch of homesick dogs make."

"Oh, don't give us that deplorable experience of yours again, Rowley," Paycock curtailed Rowley's superior schooling. "You must be getting forgetful, you know, you're always bringing up that school."

"In my opinion, if a self-respecting dog plays it cool, he won't let it get to that obedience school torment," Bruno recovered their conversation. "But as I was about to ask, how are you and Laburnum getting along with the new owner, Paycock?"

"The landlord? That's what he is, Bruno, just say 'landlord'."

Bruno duly repeated, "Landlord."

"He's behaving better," Paycock replied. "It'll take a while as *he's* from some islands half-way around the world that speak arched."

"Arched?" Rowley queried Paycock.

"Right, I've heard him too, and that's what it is, Rowley," Bruno agreed. "When the landlord speaks, he arches away. It's a lot different from old Hans. Hans speaks clonked."

"Once this new guy fits into the winery's ways here, he'll be all right. Bruno, if it's cold, doesn't he let you stay in the production center?" Rowley wanted to know.

"Yes, he does."

"Though, Paycock, how about the landlord and Lab*ur-r*num?" Rowley suggestively raised his brows up and down. "Do they get along? I mean *he* is a *male sapien*."

"With Laburnum? Just—let—*him*—try!"

"It could be good for Laburnum to talk about the places she studies, Paycock, she needs someone traveled like that. I heard that the landlord used to be a diplomat and has lived in many countries."

"She's got Hans," Paycock curtly reminded him.

"Hans didn't travel, he fled."

"He made it to other countries," Bruno reminded.

This new suggestiveness of Rowley's began to worry Paycock. "Look, friends, it isn't *sapien*-rutting time, is it?"

"No, that's early spring. You're okay for a year, Paycock."

"Uh-uh, Rowley! *Sapien*-rutting time isn't only in the spring," Bruno was dead certain. "Mel gets frolicsome Saturday nights and goes around saying his male tool needs a tune up. He sings a cheerful ditty about 'Henry and t' bucket, t' bucket, t' bucket,' as he sprays himself with that stuff that makes him smell like a blossoming young orchid. He thinks that's what'll make a female *sapien* stand still, he he! I'd like to advise him that just one drop of fresh skunk oil, and he'd have more females clambering all over him than he'd want."

Paycock lowered his voice to a whisper, "Hey watch it, Bruno, globbed goofballs *sapiens* mustn't know we speak!"

"Okay, all right! Don't look at me like that! You know I'd never forget our Canidae creed."

"We'd all turn to dust if *they* found out, Bruno! Though you might be right about the skunk oil."

Listening to his good friends' advice, Paycock dwelled on what they'd said as he silently generated some eager new protection duties, imagining two tough males battling over Laburnum till his chest thrust out handsomely!

Poor Paycock, here he was, in bad need of getting Bruno and Rowley discussing this major nuclear menace of real substance, yet more important still these heavenly spring breezes; plus if this interfering landlord was taking away Laburnum's blissful affection, he would have to get vicious and challenge him! Laburnum's affectionate caring had only ever been meant for him; and if his best friends were right, and Algernon really was an obstacle, he'd be up against one hell of an uphill battle that just might test how heroic he was! "With what you're both saying, you think I'd better keep a close watch on Laburnum?" Paycock asked.

"With this guy talking arched, you'd better watch *her* all the time, Paycock. We don't know if arched-talking can do more than that French perfume Laburnum unglues on her magazine page to rub on her neck," Bruno was trying to help his good pal.

"You're talking about this new owner?" Rowley was getting it straight.

"Yes, that's who we're talking about, who else talks arched?" Paycock replied irritated. "He's from that island over there where a man stands in front of three sticks in a white uniform and uses a flat bat to hit a ball."

"That's right? And they drink tea on the hour?"

"You mean that as they're in batting, they're holding a cup and saucer?"

"Think, Bruno! A baseball batter drinks soda here, but he doesn't hold a can of Pepsi while he's receiving the pitcher's ball, does he? Just *think it out!*"

"No need to take it out on Bruno, Paycock, just because you've a sizable job ahead of you protecting Laburnum."

"Right! Yes, right, pardon me, Bruno, Rowley. I'm afraid I get snappy if any *sapien* threatens my domestic status. Wow, right now what I'd give for a nice stinky roll in a decayed catfish!"

"It's harder still when your owner is a woman. Sentimentality is more to deal with."

"Mel is your owner, so how would you know about women, Bruno? Though I have to tell you, you usually make surprisingly good sense, despite your kielbasa body and those frayed long ears! And you're right, I'll have to nose Laburnum more often, keep getting my haunch agitating her knees. If that doesn't do it, I'll work on something stronger until she gets it into her head that I'm the only one in first position here, and this-is-where-I-stay!"

"A female *sapien* shouldn't be too troublesome as an owner."

"Just minus the testosterone's all."

"The more caressing ones, like Laburnum, make up for it with their other hormones."

"Though Mel is a good caresser."

"Caressing is essential, Paycock," Rowley agreed, "but if you want an owner to be sensitive to your needs, you'd better see that his moods don't swing in every direction. Henderson is all right as a dog-owner, though when he gets worked up shouting around about what the town council is up to, I have to watch for his boot. His legs jump about, and he kicks the table; and when he misses, he scuffs up my nicely developed burr patches."

"Then move, for hairballs' sake, Rowley! Get well away from his boot—that's just doing what you have to do as a cooperative pet. Remember, *they* choose you; it's not the other way around."

"I'm not so sure of that, Paycock."

"Bruno, both Hans and Mel have owned you?"

"Laburnum is a pretty good pet-owner," Paycock said. "She comprehends that dogs are better companions if they're properly rewarded. Her treat pocket always smells glorious when I walk beside her."

"You've had good luck getting treats and staying slender, Paycock," Bruno complimented.

"Setters don't sit too long. You're the same, Rowley," Paycock added, "Frisking helps you out when you can't rove," referring to Rowley's crawling under his cage fence and coming all the way over the fields from Henderson's farm. "Look, listen to me, my friends," Paycock got their attention, "there's something very serious I've got to discuss with you."

"Remember, if you're going to keep your rightful place with Laburnum, Paycock, you'll have to think up some ingenious moves," Bruno interrupted.

"You'd better be especially watchful when Algernon comes over. You know how *they* are—always talking up some new lunch-chow. Is there any way I can help?"

"You can," Rowley intercepted, "when you're there, and the new landlord and Laburnum are alone, if they stop talking, you'd better telephone Mel or me."

This concern of Rowley's made Paycock's lower lip foam; and in his anxiety, he forgot his substantial 'nuke topic'. Horrified by this threat to his position, Paycock needed to get this straight. "You're saying that if both the landlord and Laburnum are sitting on her sofa, and you can't hear any talk, then there's bound to be action?" Bruno and Rowley slowly nodded their agreement.

This got Paycock recalling Laburnum and Algernon during their first meeting in the vineyard, when right away they'd exchanged the type of glances that made their irises gyrate. Just remembering that the landlord and Laburnum had got along this well, made Paycock extra tense, "Uh-oh, this isn't going to be easy!" Paycock had always trusted that his most monstrous growl could scare off this new owner or any other man; but with this new guy's 'nice doggie' stuff, and Laburnum turning all winsome and sweet, it was clear she was headed for betrayal.

"Rowley's got it right, Paycock, don't forget when they stop talking; it's time to call us. You carefully try out our advice and report back in a few days."

"Right, we will," both Bruno and Paycock vowed. This pledge of Bruno and Paycock's caused all three dogs to sit still and ponder so deeply that their tails thumped.

"Make certain you keep at it, you two," Rowley summed authoritatively.

Thinking of his dearest owner, Paycock nostalgically recalled, "Laburnum loves to watch for diseases. *She* pulls down my eye skin and stares into my pupils, then *she* lifts my head to see if my nose is slimy; then while I'm still sneezing, *she* combs what *she* calls my 'magnificent oily fur'. Now I ask you two, what's wrong with a few tangles? It's canine stud-potency to have a burr or two! A good-looking messed appearance says you're a dog that's been around. After old decrepit hands has cut off your nuts, you need all you've got for attracting a good-looking park bitch. I'm telling you, when you're burred and muddied up to the withers, bitches are much better at drooling and rolling over."

"Yep, bitches will go after a real he-dog stacked with burrs and even want him to pass on a souvenir or two," Rowley said coquettishly as his refined snout raised higher in the air because he never forgot he was way ahead of Paycock and Bruno with his 'expensive schooling'. Displaying his clods of bleached fur-tangled burrs in the brilliant shaft of sunlight bursting the catalpa leaves that all three dogs kept easing their heads and pasterns into, Paycock and Bruno admired Rowley's burr tangles because there were two good-looking bitches up at Henderson's farm, so Rowley must know what he was saying.

“Oh look, haven’t we got a worthier subject to talk about?”

Which reminded Paycock, “Yes, indeed we have! And I’ve been trying to get to it! I’ve a real brain-clicking topic – it’s Algernon and Laburnum’s, and it needs our well-oiled neurons.”

Glancing sideways, Bruno gave a fearful whisper, “Silence!”

Bruno’s dire warning made Paycock and Rowley turn to see Mel coming around the barn. Automatically, they changed into their dummy good-pet postures for looking obedient, demure, and cuddly; their eyes gone all tall, naïve, and shy.

“Ah, there you are, Bruno-boy! No, stay! That’s okay! You stay too, dogsie-wogsies! Good boy, Bruno!” Mel greeted as Bruno stood with his cow-eyes pleading in a creditably cute tail wag that gave such wiggles to his kielbasa backside that he disarmed Mel and made him crouch to give Bruno many kindly head pats along with weirder baby talk. “There dum de dum, that’s jes’ fine, Bruno-babyo! There, babyo, that’s it! No lickey facey—that’s it; no more baby-waby, you sit now! Stay out here and teach your buddy-wuddies a thing or two. Okay?” Mel gave Bruno a strong two-handed patting, then nodded to each of the other dogs before turning and disappearing back around the barn.

Like all dogs, Bruno had always known that *sapiens* had this hilarious belief that dogs had vacant minds. But as he and all Canidae knew, the truth is that dogs are deceivingly mega-subtle thinkers and have been from their earliest ancestry, which is why with all their knowledge they protect their emotions by playing them down. No self-respecting dog truly wears his heart on his hock, whatever he pretends. It not only doesn’t get a dog anywhere, but it violates the terms of his domestic status and might even interfere with his right to drop into fathomless snoozes—which is where all mammals did their best thinking if they only knew it.

When Mel had appreciated their ‘good dog’ poses, the good friends were safely alone again, and they breathed out lengthily, slumping into ‘relieved total relaxation’. Paycock neatly crossing his fore paws as Rowley stood up. “I’d like to hear your seriously important topic, Paycock,” came Rowley’s authority, “as best friends, we mustn’t let our superlative intellects slip. Though, Paycock, Henderson will be mad as purple-hell if he finds out I’ve gone! Bruno, listening? Don’t forget your special job now. When Algernon and Laburnum are together, watch for it going all quiet. I’ll want a full report.” Bruno nodded importantly. “Then as we three are in need of deep neuronic irrigation, we’ll get to that substantial topic then, Paycock, okay?” As the other two readily agreed, Rowley finished, “I’m off! Bye!” nodding his farewell to each.

After Rowley had left, Paycock sat on in the sunlight with Bruno. He was annoyed with himself he hadn’t determinedly moved his friends onto that world-threatening nuke discussion. As progressive dogs, it was accomplishing to sit with the sun beating on them while they drove at their central nervous systems with plenty of stimuli. It correlated their motor impulses, fulfilled basic Canidae instincts, and kept them well ahead of *sapien* understanding. Though both dogs were at least happier—Bruno because he'd been given a specialized job he'd have to report on; and in his basket, Paycock would need to do some more disciplined clever management about Algernon and Laburnum's talk. Not having sold his buddies on it today, he'd have to get his thinking so well-advanced that his words would be irresistible at their next meeting.

Chapter 7
Supper Party

"You know I met him?" Laburnum informed Sylvia in the kitchen as they talked casually about Algernon.

"Took a while, didn't it?"

"Not surprising, look at all Algernon and Hans had to negotiate!" Sylvie used that habit of hers, cupping a hand around her mouth while leaning to whisper, "He isn't around, is he? I haven't heard his crazy sports car, have you?"

"No, I know that engine now; don't worry, he's in town. Those guys got along well. No, he's taken our list to 'Able's Market'."

Spread over Algernon's kitchen counters, Sylvia was mixing up a green sauce to pour over her poaching salmon. For ensuring a successful evening, Sylvia and Laburnum had previously talked up their good dishes; and as Sylvia stirred while sharing the utensils Laburnum used for prepping vegetables, she'd got a happy little hum going.

Using hot pads, Sylvia stopped stirring to pull the fish out of the oven, making Laburnum's appetite rise, "Perfect, Sylvie! You found that good firm salmon you'd wanted."

"Mmm, I can pretty much bet it'll taste great!" Sylvia kept sniffing it, as satisfied she put the salmon back through the billows of steaming oven heat. Closing the door, she paused to re-clip back her hair. Relaxing her stance, she said, "You know, Laburnum hon, every day I thank heaven it's Algernon! Finding that 'right vintner' came awful close, didn't it? All that 'special guy' business of Hans'? And think about it, how long have we known Hans? Reb and I would go nuts if we couldn't come out to this place—though hell, listen to me! Hey, it was a lot worse for you, hon! Though I'm positive we've lucked out, and Algernon is a real decent guy." Laburnum took the larger knife from Sylvia, "Though I can't stop thinking what would we have?"

"Done if he'd been had been some tight-assed militant?" Laburnum's flash of abject misery, "Holy Hogswort, Sylvie!"

"Hogswort?"

"A new bad local plant. Its name's sound suits scary feelings."

Sylvia kept chopping more parsley while repeating, "Hogswort, Hogswort."

Laburnum kept on, “It’s my way of exclaiming because any hard-nosed new landlord would’ve had me out on my backside, you know that Sylvie?” Sylvia handed back a chopping knife to Laburnum. “Remember that day you’d said that this British tourist might be interested in purchasing this place? I’d cranked up every morning-star spell and then some! Yes, I’ll say we’re damn lucky! This guy is not only letting Paycock and I stay on in my snug little apartment, but he’s keeping on Reb and Mel; and hey, you know, I really like the guy! He’s different all right—I mean the British aren’t so bad. And he’s traveled all over… interesting!”

“‘Different’ is all right! And you should like him. Single, the right age, a nice-looking new man from far off places—that’s *taller* than you!”

“And speaks with a different tongue! Except for Hans and Mel, who do we know from other countries?”

“Right.” It was on this ‘different tongue’, thinking of Algernon’s upper-crust phrases, that they both caught one another’s amused glances. They stopped their giggles, though as Sylvia was determined to be fair to their new owner, “I get a real kick out of talking to him at the bar. He’s such a royal, and it’s not just that accent, I mean like.”

“I know what you mean.”

“I wouldn’t mind betting he could be one of those lost princes they write about over there. Though, no, I don’t think they were from England.” She cross-chopped the parsley, “I have to admire him. It’s too bad some of our regulars wonder who the hell he thinks he is. But Laburnum, whatever our local guys say, when Algernon comes in and sits at the bar with them, like him or not, he always has something to tell and gets them going. It amazes me how he wins guys over! Reb’s for him; because like Hans, he’ll listen to suggestions. Reb and I are sure he’s going to work out just fine.” Sylvia sifted some of the finely chopped parsley into her saucepan mixture as she stirred and hummed this same little tune, then giving an enigmatic laugh, “Mind, it won’t hurt that Hans always hired good crews!” More shared amused glances.

“You’re saying Algernon hasn’t had Hans’ hands-on experience in the vineyards?”

“I doubt he’s had a lot, he’s so urbane—have you noticed his hands? And he’s always in great oh-so-casual European smart clothes! But you know what he’s got going for him? Laburnum, that guy wanted this place real bad! I think he was trying to hide how much he wanted it, but I could tell this house and the winery had swept him off his feet! That first day we brought him here, he so loved this place, he was ‘speechless’! No, I’m not joking, it took him sometime to find his tongue!”

“Algernon?”

"Anyone can be over-excited, I guess! Shrewd old Hans must've known Algernon had fallen for this place!" Sylvia said. "I'll bet our new landlord paid full price."

"Aw, I wouldn't be too sure, I heard they'd been a time haggling."

"Right."

"That day I was too scared to leave this place, Sylvie," as Sylvia knew Laburnum had kept well out of the way of the negotiating, not bearing the thought of losing her apartment and all she'd loved about Runditz's.

"I knew what it meant to you, hon."

"Yep, both you and Hans did! But oh, I was so damn scared, Sylvie."

"So, they should've haggled; along with the winery, Hans had valuable property."

"Oh right, and how can you beat a house like this? In perfect repair—thanks to your Reb—and as real estate, with our barn apartments and all those southern-sloping vineyards that Superman-Hans kept going for far too long. I'm sure they know it, but it's been your Reb and Mel keeping this house a showpiece; and I'm in with you about how Algernon will be, Sylvie. He's smart; and thanks to our stars' lineup, whatever his reasons, that man really fell for this place. You know this wouldn't have happened if you and Reb hadn't done all that talking it up you did with him at your inn?"

"I told you about that?"

"Reb did. Clever of you to get Algernon wanting to see this place, you deserve more credit. All I could do—well, who knows? My hottest spells may have helped some!" Laburnum sighed sending home the enormity of her relief as she and Sylvia exchanged more modest little glances. "And I'll say this, if Algernon has some fetish for this place, I'll bet it'll help him running the guys at the winery!"

"You mean the 'chaps'?" More giggles. "It's hard to guess what changes he'll make, but you know who'll be in on it? You won't keep Hans away!"

"You bet Hans will be here every day."

With an agreeing nod, Sylvia turned up the double boiler. "Yep, so far this real estate sale is looking fabulous!" she said, and hummed this little tune of hers again as she leaned around Laburnum to retrieve her cup of coffee from behind Laburnum's stack of vegetable peelings. Sylvia often hummed as she worked. "By the way, Laburnum, you know I admire Algernon to the skies, and I don't mind his 'chaps' or even his 'plimsoles'."

"What the hell are 'plim'—whatever you said?"

"That's what he calls sneakers! And that last letter in the alphabet is 'zed', not 'zee'!" More giggles, "But…" Her hand went up to whisper again. "You're quite sure he's not back?" Laburnum assured Sylvia again that she'd hear Algernon's wild sports car. Sylvia leaned nearer Laburnum on her pause slant-slicing her carrots. "Don't get me wrong, hon, but there's one thing I don't get. Can you tell me why he calls himself 'one' when he's talking about himself? Could it be something physical, like a problem with the roof of his mouth?"

Laughing, Laburnum said, "Oh, Sylvie, you know it's not!"

"Then what stops him from calling himself 'I'?"

"Look, we both know that once in a while 'one' is used as the first-person pronoun."

"Though thinking of yourself as 'one' *a-all* the time, Laburnum? Isn't that pretty freaky? Even culturally."

"I know!" Laburnum chuckled as she partly agreed. "But you know what I figure? I bet he's coming down from one hell of a glitzy career—far more than any man I've known! Coming here is Algernon's choice all right, but mustn't he be making one super-colossal adjustment? Did you hear that Hans knew about him making big diplomatic deals from his German newspaper? Right! And that 'one' business… have you ever thought couldn't we all have personal discrepancies we each don't always see?"

Smirking, Sylvia said, "Well, speak for yourself, I don't have any! Oh, but you, Laburnum! Those!" She was laughing so hard she had to gesture.

"You're going to say my glasses, you cat! You know my ears are different and it's… well, this way I see better, for heaven's sake!"

"They can fix them so you'd see better still! Though don't get me wrong, hon, I'll love you anyway!"

"Flattery won't help!" Laburnum's pretended offense.

"Though back to Algernon, Laburnum. What d'you think he's come from? D'you think his parents called themselves 'one'? What d'you suppose they live in? Or how about this, couldn't the Foreign Service have trained Algernon to be so detached that now he's retired he can't stop all that? Algernon is nice-looking and holds himself well—though that uprightness—have you ever noticed he has a haughtiness in with it?"

"Haughtiness?"

"Like something of him is far away, distanced, like a colonel in an old British B movie."

"Know what you mean. Yes, though that doesn't bother me."

"If he'd hit the heights with his ambassadorial work, with all he's done and seen, I suppose we can't blame him for not seeing himself like most people."

"Yet he's settling way out here in the New York State countryside!" Sylvia reminded, still amazed.

"Yes, you mean – what if he's a spy or something? You can't help wondering about him. Though that Foreign Service work couldn't always have all been so great—in embassies he'd have dealt with riots and worse! It must get pretty grim working with an ambassador when nations go at one another. Think of all those

Mid-Eastern riots. Though no, you know, I really think this 'one' business of Algernon is just a personality quirk of our guy!"

"Like those 'If you will?' people on TV talk interviews?"

"Yes, but you know, his 'one' thing sounded crazy to me at first—even comic—but when we'd got talking about early civilizations… yes, Sylvie! Can you believe it? You know how much I've ached to talk 'civilizations'! Though I can't say I'd noticed if he kept this 'one' business up."

Laburnum kept peeling as Sylvia cleared her counter end. "You think his family is from a manor or a mediaeval castle? Though it wouldn't make sense he'd leave some great picture book place, would it? You've finished with that longest chopping knife?" Laburnum held the knife by its blade to pass it to Sylvia.

"Who knows what his parents are like? Though there's got to be money—what's a Lamborghini cost? And imagine suddenly putting money out for property like this without blinking an eye when he's also forking out alimony? Though that doesn't go with him being so nice and easygoing, does it?" Passing the knife back.

"Oh Sylvie, listen to us. Don't you think we should be remembering that 'a fly doesn't get into a closed mouth'?"

Sylvia's burst of laughter! "Oh, all right, Laburnum hon, you're right, maybe we shouldn't keep on talking about him! Though it's a good way of getting to know the guy; and like you, I'm just so frickin' glad it's him."

Laburnum was chuckling at her own reproach. "We'll know more about him one of these days. Or you know who will?"

"Hans!" Sylvia chimed in.

"And when one of us is alone with Hans."

"If it's you, Sylvie, be sure to let me in on it. Particularly about Algernon's family, and where they live." With a hand on her hip, Laburnum stopped and surveyed her chopped vegetables. "Enough? What do you think?" Her steamer pot was filled with fresh colorful carrots, runner beans, parsnips, small onions, cauliflower, and pale yellow rutabaga.

Sylvia appreciatively said, "Mmm! Yes, that's plenty!" Turning back to slowly stir her mixture in the double-boiler her little tune got louder. Singing or humming, Sylvia was happy.

"Hey, I know that song!"

"You doo-OO?" crazily excited, Sylvia grabbed Laburnum by the shoulders and turned her towards her! "You know the words, Laburnum? Then help me, hon, it's been bugging me silly since I've heard it."

"That tune, keep it coming," Laburnum said.

"Da-da-de-dumming," Sylvia recalled more of the notes. She hummed over the first phrases of this tune with confidence, while into it the women heard the

Lamborghini slow down to park. "I used to know that ballad—it's about gypsies! 'She's gone with the raggle-taggle gypsies, O!'"

Sylvia was so pleased, she raised up on her toes and clapped her hands. "Oh wow!" Joining in with Laburnum, she repeated the phrase. "Laburnum, that's so-o gre-*eat!* You know more? I know you do. *Try,* come on! Please?"

"Something about—'and downstairs ran this lady, O!'"

"Who wanted to 'see the gypsies, O!'" Sylvia sung. "Just gr*e*-at! Oh, I love you for it, Laburnum sweetheart!"

Algernon had come in as they struggled with these bits of lyrics while clearing up the utensils. Taking the ice cream from his grocery bag, he put it on the counter beside Sylvia and after finding spaces in cupboards for the other groceries, he leaned on the refrigerator to check what Sylvia and Laburnum were doing, till Sylvia lifted her wooden spoon to pat his gallon of ice cream.

"Right. Where?" Algernon asked.

"This freezer up here please, Algernon!"

"Sylvie, this is the guy you need for that British gypsy song!" Laburnum remarked and sung her catchy line, which Sylvia picked up.

Algernon put the ice cream away while he joined in, giving it his full rich tenor. "'There were three gypsies came to my door…'" raising a hand, "Er, hold it! One knows it!"

As Laburnum put in her line, "–and downstairs ran this lady, O!" Elatedly, Sylvia repeated both lines, closing her eyes for getting them memorized.

Algernon rubbed his forehead. "Then… 'One sang high and one sang low'."

"Chinese gypsies?"

"Being a nomadic race the Romanies did happen to be in the Far East, Sylvia. Known as 'Luoli'—should you need to know."

"Thanks! Though no, that's not what I want."

Using his strong tenor again, Algernon finished the verse, "And the other sang bonny bonny Biscay O!"

"'…bonny bonny Biscay O!' Thanks, Algernon!" as she applauded him. "Thank-yo-*ou!* Now I've got it! That song's really bugged me, kept me awake nights." With Algernon's help, Sylvia ecstatically repeated the four lines, then she checked her watch, "Look, Laburnum," quickly she smothered her sauce over her removed fish dishes and pushed them along the counter. "Laburnum sweetheart, I've got to run. These will need refrigerating, okay?" Laburnum nodded. "Be back in a few hours."

'Byes' to Sylvia, who rushed off singing, "There were three gypsies came to my door! And downstairs ran this lady O," her joyful singing distancing as she left the house.

Left with Laburnum, Algernon checked Sylvia's sensational salmon and watched Laburnum top slivers of butter to two sheets of crusty dinner rolls,

“Lovely, oh yes, all of it! Gads! This is to truly be a ticky-poo dinner, Laburnum. Is there any special reason for it?”

“Ticky? Oh, it’s a Friday night,” Laburnum gathered the knives to wash them. “A different meal to look forward to on Friday’s gives the week a nice rhythm.”

“Righty-ho, yes! Splendid, I’d say!”

“Sylvia was trying so hard to remember that tune. I hope you know you’ve made her day, Algernon. How come you knew that gypsy song?”

“End of school term, special assembly, the whole school sang along—a traditional treat celebrating classes being over. Folk songs mostly; occasionally, a boy would solo or a group of us descanted.”

“About the Chinese gypsies, ‘One Sung Hi and One Sang Lo’?” Amusing them again. “‘Luoli’, wasn’t it?”

“‘Luoli’ was the name given them over there actually, yes.”

“Over there?”

“Shanghai back in the ’50s. Studying the Chinese dynasties, one found out about the Luoli. There’s all kinds of fascination when you go back beyond Mao, as you must certainly know, though it wasn’t the greatest time to be posted there.”

Having said this, I left Laburnum to wander through to my study to make my check of the lake’s endless inspiration through the porch door window; some gracious greens in the far sunlight, and on this day, a bleached look to the land before the shore. Relaxed gazing it, with my shoulder against the door for falling into an examination of this panoramic lake length by length, my tall body sliding into angles as I lingered on the muted ‘old masters’ afternoon tints. Laburnum’s finishing up in his kitchen sounded personal and friendly, emphasizing a pleasing peacefulness around the witch-woman.

It was encouraging not to be quite as restless around her now!

Was this because I was an ocean away from family or some mission’s rigid freedoms? After all, I didn’t need to be quite so insistently obstinate about non-involving with women now. Though this thought would need more contemplation. Over here, America’s freedom was different. Unhampered by what I called ‘networks’—networks to a mission’s frequent societal expectations, or the networks of his father’s endlessly reiterated ‘form’. Not being as hemmed in by such ‘networks’ was a nice newness to get used to. Particularly when it involved an American woman, and I liked hearing the sounds of Laburnum’s domesticity as she cleared her counter, her movements were company. As a neighbor-friend, this was likable, even though for me she was still very much a new kind of woman.

Still gazing at one's changeable lake; I knew it was due the wind-cleaned air, yet it still caused a freaky moment when the shore appeared to have moved towards me, far nearer than it actually was!! It was enough to fill one with wonder when across the lake, I saw a northern area of solid horizon hues. Wandering back to the kitchen, "Laburnum?" She turned, "Have you looked at those fine Corot colors out there this afternoon, they're quite mesmerizing. Is it possible to get tired of these changing lake effects or all this quiet? If you're through, come and look."

Laburnum came through drying her hands on a dishcloth and stood beside me to survey the spread of lake. "Corot? Corot? Soft grays and greens? No, I don't think," starting to answer one of his questions. "You know, being so used to that view, I can't honestly say. I study Seneca as you're finding it, but I'm sure my days wouldn't be as lovely if I didn't depend on that ancient water being down there."

"With all its mystique."

"Hasn't it? Over 600 feet in some places! If I ever need to look for that 'quiet' you're mentioning, I take a walk down and sit right beside it. Get a lengthy gaze going at how the weather textures the surface or scarcely alters the colors. Then if there's a change within myself, it makes that lake suddenly become 'distinctive' if that's the word. No, no, 'significant'?"

"Significantly distinctive?"

"That's it, Algernon! And if this happens on a perfect weather day. Now don't laugh, but I swear I understand the lake's secrets!" I was not laughing as I turned to look at her, and she explained, "With those depths, it's not beyond plausibility that a fanciful creature or two lives deep down." Gazing there beside him in his study as some angled sunbeams momentarily hit his bookshelves, Laburnum's eyes soon raised to his spotlighted titles as inadvertently she was caught by one. "*The Minoans*?" she asked curiously.

Seeing what she was looking at, I reached to get it down and thumb through it, "Take it back with you—written by a couple of archeologists."

"You brought it over here?"

"In that favorite books box. When you and Hans were here, you two gave me a hand with it?"

"Oh right, though I'd been in the kitchen. Were you in Crete?" He nodded. "You saw that palace with the dolphin murals?" she asked in awe.

"The restored palace of Knossos, yes."

"Where the queen had her famous flush toilet?"

Laughing I said, "Not quite like ours, but yes, in about 1600 B.C., the Minoans fabulously invented plumbing and the flush toilet! Hygiene-conscious people, they loved keeping clean and wearing beautiful clothes and jewelry." Shaking the book, "This tells you all about that," putting it in her hands.

“I admired their collective aim to make living more attractive,” she said. “Unlike most ancient defending communities, where weapons and thick-walled defenses were first on the list, I recall Minoan fascination with building houses several stories high, in itself a feat; and they appreciated living in them peacefully, as all that money.”

“Yes, all that money!”

“Kept their culture going for hundreds of years. Fabulous, wasn’t it? Algernon, I do envy you having seen so many of these remarkable historic sights! Did you see other remnants or reconstructions there?”

“In Crete? Some illuminating art pieces,” nodding to the book in her hand, “I may have left one or two postcards in there, one’s habit is to keep PCs where they’re compatible.” As Laburnum recalled more of why she’d admired the Minoans, I became impressed again with our genuine enthrall as we pooled what had especially impressed about the dolphin murals, her dark eyes of some woodland brown so intensifying they threw tiny spars. We were still discussing Minoan buildings when Laburnum gave a loud sudden, “OH-*oh*!” She looked down, Paycock had surprised her by slinking in, like a cat, to rub her knees. “Sorry, Algernon, I hadn’t meant to bring him!”

“You don’t go anywhere without him, do you? Bring him anytime! One adores dogs! One might think of getting one’s own.”

I would have liked to ask Laburnum how she had become interested in the dolphin murals, but a long jungle-like growl emitted from Paycock. “P*A-AY*-co-ock!” Laburnum wagged her forefinger at him. “No growling at a friend ever, and never in *their* house! You’re a special guest, and that was grossly unwanted! It’s time I took you home, and we’ll have a serious talk about this behavior!” Checking back at me, “Please forgive him, Algernon. I’ll take him in hand; this nastiness is unusual for Paycock.”

Laughing my politeness answered, “He’s just a dog, you know, Laburnum!” An unfortunate remark as it caused another loaded growl that made one try crouching down to speak to him. “You’ll eventually get to like one, won’t you, Paycock?” The growl repeated as I put a friendly hand out to her pet and asked, “Has he been used to being in this house?”

“Yes, that’s it, I’m afraid. Hans’ Bruno was Paycock’s closest companion.”

“Bruno the basset hound was originally Hans’ pet. Hans couldn’t take him to his cousin’s, and he was sure Bruno wouldn’t get along too well in town. So when Mel offered to take him here, Hans was much relieved. And it’s worked out, Mel is a good dog-owner, walks him, which poor old Hans couldn’t do. The only annoyance with dogs is at night if a coyote or a skunk comes around. Paycock has got excellent ears and wants us all to know what he hears, and his bark sets Bruno off. Once they’re shushed though, they stop. But that’s what it is if you hear them, just a night animal. Mel took over Bruno when Hans moved into town. You may have noticed how well Bruno's transferred to Mel? So, Paycock, there's no excuse; you are *not* a lonely dog!"

"One is too sound a sleeper to worry about a few barks after being outside all day, and it's good to have built-in dog protection!"

Laburnum agreed as she returned to the kitchen to make room in the refrigerator for Sylvia's fish dishes and lift each in. Then shouldering her colorful big canvas bag, she started to leave, "Paycock and I'll be getting along. By the way, Algernon, I've told you about this poet friend of mine who entertains with his ballads? Rafferty is coming to my place Saturday evening. I've talked him into having an audience of two if you're interested?"

"Ballads, you say? Delighted! May one bring the—er, grape juice?"

"Thanks, no, I'll have beer for you guys, and anything we'll need. Just come at 7:00. In the meantime, we've this great supper ahead of us. Sylvie has to bring her special homemade dessert. I'll be over to set the table as soon as I've done some things and bathed."

"Can't one take care of that? Setting the table, one means?" Smiling at one another as Laburnum shook her head, I rubbed my hands together as she left and checked out the food again, with pleasant new thoughts of Laburnum and oneself at her friend's poetry reading—an aspect of American country culture that surprised me.

Later that afternoon, I was yanking brush with Mel and company in the unremitting sunlight when in a sudden burst of unusual heat, the temperature quickly rose. We all welcomed this forerunner of summer as we wiped at brows; though having put in a heavy morning out here, I was surprised at how profusely I was sweating! Neck and brow needed constant handkerchief mopping as I determined to get at least this row finished. Swiping at my forehead again, I yanked out a stubborn bunch of Queen Anne's lace while this new extreme heat returned me to my former elite life—and brought back one of my most worrisome experiences! Unforgettably, with one particularly concerning incident! *It was that famed game when I'd rashly challenged the top Burmese negotiator to a championship game of tennis. Oh and hadn't I indeed! It had been during a gridlocked conference, and... why in heavens I'd got in that deep? What in Great God Pan's name had I been thinking of?*

One was challenging the opposing nation's leading negotiator, known to be a difficult man that easily displayed shrill intolerance if he didn't come out ahead in whatever he did! Thank any other divinities as well as Great God Pan, I'd been shrewd enough to see to it that I 'lost'. Which turned out to be a reverberatingly clever move later at the negotiating table! Though even one's sweating wetness here in this Finger Lakes vineyard couldn't compare to that bodily meltdown during this much-touted tennis match with observing nationalities loudly cheering on their leader! One's fine English skin had tanned to crisp burnt toast as one knew that his politically inane acceptance of that match could direly injure his diplomatic esteem. Though, there had been great remarks on one's sportsman's gallantry as a loser! *Yes, one had truly been gallant!* Which had even intrigued the curiosity of my opponents in all their much-copied Anglican old-boys team spirit; and with generous hearty congratulations, he shook his victorious opponent's hand looking him in the eye! Still—all the same—*frightful!* Thank heavens that here in these Finger Lakes even sweating undammed sluices and repeatedly brow-mopping only meant that he was accustoming to the day-long use of his muscles working well in this fine little Runditz vineyard!

Scarcely a breeze softened the brazen sun's stabbing as here in America I counted the vine rows yet to be worked. Sylvia and Laburnum's cooking smells teasingly blew from the open windows, as their special supper had everyone eagerly looking forward to it. Finishing up, I finally got out of the vineyard broil and went up to the house.

One severely spoke to oneself about one's personal behavior with this next Runditz get-together. I was not—not on any account—to talk about my wretched father! One had learned one's 'lowliness' limit from that first time; and with all the effort the women had put into this meal, nothing must stop it from being a Runditz Winery week's end happy celebration. For myself too!

Enticingly, the baking fragrances of that poached salmon went through the house and up the stairs. Showering and pulling on fresh garments had seemed like a lot to bother after that draining heat; but owing my new friends looking fresh and 'landlord'-groomed for this well-planned change of pace, thinking of a certain superb wine of Hans', my hungry envisioning was matching Sylvia's poached salmon.

On this mellow spring evening, Hans, Reb, Sylvia, Laburnum, and Mel met up with him again in the elegant country dining-room around Laburnum's flower-decked table. The respective dogs had been fed and had settled in ridiculous slumped attitudes under the table; and like the dinner here for one's welcome back from England, the cloudless end of day dimmed its riches through the spread of bay windows that silhouetted lulling branches of a willow and nearby catalpa tree. The delicious dishes were passed, wine and grape juice poured with Laburnum's teetotal preference going unobserved as attentions focused on Hans' insistent concern that I was not far enough along with the brush-pulling! Making sure that Hans heard, Mel loudly repeated which vineyards had already been properly cleared; though Hans wouldn't accept Mel's word as his decades of managing each season's rounds of work wouldn't let go of him. Everyone understood this, but Reb, who had helped organize the local brush-pullers with Mel and put in all his extra hours after his town's carpentry job, also attested to Hans that they had at least the same amount pulled as former years. "An' it's done thorough, the way you'd yell at us!"

This silenced Hans, though he sat stubbornly skeptical; his doubting eyebrows raised fixedly as he wouldn't touch his plateful.

Mostly though, I was increasingly admiring of one's new friends, who were as mindful and concerned as he about aging the collected grape juice. Lapping up their varying personalities again and their informal little in-jokes, I noticed that each had an immovable seriousness about their full or part-time field work, and as I welcomed getting to know more of 'lowlier' humankind's achievements—all still so new to him—it pleased one I was forming more vivid insights into their individual levels. Though I did have moments of worry that these insights with my new friends might be costing me my 'worldliness', and all that skillful interaction I'd been known for on other levels—'worldliness' was the pro-diplomat's precious conditioning of a lifetime.

Ladling Sylvia's delicious chocolate cream pie onto my fork, I found little surprise lumps of chocolate within. Eating heartily I drank up, tossing in a question or two as one tuned in to their information about what could be the effect of drought on vines. Questions that would have seemed blasé had I been seated next to Laburnum.

Though Laburnun– *oh my God!*

Just look at Laburnum! That wasn't?

Oh no, it couldn't be? But—oh yes, it was! A disgusting little something was hanging from her left nostril as she went on animatedly talking to Reb! Surely this twit-witch woman could feel how repulsive she was? How more socially uncouth could one be? Maybe allowable at a drunken stud party, but in a respectable woman—utterly unforgivable!

If Reb noticed this grotesque embarrassment, he made no show of it, possibly because he was apt to talk to the tablecloth. *Though what could a man do when a decent woman wouldn't use her handkerchief?* Get Sylvia? *Oh praises be! Sylvia had got up and was going to Laburnum with a handful of tissues.* Laburnum paused to look at them inquisitively; and at last realizing she needed them, she almost nodded her thanks to Sylvia, who discreetly sat down again.

Without verbal exchange, the incident was over, thank all celestial orbs as one took in Laburnum's complete unawareness of how physically disgusting she'd appeared to others; and that her being oblivious of her appearance was what everyone here expected! Her intensity behind those crooked glasses was undoubtedly because she was mentally never too far from whichever ancient civilization had her mind in grip, though not even her scholarship could excuse her revolting dinner table misdemeanor. One's automatic finesse around everyday civilities made one wonder how much I had more honestly enjoyed Laburnum's company.

Sorting this thinking about her later, hoping I'd be fair-minded, I reminded myself that the careless twit-witch also knew an astounding amount about the Minoans and had unerringly probed her studies of them and other outstanding civilizations. Was it only his own far finer dinner manners that had been so crassly offended? Due to his varied work, he'd had to deal with quite enough bloodiness or gruesomeness, which was never to be confused with civilized scenes like this special dinner. Though 'civilized' had to be kept monumentally separate, yet the witch-woman had so grossly nauseated, one hadn't been aware that I'd drawn my own napkin up over one's nose and was needing to remind oneself to take it down. *The question was – now he was getting in on this lowlier plane, should he be forming judgments of her? Socially people here saw this 'misdemeanor' as tolerable, so should his disgust with her simply just be accepted?*

Very likely he could be comparing Laburnum with the type of woman of privileged background one frequently met at embassies – some Foreign Service co-worker's daughter who was inevitably writing a '*Don't tell anyone'* kind of book exposing secrets of overseas Foreign Service excesses! Which was unfair – as in all honesty, Laburnum's insatiable 'civilization' interests had done a lot to wake him up and had even made him quite wonder how she'd become so involved with foreign policy.

Oh, Algernon, dear old bumpkin, what a troublesome time you do have with the gentler sex.

Acknowledging that in 'lowlier' circles social dinner table, niceties might be less of a concern, especially when everyone here knew that a woman like Laburnum easily over-involved with her studies. *Though, what did I mean by 'a woman like Laburnum'? Did I mean that if I'd come across her while into my career, one would not have found her interesting?*

There was no doubt that Laburnum would not have made it into a mission's elite milieu. Not without the background and polish of an eminent husband or a top-name school or two. Single diplomat colleagues accepted that mission women, wives mainly, formed a group—a solid abutment for staging jolly dances, holiday parties, and bridge-evenings with prizes, et cetera. Any other good-looking single women usually arrived affianced.

More seriously, could one ever imagine Laburnum being any part of an overseas mission? Hitting it off with well-heeled women loaded with ex-pat. Savoir faire, and illustrious contacts who made torrents out of small talk while dropping a name or two? One could only meet a new attractive woman if one was introduced to a colleague's sister; and once one had this privilege, then in all its glory Foreign Service 'form' whittled you into the appropriate kind of partner through compressing, stamping, and approving by rank's intractable consensus! Which meant that any woman seen as a prospective partner had better come from 'family'. Well-known and 'old'. 'Family' that equated societal acceptance! Despite one's eligibility in having 'old family' of one's own, one's disciplined off-handedness with women let me observe that the women drawn into mission cliques had been monotonously tidy-minded with neat mental drawers containing every kind of manual for resolving every possible overseas situation.

Laburnum fitting into that tiny space?!

This thought amused me as I rested my eyes through the bay windows on the thickening outside dark. Altogether though, he summed that Laburnum was really rather comic. He'd tried to stop short at his surfacing word—*'uncouth'*—in assessing Laburnum. Forgetting to bring her handkerchief had kept him distastefully diverted from her, as instead he gazed the grander closing down of where they had worked now being affected by night time's elements. Though, if as a woman, Laburnum had been offered those overseas wives' kind of 'sophistication', would it have been her choice? Not as the woman Laburnum was now who sought peace, serenity, her dog's companionship, nature walks, and a writer's paradise. In this as a woman, she was elaborately different. Although often quite fascinating, those 'differences' might mean she might take a lot more getting to know—*should this be what he wanted?*

Laburnum's good friends at Runditz's loved her for her independence; her knack with color, her harmonizing hues, all were appreciated—as demonstrated by the gorgeous mix of peonies she'd cut low and arranged mid-table. He had to admit that aside from Laburnum's table manners, she did have a talent for decorating. Often there were quite stunning colors to her patterned shirt, skirt, and necklaces—all of these.

Still unwilling to look Laburnum's way, I'd found the darkening vineyards captivating. In this smothered twilight, one could just pick out the nearly indistinguishable rows of vines they had spent this day freeing from nutrient robbers. Vaguely there the rows lay, with their ghostly symmetry letting through their work's satisfactions, all aptly starting to rest now under that kindest of cozy night blankets.

The sleeping vineyards contrasted with the affectionate teasing going on, and the well-told stories coming from around the table, even as I tossed in my own quip or two. When the boisterous laughter during one of these tales subsided, one happened to look over at Hans. The former owner of this estate must have been studying him because on eye contact with the elderly German, I caught his discreet foxy, wall-eyed wink! Given just to oneself with his surreptitious smile!

Had Vintner Hans known similar private thoughts when he'd managed this estate? Verbalized enrichments and incidents here in this same room, at this same table? Which also must have mixed in with some of that history that only that sagely old scoundrel had amazingly survived.

One's inherited owner-management was developing directly out of Hans' creator-owner-management and his systems, and this fine elderly gentleman's fame for saving this heavenly 'Habitat' from Fire Department conflagration. Looking back at Hans, I hoped that on former contenting evenings like this, Hans' own indulgences had fed him at least as many satisfactions, as furtively I returned his extraordinary old friend's special wink.

Chapter 8
Rafferty

Laburnum's poet friend Rafferty.

Molding what his mind's eye was seeing in the air before him, Rafferty couldn't restrain from gushing his Victorian ballad till one needed to affect letting my head fall onto my propped hand, as I was fearful of offending Laburnum too if one howled with unforgivable laughter. This 'entertainer', as Laburnum had rightly called him, had selected galloping ballads for yanking his delusions out of Laburnum's drapes or pulled down from her ceiling, or they'd got extracted from her caressed standard lamp's shade. His lanky elegant hands carving credible dimensional forms as his eyes widened with his own stricken disbelief. Seated on her scarlet sofa beside Laburnum, one made a bigger effort to listen rather than watch this American poet's antics.

In so many areas over here in America, there was such a great deal that was different!

Then oh God help us! Here it came!

Rafferty's, "Sai-ai-aint Agnes' E-eve-"—three silent beats—"A-A-A-a-ah, a bitter chill it was! The owl, for a-a-all his feathers, was a-cold." Unloading fearful shivers on 'bitter chill' while earnestly sculpting the lovers into 'existence' from some trap door in Laburnum's beige carpet, or the lovers were forced into communicating by his graceful exceedingly long hands, that made sure of the dramatic effect his 'St. Agnes' Eve' lovers had on his audience, Rafferty's gestures so suddenly startled Laburnum and Algernon's acutely tensed feet that the whole sofa backed up by inches.

Oh dear! Most likely Rafferty was undoubtedly a lonely, reclusive poor soul. Though his choice of performer's gear!

Frayed trouser cut-offs displaying spindly long legs that turned profile became poles topped by a jutting, child-like rear-end; and for style rather than being button-less, Rafferty's dinghy checkered shirt was sportingly left open to his waist so sundry tufts of gray hair bedecked this opening. This thick hair also crowned him as it jutted straight up from his cockatoo-like cowlick. Continuing his bird affinity, his well-shaped strong beak rose protuberantly from his quite pleasant face.

ENOUGH, Algernon! You should NOT have come!

The English Lake District poets were favorites for everyone who appreciated that superlative boom; and one was among them, as I reminded myself that rustic eccentricity was not limited to any one country. Which I knew, having been befriended by a charismatic story-telling old fellow that one's father and brother Gillie constantly made the butt of dinner table jokes. One's family's jeering had deeply offended one because the affectionate old fellow could fascinate my young mind, describing colorful village incidents as he magically showed me how to splice two ropes into one. Recalling one's youthful need to defend this old chap at the manor, sitting here on Laburnum's scarlet sofa before her poet friend, I shamefully tightened my abdominals; because being a 'fair-minded man', I cared enough for Laburnum and her poet friend to not disgrace them all.

Rafferty certainly entertained—mesmerized, more accurately; but all I could admire was Rafferty's remarkable memory; and when he could remove the histrionics, the extensive scope of his voice was pleasantly agile. I had always treasured that beloved classic 'Gunga Din', and I began to dread that Rafferty was working up to a major killing of it. But no, luckily, a good deal of Gray's 'Elegy Written in a Country Churchyard' kept this verse-obsessed fellow fastened to his flooding inner scenes. Oblivious that he might be desecrating anyone's precious imagery, that 'moping owl' of Gray's sent Rafferty's eyes into a protractedly awed roll.

Rafferty's verses cascaded on with burlesque profusion as one asked myself whether this 'poetry evening' was really what I had been seeking for my metamorphosing into a lowlier life? No doubt I should be continuously relieved with leaving the intensity of world summit dealings, and all that they entailed, yet here as I sat beside the scholarly clairvoyant herself, buried into this unusual interpretation of the British romance poets eccentrically sung out by Lady Laburnum's lyrical country friend. *Oh greatest of over-appealed to deities!*

Joining Laburnum's eager applause, I felt sure that she too must be sharing my need for Rafferty to hurry up and conclude his recitations—making me unable to glance her way. I tried not to fidget as more verses got spouted while he and Laburnum, again with their hopes high, enthusiastically stood up to applaud—*but, oh dear, no – here it came!* Striking the pose of Laurence Olivier as Henry V addressing his troops before going into the St. Crispin's Day battle, Rafferty got 'Gunga Din' going with a wallop! "You may, talk o' gin and beer, when you're quartered safe out 'ere." I repositioned for Rafferty's pseudo cockney charade, yanking in my stomach to brace for all poor Kipling's soldier was to be put through, until, using all his effort I closed my eyes and only attended the words—*oh better… far, far better!*

Why hadn't I thought to close them earlier?

Who couldn't adore the impudent jabs and sluicing wit of this rollicking barrack's ballad? Not seeing Rafferty's overdone gestures, his voice certainly was talented, and one quite enjoyed revisiting these droll lines all the way to Kipling's fateful bomb-shell. "You're a better man than I am, Gunga Din!" More appreciative of Rafferty's presentation now, I also saw that in with my own 'going lowly', I was discovering that people over here had surprisingly spirited interests. When I inevitably opened my eyes again, one saw that at last Rafferty was into a loose droop from his waist—*conveying that his recital was complete?!*

Making sure it was, Laburnum was standing to heartily applaud and tidy the tray of bottles, beer mugs, glasses, and cheese she was to take to the kitchen. Rafferty though, being overcome, had fallen backwards, alarmingly, into Laburnum's scarlet armchair, flopping across it, like a deflated dinghy, as his vocal muscles relieved with the stress of all that memorizing being drastically extinguished. No further word or other gesture came from the poet, till worrying, Laburnum put the tray down again. Laburnum and I continued telling Rafferty how much we had admired all his effort as we plied him with gratitude. Though not responding, Rafferty slid further down in the chair into unnatural-looking angles. Laburnum and I were concerned and kept up even louder encouragements until our poet toppled sideways, like a rag doll, and his head flopped over the chair's arm.

"Oh! That's just what Paycock does," Laburnum observed.

Had he fallen asleep?

There was no doubt that this ballad lover was asleep all right, as studying him Laburnum and I continued talking to him. Then we looked at one another. Laburnum shrugged, though I looked at her more questioningly. "No, he's not expounded quite as stupendously as this before, not to me he hasn't," she answered my non-asked question.

"Where does he live? How far has he come?" I asked noticed the shreds Laburnum had made of her shawl's fringe, as one assessed that on Laburnum's part anyway, this 'friend' of hers was just that, without much likelihood of becoming more.

"He can sleep there, or on the sofa, Algernon. When he's got his strength back, he'll go home. He lives up on the hill across the highway—to answer you."

"*Across* the highway?"

"Yes, and don't worry, I'll be at my 'desk' anyway; and I'll see that he's fully recovered, then Paycock and I'll walk him home."

"Give me a call, I'll join you."

"No, you're tired."

"One's retirement perk is that there's no need to be on the job at a specific time, and so it should be for you! By the way, where is my growling quadruped?"

"He's been allowed his rug by my bed tonight, which miffs him as he loves company. But he knows it's because of his rude growling, and Algernon, he does regret his behavior to you."

Nodding, as we both looked again at the unconscious Rafferty, I remarked, "That was a very large number of pages to memorize; it's no wonder it's done him in."

We concerned that the evening had literally knocked Rafferty out. "I think he put on his best performance knowing he had a double audience," Laburnum whispered, though it didn't look as if Rafferty was hearing. "Poor Rafferty, it's best he sleeps."

"Have you known him fade out like this before?"

She shook her head. "Though I went to *his* place that last time, and he wasn't as overcome with just me. I think we got his entire repertoire tonight."

"A commendable feat. Though no 'wraggle-taggle gypsies'!"

She smiled, "British standbys tonight, knowing you were coming." She had put down the tray, but when a growl came from the bedroom, she picked it up again.

I placed my hand across Rafferty's forehead, which the man didn't appear to feel; and thinking it a good idea, Laburnum took the tray to the kitchen and returned to try timing his pulse; but wearing her watch inside her wrist, she had a time feeling Rafferty's vein's throb while checking the watch face. She finally gave up and moved Rafferty's wrist to me, and I checked it to my watch. Nothing was abnormal other than Rafferty remaining soundly lost to his dreams.

Looking at Laburnum, I asked, "Will you be fine?" She nodded. "Look, I'm planning to read too. Call me when he wakes?"

Laburnum's phone call to me came through well after one o'clock. "I saw your light still on, Algernon; and just wanted you to know that Rafferty has woken up fine, so there's no need."

"*Be* there!"

Cutting her short, I was pleased Laburnum had called, as I stepped into my loafers. The waning moon's late rise made it a black night with only stars to give any light; and out in the cooler air striding over to Laburnum's, I met her already waiting outside with Paycock leashed up. Under her outside light, Rafferty leaned against the wall, fairly upright. In my ongoing effort to befriend Laburnum's dog, I offered to take Paycock's leash; and as Laburnum was to shine the flashlight, she let me take it.

After Paycock's dimmer growl as they set off across the lawn, Laburnum remarked, "Rafferty, Paycock is not too fond of you either, is he?" If Rafferty answered, I didn't hear him, though one was recalling how much a male dog wasn't usually too overjoyed if his female owner's attention was taken over by another male. Diagonally zigzagging the dirt tracks that cut south and west through underbrush and along a farmed field—*weren't they on that same track he had seen Laburnum take on his first evening back from the U.K., when she'd gone to hear a poet as one guessed that Rafferty was the man she'd met?*

We three walkers limited our comments to getting our 'night eyes' on this moonless night, and avoiding face-level long brambles, or treading around a mainly buried rock that Laburnum warningly illuminated with her flashlight. Laburnum knowingly moved along with ease, not needing the light that she mainly flashed behind her for the men.

"Why hadn't we thought of driving?" One asked aloud, and Rafferty strongly agreed while avoiding a swung-back twig.

"Oh no, walking at night time is so lovely," Laburnum expressed, "particularly along these footpaths."

"You can think like that if you want to," Rafferty spoke out stumbling on the rock she had just thrown her light on. In exclaimed annoyance, he gruffly informed, "A better way is how I came, by the roads."

Rafferty didn't need to be so gruff; he'd only stumbled, hadn't fallen. Listening to him grumpily making it clear he wasn't at all pleased with Laburnum's choice of route, one put Rafferty's annoyance down to his waking up still tired from his evening's major achievement.

Making an effort with the man, I suggested, "If one walked in front of you, Rafferty, one could warn you about rocks."

"'O-o-ONE'?" Rafferty loudly mocked. "You're meaning, 'you', aren't you? Are you saying that 'you' would stop me from falling?"

"One had just explained that to you, yes." I did not need Rafferty being insupportably rude when Laburnum and I were giving up our sleep to get this siphoned-off poet home.

"But 'one' is wrong grammar!"

"*RAFFERTY,* dear," Laburnum's call came brightly, "as Algernon's had the best of upbringing and schooling."

"...and he's from England."

"Not that any of that matters. It's personalities that differ," I defended.

"Huh, if you ask me."

But Laburnum drowned Rafferty out. "There's A GREAT SAYING," Startlingly loud, she called back, "A JOURNEY OF A THOUSAND MILES begins—begins—with the company HE KEEPS?" One held back one's laughter!

"That's a-all *WRO-ONG!*" Rafferty yelled at her through his groans. "What you're meaning is, 'A thousand miles starts with a single step'."

"You're sure?" she twisted back to ask.

My laugh at her muddled proverb had broken our tension, though I'd guessed that Laburnum's shouted effort might have been to protect my 'foreigner's worldliness' from Rafferty's ridicule.

Rafferty corrected her, "And it's, 'A MAN IS KNOWN BY THE COMPANY HE KEEPS'. That's everywhere! I thought you'd have known that one!"

"Oh! Yes, that's the one I'd wanted," Laburnum assured him as they came to the completely empty high road, and all three crossed it.

On the other side, Laburnum and I saw Rafferty safely back along the road to his house till Rafferty announced, "It's okay here. I could've made it, you know?" They said their goodnights assuring Rafferty again that they had very much enjoyed his special evening.

Laburnum and I turned to return home, though Paycock wanting to keep going with Rafferty suddenly yanked! Snatching his leash from me, Laburnum gave her pet a few curt words. Getting back to the highway, we had to wait for a couple of tractor-trailers before crossing. Despite this black night, and the many lengths of hedges edging the farmed fields, Laburnum knew exactly where to enter for their track again through the underbrush; and once into it, Paycock led the way, and she and I walked singly. Turning back to him, "It was kind of you to come, Algernon."

"Very kind of you to dig through your, ahem, proverbs repertoire, and save one from having to make personal explanations, Laburnum. I appreciated it!" She laughed merrily, without Rafferty in this striking stillness, intimate though it seemed in this night's blackness; each of us were relieved with just the other's company.

Passed the first field the more even ground let us walk side by side, and I suppose as I had brought this 'one' business up, Laburnum saw her chance. "If you don't mind my asking, Algernon, what would you have explained to Rafferty?"

WHAT?

I was severely jolted by the utter crudity of Laburnum's extremely personal question. One had to remain silent for some paces.

Such a lengthy pause may have made Laburnum wonder if she should not have asked this. One was recalling that in America, everyone believed in asking whatever questions they wanted to. In Europe, Americans were known for their 'tell-all culture', which to Algernon ignored other people's sensitivities.

Struggling for circumspection, I finally said, "One is noticing that over here, there's a concern for the style of one's speech."

"The *style*?"

"You don't think so?"

"I'd say that people here aren't used to you referring to yourself as 'one'."

Disastrously hit, I exclaimed, "Youser!" God, how could a decent woman like Laburnum be so personally offensive?! Her resorting to this intimacy was not at all what one cared for. Scholarly she undoubtedly might be, but scholarship didn't qualify her to. Oh why in all heaven didn't Paycock give a good hard yank and demand her attention? Though, wouldn't this be the one time her disobedient monster-dog behaved???

Still silent, though I became mindful of one's hard-earned tenet, *all differences can be negotiated,* as the automatic-gentleman in me continued to hold twigs back from Laburnum's irritating face.

Did this situation mean that his only recourse was to take a stab at the lousy inquisitiveness of this impudent woman? Gathering one's thoughts, though going from one possibility to another, I became lost! LO-OST! Crikey! Over here I'd rarely experienced such an abundance of youthfulness so dousing and annoying that this much younger country lacked such personal insensitivity! Most likely due their destabilizing lack of queen and country. Though, oh Lord! It went against one's nature to leave this talk with one's neighbor up in the air. Though hadn't it been her damned audacity that had got this going? Gathering one's wits, I'd at least attempt to answer, "There has to be an objectivity, Laburnum. A distancing of oneself to fully assimilate a subject."

"A 'distancing'?"

Bally-hell this infernal female! Should he try snarling, like some angry animal, and get Paycock fired up? One paused, then after righting a coughing spell,

Oh, come off it, Algernon old toad! More reasonable behavior, please!

Still prevaricating, "Mmm, one would prefer that; now this is just to you." Another uneasy cough, "See, settling after decades, to really be settling in just one place… well, one realizes, being scrupulously honest, that one has the deadliest fear I might be losing—or that *God help me,* I could become, could be becoming *provincial!*"

"*Provincial?* Oh gol-ly, you mean like me? Or Hans?"

"Ha, you're giving one a lot to think out!"

"But you can't mean you'd become provincial just because you're physically settling in another place?"

More strides, more bramble untangling, another lengthier pause. "That's what one isn't sure about. And as you must know, one didn't mean that you and Hans are provincial! You've traveled, lived in other countries, and obviously, Hans."

"For me, a year in Portugal is all! Not much else. A week or two in Mexico. But I don't consider my views narrow if that's what provincial means?"

“For oneself, that’s just what one means! You’ve lived in Portugal, known a country that wasn’t your own, used its language.” *Better keep her on this tack, Algernon old chum.* “You’ve known other people’s love for their country, found it as deep as the love you have for your own homeland. Understanding this is an absolute; what other way can one make sense of different anthems, unappetizing foods, religious carnivals, political extravagances? It’s preposterous to expect tolerance from foreign countries if one hasn’t gained some knowledge of the immensity of their culture!” I *was refusing to get breathless,* though suddenly stopping. *What in hell was I doing? In answering Laburnum’s far too personal question, wasn’t I transmuting my offence? What on earth did it matter if I’d been personally offended? Wasn’t I shoving my anger onto—what? who?* Even though she’d been the one to get this going! A*nd she blasted well wouldn’t stop ‘yes, yes-ing’. He saw he’d better keep this thought-flow going only to one’s self.* Aloud, one said, “In my work, Laburnum, when one needed to understand what was irreconcilable, one had to get under the skin of the citizens of that country, its representatives, its aims, one’s had to feel out their wants, how their ideals had evolved, become sacred. This is an intrinsic starting point in international antagonisms.”

As I personally still rankled, I saw that if I was to get back onto a surer footing, I’d have to keep her safely maneuvered onto one’s former work. Being the target of this unfamiliar intimacy, most honestly, I knew that one’s answer’s evasion could become one for that ridiculous book of records of Guinness’, let alone for this impertinent twit-witch, though, eventually there could be more to all this? *For instance, could he be missing out on more perceptive American thinking? You must be thinking you could be, Algernon, you old Fidus Achates.*

Trying again, “Yes, Laburnum, and if you’d thought one was afraid of losing one’s worldly proficiencies settling over here, you’d be dead right! Having a very sound idea of how differently people live in some of the most outlandish countries, one has to say, it does seem thoroughly peculiar to be settling in a place where one might ultimately need to build a single loyalty! For persons like oneself, this just cannot easily be done.”

“Because of all your cosmopolitan experience? No, Algernon, I see it wouldn’t be easy,” she said, kindlier. “With all your dedication and insight, I’m getting an inkling of what those diplomatic years must have been for you. Breadth of thinking like yours is praiseworthy, and I wish all of us had more of it. Though with this ‘worldliness’ of yours, I have to ask—probably another silly question—but, where does nationalism fit in? All nations with any pride do their share of flag-waving.” *Ha! This more general question of Laburnum’s was balm to one!* Though as she asked this, she kept receiving sharp pulls from Paycock’s leash and repeatedly had to reach down to pet her dog.

As I spoke, I breathed more easily. "Pride in a country helps build its identity certainly, particularly for developing nations. Though even if newly independent, when nationalism gets too fanatic; yes, it can certainly disrupt a climate for debate." Then at last came his more rote reply. "One isn't saying that national differences shouldn't be; with groups of people anywhere there'll always be differences—desirable, obviously. Variety enlightens, enriches." One waited as Laburnum pushed Paycock away from rubbing her knees. "Though yes, agreed, the other side of nationalism is that it can become maddeningly tricky. Which is why personally, for one's self, one's aim will always be 'internationalism'."

"A leveling of the global field? Oh do STOP that, Paycock! Behave now! I've given you a nice cuddle!"

"Internationalism isn't new, Laburnum. Here, Paycock. Good dog," I. rubbed Paycock's ears as the dog stiffened, though he didn't growl. "Yes, in trading with other nationals... well, as you know multi-national shipping merchants established all that way back in large ports, like London's, or the Silk Road, trading not only created wealth but provided needs while spreading international influences. Similarly, today, one doubts you've studied wine labels, Laburnum, but wine now comes from hundreds of different countries." *Oh- good Lord, what was I talking about? I was rambling and only 60! Automatically, I kept it going, though.* Only just then my flashed light caught the large buried stone Rafferty had stumbled on, and without mentioning it, each of us walked clear around it.

Laburnum replied, "There's no doubt that international cooperation is a must, Algernon. And I know I keep on about this, but any further enjoyment of life will always be inhibited by those stockpiles of massively destructive weapons. Whatever else we deal with, that's always in front of us, isn't it? That we could obliterate or be obliterated. All of us live in this unnatural fear."

"Which may take forever to resolve, Laburnum, but hard as it is controlling those weapons, don't forget that nations do have other urgent needs. Battling air pollution, for example, preventing the spread of infectious diseases, pooling expertise for growing crops on unwelcome terrains—heavy amounts of diplomacy goes into reducing nations' logistical differences on these and other fronts. The beneficial greater objective being that as they each get resolved, they form sounder economic networks for maintaining peace in each other's countries."

"Ye-e-s," Laburnum uttered slowly fitting this into her perceptions. "Yes, I do see how valuable your 'worldliness' must be."

"And why one aims for 'internationalism'," I continued past her. "This isn't to say one doesn't dearly love where one was born as much as anyone, or that I couldn't develop a profound love for, say, the Finger Lakes."

"*OH, WHAT* did you just say—'*I* couldn't develop'?" Laburnum's surprised exclamation as she turned to me.

I laughed weakly and politely, then continued, "I do use both pronouns, you know. Though down deep, *I've!* Oh listen, *'I'VE'!* See how you've inhibited me?" One eased enough to be amused. "I meant to say, all that *ONE* has taken on here in the Finger Lakes!" Laburnum and I spluttered with more mutually understood laughter.

Our conversation had hit this sudden insightful height, yet Paycock would keep pushing his snout into Laburnum's knees, or her hand, or he slurped against her skirt, till her dog's irritation got her to stop walking. Stimulated with Algernon's conversation, she reproached Paycock as her strong fingers rubbed at her dog's spine consolingly.

Re-starting to walk again, Laburnum returned me to our talk, while by the flashed light one shone for her, as she was tending to walk slower coming in sight of one's house lights. "So much of your 'internationalism' sounds incredibly hopeful, Algernon, though I imagine when a conflict resolution flops—and we all hear about those—it must put you through an unbearable hell! *THERE!* Now Paycock, *THAT'S IT!"* Having given her dog another last loving pat before turning back to me, "I don't know how much I'm like other people, Algernon, but when so much of the news looks hopeless, and any improvement efforts like yours only happens behind closed doors, how can I see any hope of 'bloodshed' ever being over?" Grudgingly I agreed. "Good! That we agree, I mean! Because, I have just one more question!"

"*One* will put on *one's* armor!"

"No, it's not personal!" Laburnum assured me, "Oh, all right, I know I'm being opportunistic, but I wanted to ask." One braced. "After your extraordinary poetry evening and watching you administer admirable health care to the poet-performer Laburnum, you may ask what you wish!"

"Yes, I must apologize."

"No, no apology. Though after your poet's recital, we do deserve to fully return to being ourselves. Your question?"

"*'Return to being ourselves'?* Yes, lovely! I wanted to ask you; on your Mid-Eastern travels, did you see evidences of Mesopotamia? The ziggurats or the divided states? For me all those ancient 'cradle of civilization' efforts keep me in constant awe."

"The cuneiform hieroglyphs are truly awe-inspiring, yes." Her look at him in the thin outside light was as if his brightness of mind might be stretching his skull.

"Oh, and the Code of Hammurabi?" Getting his affirmation, she was duly impressed. "Yes, that Code! Algernon, could you give me your first-hand 'impression' of it sometime, rather than its description?"

As my brief recollections caused her to frown, and she seemed to mumble to herself, I saw that I could be up against a lot more persistent probing from this conniving woman, particularly when she muttered 'the more I research'.

"Keep in mind that ancient evidences are few, Laburnum."

"Yet as a testament to the earliest structured societies, they do exist. We can tell this from their hierarchy, their frame-worked social levels, and Algernon…" as Paycock kept demanding, "…wouldn't you agree that in many ways the influence of today's powerful corporations run a parallel to those movers of that first ancient boom?" *Oh, why didn't she see that one wasn't up to much more?* "What I mean to ask is, what headway have we made as human beings, in—for instance—oh, *what say,* low income? Has any golden era managed to resolve that there's always a percentage of society trapped on that lowest rung? Could keeping a lowest rung be what keeps economies going? Do you recall what that ancient Code had to say about that?"

"Indeed, there were all kinds of protections – fixed rates on commercial services and rights regarding property, legal procedures for personal injury—you could look up others." *God, I'll enjoy being away from her.*

"You know I love all that ancient data and getting just a glimpse of how different an average woman's life would've been back then. I mean, look at the depiction of women at Persepolis."

"The Gate of Nations?" I asked, though becoming tired, I just aligned with whatever Laburnum was after. Then making more effort, though… *Oh Lord, why didn't she just shut up?* "Yes, one has stood before those enormous bull reliefs. One's sure you're well-versed in those Persian ideals."

"Some, but why do we keep overlooking that so many of their ideals *did* work?" I was going from one foot to the other as she kept on about King Darius, then Alexander's policies after invading. Oh merciful heavens, one may just drop. "Then out in part of that much smaller world, Algernon, fabulous Persepolis! You mentioned that you've stood on that vast square among its imposing minarets and columns? What must it have felt like? You must have had remarkable sensations! After all, it was their honored place for special rituals."

"Rather than for everyday living, yes," auto-politeness somehow kicked in.

"For outstanding occasions or momentous burials and—as you say—kept well away from everyday living. But you've actually *stood* there? When you'd looked around standing on those hallowed ruins, you must have tuned into those long-ago events?"

"One is sure that you would have come away from it charged with its ancient meanings, Laburnum. For oneself though, one was mainly impressed with the magnitude of its design. I'm not sure I can provide you with deeper insight."

"Though through your internationalism?"

"Right, that was there at Persepolis." *God, I might hit her.*

Paycock was still butting Laburnum's knees as we stood by her door. Before saying goodnight, one shook Laburnum's hand while muttering I'd take Babylon up with her another time.

A slightly uncomfortable leave-taking, but I felt I'd done all I could for Laburnum and her poet friend; and as I was so pulsatingly needing solitude and my lovely understanding house, I quickly returned and switched off my porch light. In a hyped fuzziness, I went around to one's favorite chair out front and put a foot up on the porch rail. Breathing out an extensive double sigh of relief, I rested elbow to knee. Shortened viewing to my night-eyes in this blackness though now he was, *oh God, thank you!* One was—*alone!* The complete darkness of this night rinsed me into absolute solace—which was all that mattered! Direly relaxing one's tense body, I slid down into myself to let the night's coolness with its spotty firmament enclose me in its annihilating comfort, as I saw that what I really needed was to let one's newer uncontemplated feelings completely rest.

Later I would contemplate why returning from Rafferty's, I'd baulked at any intimate talk with Laburnum. I certainly knew she was too pushy, no doubt of it, but heavens I'd known plenty of that kind. Could it all be cultural? Would I meet more of this here? Was I reluctantly facing that I could be into some new immigrating school for retired diplomats? All in all, was one doing as they say—'what he was put here on this earth to do?' That mega question?

Laburnum had intimated, or rather stated, that his language, particularly his personal pronouns, were not understood by rural Americans. *Could she have meant that he wasn't being understood by those people who worked for him, and that I was expressly getting fond of? Though, surely, that couldn't be right! Could that mean I should have to generate more flexibility?*

Keeping in mind that Laburnum was the kind of person who not only conversed with her dog, but who undoubtedly took her dog's advice seriously–which showed she had a healthy sense of humor! Though, during this profoundly intimate criticism of me and my employees, I had *not* got the idea that she was just being amusing! *What had most amazed me was that he had gone to the painful trouble of explaining his provincial fears to her! This had amazed him because of his beliefs in all he had been so vehemently against. Amazingly, in all truth, it hadn't turned out to have been all that agonizing – not grossly, anyway, not once talking had 'taken over'. How utterly extraterrestrial! Nor was I aching to reproach myself for so perversely airing one's private feelings anti-Foreign Service style, either! Insane! Incredible!*

I'd permitted our discussing my 'worldliness' because… because her inquiries typified her decently inquisitive mind. I had apparently defined to myself that she was an appropriate person to tell my more hidden feelings to because even though she'd been so vulgarly critical of him, living out here I might still value her as a companion—enough to ignore her insolence? *Possibly, eventually. As the fair-minded man one was, I might even find that her opinion, though it's hard to believe, could become helpful.*

What the leveling Laburnum may have done was to re-direct me to look more carefully at who one was as one adjusted to this 'lowlier' retirement happiness here; and for this, well, could there ever be a day when he might quite graciously want to thank her? Tonight, though, he didn't think so.

Yawning—nor was it likely to be tomorrow! Yawning again, oh dear!

When one explored one's appreciation of rural Americans, one rarely forgot that one's happiness had rocketed out of that very first day before that epiphany of his 'Supreme Habitat' had towered above him as he'd remained glued in his Lamborghini as if from a lightning bolt—digesting what his doodling had done back in that boring Moscow meeting. Over here while learning to grape-grow and make wine with his admirable new friends– he'd needed to accept that in life, there could be the most odd and rare events that could not be explained! His Supreme Habitat epiphany had unquestionably been the most resounding nerve, heart, arteries, and bone-shaker he had either known or could ever have wildly imagined!

Getting to know the witch-woman and all our friends in this enthralling lakeside environment, one had learned that I was truly seeing lowliness in their loving, yet immensely straight-forward interaction. Loosened to it I saw that I might very well find out how these fine low-profile people had built such enviably useful, playful, loving, and wonderfully peaceful lives without the least touch of pomp and circumstance—which I still could not quite believe! How on this phantasmagoric earth had they ever done it?

Chapter 9
The Gift

A valued bond between present and past winery owners was the examination of some particular wine's complexity; and even if one had to fetch Hans in one's Lamborghini, we both made sure we kept up this occasional treat. On one warm late afternoon, after a client-friend of Hans' returned from France and given him a bottle of the finest Sauterne, when the visitors had left the tasting porch, Hans headed for their end table to enjoy this much anticipated 'rare Sauterne'. Our sipping was as much for evaluation as companionship as Hans had taken himself off his pills knowing his tasting abilities to be more acute without his pain medication. Leaving his cane on the next chair, he eased down onto the upright chair, I kept for him that was best for his back, from the dining room. Hoisting his left leg up on the next chair's seat, he got his body settled comfortably. Smiling at one, he took a good deep breath, then stated formally, "Ready!"

Only too aware of Hans' excellent tasting abilities, I determined to work up my own more acute tasting buds for analyzing that bedrock distinction to this variety of the ancient beverage. Along with all Hans' achievements, that drew adulation from far and wide, was this serious respect for his tasting sensitivity. One always learned more about tasting from Hans, but one day—just once—I would love to outdo that wise old rascal!

As I poured the precious wine, both our eyes' glinted, like the whitest of sun-brightened diamond chips. In religious anticipation as connoisseur good friends, in feverish expectation, we both sat straight till formally raising our glasses greeting one another. Holding our glasses high, we studied the wine's swiveled pallor, appreciatively swilling the liquid higher up the walls of the elegant glassware to lingeringly inhale and re-inhale its bouquet. In protracted pauses, we each went into fathoms of labyrinthine assessing before inhaling again. Sipping, we kept the fine wine in our mouths as we two vintners deeply contemplated its qualities for some beatific closed-eyed, near comatose moments.

Hans finally stated, "Temperature—he is perfect." Hans was appraising the bottle he himself had prepared. After further rumination, "Honeyed all right, dried honey!" After another inhale, "He a little round…"

"Round, mmm –" Though I had to agree. "A slight molds aroma, and it's a bit short."

"Ha! The question—it can be round and short?"

"You see one quality obscuring the other?"

"It's what can happen."

Unsure I agreed, I raised my glass again. "Mmm, one has to say it could titillate illicit intentions!"

"*Ja, ja,* that so! Because he not fat," Hans answered. Ever alert to my next drilling-eyed sip, Hans asked with a maddening smile, "Are we back to personal taste dilemmas again?"

One's taste buds were too preoccupied to answer. Even as one penetrated the beautiful beverage, one could no longer get obsessed about it; though damn it, Hans had hit it with 'dried honey'! Seeing that his rival was again likely to be the first to arrive at a satisfying analysis, he just had it in him to, the rum Old Saxon rogue! One tasted again, determined to at least see exactly what Hans was seeing.

"It's the touch of…" Hans' wide-apart eyes roamed the porch ceiling as if seeking. Closing them, he dove again into its flavors, "What is it? That fruit, it in orchards?"

"Orchards? Apples?" Hans shook his head. "You're not meaning pears?"

"No, no!" Then he had it, "More superior. It *quince,* Algernon!"

"*The devil!*" I muttered.

Ripe *quince!* Spiced. With nutmeg!" Then announcing it as top priority news, "*Quince with nutmeg,* it is!"

Blast this Teutonic Tasting Terror! Hans had it exactly! "Nutmeg! Lord above, yes! Quince it is, damn you, Hans! Precisely right, yes most certainly *quince!* You've got it! With just the right aging. Barsac, you say?" Knocked again by Hans' immaculate tasting abilities, and his quickness identifying, I tried to get in on Hans's vibration.

"Perhaps it is the aging that is good," Hans added. "Though a fraction more wouldn't have hurt. Barsac, yes, of course! What else, a wine like this?"

One took another sip. "You're saying, that the noble rot."

"Had been caught in the nick of time! *Ja*, perfect! Had to be—I don't much care for tinny tasting Sauternes. Less noble rot, he go metallic."

"A tough challenge catching noble rot before it raisins out."

"Fungus—has to be interrupted." Hans paused and looking again at his glass' pale liquid. "Very fine! I really think now—it's hard to beat. His aging too, even—yes, I am changing mind, he's got it right. You can tell after the swallow!" Tapping his throat and widening his eyes, "You know I'd been save this bottle till you back from U.K.?"

"Very fine it is, Hans. I thank you most heartily."

"*Ja*, an exceptional gift! None better."

Reb was coming around the corner of the house from the vineyards; his head tilted for mopping his brow on his short shirtsleeve. With his head turned, looking up, he saw them. "So here's where you two are hiding out!"

Hans swung his arm to Reb. "You to know this rare Sauterne, Reb!" My cue to pour him a glass.

"*Hold* it, Algernon!" Reb said. "Hang on, Hans! Anything special?"

"For to educate you! It great informing, you'd better to know it! Come up and try!"

With a mixture of slow smiles, Reb gave in to Hans and came up the steps to straddle a chair between them. One poured him the Sauterne as Reb elaborately stretched his arms out wide, then shook them in a witty pseudo-preparation for this wine examination. Becoming serious with Hans, and I confidently awaiting his involvement with the pale liquid, we anxiously watched Reb thrilled as he discriminatingly swilled, sniffed, and at last tasted! Finally, swallowing slowly, Reb's eyes opened wide. "It has a supple nose. It's a Bordeaux."

"Which commune? Sip again, please. Make guess?"

"It's a Barsac!"

"A-ah, you knew Marcel, he came?" We all enjoyed this as Hans explained, "Before you were here, Algernon, when my old friend Marcel, he came to buy cases, always he leave me a bottle he brings from the Bordeaux estate."

"Still, I'm frightfully impressed, Reb," I remarked.

"But he exceptionally poised, you agree?"

"Knock-out!" Reb shook his head, too weary to delve. Then seeing Hans' disappointment, he tried, "O-okay! I'd say woody… oak. An' there's more I can't get. Spice maybe, nutmeg, but it's round."

"Round," one repeated, as Hans and I both kept approvingly raising our brows at Reb.

Reb sipped on, still scrutinizing. "From that region with that warm dry fall that gets mist at night."

"Exactly right!" one agreed, surprised. "Between two rivers that have different temperatures. Their unique geography makes the mists develop the fungus. Reb, one is certainly impressed!" Reb listened as Hans filled in his knowledge of growing this superb Sauterne while we continued eking out this wine that each had first known earlier traveling the Bordeaux region.

Reb turned to Hans saying abruptly, "Algernon knows about Sigmund?"

"I was getting to it." Hans' brusque long-faced retort implied that Reb could have been more tactful about bringing the Sigmund question up just now.

"Sigmund?" one asked. "The viticulturist?"

"He won't return this summer after all, Algernon; I most sorry to tell you! He had planned to continue here before you bought winery, as I told you. He much likes it here, but he has to work out management muddle in his father's Riesling estate. My guess is he will be back when he has settled family situation there in Germany. Listen, I most sorry, it not what I said. It much upset me it not what I'd said, and it must much disappoint you. You've tasted Sigmund's good work, he worth waiting for—he has given us excellent wines. Not every viticulturist get their wines recognized by what we call the 'reviewers and awarders'."

"Sigmund's instinct is a lot like yours, Hans?"

"*Ja*, Reb, but it not been my livelihood."

"It could've been," I insisted, as Reb lustily agreed. "Hans, you're worrying that?"

"No Sigmund, he will be back, I know he will be," Hans dominantly needed to believe this and to overcome this dire winery disappointment. "It not how I claimed it be for you, and that not fair of me, Algernon. I most sorry."

For Hans' sake, I did my best to temper this major bad news. One had too great an admiration and fondness for the wine-soul of this unique extraordinary refugee vintner. "There are surely enough varieties from these last years to last awhile, Hans? And if need be, as Reb says, you certainly have a great deal of Sigmund's talent."

The import of this news was sinking into me, but as so much else here was going smoothly, I kept to myself that I might get drastically upset. Feeling the weight of being a vineyard owner and the moods of my employees, I hid my disappointment and swiftly talked up our alternative. *Though as all this sunk in, I saw that the reputation of Runditz's fine wines could undergo a severe drop.*

"A-aw, Hans is as good a taster as Sigmund, you know it, Algernon?" Reb insisted.

"Look," I said, determining not to let this overwhelm, particularly after they'd been so happy with the most special Sauterne. Obviously, Sigmund had done much to increase the wines popularity. Though having had Hans' word with the estate purchase that his unusually good viticulturist would complete the winery—not that it could have altered my purchase of his 'Supreme Habitat' mansion and all its extrasensory commitment—ha, how could it? But as they all knew, an excellent wine-taster could be the key ingredient for a winery to soar – "Look," I started again, "on days you're well enough, Hans, come and do trials for us?"

"It means I not to take my dumb-dumb pills?" Hans was agreeing as he swung his arm down to his raised leg. "On 'good days' only? Then, *ja*, *ja*, I could."

"On those days, your excellent analysis would give us that push we need, and you'd have Reb."

"*Ja*, that is so! Reb, he develop excellent tongue." Hans wanted to make amends.

"Hey wait, I don't know your European vintners!" Reb reminded. "You guys know all there is to know about all those types of grape growing."

Whatever excuses Reb made, I was sure that Reb really wanted to do it, and persisted. "Working alongside Hans, Reb?" He got Reb envisioning what this would be like with his 'father' Hans, and he soon had Reb's conditional nod.

"You've Mel," Reb reminded.

"*Ja, ja,* Mel very good too."

"Hans, you'd been talking up a new ice wine," I fleshed out this replacement plan. "Why don't we slow down on that? You haven't been rushing any other new wine here?"

"No, and not to hurry. Never to rush a wine, no, it not good. Now Mel, Algernon, he no Sigmund, but with suggestings, Mel hits it."

"Let's not go for a new wine for a year or so, and we'll hope Sigmund will return. With your *damned annoyingly* excellent nose," I teased Hans, "we'll keep the winery going, then," indicating Reb, "chances are we'll do very well with our alternate taster talent. So, Hans, let's not get too worked up about Sigmund," I soothed.

"Ha, that what I hope you say, Algernon."

"None of us want to see a new Runditz wine launched before it has its optimum sophistication." *Hans' wines had always had an excellent wine-taster and were exceptionally attractive to a wide range of customers. Particularly Hans' circle of Europeans, who had spread the word about Hans' unusually good wines and who expected to travel here for their several cases.* With all this, I saw that the winery would do pretty well as Reb and Hans reached to meet his effort. "It's settled then? Now, will you sleep tonight, Hans?" As *I'd become increasingly concerned about this unexpected setback to our changed plans.*

Other lively considerations came up till coming from the fields Mel walked past. Hans and I called him up the steps as Hans tipped him the last of the special Sauterne. Mel waited beside them as I told him about Sigmund not returning and our provisional 'group viticulturists' plan led by Hans on his 'good days'.

Mel gave a long relieved shrill whistle because he'd been wondering how the winery could continue as he raised and lowered his shadowed head, his neck ever fluid as his worries kept expelling in a noisy enthusiastic hum, "Good, mm, yes fine, mmm! You want me to? O-ho! The idea's good, but we'll need to talk. Better though, yes! Good!" Casually accepting this last glass of wine from Hans, Mel pulled up a chair beside him and incidentally sipped. Suddenly, his large brown eyes rolled, making the other three gleefully hoot! "Oh Yi-ipes! Oh-oh… Oh, I know! Marcel was here, Hans?" And laughing, "Jeez, it's superb!"

"What do you see in it?"

“Aw, it’s fabulous!” Though as usual with more analysis expected of him, Mel held the glass high to study it more; then tasting it, he pondered it incredibly. “Oh! It’s round! Has an oak tint. Bet that’s what *you* said Reb. A touch of mango?” Mel managed, though like Reb on this end-of-day, he had to keep mopping his brow. “Well, of course it’s excellent! And about the other… the ‘group viticulturist’, I mean. You’re a taster as much as Sigmund is, Hans! You’ll do to keep us going!” breaking their concern. “You’d never let a wine go till it has everything it could have.” Getting the others’ eager agreements as he savored more of his wine, “Sigmund is to come back?”

“*Ja ja*, you know it.”

“We’ll know more then?” Reb’s stated question assured.

“*Ja*, naturally, *ja, ja*.”

Much as Reb and Mel had been reluctant to say it, they saw that these secondary plans would slow the winery’s steadily expected yields, which still were causing some concerned expressions. Cursorily inverting the Sauterne gift bottle, it was emptied of every drop as Reb studied its refusal to drip.

Well aware that adverse personnel situations like this were bound to happen, though, with all the carefully nurtured stages to Hans’ wine production, my hope had been that by next year when the Runditz label was due to change to ‘Cholmondley-Rute’, some exceptionally fine wine would be under one’s name—a wine worthy of presenting to his father? Instead though, Sigmund’s news made him see that to keep the winery prospering and his employees content, he might have to work on a much more winning ‘plan B’. In with this disappointment, it did occur to me that foxy old Hans may have had some idea that Sigmund was capable of letting us down—he’d been his protégé after all, as I too had fixed to Reb’s drained bottle; and willfully ignoring any more of this concern, I stood to emphatically state. “Well, it has to be done!” *With the tantalizing gift bottle quite emptied, it wouldn’t do them any good to become more dispirited. Enough tentative planning for now!*

“Make it some terrific European dish, Alg’non, okay? Hot dogs n’ fries would do it!” Reb cockily suggested, which reminded the others that the plan tonight was that one was to try my hand at cooking. I’d been longing to cook some tasty dishes in the kitchen. I’d watched the women and was encouraged by the men’s thoughts turning to food. “Don’t worry, Reb, I doubt I’ll steal your thunder.”

As they didn’t know Algernon’s cooking, Mel agreed that he was safe, “But after that Sauterne, you’d had better come up with something knock-out.”

“Oh, you’ll all be asking for seconds,” I said, taking off for the kitchen, and leaving Hans Reb and Mel without much to say.

For looking the part of tonight’s chef, I pulled on Sylvia’s big floral plastic apron. I’d been inspired by Laburnum and Sylvia’s enticing special meals and had envisioned a deliciously whipped up far simpler little supper, having selected groceries from Able's. Using what I'd seen and read about cooking, into a saucepan of boiling water I dropped in the commercially cleaned baby carrots; while in the largest cast iron skillet, I melted plenty of butter to sauté the pork chops. I'd read that marjoram-and-thyme-benefitted pork, so shook these in with a generous cup of Chardonnay. This all sizzled and smelled good, though I was sorry to see the browning chops blanching because of the wine—though patience… just wait! The meal was to go with Sylvia's tall bottle of her homemade applesauce, which I opened and stuck a spoon into it to put it out on the table with a bread basket full of knives, forks, and napkins.

"You'll need sharper knives," Reb suggested, as he brought through four, while one arranged their four plates on the kitchen counter and turned the chops.

"Good thinking," I said, feeling quite professional, as one tossed the spatula in the air and caught it! Placing fresh bakery rolls on each of the plates, I heard Reb outside telling the others. "He must know what he's doing—he's just caught the spatula he'd flipped up near the ceiling!"

As the wine evaporated, and the chops started to nicely brown again, I served a large dollop of carrots on each plate, then dished one large chop beside each. Believing myself very much the chef, I saw my first dinner doing much to balance our erratic evening; and with Hans nicely settled out there, I took the appetizing plates to put one before each of them at their outside table in the fading daylight. Reb already had lit the citronella candles against little creatures.

Enthusing about my good-smelling meal, Hans cut into his chop and chewed a couple of mouthfuls well. Then he rated my cooking, "He get a 'seven', Algernon! Seven out of ten!" Hans' assessment received quasi-serious teases because Reb and Mel simultaneously stood to return their chops to the frying pan, making cracks about 'e coli' keeping them out of the vineyards.

"Sylvia makes a great applesauce, Alg'non, but I can't say your cooking is up to Hans' special Sauterne."

Reb was gruffly told to be quiet and get out there and make the coffee!

Bringing out mugs for the coffee, I had another 'personnel' question I needed to know about. "Hans, didn't you tell me that you knew of a woman that would house clean?"

Hans put his knife and fork down. "Sally-Anne, yes. She been here already?"

"No," Mel answered, "she didn't know when Algernon would be back from the U.K. She's at her sister's in Pennsylvania. Want me to give her a call?"

"I'd heard from Hans of Sally-Anne's competence for 'filling in'. "She also doesn't mind if dishes and saucepans from the night before get left in sink. She was to deal with a meal like this one *and* keep the house clean and tidied."

"Hans, you mean on an evening like this, Sally-Anne would wash up my sink full of dishes?" I asked.

"She like them rinsed good, but yes, she do everything! She good energy as well as good sense. She good at washing curtains, bed covers, rugs—*every*thing!"

"See how soon you can get her, Mel. Does she live in town? You *will call her?*"

Mel nodded, "Newt travels, and she likes to keep busy. Sure, I'll call her as soon as I'm back at my place."

"Newt's her husband?"

"He is, Algernon, and get going, Mel, I'm on K.P. tonight." Reb glanced at Hans, "And Hans is to come home with me." Hans nodded recalling Reb's arrangement.

This unusual evening of exceptional tasting had mixed with the disappointment of Sigmund not returning, but they had agreeably talked up the best alternative tasting plan they could come up with that made us all feel better—tentatively. Though I'd want to think more on that. Also, I was to get a much-admired housekeeper, who they all knew and recalled how well she would straighten out the bouts of unenthused 'habitat' housekeeping. All these were good, and I didn't mind that my pork chops were a little underdone and had to be re-cooked, but everyone complimented their flavor—I would know more for the next time.

With our men's evening drawing down, they sat over Reb's dependably good coffee under the darkening sky's fair-sized moon that kept brightening to a stark white above the far horizon. A gibbous moon to gloat over them, leaving behind an abstracted indigo twilight cloud between pale patches of cloudless sky. It reminded me of a particular Lake Seneca painting of Arthur Dove's I'd admired at the local museum—Dove was the famed local painter here who had once lived in this area. Watching the clouds slowly change, the men stretched and yawned as their energies too were drawing down. After their full day's work, they agreed that more than Algernon's cooking, their pleasant drowsiness was still being encouraged by Hans' good friend's special gift of finest Barsac Sauterne.

Chapter 10
Alarm

During the night, I awoke with a start, wondering if I was hearing voices outside. Alert enough to know that Bruno had barked, I made out two voices. With moonlight coming through the windows, it had to be well before dawn. Concerned, I scurried out of bed, pulling on jeans, going to the window. Below in the shadows, two men. One was Reb—*Re-eb?* Reb, hurrying to someone—*something's wrong?* Into my loafers, I dropped down the stairs two at a time, falling against the banisters as one yanked yesterday's T-shirt over my head, worrying what could cause them to be up. Outside in the barn's shadow, one made out the fluid gesturing, unmistakably Mel's. "Is anything wrong?" I called descending the porch steps.

The men checked one another before Reb asked, "D'y hear that?"

Getting to them, "What?" I asked, but only met their shadowed silent frowns. "What's one listening for?"

"Paycock." All listened as I heard a distant dog's howl that might have been any farm dog.

"Laburnum goes on meets in the woods," Reb informed. "Barking isa from up past Henderson's someplace."

"Laburnum? In this dead of night?" I queried, awed, wondering about Reb being here. "Mel, you'd phoned Reb?"

"Reb knows more about this."

"Something has happened to Laburnum?" I interrupted thrown by the weirdness of the situation. *Reb and Mel were recent American friends that I hadn't known here long enough to trust what a night-time concern over here could mean. I felt the strong eerie input of being in an obscure night situation in a country I didn't know enough about, that at this moment seemed minatory. Peculiar sensations ran me, though, heavens, this was a civilized country—one shouldn't expect anything gross.*

"It isn't good Paycock howls," he said rubbing his eyes. "I'd guess that bark is up beyond Henderson's, but she goes other places."

Impatiently, Mel cocked his head at Reb, "Hadn't we better?"

"Yep, let's go! Come on, Alg'non; it's better with more than one guy," Reb said this hurrying to his Lincoln, "The kid's dirt track is first."

"Reb, hadn't you taken Hans back to town?" I was trying to understand, while keeping with them.

"Yeah, I'd got Hans back and was sleeping more than a newborn babe at Sylvia's when Mel called."

Quickly like them, I got in the passenger seat next to Reb. Seeing Mel packing his knife in his belt sheath in the back seat, this sinister air continued as the car got going. *Though, whatever she'd done, this was his neighbor-friend Laburnum that something had happened to!*

Recalling how at ease Laburnum had been that night time walking from Rafferty's, I needed to know more about Laburnum's night-times – "'Meets', Reb?" I asked, "Sylvia had said."

"Laburnum has other powers."

"Some think that," Mel stated querulously.

"Mel, she certainly called it the day I was to arrive back from England, and you all made that frightfully good meal," One reminded beginning to perceive more with them.

"Knew it when Hans took his fall too," Reb agreed. "Right to the minute I got him."

"She was right?"

Reb nodded. "She was right. It was me wasn't quick enough. His leg hasn't gone right since."

"Hans had pains in that left leg several harvests," Mel reminded Reb. "Aw these 'other power' miracles maybe nothing more than noticing what's been happening and making a clever guess. I knew more about all that than I'd wanted once."

"Could be, Mel," Reb accommodated, having taken a right turn onto the highway. One noted Mel and Reb's different attitudes towards Laburnum's clairvoyance as Reb went on, "Problem is she's a helluva walker; and if she has some medium friend needing her, she'd get others."

"*Others?*" I asked. "How many?"

"Just another odd one or two, maybe three. Folks like her, 'Paranormals' she calls them."

"Witches!" Mel opined. "And tonight isn't the only night. Should've suspected it with the moon still big."

"Just one other time, as I remember it, Mel," Reb elucidated turning left to go up on a road that took them passed the Henderson farm and on into the hills. Algernon was agreeing that Laburnum must be a 'helluva walker'.

Coolness whisked through the car as Mel rolled down his window to listen. "Not hearing Paycock," he said.

Feeling very much the unhelpful outsider, I asked, "Is Rafferty a medium?"

Loud guffaws from both guys. "Rafferty might be smitten with plenty of imagination, but he ain' got no sixth sense!" Reb said turning onto a grassed track that had to have been well used with his car still riding smoothly. They passed a moonlit knoll. "Doubt Rafferty knows anything about Laburnum taking night walks."

"How about Hans?"

Reb was thoughtful as he brought the car to a stop. "Laburnum was sick back when she first came here till Hans and Eva got her going." The men got out, and their slammed car doors echoed into the scarcely moving summer's moonlit flooded air.

"Hans' over-compassionate, you know it, Reb! Any other landlord would've sent her packing." Mel hadn't liked being wakened.

"Laburnum, though?" my disbelievingly pursued.

"They helped her out. You weren't here then, Mel, but Laburnum was a wreck. Listen, you still hearing Paycock?"

"What made her a wreck?" I persisted following Reb's path into a dense wood that blocked the spread of moonlight and made seeing and walking difficult.

"Had a bad time in—Colorado, think it was."

"It was," Mel said.

Walking, I realized that I too was becoming as concerned as they were about Laburnum. Laburnum, the insolent witch woman?! Why had she taken such ridiculous chances in this dead of night? With her occult proclivities, couldn't she have foreseen danger or drummed up some good sense? He'd begun to have some intermittent respect for this prescient night-roving female twerp, which I amended to *a scholarly American female twerp*. After all, dealing with Rafferty's overwhelmed faint, she'd shown sensible management, so why this dead of night scariness? And if he was as concerned about her as Reb and Mel were, I realized, *it had not been his intention to take this peculiar woman over-seriously.*

"Listen!" Reb ordered. Getting used to the opaque darkness, the three stood still struggling to hear. Out of the silence, only the distant hoot of an owl, till Paycock gave a single pathetic wolf's note not too far away.

"God!" Algernon muttered, "You say she's done this before? Any idea what it means?"

"We'll find out." As if knowing where to go, Reb pushed through to a broader path between underbrush and broken branches. "Don't get upset, Algernon, it isn't animal sacrifices, just something a few people do over here that doesn't always go right. Don't suppose you've much like it over where you come from?"

"Worse! Some practitioners try to sacrifice animals, though the police and animal rights groups raise all hell." Mel and I had silently halted as Reb stopped stock still; his hand spread wide by his ear as closer now they could hear Paycock's tired whine.

Reb called through funneled hands, "PA-AYCO-OCK? LABU-URNUM?"

Unclear responses came from Laburnum and Paycock somewhere well ahead of them! Laburnum just distinguishably saying, "Can't move, Reb! I'll, I'll hum."

I heavily breathed out, thankfully hearing Laburnum. I was even more relieved believing she might be using some of their 'wraggle-taggle gypsies' tune. *Wasn't it?* Though, too erratic, too throaty to tell!

Watching my step as our feet crackled twigs and bodies snapped branches through what was only a rough path, or had been, as I kept myself with this kind of happening and moved along with the two men. Having agreed to come—as the Runditz Estate owner, I owed helping Reb and Mel—so like them, I kept pushing through branches inordinately hoping Laburnum was not profoundly hurt. Actually, I was hoping this to such a point that one had to reproach my jarring head noises. Neither Laburnum's humming nor any other music jingling one's brain now could come through with this much tintinnabulation going on, as with all my might as her friend, I hoped she would not be set back by sickness or some unimaginable injury. Bodily injury could mean 'x' amount of recovery that, sadly, would push into her unique quest studies. As her 'landlord', only just getting to know Laburnum, like the other two fellows I'd felt driven to attend whatever this incident was that was happening to her.

Mel and I followed Reb until we were met by a brushing sound, and oh—great conniptions! Paycock bounded out to us! All but dislocating his over-excited tail-wagged body! The dog rushed to Reb to lick his hand, then to myself and Mel! More avidly listening for Laburnum, we headed for the gap Paycock had come through; and in the scarcity of dappled moonlight, soon made out a very sad-looking Laburnum awkwardly prone. Nearer her they could see she was struggling to raise herself from a mash of old leaves and bark. Seeing her better, her shoulder was propped against a tree trunk as she desperately stretched both hands out protectively—to what? *Cover an agonizingly painful leg?* Leaning from the tree, she called in her throaty groan, "Don't *TOU-OUCH!"* Her begging becoming a shriek! *"PLEASE do-on't!"*

"I'm *not.*"

We three fellows leaned or crouched around her, each man making suggestions of what was to be done while dealing with Paycock's anxious rubbing. It was obvious Laburnum needed hands-off care. Reb bent closest, frightening Laburnum, *"DON'T touch! PLE-ASE,* Reb! It's my shin, I know it is." Hearing Laburnum's wonderful velvety voice turned throatily harsh, as Reb kept assuring her he'd be extremely careful, promising only feather-light touches. Watching this, one's visceral pain bolted through one to stop, like a rock blocked by a cement barrier that had rolled down a cliff. Standing back, I watched Reb lift Laburnum's leg as softly as if it was a priceless bird's egg for examining her damage. One's held breath eased as I looked at Laburnum, Reb with her. *I'd seen all this kind of thing before, hadn't I? No, no... all that had been far worse – I meant, I'd seen it in grossest numbers of people.* Finally, with an unbearable grimace, Laburnum's head went down for forcing herself to give in to Reb's gently probing hands as she tried to trust him. Mel stood by as Reb derisively muttered at her untouchable swollen shin and ankle. Mel was assuring me that Reb had had some medical training.

"Oh *GO-od!*" Laburnum agonized pulling from Reb, "O-Ow! Damn, oh cr*a-AP!* Sorry, Reb, but *da-amn* the thing!" Paining as she took in that, Mel and I were there, "Oh good grief! Sorry, you guys! I'd have done anything. *Sorry!* Guess I'll owe—guess it'll be special dinners for all."

"QUIET!" Reb commanded her, not so jokingly. "We're going to get you back. How much weight can you put on it?"

"It's just *he-ell!* Oh, all right. Maybe if? Look, I'll try. See, I know it's."

"It's broken," my lengthy exhalation assimilated her condition.

"Right, Algernon," she breathlessly puffed out and overcome, sank back.

"We'll find out more when you're home," Mel suggested. "If you two will get her to the car, I'd better walk Paycock back?"

"Too far!" Reb commanded. Then to their amazement, Reb couldn't stop a strangely garbled laugh. "No. It's all right, Mel, don't worry. I just had an idea. Alg'non could fetch Paycock in his Lamborghini!" The impertinence of this suggestion broke through some of the misery of Laburnum's predicament, though it didn't begin to obscure her awful pain. "Okay. Now we'll get you to the car. You're to keep that leg out straight—well, all you can." To the others, "Laburnum will be in the front and Paycock."

"On my lap in the back," I suggested.

"There's a blanket in the trunk, right Reb?" Mel asked, and going closer to her, "Crazy of you, Laburnum! Tripped on a dead branch or something?"

"I don't know, Mel. More like metal—a chunk of metal."

"Weren't the others with you?"

"They'd off on their motor-cycles... couldn't hear."

I saw that they weren't settling how Laburnum—a badly injured, quite-tall woman—was to yet be taken back through this thick dark underbrush. "Any of us bring a flashlight?" I asked. "How far have you been dragging that leg, Laburnum?"

"Not—oh—since back at the clearing."

"That's how far?"

"Aw, a half mile."

"Half a mi-*ile?!*"

Laburnum suffered as Reb and I helped her get up on her good leg. Putting an arm around each of our shoulders, she tried to walk; but as soon as her weight went onto her bad leg, her groans turned to a shriek. We held her upright as she got her weight back onto her uninjured leg. My suggestion was to cross-arm-chair her, as Mel was already going ahead with his knife cutting away vines and thorny branches; but not being delicately boned, Laburnum quickly couldn't take it – "*Please!*" she gasped, "No more, *guys, ple-ase!* Let me just *lean* on one of you?"

"Next time you do this, lose some of that damned weight!" Reb kept at her unresponsive spirit as she fell heavily against him.

Easing her along slowly, painfully getting her out of the woods as Mel's, "Nice boy! Good old doggie-wog," helped simmer Paycock down.

Finally getting Laburnum out in the bright moonlight, they saw how pain had left tear streaks down her shined cheeks.

"Well done, Reb! Though it's the hospital for this lady!" One announced what they all knew.

Getting her to the car, Reb gave quick little orders; and having pushed back the front passenger seat, I firmly held Laburnum's lower body for carefully ladling her in, as Reb kept her injured leg lifted, like finest crystal. Having got her into the car, Reb told her, "You're a helluva nuisance, you know it?" Which received her weepy, exhausted, but whole-hearted affirmation with grateful nods. Going around the car, Reb asked, "Drop you and Paycock off, Mel? 'Hans's avenue'," as it got called. "You too, Alg'non?"

Mel wanted to be dropped off with Paycock. Responsibility made one decide, "Thanks, no Reb, I'll come with you."

Laburnum feebly objected to them giving up their sleep as Reb drove, but all she got back was Reb's fake-disbelieving. "Oh yes, yes, ri-ight! Right, she'll never go night-roving again; you hear that, don't you guys?" He said this while envisioning his side of Sylvia's bed remaining empty for another couple of hours. "Though a couple of your shrimp and macaroni salads might coax us to be more forgiving!" Reb had Laburnum almost smirking beneath her ringed hand that they could see by the front window's moonlight remained clinging to her face.

In the back, Paycock was only too happy to get a car ride sphinx-style on Reb's car blanket—front paws on Mel and the bulk of his weight across one's thighs. Nearer home, Reb pulled his sullen passengers over off the highway to drop off Mel and Paycock. Leaving them, Mel wished Laburnum well, and she raised some accepting fingers to him off her forehead.

Concerning only for Laburnum's sniffed-back pain, Reb was simply to get Laburnum and myself to the hospital and drove cautiously, though quickly. Through the car windows, they all saw the lake's thin sun-edged dawn clouds orientating them to this night hour spreading spottily across the eastern dark. Seeing the changes to these pallid dawn patches, Reb gave up trying to cheer Laburnum, and he and I sank back into our own thoughts more comfortably now in Reb's smoothly riding back seat without Paycock's weight on him.

Stratocumulus scarf clouds of lithe temporal beauty lengthened some of the pallid dawn patches, though I was too enticed inside the car to my rear view of Laburnum's stiffly angled hand that clutched the curve of her cheek. Fixed to her tautly held rings within her fingers clutch, as she only gave an odd heave or two now, although I noticed that my own occasional visceral thud still menaced. I concerned with Laburnum's oncoming misery knowing what her pain could become, though what more could've been done? Much as I had instinctively ached to get both feet in on this whole situation and direct her, I knew that Reb's handling of Laburnum—having done all he could—had been commendable. As her longtime friend, Reb had naturally risen to taking her over; and by all that I knew of these good people, Laburnum's management had needed to be Reb's.

Bodily easing down into the car's soft seat, I mused.

Laburnum?

A woman whose foibles could irritate at times, certainly did, though I mainly liked my 'neighbor'. Her civilization studies she worked at and her excitement for them fascinated all right, *which was another reason it hurt I couldn't harness my once well-used directorial abilities to do more for her. So here I was again—up against that distressful sickly ambiance! That ages old, forcefully disciplining 'compassion' of mine! How often had I been aware of my lifelong demon urge, that finally, under Foreign Service auspices, had been strategically honed for organizing traumatic needs out in field carnage zones.*

Viscerally, I was still rebelling—*was this because when we found Laburnum horribly incapacitated, I'd been professionally aching to do more for her? I'd winced at this fiercely interfering emotion of mine*; *my astounding 'over-compassion' that always stimulated my strenuous desire to help, to direct, to plunge deeper into the situation for incisively making a difference, whatever sarcasm one's colleagues had once berated me with. Why did he? Because I'd cooperated with dedicated allied forces, that rallied newly arrived aid for most effective reinforcement?* Habitually, I'd made sure I'd been in on ordering them in to the rescue of that enclave of casualties during those grim insanities—of those mind-numbing numbers of indiscriminately aged victims barely surviving those satanic warlord's slaughter.

Massively victimized tribal fleeing demanding that their God ends that barbaric critical struggle. Desperate jarred field phone calls for boosting inadequate medical aid, prolonged waiting for confirmations as relaying armies were reduced—spread thinner. Re-strategizing these new attachments while juggling any other re-grouping that made a step towards strengthening their sub-maintained teams for that stubbornly veiled end to all that over-extended Central States' savagery in those atrocious, bloodiest wars.

Journalist recorded, as much of it all had been.

Oh for Lord's sake, Algernon, you bastard! Why allow all that back again? It hasn't any bearing on what's happened here in this American wood today! *Although.*

Those far-off battles *had been lived! On*e had survived them, seen them through.

How had I? Had I seen that if I'd been stable enough to compartment who those poor wretched victims were—mother, lover, infant, child—from whatever governance or God they'd belonged to, that had once loved and greatly appreciated their 'lowliness'?

Though that wouldn't have worked back then, though Algernon, would it?

Not in the way that would've been meaningful to them, although, I had not understood this—not while immersed in that steady bloodiness. No titillated by the expectation of being about to get relief as his body's defenses prepared for what else to expect next—*Why?*

Because droves of terrorized victims had by their sheer numbers re-acted to the collective compassion he was a part of—beyond all words like these.

Now though, this moment, here, in Reb's car—this peaceful Lincoln Town car—I saw that much of all that had been on a shattering other human level. A level I wouldn't have known if one's 'compassion's' chromosome hadn't been frantically honed, transformed for it. It always came down to that ages-old strengthened 'compassion' that begged to bring order to survivors in even the ugliest outrage?

Laburnum was neither his kin nor remotely a *committed* friend, though her eccentric civilization studies had shown him the possibility of *what?* A more personal bond with her? Was I seeing all this coming out now because one could be *discovering that I really quite liked that lowlier female human being in front of one with her ringed fingers still clutching her face? Could it be causing her value to him to become more intrinsic?*

Listen, aren't we rushing it a bit here, Algernon?

Coming from her agonizing woodlands terror, she had shown him her terrified 'lowliness'. Wasn't that it? 'Lowliness' that he too, was greatly needing, was learning. *Living meant he had a prioritized physical body that 'lowly' or not—as in each of us, we struggled to know better. Laburnum had been left in that woods on her own and had been sinking badly, with injuries threatening worse suffering. In her most human state, I'd sensed my common ties to her. Though, oh my God! Here's the outcome—Laburnum would survive her injuries!*

Away from the subhuman experience of bloodiness and battle, this night he was seeing Laburnum yet again- *Algernon, do keep uppermost that she was on a far lowlier scale, and that this whole situation was on quite another 'compassion' level. Through the car window… a-a-h, the changeably soft dawn clouds that at last eased his raucous thinking.* Clouds that actually comforted, because ritually they could return on other dawns. Solace! Seeing and knowing more of this American newness of what could happen out in a night-time wood here, he'd had to ask himself, *how many human beings had I, Algernon Cholmondley-Rute, actually felt responsibility for or truly cared about?* Though as he wrangled with his lowlier compassion's inexperience, his demon-urge's 'compassion' though lessening still flowed in him—which was why he kept repeating to himself that although this Laburnum incident was a single lowly heartrending situation, it was 'mendable'.

On this dawn, over here in the Finger Lakes, New York State, U.S.A., with Reb hurriedly driving Laburnum to get her medical help, and the pallor to those wispy, slowly moving dawn clouds daylight-strengthening, he had again scanned to get at the cause of what his rivals had called his 'contemptible emotion'.

Naturally, once his compassion had been controlled, it had been a highly valuable attribute that had re-directed him and his work. Yet this still didn't explain what had made him one of a small brotherhood to be endowed with this invaluable quality. Didn't it for heaven's sake? Algernon, old dolt?

Although – *all right!*

Truly he knew where that 'contemptible compassion' had come from, didn't he? If he honestly thought hard, he could fathom the motivating seeds to this frustratingly needy asset. Come on then, out with it, you battered old Ironsides. Though—oh.

Ahead were the bright lights of the Emergency's carport, thank the Lord! And at last Reb had slowed down.

We were here! Laburnum was to at last get help!

The kind of help the poor soul direly needed. She would be all right! And one's depressingly rummaged past would cease. Hooray! All praises be to the king of kings!

The Lincoln halted and one's gaze was still lingering on his rear view of Laburnum's rings on stick-like angled fingers that still held back her pain—pain that could be about to be felt more acutely when she's moved. White hot his empathy pulsated annoyingly as the Emergency's bright lights defined Reb's navy sweatshirt as he'd jumped out to hurry for paramedic assistance. One also got out of the car and breathed in the dawn's freshness while willfully throwing off one's bloodied phantasmagoria. Helped by this bracing outside air, I opened Laburnum's door to let her too sniff this dawn's freshness—though as her head was down, one couldn't tell her response.

Returning, Reb was hurriedly forewarning two medics with him of Laburnum's agonizing leg. Standing back I listened as Reb added to Laburnum's croaky beg for understanding that her pain was making her pass out. Assuring her of their extreme care, the medics used her directions. Pedantically soft spoken, the white uniformed fellows slowly and methodically extracted her from the car as her sad features furrowed on every least move; yet while in and out of consciousness, these paramedics knew exactly how to get her out and up onto a stretcher.

Once wheeled inside, two emergency room nurses took over Laburnum to routinely check her vitals, and administer pain killers for quietening her to take her down to X-ray, which they did. They answered her as these actions were accomplished. Back into an allotted bed in an ER cubicle, propped by pillows, nurses curtained her off to attend her leg. Between groans from behind the curtain, Laburnum fitfully struggled to answer another nurse that filled out her admission forms. This nurse had burnished red-gold hair piled high and sat close to her behind the curtain. When the curtains were pulled back again, Reb and I were relieved to see Laburnum looking given in, lying back at last, though she was a ghastly white and dazed as her medication grudgingly took effect. Sliding into what looked like sleep, Laburnum was at last lulling down heading for being knocked out. Though on moments coming to, in that muffled, former sultry tapestried voice, she attempted to express her flooding gratitude she'd been 'rescued' and was finally in competent medical hands.

Meanwhile, as I wanted to stay with Laburnum, Reb offered me his Lincoln for returning to Runditz's and went off to phone Sylvia to come and get him. Sylvia got to them while Laburnum dozed; and as soon as this best of good friends came in, dazzling in her summer mauves and pretty rose lipstick, their tensions relieved. Sylvia leaned to cup Laburnum's face in her hands, all reproachful head shakes and smiles, and extremely careful not to worsen Laburnum's pain as she smothered Laburnum's mumbled apologies with the sweetest pretend kisses and deepest regrets. Though, "*Stop* that, Laburnum; you know very well that as soon as you're out of here, you'll be planning to keep everyone up with more of your night-time whoop-ti-does!"

"Never! No, never again!" Laburnum's words though muffled came out more clearly. "I've learned my lesson, Sylvie dear."

"Oh-ho-o! Till some nice quiet dead of night when I've a super-special supper waiting, and you'll be out in another forest full of the wildest critters while Paycock howls for Reb—you know you will!" And laughing, Sylvia looked Laburnum's covers up and down, "Ha, a broken leg, is it? You only do these nutty tricks to get attention, Laburnum hon, you know you do!" Sylvia's laughter was so infectious, Laburnum tried to chuckle.

Reb and I watched this fond rapport as the nurse returned with the abundant burnished red hair. Laburnum's hand fumbled for her glasses from her side-table, which the nurse took from her to put on her. Her glasses' characteristic slant landed lower still over one eye, and looking at her patient, the nurse took them off her face and put them on again straighter, as she suggested she get her spectacles fixed—causing much laughter. But as Laburnum lay there frowning, as soon as the nurse had left, she replaced them herself; and with her glasses arm more crooked, she looked more her old self.

"They're better wonked!" Reb said. "When you're using your crutches, they'll match your limping."

"Well!" one exclaimed leaning the wall, "One must say, there's a good deal more to learn about what Laburnum gets up to on moonlit nights! Someday she'll owe us a whopping explanation!"

"You'll never squeeze a word out of her!" Sylvia remarked. "She loves keeping us all guessing; doesn't she, Reb?"

"But she can't when three good chaps tramp the woods after her for half the night!" I let go, "For old Beelzebub's sake, I'll be driven to discovering what other practices she keeps to herself!"

"Oh-ho-o!" Sylvia exclaimed smiling, "You heard that, Laburnum? Algernon just said, *'I'll* be driven'!" She stressed this personal pronoun again, repeating it as she exchanged an incredulous smirk with Laburnum's managed smile! "Great, Algernon, I hope you try it! Find out all you can and clue in the rest of us!" Then fondly looking up and down Laburnum's white-sheeted length again, Sylvia curiously looked under the sheet. Laburnum's huge black and purple leg had been packed in ice and raised on pillows. "That's cooling the pain some, hon? By the way, you do know how much I care about you in re-*ali*-ty, don't you, you annoying witch?"

"The leg is doing better, Sylvia; and yes, I know you don't care a damn what agony I suffer!"

"You heard that! She's better already!" Reb said. "And why won't she be? Look how it'll be! She'll be sitting in the shade all comfy, like a potentate, reading her big books while we're sweating in the burning sun doing her vine rows."

"Uh-uh, give me a week, and I'll be out there with solar tea for you all."

"O-oh, cool! Algernon lo-oves solar tea!" Sylvie's cynicism stimulated amused additions.

This aroused one's defense, "Now let's get this straight! The only brew one absolutely detests over here is that king-size water bottle of yours, Laburnum, with a rotting bunch of teabags stagnating in it for all hours in the hot sun!" Which brought on another slew of retorts. "Now if it was your American coffee, your sodas or your delectable milk-shakes? Though one has yet to find anyone here that can brew a really decent pot of tea, or that even sells worthwhile tea leaves! If one didn't have a kind sister-in-law sending one sealed boxes of Darjeeling's best that hadn't been basking on a shelf since Teddy Roosevelt was president, one would've lost one's sanity! There's more flavor running out of a rusted eaves trough than in a U.S. cup of tea!"

"Huh, that woke yew up, Alg'non!"

"So that's why you're always hugging that thermos flask?" Sylvia asked.

"Like fine wines, Sylvia, really good tea isn't for everybody! It takes muscular strength and a stable libido to savor a decently strong cup!" Reb and Sylvia doubtfully tossed this around; then as sleep was dragging Laburnum from their foolery, Reb gave Algernon the key to his Lincoln, and he and Sylvia lavished more pretend hugs and special well wishes on their patient. Sylvia blew her kisses, and Reb announced, "Oh come on then, you've earned it," as he went to plonk a good friendly one on Laburnum's cheek before he and Sylvia took off.

Soon after Reb and Sylvia had gone, the cubicle resonated emptiness, tranquility, and the unfamiliar early-morning functionings of a hospital. Laburnum was still a drained white, but as there was lessened noise from other admissions, in her great need of sleep, she dozily fell into what looked like at least times of sounder sleep. Looking around the nebulous curtained-off cubicle, I was soon into the tedium of the air of medical sterility, efficiency, and Laburnum's annoying divider curtain with its pale pink oblongs overlapping that bugged my eyes as they kept being kinetic. Avoiding this sight irritation, I would make use of Laburnum's sleeping quiet to catch myself up.

What a bizarre night!

So how had it come about?

Having suddenly awakened when last night's moon was very bright, I had agreed to be sucked into Reb and Mel's compulsion to search for Laburnum—no calling in the professionals, the police for example. Then finally discovering Laburnum in that pitiful condition, having suffered fearful pain for far too long, who wouldn't have felt for this woman that really the fellows' most deeply respected?

It was pleasant-knowing I could drive Reb's Lincoln back to Runditz's any time; but even though vineyard work had to be done now there was daylight, stuck being relaxed here beside Laburnum in this chair, some unarguable instinct kept me here.

Could I bring back that personal overview I'd got going while Reb had driven us here? As I still hadn't fathomed the causes of one's notorious 'compassion'. Even when allowing in those gruesome Rwanda battles, believing I had been onto something.

Oh yes... one had been asking why, in all Valhalla, it had been me- Algernon Cholmondley-Rute who'd had all that consequential 'compassion' dumped on him? Refusing to believe that my 'compassion' had been out of my blue-blooded chromosomes, I recalled seeking where this fireball emotion of mine had come from. *All right, how else could I, Algernon Cholmondley-Rute, have got that most imperatively useful emotion before those directing me to be so well professionally honed? Why me? Why had this chance been missed by my old chums?* Oh piss! Just getting it going again and some heavy footsteps—*coming in here?*

White-coated and too self-involved to look up, his hand flipping his clipboard's papers, was it the 'on-call' doctor who stopped suddenly and stayed standing still glued to his papers—for Laburnum's case? Her name? One helped him. "Shock, leg broken. Just arrived," his voice unfortunately awakening Laburnum.

"Laburnum Braithwaite?" the man asked. Laburnum scarcely managed to nod.

Was this man who was still tearing himself from a previous patient, stethoscope dangling, medical?

"So, what's up here?" this doctor was all business.

Directed to her, Laburnum struggled to speak, "I'd badly needed help."

"Help? Yes, well, what did you need help with?" Impatient, sharp.

Laburnum was momentarily tongue-tied. "You *are* the doctor?" I queried him.

"Doctor Ekid," he announced taking a long stride to quickly put his hand out to me rather than Laburnum. "Now, 'Laburnum', is it? Explain why you're here."

"I..." she excusing her yawn, "tripped in the woods."

"The woods? When was this?" The look of semi-conductors colliding expressed on the face of this hurried medical man.

"An hour or so ago."

Checking his watch, "You wouldn't have been out in a wood at 2:00 a.m."

"Walking my dog."

"This is a night habit? Someone was with you?"

Laburnum, trying so hard to get words out, looked to be about to weep.

"She *had been* with other people, Doctor. Having had a bad fall, she'd dragged herself for a half mile or so desperately needing medical help. You may know she's been X-rayed."

"They'll be here any minute. Husband?" he shot the word at me.

"Good friend."

To Laburnum, "You'd better train your dog to do his business earlier in the evening." Just then a boyish young medic came in and handed Dr. Ekid an X-ray envelope. Accepting it, Dr. Ekid dismissed the young man. "With some common-sense, accidents like this can be avoided and save all us all." As this doctor wasn't looking at Laburnum, he wasn't seeing the tears rolling her cheeks, which made her snatch tissues to her face. Compulsively, leaning I soothingly kissed her forehead. When she and I looked up, the doctor was holding her X-rays to the light.

"Two breaks. Profound. Best you're admitted upstairs for now." 'Doctor Ekid' was being called over the loud-speaker. Before hurrying off, he said in his whipping cold voice, "Be in to you again later," and was gone.

"Don't worry, we'll get someone else, Laburnum. That man wouldn't warm to his run-over mother!" Despite her frustration, her offense, Laburnum turned her head and through her tearful misery smiled at me. She was relieved and enormously thankful I'd been here. "Silly, old, over-officious commandant!" I cheered her as she put a grateful hand on my arm.

The nurse returned.

"Dr. Ekid, Nurse?" I asked, "Is he always so tactless?" The nurse grinned and put her forefinger up to her lips before nodding.

Wanting her own doctor, Laburnum asked the nurse about him; and speaking softly, the nurse promised to phone him. "You have an excellent doctor there. He's the best for broken bones. He'll have you up and mended in no time."

Laburnum thanked her, and once her blood pressure had been taken, much relieved, she turned her head into the soft pillow and let sleep slip over her again. With that insulting situation over, as Laburnum's eyes remained closed, I wondered where I'd got to with my thinking before the head vampire consultant's visit. Laburnum was thankfully feeling secure enough again to drift deeply off into sleep again—*best thing.*

Avoiding the curtain's pink oblongs, I willed myself back onto this subjective history, which was not for anyone else.

Yes, it had been eons ago.

My intrigued imagery went back to being a student splashing around in the Cam, when Thaddeus and Hockney would keep socking it to me that one was irrationally far too soft at competitive team debating. They'd dubbed one 'E.C.'—'Excessively Compassionate'! This was when, naturally, we had all been expected to display exemplary behavior to the rest of the 'lowlier world'. Exemplifying 'gentlemen', several of whom saw foreign affairs as a preferred route, and which may have been my own choice too with my love of travel. Though, more accurately, oh yes, it had been a family incident that had hurried along one's future!

Father had been lavishing jewelry and expensive gifts on a titled heiress he was setting up for dear old brother Gillie! She'd been from a family of formidable wealth, needless to say; but despite this lady's acquaintanceship being enticingly fanned by Father, as she got to know Gilmore, this—Lady Hortense was her name—amazed us all by instead taking a fanatic liking to oneself! One has to say that commendably, Father only delivered a few terse words to me before one suddenly found oneself employed at the Norwegian consulate!

One's sardonic greatly amused university chums kept instilling in me that my 'excessive compassion' would have other more loaded 'drawbacks'! Though this was only till well into one's career when Franklin, one's honorable mentor, seized hold of one's notorious emotion to iron-fistedly guide it—pruning one's over-garrulity to orderliness, and sharpening one's focus to targeted usefulness, only! All when one was distressingly unaware that my rambunctious 'compassion' had already been given the best guidance, not only by one's perceptive and extraordinary mentor, but also by one's dearest and most beloved deceased mother! Yes, Mother it had most honestly been!

Huh—the polytonality of skills unperceived!

Lord, hadn't it been though, Algernon, old turd?

One had not understood this, humiliatingly, but indeed it had been Mother who had led one into an understanding of societal innuendos, and an acute sense of morality that one strongly applied while climbing that ladder in the Foreign Service. So much so that all that edifying I had received from Mother that had been buried under all the noisy antagonism happening in the manor had made one wonder—is this what everyone undergoes growing to adulthood? Because the more I thought about one's compassion coming straight from Mother, the more one saw that it had most certainly been dearest Mother's unappreciated, resourceful, clear-minded, clandestine policies and politics that had so often pushed through much of her kind and most lucid counseling! Mother's darting-eyed empathies nurtured and endorsed by Granny and Grandpa, her fine parents, who had been banned by Father from the manor. Yet Mother! Silently, she had been that illuminating kernel I'd been constantly searching for of one's earliest compassion's development.

Returning to me was one's rapturous childhood and Mother's solid, though softly spoken cultivation for fair dealings, kindnesses, and far-reaching suggestions. All from her and my grandparents – most certainly NOT from Father! She'd suggest to one so graciously, so alluringly, one had trusted its validity. Though more obstreperously Father and Brother Gillie never missed every guffawed chance to desecrate one's dearest mother's words, because she happened to be a—yuk… woman.

Oh so unpatriotic, so horribly uninformed!

With all I knew now! With one's mind clearing, there could be absolutely no doubt! Dearest Mother and one's wonderfully wise grandparents had believed in that 'compassion' that had bestowed so much admiration on me! By all that they had discussed, taught through gift books, or through their subtle examples—of whom they were electing, or had deserved public praise—had raised one to their formidably high standards! Just as so often going up that little spiral staircase to her stifling little library, Mother's ideas had rattlingly impressed me!

Yes, indeed, who else could one's compassion have come from but Mother, and how fantastically one owed that sagacious and brilliant woman! One had never given enough magnitude to the perspicacity of that most loving and kindest of parents!

These thoughts so churned me, they startled!

Instead, distressingly knocked sideways by Father and Brother Gillie's corrupt dominating, by shunning Mother or competing to humiliate her and her far-finer, more distinguished family brought to mind much more of that most angelic of mothers and her sweetest parents. One was mortified it had taken all these years for one to see that it had been she that had given one this biggest, most priceless Freudian and even Robin Hood's immortalized influence. *Though, oh dear!* Reliving these parental memories inevitably one was being led into that.

Oh no-o! Not that ugliest of all days! A day that one would have to, yet it would take all one's courage. Algernon, just do it.

All right! As the bells still tolled for Mother's funeral ending, Father and Gilmore hadn't got out of the church when Father's soprano voice jarred everyone with its loudness exceeding the tolling bell, as it commanded Horace. "Get 'young pulverized brain' into the car and ruddy well make sure he's driven back to school and stays there!"

Such embarrassingly raucous orders cowed one before one's bereaved aunts, Uncle Ollie and Auntie Prue, cousins, family friends, and a few various arm-twisted notables that Father liked. Not that Father cared a hoot about what he was in church for, but he was making sure that I, his second son, would be kept well away from anything my beloved mother might have wished for me. Wasn't that what it was all about?

Dearest Lord, that anguishing day.

Heart's revving wouldn't let one forget how greatly one was about to miss dearest Mother's lovable informing and her dependable caring. Coming out of the church into that all-swallowing void with reality jolting the barbarism of that blessed parent no longer treading this earth, I was discovering how infinitely I could *not* live without that most sagacious of mothers.

Then why Father and Gillie's inhumane stupid secrecy? On a day like that, what could their ulterior plans be?? And couldn't they have at least kept their treacherous voices for after Mother's funeral bells ceased?

I was deep in wonderment about all this as my eyes dizzily still jumped around on Laburnum's divider-curtain, with those absurdly overlapping pale pink oblongs!

Because I was realizing that I had deliberately let that *Götterdämmerung* day's vividness inflame one all over again!

One's prep school rule for boys when a student lost a parent, was that the bereaved boy was to spend days at home with his saddened family. Instead, for me, Horace drove one back to one's legendary school without saying a word! Blindly, I'd walked in on the ending Latin class, where I stayed sitting on in the emptied classroom, fixed into a bodiless state, staring for an age at—nothing. Finally, a prefect must have found me because neither hearing nor seeing him, I had been kindly led upstairs to matron. Matron, that beloved mother substitute for boys with traumas, who cradled me against her sweet-smelling bosom until her melodious sensible words broke through my iron-discipline, and my agony erupted.

For Mother's sake, too, I needed to become a great deal more analytical about this quixotic emotion of mine, of hers—*of ours!*

Though enough! No more right now!

Oh my God, Algernon, what a ludicrous old lumberhead you've become! What has age done to you? Are you really needing to re-tread this grossly upsetting personal history? For heaven's sake! In one's retirement, what a God-awful, culpable, old memory rubbish-bin I've become! *ENOUGH! For all idolatries' sakes!*

Yes, it most certainly was enough!

Those up-churning scenes had lain waiting in one over all these years! Waiting for one's retirement and the *leisure* to re-live them? With all that I was being shown, the truth was, it had been because of Mother that my finer, more controversial compassion celerity had steadily emerged.

Could these have been memories one could have related to one's friends?

The red-haired nurse returned to check Laburnum's pulse and blood pressure; but as she left, I pulled the bedside chair up closer to my dozing 'paranormal night walker'. Wearied by one's starkest memories, one had taken Laburnum's hand to hold her fine tapering fingers before—deciding that this gesture was nothing more than a kindly action, picking up on what each of us had liked about the other. Simply a decent little expression!

Wakened by the nurse's ministrations, Laburnum kept her eyes mainly open before looking straight at me, curiously. With her pain subsiding, she seemed to be amazed I was still here!

Laburnum wasn't a woman to fool herself, "*Al-ger*-non?" She almost cooed. Though what reason other than my being her landlord did she have for one's kindness being lavished on her? One's goodwill? Her muffled voice echoed, "*Al*-gernon, this feudal concern."

"'Feudal'? Oh no Laburnum!" One's offense was inexpressible.

"I meant, this overseeing? It's very thoughtful of you to be so concerned." Though as she tried to think more, a cloudiness slid her mind till her narcotic-loaded eyes involuntarily closed.

Expecting only intermittent contact with her, one continued one's vigil anyway, as one was content to just sit there with one's various new past comprehensions settling in on this strange non-night. Tenderly, I wiped a strand of Laburnum's dark and gray hair from her full lower lip, as still holding her fine hand, she slept again and slowly, I relaxed back against the back of this bedside chair. *No, I did not have to stay here. Reb and Sylvia would have made sure Laburnum was well looked after. Though, here I was adjusting my elbow for continuing to hold her hand and stay here sitting!*

One hadn't re-assessed one's long ago mortared decision to never seriously mislead any woman—a discipline that had been automatic since my three-ringed marriage circus that I'd practiced for so many years it had become a given, even on my first meeting with Laburnum in the vineyards.

Laburnum!

Admittedly, her table manners could be distinctively repulsive—ghastly! Good God—*forgetting her handkerchief?* Though much more often, I'd looked forward to our meetings and was ever grateful to her understanding that in coming here to America, I'd coasted down from that grandest of world heights to this very desirable lowlier self-exile. Irritating as her interjections could be at times, Laburnum had gratuitously helped one. Which made one see that maybe my liking for this woman was not completely casual? Abruptly, Laburnum's louder exhale broke through my thought, making me lean to watch for her breathing to regulate again; her jaw and lower lip to re-slacken.

Moved by Laburnum's sad state, one surprised oneself by impulsively bending to her beautiful tapering fingers still lying in my hand to brush my lips across them! One wasn't planning romantic involvement—one had far too much to learn from Hans about managing the wonderful world of wine. Then, after all, was such a thing as genuine romance ever planned? One sat back again, glad to simply study Laburnum's fine fingers while still awed that my instinctual embracing of them had actually beaten out any mental decision!

Chapter 11
Recovery

A heavy downpour drove Reb and oneself out of the vineyards. Hoping to return later, the hired field crew took off as the torrents set in. As Reb had finished his commissioned carpentry job, he said he'd do today's other chore—with his Lincoln more spacious than one's 'glamor car'—he would fetch Laburnum from the hospital. Telling me he was off for her, instead of joining him, I used the time for giving Paycock a good wash down on the porch. "You know that Paycock's long hair will have to be blow dried before Laburnum sees him?" I caught Reb's smirks at this useless beautifying of Laburnum's rambunctious pet.

The rain continued without letup, which the vines needed; but with Laburnum weak and on crutches, her leg heavy in a large plaster cast, it wasn't easy for Reb to get her around the puddles into her apartment. Juggling an umbrella over his patient while putting a firm arm around her shoulders, he maneuvered her inside, where she shook off the rain; and with my help, awkwardly backed herself onto her scarlet sofa. Reb lifted her heavy leg up on the sofa before she sighed, smiling gratefully; and with a fatigued thump, gave way against her cushions.

"You're looking far better. Wonderful to have you back!" Bending I kissed her forehead.

The rain slashed on past the windows; and though Laburnum was glad to be back, she was more tired than she'd expected to be. Reb had to rush out through the rain, bringing in Laburnum's bagged possessions, and her cheer-up flower gift vases to put around her living-room.

She turned to me, "Algernon? Paycock!?" As one had taken over Paycock's walking and feeding while Laburnum was away, I'd quite enjoyed teaching her dog some manners. No more barging through the front door first, he must let adults go into Laburnum's apartment ahead of him—this took some practice. In Mack and rain hat, I'd brought the beautified Paycock over to Laburnum. Once inside, although Paycock was joyful to see Laburnum, one was pleased that her pet had the decorum to just stand and stare at his owner as his tail wagged till his whole rear-end virtually rocked off. Laburnum received my welcome back embrace, and looking at Paycock, she said, "Oh I do appreciate the grooming,

Algernon! Lovely!" and to her dog, "You most handsome quadruped!" Even when Laburnum repeated her dog's name, and he coyly went closer to her, Paycock thoughtfully just kept it to nuzzling. Then abruptly, not satisfied, he almost lay on the sofa with her. Pushing him down, Laburnum explained to him that her huge plaster cast was there for mending her bad leg. "It's broken in two places, Paycock, so you must understand and not get too close, because inside down there it hurts." Listening to his kind stricken owner, Paycock gave her scores of happy little arm licks instead that tickled and made her laugh until with my help, she could back away from Paycock and rest against her big patterned cushions. With a better understanding of Laburnum's change, the dog behaved. Though I knew by the looks pet and owner gave one another that each were undergoing some memorably crucial moments!

Laburnum saw what Reb was doing. "Oh Reb, no-o! No-o, the pink carnations will look best up on those book shelves." Laburnum directed her kind dripping friend, "Daisies and bachelor buttons on the table."

"Ple-ease? Or these'll get tipped over your head."

"*Please,* Angel Reb!"

Laburnum's orders had been to limit movement and take lots of resting her huge leg over a cushion. She was extremely pleased to be back here at Runditz's and in the snugness of her own little living-room with her familiar pictures, lamps, and her furnishings' heartening bright colors; and even the functional look of her special notes pinned to closets—all were safely here for consuming her again! Especially soothing to her needful spirits were her shelved books with their well-worn spines, tall and short, geographically organized. Just the familiar look of it all that was in this warm nicely cleaned little apartment diverted her momentarily from her unpleasant leg aches and her miserable limitations.

When the rain slowed, Sylvia, Mel, and Hans visited. Laburnum sat up straighter on the sofa to give each a hug. Hans joked about needing to try out her crutches, and he had brought her a newspaper with an article that referred to some work I had once been in on. Though as Laburnum's German wasn't good, she left it for now. Much as Laburnum adored being back here with Paycock, her 'desk' again, and these very best friends, she soon found that all this embracing and catching up tired her.

Back on that evening of Hans' fine Sauterne tasting, as promised, Mel had made his phone call to Sally-Anne in Pennsylvania. Wanting the job of housekeeping for the new owner of the Runditz Winery, Sally-Anne had promptly returned. She and Laburnum had known one another from Sally-Anne's being here earlier for Hans. Though today, seeing what care Laburnum was needing, Sally-Anne took over helping her to the bathroom and getting off her still damp clothes, and into dryer garments. Ingeniously, she cut the leg elastic of her marigold panties, so Laburnum could pull underwear on over her huge cast.

Sally-Anne was helpful in many ways. Being neat, petite, and energetic, while Laburnum was hospitalized, she had cleaned and polished her barn apartment while singing away, rubbing up the window panes to a new transparency front and back and opening them to let in the heat of the wet day for freshening the Paycock-stifled air. Sally-Anne quickly proved to be the wonder-worker Hans had said she'd be and, like Sylvia, was cheerful and enjoyed singing popular songs as she dusted. I requested she used Laburnum's varnished stone paperweights for anchoring her ongoing work on the 'desk-end' of her table, which she did, carefully respecting Laburnum's piles of jottings and notepads. Reference books and boxed reams beside her computer, all got neatened and dusted. Good at housework, Sally-Anne was another country woman who excelled at making meals. Dividing the food for Laburnum and myself, she delivered them to each; though if she made supper in Laburnum's kitchen, and I came to help Laburnum to her chair at the food side of her table, glad of each other's company, the three of us ate together. Laburnum though didn't want much to eat, and thanking them, she would quickly ask to go back and rest.

Having Laburnum back nicely completed the estate again, though what took more time than one had expected was grasping that she was barely managing her painful movements as prescribed by her therapist. Theoretically, I knew that if she was to get back verve for her studies or for conjuring up special meals with Sylvia again, she'd need plenty of Sally-Anne's good care and lots of rest; and I did my best to liven up her long days with a fine vase of birds of paradise, and having checked that Laburnum didn't own it, a splendid book on Persepolis. But giving these to her, she yawned, thanked me, then rolled over and went back to sleep again. I thought she'd be sick of sleeping; though no matter what I said or found to amuse her, sleep seemed to be all she wanted.

Accepting some of this as necessary, still it aggravated that Laburnum wasn't the livelier companion she used to be. One was an immensely charitable man, but it bothered me that between sleeps she lolled about for most of the day in her dressing-gown—or 'robe' as it is here—and that my carefully selected cheer up gifts hardly kept her eyes open. I'd done well with an orchid plant. Laburnum enjoyed letting her eyes roam its elaborate form, its cream and peach petals, and awake one time she said she'd appreciated the bowl of fresh fruit that Sylvia and I kept replenished handily on her coffee table. Apparently I had built up more expectation of our resuming friendship, though I did my best not to let her see one's intemperateness. Throwing myself into longer hours in the fields, or taking Paycock for several mile hikes, I kept finding any excuse to check Laburnum's lights from one's living-room window or porch, hoping to see her up and moving around. On every visit to her I paced her living-room, which grew smaller as one conscientiously avoided bumping my head while she lay so inert, eyes usually closed, until it poignantly irritated me she was not getting back her 'old steam'.

Sylvia noticed Algernon's restlessness and asked me if I was losing weight. She and Reb kept telling me that Laburnum's recovery needed time, and why didn't I concentrate on getting done all I needed to in the fields and relax? Another day, Sylvia, seeing me looking utterly forlorn, suggested that if I really wanted to help Laburnum, maybe I should stay away from her for a few days? Loathe to agree but ready to try anything, I agreed that one's pacing impatience wasn't helpful; and I forced not visiting her, though this too was defeating.

Amazed that my famous old Cholmondley-Rute blue-blooded strength wasn't chipping in—after all, Laburnum was just a good friend. Adding to the disappointment of not having Laburnum's eager friendship was yet another aggravation. I would keep thinking about what a real intimacy with a woman could be, ideally. Which instead kept bringing back one's ugliest husband experiences with Francesca, till it occurred to one, *what would retirement have been if Succubus Francesca been here with him? Oh God! This Supreme Habitat with Francesca? For heaven's sake, most inattentive Lord!* The mere thought of Francesca anywhere near here desecrated his paradisiacal 'Supreme Habitat'. *Augh!* She'd have dragged this heavenly spot through that *Inferno* of Dante's! Clawed carnivores from unexplored jungles would have had more tenderness than that barbarous harlot, but… *Uh-oh, wasn't I supposed to be putting that mindless cheap whore behind me forever? For all those gods on Mount Olympus's sake, Algernon, good old mate, try harder! A lot harder.*

One night returning to his house after dark, I restlessly walked up and down the porch, only sitting after noticing how much one's breathing wasn't rhythmic. I'd often sit studying the opposite shore's lights streaking golden needles at me across the night's polished water, a sight that should have diverted as I pondered that witch-woman reclining away over there on her scarlet sofa. Or on an afternoon's end, I'd walk Paycock till the poor dog's look at me pleaded to return home. Going back the long way by the shore, I sat on a whitened driftwood log to cursorily throw Laburnum's precious pet a stone that sent him vainly swimming around looking for it. Hardly consoled by the water's laps one's gastrointestinal system also rebelled, *this too because of his penchant for getting mixed up with an 'erratic fortune-telling' woman?*

One knew that not having properly known a decent woman other than my wonder-mother, who had drenched one's early boyhood in unforgettable curiosity or rapture, making it harder for any other woman, I lamented. Overseas there had been a few business relationships, or an occasional almost intellectual talk with a wife of a certain nob, though really I'd only ever looked for wanton women. Thaddeus, or my other secretively licentious playmate, Telford, and I, purged our sexual needs by making use of those 'oldest profession' women, generously paying them to allay our 'peccadilloes'. I'd had no knowledge of these women, no interest in knowing who they were. Which may have been why Laburnum had become an enigma to me, as according to Sylvia, she had surmounted rotten adversities out west before coming to the Finger Lakes to so admirably manage her later scholarly years.

One's sensitivity to Laburnum was at best irregular, because if one did visit her, her indifference would tumble my thoughts into greater disorder. There had been a time in my youth when I'd innocently harbored some splendiferous marital ideals. Wonderments of husbandry that his decency, integrity, and his dearest mother's remote memories had willfully conjured. All fine until dipstick Francesca obliterated his every ideal, but recollecting this only accentuated that erudite woman over in wonky glasses in her barn apartment having this nerve to take such an utterly distraught length of time for getting well!

While working the vines, earlier former images of Laburnum plagued one till I'd begged her to—*what?* Let him find some miraculous doctor for healing her? To fly her off to Aruba to watch her heal at a luxurious health resort? Herb-obsessed Laburnum wouldn't hear of his medically interfering. Then one evening paying bills at his study's desk… *had that been Laburnum's lovely tapestried voice calling his name? No-o? More likely an audio hallucination that made his head choke. Or he would discover himself in the clownish position of an Italian marble roof-top statue gazing dazedly at the lake through his porch door window;* and while working the fields, reading, or taking lengthier hikes, I began to see myself as that agonized remnant of a human being in Edward Munch's *The Scream*, with my mouth braced wide open in a shriek so virulent that through one's dilated gullet one could actually view my trembling entrails! *Oh for all the ashes of burned up martyrs, Algernon, is this being level-headed? Helpful?*

Greatest of deities, what is the matter with me?

I'd even got dearest Sylvia worrying about me!

Until one morning, I woke realizing, *Great Lucifer, was one's Cholmondley-Rute manhood made of Titmouse piss? How frightfully shameful! Oh but think, Algernon!* All one's assets and achievements have been well proven and published, even in voodoo right-wing newspapers. *For God's sake, listen to me, my dear good man! From now on, no more of this unsociably feeble whining just because she's a woman, for mercy's sake! Take yourself in hand! It might be that this lowliness business has come on too fast? Has eaten up some of one's testosterone? Then let's slow it down?*

Though disentangling one's emotions was a whole muddled drum of monofilament fishing line yanked off some water-logged tree trunk from the bottom of Lake Seneca.

Taking Sylvia's sensible advice, I'd only visited Laburnum every two or three days. Not having seen her lately, one believed that as my aristocratic manhood could be inching back again, but sadly, there was other news. News that made one at least believe that dutifully one owed Laburnum a visit.

Knocking as I entered... *Ye gods! Greater than the Hanging Gardens of Babylon and all the other world wonders, one was bowled over with delirium!*

THERE SHE WAS! The injured witch-woman was actually out of her robe, dressed, and sitting at her 'desk'! "Greatest Suppurations!" one exclaimed trying to contain my sclerotic elation. "What can have happened?" Not having seen her lately, I was surprised too because she looked up at him smiling broadly. *Smiling!* The title of her opened notebook that one read upside-down over her shoulder was 'Egyptian Notes'! Assimilating her incredible improvement, still believing it an illusion as one walked around her, then back again, stopping myself from pinching her! Though she was flesh and blood all right! Here she was, she'd not only made it to her desk, but she was looking pleased I'd come to see her! Gone was her sick old refusal of one, her eternally depressing super-introspection. *Heavens, what more marvels could there be to this over-excavated world?! The perennially feeble female yanky-dingbat actually had the mending qualities of a human being!*

"Oops!" one exclaimed wondering if one's breathing had stopped. "Oh goodness, Laburnum, you look really lovely!!" I tried to catch up with all I was seeing, but all I could say was, "Throw her in the teapot, said the dormouse."

Ignoring one's supercilious quote, she replied, "I've always been a sturdy walker, Algernon! I'm sure you must have known that all I needed was rest."

Shaking one's head awesomely getting used to her better health, one went into a catatonic stare at her and dropped into her armchair to slouch back the way she used to like me to. Still disbelieving this reincarnated scholar-fortune-teller's enormous difference, I finally recalled why else I'd come. "I imagine you've 'heard' about Reb, Laburnum?" I asked a little facetiously because of what she'd already 'know'. I had just met Sylvia and had heard about Reb's car accident. "In fact, Laburnum dear, Sylvia said that it was you who first 'heard' about our very good friend?"

Adjusting her bad leg, Laburnum sat back from her notes. "Yes, I was the one who phoned Sylvie, Algernon."

"Sylvia was overcome with thankfulness that you had! I gather Reb's smash-up could've been far worse."

"You know he hasn't even a bruise?"

"Thank all the strings activating us from above."

"It'll only be fender work, and that's reparable. Understand, Algernon, yes I was the first to 'know'. Though, I don't like receiving pictures that happen out of nowhere to one of our group, like that. Particularly when I can't just jump on my motorcycle and go help the guy. But Sylvie has got back to me; they're dealing with the car and the drunk driver that side-swiped him."

"Nasty!"

I got up; and despite this news, happily paced to look out of Laburnum's window and came back listening to her describing more of Reb's near miss, just as good old Paycock slunk over to lick one's hand.

Since I had got to love Laburnum's pet, Paycock couldn't have chosen a cleverer moment to distract one as the suddenness of his beloved's truer recovery wouldn't let much else in. Laburnum recalled Reb's confident countryman's good-heartedness, and like everyone here, I was saddened and concerned by Reb's accident. When Sylvia had spoken to me earlier, she'd made it clear that there wasn't anything I could do; Reb and she were handling all they needed to, thank you all the same. I had not wanted to impose or be seen as 'feudal', as Laburnum had called it, yet I would have helped in any way I could as everyone so-so wanted Reb to sustain that immeasurably gratuitous persona that had earned him the warm fondness of the Runditz family.

The dog's caressing licks were quite pleasant as it also became clear to me that Laburnum must apparently be quite highly developed as a medium, having caught so precisely into Reb's telepathized terror. Due to Laburnum's phone call, Sylvia had hurried to the accident scene and just as Laburnum had assured her Reb would be, she'd found him physically unhurt. This hadn't been late, only at about 8:30 last evening. Sylvia had found Reb leaning against his car, shocked, saddened, and angry while trying to recall the other car's license plate and examining his badly crushed fender.

"Have you seen Reb, Algernon?" Laburnum asked.

"He was at the garage where he'd taken his car this morning. Yes, I saw him; and as you'd expected, he's okay but sick about his fine Lincoln. As I left, Mel had got there. It was damn good you called Sylvia last night, Laburnum!"

"As you know, my 'seeing' isn't always reliable; but last evening it was so sharp, it even had an odor of gasoline to it! Yes, and as it was still long before Sylvie's bed-time, at least I could help her find which section of the highway."

"You'd 'seen'?"

"Enough to recognize that stretch with Jensen's silos. You'd have known them too by their odd heights. Sooner or later someone would've passed and phoned Sylvie, but Reb was in bad need of her; and I'm sure you know how deep the connection is between those two."

"Well-merged, yes. How did that much psyching affect you?"

“Me? You mean, did it tire me?” That was what I’d meant. “A bit, it’s another kind of work, a concentrated use of another faculty, isn’t it?” One was sure it was.

Paycock was needing my attention. “You want to walk, Paycock?”

“Good of you, Algernon.”

“Don’t get over-confident with your crystal ball, though it’s splendid seeing you up and about, Laburnum! Okay, I can tell when Paycock needs masculine company—we fellows need to give one another boosts. Come, Paycock!” Paycock was already waiting by the leash that I took from the hook to fold for carrying. I checked back at Laburnum. “Keep up all this wellness, Laburnum. See you soon!”

Leaving Laburnum to her ‘Egyptian Notes’, I took Paycock for a good long ramble around the vineyards and down to the lake before returning, feeling more himself at last, though he was hot and thirsty.

“I meant to ask you, Algernon, is the brush-pulling completed?”

“There’s not much left. Heavens, it’s good to see you as your old self again, Laburnum! Yes, the fellows are trucking in manure now. When we’ve got all that on, we’ll slow down to sit and watch the first grapes ripen. May I help myself to lemonade? You too?”

“And check Paycock’s bowl, will you? My apologies for making use of you.”

“One will find a way you can repay me!”

Once both were set up with the cold drink, one asked, “Into Egypt again?”

“As I woke up this morning, I was putting together Ra and Ba.”

“Ha, yes the two parts to the human soul! I can understand where you’d get tangled up in those.”

“Not tangled, but it did become an incentive! You know all of this, Algernon,” indicating her notes. “Weren’t you at the Cairo consulate? As one of the earliest civilizations, I keep coming across more to marvel at of their society’s tolerance—family life revered, yet marriage didn’t have to be by contract!” Checking up at him, “Can you imagine? There could be divorce, not just for noblemen but for their servants too! A woman could divorce her husband for mental cruelty or incompatibility! How many other civilizations thought like that? Wasn’t that about as progressive as you could get? Though, the divorcing Egyptian woman might have to forfeit money. Yes, still far from ideal for women! Then the same old blaming them for not producing the wretched son and heir. However, I’m in awe of how greatly their living was directed by.”

“The afterlife?”

“Damn you, Algernon! How unfair it is that certain persons get favored with all that wonderful hands-on edifying!”

"Grossly unfair yes, perfectly right! It's enough to make one have to drum up endless patience with persons who put together sociological ideals from their ancient civilization studies."

"'Sociological ideals'… Lovely, oh lovely!" Jotting herself a note. "You can count on me listening to every least bit of what you know." Then adjusting her position. "It might be my occult leanings, but a civilization that's as driven as they are by the afterlife, with their idea of judgment showing them how their daily behavior might improve."

"Not so unlike other religions?"

"But with no one spiritual leader?"

"Don't you think that this was a reason the pharaoh immortalized himself?" I was again drawn back into what I too had once hotly intrigued with at one's Cairo mission and relaxing here with Laburnum again, bringing Egypt's culture and beliefs back under more magnification—that Laburnum couldn't get enough of—was more like those earlier pre-accident afternoons that she and I had so enjoyed! I was glad it was this Mid-Eastern mystical culture stimulating her again. Looking at her more carefully, the pain that for weeks had noticeably mortified her fine dark eyes to a sickly dustiness was at last gone! In my gratitude, I had started putting together the story behind the Cheops Pyramid for her—just as Reb walked in!

"Should've knocked harder."

"Oh Reb dearest! Never mind! How are you? It's so good to see you!"

"Listen to her pretending, Alg'non! You wouldn't believe she'd seen my smash-up, would you?"

"I'd say she hadn't wanted to receive anything that horrible, though just look at her, Reb! Using it must have done her some good."

"Yep," Reb agreed, and to Laburnum, "Did you see anything on your psychic screen of that rusty-minded washed-out old drunk that took care of my car?" Laburnum shook her head. "Aw, so what should I expect, the roads are full of 'em! How's a man to sleep nights?"

"You got his license?"

"Four letters and two numbers. Maybe that's enough."

"You mean the cops have some idea?"

"That's what they tell me, Miss Potentate, so unless you can come up with more, I'll just have to sit tight and see what they can do. Which reminds me, I've come here to thank you."

"You've done a lot for me, Reb, I owed it you."

"The truth for once—yeah! This time though, it helped Sylvie."

"Can you calm down so you'll make up your sleep tonight?" I asked.

"Sylvie's mixing me one of your tonics, Miss P. Using some of your 'erbs."

“Keep sipping away at it, Reb, that’s what’ll do it. Stay off the alcohol tonight, and I’ll guarantee you’ll make up your sleep and more.”

“No wine? Only if you say so, I guess. I can’t miss Sylvie’s early morning hot cakes and sausage, or how’ll I put in an honest man’s day?”

“Algernon’s no task-master, Reb.”

“No, but after taking the day off today, I expect more of myself.”

“Give yourself a break, old chap, you had a nasty accident, and you’re extraordinarily lucky it’s just a fender.”

“Right. I’ll know more after I find out what these ’erbs of hers will do.”

Reb paced about before leaning a straight arm to one of Laburnum’s labeled closets. Then standing straight, he arched his back as if to get his muscle power returning along with his usual better posture, and slowly he rolled the stiffness from his neck before turning sharply. “See ya!” he said as he went off again as suddenly as he’d appeared, leaving Laburnum’s mischievous affection shaking her head as she caught Algernon’s eye.

Chapter 12
Dog Concerns

Paycock's good friend Rowley was out on a happy rove, having crawled under Henderson's cage fence. Lost to patches of long grass loaded with morning dew, he pushed through it slower than a sick cat for letting it more gloriously cool off his hot fur. Next beside such fetid footpath and tractor trails that no dog that's been to obedience school could refuse, Rowley changed his mind—that coveted prerogative of dogs. Instead, he yielded to an instinct-telephonic to turn in at Runditz's as the three had Paycock's hot topic pressing to be aired and spent some best friend-time with Paycock and Bruno.

Meeting up, the three dogs saturated their togetherness pleasure with plenty of rolling on backs, sneezing. Paycock stretched out his long body on the grass to exhale little puffs of awakening breaths that beat the fragrance of a pig farm in a downpour. Though Rowley, into the same stretching and puffing rites next to Paycock, was aroused by his friend's insta-chromatic breath—it extended his enjoyment into snorted 'harrumphs'. Being older, Bruno was the last to back roll because his hearing wasn't too great with his long ears muffling his companions. Today, instead of letting his long ears flop, he'd styled them out wide above his brown cardboard color fur to make his tiny black snout look as if he was snottily peering out of a carton. Paycock and Rowley couldn't look straight at Bruno when he did this without getting stomach aches with laughter till Bruno raised his paw with something to say, and both his friends had the courtesy to stop laughing.

"Talking of Laburnum."

"Were we?"

"How're you managing your new landlord, Paycock?"

"I have to terrify him with thunderous growls to make him watch it with Laburnum."

"Good, keep it up. You've worked hard for your status; you mustn't let him threaten it. By the way, has Algernon jumped her yet, or does her leg cast scare him off?"

"No, he hasn't, and he'd better not try to take over my position!"

"Laburnum could move her plaster cast out sideways," Bruno suggested. "After all, she's getting older, it could be regrettable to wait."

"But *they* haven't-been-left-alone, Rowley!" Bruno loudly repeated. "I've seen to it! Paycock message-telephonics me if Algernon visits."

"Though Laburnum's got good smells, she could still have a sizable litter."

"*Sapiens!* A litter, Bruno?!" Paycock laughed so hard, his front paws gave way. "*They* would have a 'family', Bruno. Say 'family'."

"Family. Though *Sapiens* may live a lo-o-ong time, but even for *them,* time eventually passes."

"When she's not looking, he could surprise-jump her from behind?" Rowley suggested thoughtfully, "So they can smoke a cigarette."

"Uh-uh, Laburnum hates those fire sticks!"

"Because she's not being rutted!" Bruno knew. "She'd like fire sticks if he gave her a good shagging."

"*They*'ve got to sniffing out one another," Paycock felt obliged to defend his kind owner. He'd always believed Laburnum was more kind than other dog owners, though admittedly, Mel was good to Bruno. "Algernon walked Laburnum outside a few steps yesterday."

"They take you with them?"

"Had to, Sally-Anne can't get my urinations out of Laburnum's beige carpet."

"Another way for getting you out with them is to heave around, making out you're about to vomit," Rowley elaborated.

"Yes? Good, I'll store it. But back to their rutting, Algernon is getting hotter for her! He's slow, but I don't think we need worry. I walked him down to the lake yesterday, all sweated from working the vineyards and visiting Laburnum. He removed his shirt and shorts till he stood in what *they* call a Eurobikini, which he might as well have taken off too; but not losing a minute, he waded out and swam wherever I did, so I swam fast and a long way out. Have to say, Algernon's a pretty good swimmer."

"Cooled him off?"

"As he doesn't jump her, he needs to, doesn't he?"

"Elementally speaking."

Having aired any immediate concerns personally affecting them, the three warm slothful dogs nosed their muzzles into any nearby chlorophyll rich grass or beneath their thighs for indulging in some delectable dozing rights.

"Listen you two, let's forget Algernon right now, we're overdue for a much more serious talk." Just as Rowley had expected, Paycock was exploding with his need to share his well-chewed-over topic as loaded with all his night-time basket-thinking; he was bouncing up and down. "All right, Bruno, Rowley, now for battered briskets' sake, let's get down to this nuclear disarmament test ban treaty before we're all regretful?"

"Er – then it's better to skip 'chatting'?" Bruno asked.

"I've been waiting for you and Rowley to come over, Bruno."

Instead, the three did some quick polite togetherness vibrations to settle down, before Bruno and Rowley attended to Paycock, who was sitting bolt upright in his magnanimous setter posture—his snout at a half point as the sunlight showed off his cordovan coat's bonfire glow with its envied scummy sheen.

Bruno and Rowley were making thrilled little moans because they too had been longing for some real Rolling Stone philosophies to jam their incisors into. Getting comfortable opposite Paycock, they prepared to do some conscientious listening.

"At last! Good!" Paycock said remembering his superior setter's patience. "Now what that new *sapien* nuclear treaty means." This statement of Paycock's immediately drew Rowley and Bruno's acute concern as he lured them into Algernon and Laburnum's struggle with foreign policy.

"Yes, Paycock?"

"What this treaty means is that those years of attempting to blast another continent out of the universe, o-or getting the continent we're on return-blasted out of ditto, could now be officially *over!*" Paycock was well-geared for this, having distilled Algernon and Laburnum's discussion while pretending to be asleep in his basket. "That is, *sapiens* are finally seeing that mega-blasting on this ultimate scale means farewell Planet Earth."

"Yes, eternal vacuum! *The Death March* of Saul!" Bruno tensely exclaimed.

"Nothing on and on!"

"Death march of…?" Paycock queried; his ears raised as much as a setter's ears could raise.

Rowley told him it was a funeral march. Being highly reputed for his Westminster aspirations, Rowley valued his porch-talk education lying at farmer Henderson's feet hot evenings, listening to him and his brother getting all politically worked up and inducing Rowley to contemplate his own political opinions.

"The trouble is, *sapiens* have made such an unadulterated mess, thinking that as they're friendly and cooperative with other countries, *they've* been forced to make this treaty!" Paycock continued from his night-time distilling. "We three know it's a step in the right direction, but now—and this is important—how did *they* ever get into such an abominably fouled up mess? It takes a long time to get that politically constipated." Paycock and Bruno kept nodding their agreements. "Having thought hard about this, I'll tell you two best friends why *they* are." Paycock sat even straighter. "The fallacy of *sapien* thinking, and all *their* globe-trotting hopelessness, is because *they* pop out of the womb programmed to *compete!"* Paycock hesitated to let the loftiness of this disputable word sink in, before reiterating, "Yes, you heard it right – '*compete!'* Which is a brutal quality to deal with because *sapiens* have been ancestrally competitive long before birth."

"That's *their* programming, Paycock! Why, just last week on Mel's radio science program, *they* were bragging that competition has been found to exist in *sapien* fetuses! Meaning, that even before *sapien* infants pop out, *they* please their parents by competing to make more vomit and defecation than the next puppy."

"'Infant'. Say 'infant'."

"Infant. Though do you know a country where they don't compete, Paycock?" Bruno asked.

"The ones that aren't shooting rockets off to other planets?"

"Right Rowley," Paycock agreed. "Laburnum said that before China had that big production Communist leader with his little red book, the Chinese used to peacefully swap music, pottery, songs, and paintings so contentedly, *they* didn't bother with money!" Paycock informed. "When Laburnum and Algernon talk about the ancient peaceful Chinese, Laburnum refers to *their* behavior as 'indefinite'. She says that thousands of years ago, long before that big production Communist leader, Chinese *sapiens* found that goals didn't need to be competitive, or fierce, or violent. They called this being 'in-definite'."

"'In-definite'? To get in-definite, I wonder, did they have to core-meditate like us?"

"That's just what those ancient Chinese did, Bruno," Paycock knew. "Laburnum has read books on 'Definite' and 'Indefinite'."

"Which is exactly what our creed did for us canines back in Pedagogy if you were both paying attention, and look how blissfully contented we dogs are. Sadly, this is not the same with *sapiens*."

"You know, Paycock," Bruno raised his face up from between his long ears to speak with more mature authority, "You're right about *sapiens* competing. It isn't just Lamborghinis and Lincolns, it's parties in election times, fast racing cars, huge international prizes, beating out other siblings at the dinner table, or flying up the ladder in a corporation, because *they'll* use *their* fathers to jump ahead of other employees. It might be true to say that *sapiens* need to be highly competitive just to keep *their* next breath coming."

"*They* don't have to—not that way. Like Hans, *they* could just live peacefully in the countryside," Paycock pointed out.

Bruno spoke, "I've done some advanced studies on this 'definite' and 'in-definite' business, because I heard Mel tell his girlfriend that she was too bright to be rutted," which made Bruno double laughing, "Ha ha ha!" Though he tried to be casual about his comic information. “Like you, Paycock, Mel thought that when nations decided to go ‘definite’, *they* made huge, terrifying defense aims; and paying for them everyone got taxed so heavily, there was always a large group of people that had to go without food.”

“Unconscionable! Shocking, Bruno! Unless—unless—*their* nation had had to become ‘definite’. Like, supposing an avaricious neighbor commanded his armies to run over another nation’s homes, shops, roads, and lovely odorous alleyways,” Rowley commented—a thought Farmer Henderson and his brother talked up.

“Avarish? Er, greedy?”

“Or when an insane ruler uses his armies to force everyone to think the way he does.”

“Forcing *them* to make ‘definite’ goals for defending, you mean, Paycock?”

“There could be good reasons like those when a country needs to go ‘definite’, Paycock.”

“Unless the competition gets so high-powered, it turns irrational? *Sapiens* will need to learn how to catch it before it turns irrational.”

“Right, Rowley! So the big-picture question is, what can be done to get *sapiens* back into more of *their* ancient ‘in-definiteness’ again, isn’t it?” Paycock asked from his night-time’s wrestled thinking. “Then *they* can exchange things the way *they* used to and sing and be happy and playful.” Paycock paused needing to take on a more professorial air. “The frightening concern about ‘definiteness’ is, once it really gets going in a nation, it’s very hard to stop. Look at the global amount of non-benevolent inventiveness! ‘Competition’ on our national scale.”

“And on the international scale. Like what is non-benevolent inventiveness?”

“Medicines with bad side-effects? Phoning while you’re driving?”

“Internationally too, yes, right! How can we keep up with it? It sends hastily advanced non-benevolent inventions way up over the hill of control.”

“Oh yes, *they’re way up* over the hill of control!” Bruno repeated.

“And out of sight.”

“Gruesome, because there’s no danger-checker. I mean, not officially, not internationally.”

The three good friends were so horror-struck, they needed to lie down and get their snouts beneath some good aromatic armpits or haunches for re-balancing. As the good friends cooled their equilibriums, they each stood up and shook off their coats in long sumptuously wriggled shakes until they felt better.

“The problem is so deep down inside *sapien* body chemistry that the only way to change *their* competition-fanaticism would be when *they* are infants.”

“As helpless *babies, they could* be molded?” Bruno asked.

"Right, Bruno. Oh Rowley, Bruno—wait! *Oh listen!*" Paycock's paw went sky-high because he'd had a flash! "Do you two think that this could be why Algernon and Laburnum are digging into all this?"

"You mean if they're really thinking about making an infant, it would be sensible to know what's ahead for him? It?" Rowley was back into his stride. "Yes, it would all greatly change if babies were re-indoctrinated while *they're* helpless. It could make a big change to all that hopeless competition you talk about, Paycock. Think about *sapien* babies now; their parents make them do logarithms when *they're* just a week old."

"That's true! *They* don't understand how hurtful over-smartness can be! The computing brain is such a small segment. Listen, have you ever heard of a *Sapien* parent giving *their* offspring advanced education in kinetic sight development? Or expandable variable flavor sentience?" Sitting tall, Rowley shook his collar fur and asked, "Paycock, can you imagine what it would be like if competitiveness had never been invented?"

"Great juicy bones! *They*'d all be figuring lovely exchanges in food, making high-styled burrow-shelters for one another, and *they'd* think out seasonally useful jewelry and custom-built clothes," Bruno contributed. "Whew! Do you two realize that all this could make *them* a genuine democracy—like the Early Greeks?"

"Democracy? They'd all be sitting around discussing new projects more carefully, planning ahead with detailed drawings—*oh!*" Paycock grunted, "Silence!" he said this alarm-word so only his two friends heard. Automatically, Rowley and Bruno got into perfect pet postures as Mel looked in on them.

"Good doggie-wogs," Mel was pleased with their excellent behavior and complimented them for being exceptionally good dogs. Signaling to them how well-behaved they were, he turned and went back to the production center.

The trouble is, there's a freaky belief with many adult sapiens that canines are mindless.

Such a delusion! From our earliest ancestry, dogs have been deceptively ultra-subtle thinkers and always will be. Which is why dogs like us play down our real feelings. No self-respecting canine wears his heart on his hock, whatever he pretends. It not only doesn't get a dog anywhere, but it violates the terms of his domestic status and might even interfere with his right to drop into fathomless snoozes—which is where all mammals did their best thinking if they only knew it.

"Great unremoved gonads, am I grateful we Canidae aren't pitifully driven by *sapien* competition!"

Feeling immensely gleeful he wasn't a *sapien,* Bruno said this as he looked out from his snotty cardboard box ears again. Seeing him back looking preposterous, Rowley and Paycock whirled with laughter again till they had to bend sideways.

"Whew!" Rowley agreed. "What would *sapiens* do with all their time?"

"*They'd* do whatever anyone does best that's creative and satisfying, and *they* wouldn't need grand prizes because the joy of using *their* real talent would saturate *their* potential."

"*They* would love every bit of each day and dance around a lot; *they'd* be so happy! *They'd* even make each other presents!"

"Yes, but Lamborghinis and Lincolns, though? We'll have to think about *their* psychological immaturity."

"As it's terrifying! Exactly, Bruno!" Rowley agreed. "Though if the tax monies weren't shooting rockets off to other planets, there would be money for lots of food, and there wouldn't be hungry people."

After all this lovely synapse-provoking, the three dogs moved into more comfortable assimilation lazes. Paycock stretching out his long body to the grass to exhale little puffs of that strangely colored breath that Rowley liked and got beside him for, though sitting up, Rowley worried that Henderson would find his cage empty. "That treaty you told us about, Paycock. It could be exceptionally helpful in slowing down the arms race. What's more, *they* will have to make sure that all *their* blasting materials are dead-bolted in a high-walled, armed forces Pound," Rowley had heard this on Mrs. Henderson's NPR news.

Bruno groaned at this 'P' word, but he only trembled slightly. "Best place."

"Impossible!" Paycock came on strongly. "It just takes one pound police guard with fungus blight between his ears to sell a smidgen of it after dark."

"A smidgen?"

"That's all it would take," Paycock insisted pleased with this rare and wonderful new word he'd heard Algernon use.

"And if that hasn't been enough, now we're gut-scared that those blasting ingredients will be stolen and start the whole rotten…" taking a deep breath, "…scary, totally illegal, mercilessly uncivilized, utterly insane inducement to barely half-living all over again!"

Paycock and Rowley marveled that without trembling, Bruno had managed to say all that in one breath.

"It shows that *they* are trying to make that treaty, and that's in the right direction."

"Whatever helps," Rowley agreed, "Though thank all special treats that as dogs we've have not inherited competition. Having to always compete must be like being imprisoned. We've never had to compete to breathe—dogs keep breathing out of our pure uncorrupted reasoning."

"'Reasoning'. Right, yes!" Bruno agreed.

"You're correct, Rowley, we're the only species in nature to have adopted reasoning's. Explain and Conclude!" Paycock agreed.

"You mean like when Mel's girlfriend comes to the door, and I bark, it's because I'm reasoning Mel wants to see her?"

"Bravo! Excellent, Bruno! She came to the door, and you concluded that Mel would want to see her! Listen friends, *their* competing is strategically the same. If *sapiens* build weapons for destroying a continent, the victimized continent will build weapons to destroy theirs. Cause and effect! Sensibly reasoned, you agree?"

"*Their* trouble is that *they* don't notice that this makes everyone in the whole wide world tremble, and who likes to live in a neurotic system that trembles?" Rowley added. "Imagine what it would be like if that *sapien* treaty had made much larger rules that no one anywhere was allowed to build weapons? Can you imagine us all living without our nerve cells in conniptions?! And you know reasoning like that is so simple. Why have *they* found it so-o hard?"

"It's because *they* aren't even aware that *they* compete, just as I told you!" Paycock loudly reiterated. "From babyhood, *they* grow up competing instead of reasoning, and if *they* can't recognize *their* own regressively abhorrent competitive qualities, it's because each new sapien generation keeps *their* bad competing habits growing deeper into *their* corpuscle molecules."

"Well-spoken, Paycock, Bruno!" Rowley agreed. "Competing blocks out reason, and when reason goes, corruption grows—*oh-ho!*" Pleased with his cute rhyme, Rowley repeated, "When reason goes, corruption grows!" using his front paw to tap out the beat of his catchy jingle till his friends beat it out with him.

Paycock got back to it. "Reasoning is lost too because competing might mean *their* name on the news channel or in history book kindles. It's no wonder the military of the world over spins off its rails."

"Weak-minded!" Rowley and Bruno each respectively endorsed, pleased to be refreshing their superior dog overview.

"It's a lot to think about!" Rowley said giving a back-leg scratch to his right ear and taking a few long leisurely breaths.

"Good. With this little discussion-zapping, we're each thinking better. We'll meet here in a week and find out how our individual thinking is coming because it's going to be up to us to get some strategic guidance going in our owners."

"And that's hard. Though no one else will do it so. Right, yes, we'd certainly better," Bruno agreed. "Next week it is then."

"Unless there's any more conspicuous news," Paycock suggested. But Rowley and Bruno were each needing nice lonely spots to thoroughly ruminate the 'definiteness' and 'indefiniteness' of this nuke treaty with Paycock's competing. Agreeing with Paycock, after giving good-friend paw-waves, each got off to their imaged 'nice lonely spot'.

Chapter 13
Laburnum

One's cheer up gifts for Laburnum included a mechanized golf cart for getting her out to ride around the vineyards, but my carefully planned idea was met with surprising ungraciousness when Laburnum elegantly condemned it as 'a light-headed luxury!'

"Think of it as a mechanized cart for the Runditz Winery, Laburnum. For anyone that's ailing, or it could be helpful for making haste to a 'Porta-Potty'," one persuaded.

"We've managed without that, and it does us all good to walk," although she smiled glancing down at her leg cast.

"Well, as you mustn't walk much yet, before one takes it back, let's try giving Paycock a 'walk' with it."

"Good grief, you don't mean you want me to get in it! Won't it be bumpy?"

"No more than a golf cart if you'll trust one to select the smoother tracks?"

One had no intention of returning this marvelous 'Gadabout' as I'd named the machine to Reb, Sylvia, and Mel, who were all amused with it. These three happened to be outside at a picnic table lunch break when Laburnum was finally persuaded to take a short ride. Hobbling out using a single crutch, she refused my help as she climbed up onto this Runditz Winery vehicle with even a touch of grace! As one got in beside her and started up the machine, Paycock too was fascinated and happily sprinted around us. All this was entertainment to the lunch table group and other summer-time help at the second table, who called to us encouragingly and waved us off!

Taking a grassy tractor track that came out from between the barns, Laburnum held on so tightly, her whitened fingers curled her 'Gadabout's' seat; but when the ride didn't prove to be bumpy, she got used to her very first proper outing since before her accident; and turning to one, she *couldn't stop laughing!* Discovering this adventurous new freedom to be quite safe, her laughter abandoned; her trills scaling plentifully! Recklessly, she went on laughing, despite her prior scorn, with the richness of her once well-known laughter peals—with all those mystifying tones that prior to her accident one had found so various and beguiling! Little scales descending riotously deep or rising into a sudden set of broken belle canto chirps that thrilled one. Having done all I could to persuade her to come on this trip, this earned success was making one feel quite wicked! In fact, Laburnum's unexpected joy made me so ecstatic, my own amazed laughter quickly joined hers. A joy that loaded one with the belief that on such a fine summer's day, it was surely one's forte to be driving this buoyantly happy woman, though *mind* the ruts! After all, Laburnum may laugh, but she was still recovering.

Maintaining Laburnum's unexpected 'Gadabout' acceptance became all one concentrated on with everywhere looking so sunnily beautiful, almost beyond articulation! Even where the recent heavy rain had blanched the mid-day's long sun-doused lake views. Keeping one's maneuvering slow, with Paycock leaping ahead, not caring how humid and hot it was. He ran circles and checked back at us as Laburnum's retrieved spirits imbued her with an ostentatious radiance as the sun glowed on the smooth skin of her pronounced forehead and cheeks; and with her skewed glasses, a returned look of Laburnum's true former self more fully rewarded. As did her shirt buttons incorrectly fastened, making its frontal gape hard for one to avoid seeing her well-filled black lace bra. Coming to a wobblier downhill track, one slowed into the shade of this slope's trees till we were stopped by a stream and sat happily just looking at where our tractor path would have continued if we could have forded the stream and gone up the opposite steeper side before it turned off abruptly. One cut one's successful new machine's engine; and without its hum we remained sitting, looking around in this cooler tiny valley at this peaceful little spot, adjusting our hearing to the summer's buzzing stillness enriched by a cardinal's two-noted greeting.

"Oh thank you, Algernon!" Laburnum gushed. "I must say that was an amazingly comfortable ride, thanks to you for steering so nimbly and moderating our speed; and I have to admit—well, I'll just say—I can't tell you what a relief it is to get out like this! Really thrilling! You might have guessed I would be after being so cooped up, but I hadn't expected it to be! Oh, this is really wonderful!" And laughing now at her girlish enthusiasm, she gave me an insouciant glance, "I can't think why you thought I wouldn't appreciate it." Her closed-eyed grin. "And while I'm at it, seriously now, I do appreciate all your thoughtfulness during my recovery, Algernon." And as she wasn't getting my immediate response, "Am I coming through?"

All I was answering was 'Hmm'.

"'Hmmm'. You aren't accepting my appreciation?"

"You don't need to be so appreciative, Laburnum. We'll all benefit from this machine, and everyone here wants you strong and healthy," as one was very glad she was becoming companionable again.

"But you should know?"

"I do sense."

“Oh but sensing’s not enough! Ha, though I must say I like the personal pronoun!” More unconsciously, lately I wasn’t as likely to refer to myself as ‘one’. “Algernon, may I ask? In your career, were you used to people not expressing their appreciation when you were kind to them or gave gifts?”

This pert question of Laburnum’s got one thinking. I was apt to tighten up when she asked a question, as her questions were often far too personal. I wasn’t ready for this American extroversion. Then thinking about it, it had only been one’s sister-in-law Jasmine who had reacted with any gratitude if anyone helped out with his belligerent father, and as for his Father? Appreciative? Of anything? Never! Or Gilmore? Highly unlikely! And out at the missions, having laid gifts beside formal dinner plates of consulate wives who were politically aware of his presents, he recollected that they hadn’t thanked him either.

Algernon and Laburnum had been sitting awhile in this curious medley of gently flowing water and the cardinal’s jubilant song.

“You are comfortable?”

Checking down at her cast, Laburnum assured me she was. “It’s all inside that lower leg now, which even if I don’t take my chloroform pill, isn’t as painful. My ankle’s taking the longest.”

“Yearning to flex?”

She nodded looking the loveliest I’d seen her in the undulating branch shadows. Unaware that she looked seductive too, with those glimpses of black bra making one’s eyes wobble till hoping she thought I’d been studying the cardinal as one quickly raised them. It was a pleasure to us both to just sit here contentedly with the other’s presence and so much looking summery under the dappled light and the dusky shade of an ancient apple tree. Our entertainment was multiplied by a flown in woodpecker testing his virtuoso castanet above us on a dead apple bough, that one also studied, if one wasn’t desultorily watching Paycock paddling the stream, intent on finding deeper water to slake his thirst. Breaking these tranquil moments I asked, “Laburnum, you don’t have to answer this—after all, it is your right.”

“Am I completely returned to my studying yet?” Assuring her that I certainly wanted to know if her work was compelling her again, but no, this time she hadn’t read one right! What I’d had in mind when she so discourteously interrupted one, which she did again, was: “All right, I know what you’re going to ask. What was I doing on a moonlit night in a woods three miles away from Runditz’s?” Having rightly guessed what I was asking, she remained looking out over her cast, then at me. Smirking, I waited for her answer. “You’ve done so much for me, Algernon, I owe you an explanation. Most of all for letting me stay on here.”

“That was a convenience for me too and has little to do with why you were roving that far off where coyotes or even bears might have come across an injured, frightfully helpless woman.”

She laughed, “Bears or coyotes have other agendas. But do you really want me to get into that? I mean *why* I did it is a story—an all or nothing type of story.” *Algernon old chap, what are you getting into?? Was this really what you want as a lowliness example?* She went on, “I ask because you might regret it, taking time.”

Born ever to be polite, “That’s fine,” one uttered, nodding, *well and why not? I’ve taken the afternoon off anyway, and I get along with Laburnum.* The next nod I gave her was to get her to start, as she re-arranged her other leg; and then, for a reason I didn’t bother to fathom. *I was suddenly, most incongruously, giving my attention to one’s earliest young dreams of ‘husband ideals’! As images of those ideals bombarded*—but just now?! *Why? It surely wasn’t because one was ready to mean far more to Laburnum*—was it? *No, rather, the flashes from those long ago rapturously envisioned youthful ideals were because of all one had longed to so sweetly and biologically experience with a woman. Naïvely? Youthfully, must be! Because of all one had once dreamed of idealistically that had been outrageously snuffed and publicly mocked by Succubus Francesca! Which could still distress! Though I wasn’t sure why I hadn’t prioritized putting a stop to all that! Could it be that right now I’d been assuming one could re-develop an esthetic interest in another woman? Or that there was any possibility that one’s feelings might matter to Laburnum*? *Though was I being wise to get interested in getting so dangerously close to this woman beside him who kept prying into what was personal when she was only recently a friend? Didn’t all this seem a bit too pushy?* Gauche?

All these concerns aside, his old Eton-Cambridge irrefutable gentleman’s training et cetera made him assure her not to worry about time, and that of course she had his fullest interest. *Was that what he’d meant?*

With an accepting nod, Laburnum leaned back to rearrange her good leg while forming her story to start it, but then, “Some years ago, I was waiting to get my hair trimmed at a beauty salon. Bear with me, Algernon; it may not sound like it, but I am getting there.”

“One expects some preamble.” *Though for God’s sake, don’t take all afternoon.*

“Another customer and I were both after the same magazine,” she’d got it going. “The front cover was ‘Metaphysics – Miracles or Illusion?’ This woman and I had been talking, and I found that—‘Tillie’ was her name—Tillie did palm-readings and went to meetings for ‘Paranormals’, as we call ourselves. Yes, Algernon,” to my quick questioning head turn to her, “there are small groups of us, and yes, to answer you, there was a good reason for our meet on that lousy accident night. Tillie's sister had been badly beaten up by her husband. Witnesses caught him beating her and called in help. She and her six-year-old son fled to relatives, but the brute husband caught the boy coming out of school and took him off with him—somewhere." Laburnum's fine hands arose helplessly, unknowing. "No one knows where. Tillie's sister had custody of the boy, and the police and truancy people were after this kidnapper; but as he passionately hates his wife, the fear is that by harming the boy, this crook would get back at Tillie's sister. That's the kind of crank he is. Tillie's sure that the boy wasn't with relatives or friends, nor had the school seen him; so to aid her sister, what could Tillie do? She phoned two other mediums in this area as well as myself, and we all met. Now this may be apparent to you already, but its best you know, Algernon, that our group concentration is always best if we keep what we're doing just between ourselves. At that meet up there in the woods, away from everyone, we got some potent concentrating going using the kid's pencil case and his matchbox car—little possessions."

"The results of that meet?" *Uh-oh, was I getting sucked into this?*

Laburnum shook her head. "Nothing! Tillie came to see me at the hospital, you remember, and told me that our friends had made other night-time efforts, but so far… not a thing."

"The boy's little possessions? Did they give you an idea whether he's being held nearby or far off?"

"Tillie and another medium, Fergie, think they might be narrowing it."

"Surely, the state police?"

Laburnum shrugged, "The police are onto it, but they say their authority is undermined if we get into it."

"Unconscionable when a helpless child is at the mercy of this lunatic."

"It happens though, and the husband might be a psycho-case, but he has enough wit to cover his tracks."

For some time, I had been eager to understand all one could of occultism, but I'd only wanted to learn about it from big-name clairvoyants. One liked and admired Laburnum but was hesitant about over-involving with this odd woman sitting beside me so cozily. Who, one remembered, despite her proudly proclaimed dislike of his 'Gadabout', had actually made it out of her apartment to clamber up on it, bad leg and all and liked it!

Laburnum's clairvoyance dealt with a segment of the psyche that I knew existed, because I couldn't deny the metaphysical on certain extraordinary occasions. Most of all with my overwhelming confrontation with the incredible Supreme Habitat! A monumental mystery that maybe I'd never understand. Then long before that, while examining a museum's ancient Mid-Eastern sculptured jar, I'd experienced vivid perceptions… exotic images of unrelated scenes from Egyptian history; and though they'd been dramatic, I couldn't get them to come clearer, yet a history book verified those scenes and so those joltingly strange moments had indelibly stayed with me.

Laburnum was staring out at Paycock as she went over Tillie's sister's story that she had so blithely related to this ex-Foreign Service diplomat, named 'Algernon'!

"Well, you certainly had a reason for being in the woods that night, Laburnum. Awful! But this doesn't explain how you discovered that you yourself had clairvoyance. Was it through some unusual event?"

"All right, yes, the original cause?" *Nodding to get her to gi*ve it. "As an adolescent, I lost one parent when my father had a fatal bicycle accident, and soon afterwards my mother died of heart. They had been a very close couple, and Algernon, adolescence is a terrible time to lose all parental direction in this often beautiful, but just as often treacherous life. Especially if they'd loved you. They had been conscientious loving parents; and without them, I—I went a bit crazy! Desperately missing their love and concern for me, I gave in to an older boy. A girl friend helped me with the abortion as neither he nor anyone else I knew had any notion of how to help."

"You wanted the child?"

She gave me a supercilious look, "You may have noticed I have fairly normal biological feelings!" Grinning, I looked away from her gaping shirt, as she continued, "That was all horrible—hell! But I didn't want to be responsible for some kid going off the rails as I had, so I just made that decision. Grandma, my father's mother, lived on one side of my parent's double-house; and by some miracle, I managed to keep the abortion from her. This solution wasn't ideal, but it was the only way I could finish high school. Grandma sold my parents' half of the house, and I moved in with her on her side, and soon saw that I was in her way. Apart from Dad's death hitting her hard too, she was frail but damned obstinate and so critical of me that I stopped trying to talk to her, and all I could think about was getting away. Look, Algernon," Laburnum turned to face me, "I am remembering your question."

Smiling, I instinctively took her hand—that dratted compassion of mine! But she'd got this going, and as the tragic younger years of an attractive American woman, they were certainly interesting.

Looking at me, she murmured, "Thanks," reminiscent of her similar soft-voiced gratitude when I'd taken her hand in the Emergency Room. Relaxing now she'd got it all going, Laburnum resumed. "We'd lived in Chicago, and as soon as I could take out some of my trust money, I took off for… anywhere! I decided on Central City. My Spanish mom had been a flamenco dancer in Chicago. She was wonderful—slender, flashing black eyes, exotic—accounts for what's left of my dark coloring, doesn't it?" I agreed it did. "I didn't see why I couldn't teach dance. After waitressing, clerking, assisting at a nursery school, and God-knows what else, I landed a job in a dance hall. A sleazy place, as you might imagine; and as I soon got fed up with incompetent guys 'making it big' panning gold, I needed a job that would see me through. Knowing ballroom from my mom, I liked it there well enough. But what really held me together were *books!* They always had. For me, reading was breathing; and it couldn't be just any old book. Father was a museum curator and had always supplied me with challenging reading. On my own, I still read well-written books—self-help—one by a rabbi, another by some wise woman… I forget her name. These gave me plenty to think about idle hours, until, one evening."

"Intriguing, Laburnum, but how did your occult fascination get started?" As Laburnum's eyes softly closed, it looked as if for once I was the one asking a question that was too personal!

Apparently, she was debating about giving her next thought. *Though it might have been the bird-sound stillness, or as he'd been known to be a good listener, though more usually over drinks in a bar, but he liked to think that Laburnum could have found his listening to her opportune.*

Laburnum must have 'seen' what she'd needed to, because her head raised, and she more strongly re-started. "I'd stopped for a sandwich at a diner I'd go to. This was late, not many customers. I ate reading, and when I glanced up from my book, there was my mother sitting opposite me in the booth! Yes, it shook me too! It's hard to accept, I know, but there she was. I tried to study what at that moment I really knew was an apparition. But her black-eyed gleam had impact, even as I accepted she must be some freaked excess of my imagination." This move into this delicate intimacy of Laburnum's story had a dizzying effect on me. I'd been used to sharing sacred secrets, with a man, classified mainly, yet I hadn't known this spiritual side of a woman.

Daring to look at her, one saw that my unusual good friend needed to compose herself. I rubbed her hand, desperately sorry for all the trauma she'd known. After a deep breath she said, "Well, this is what happened; my dearest mother had far too much she needed to say to me; in fact, she started in advising me the way she had long before, yet—hey, Algernon," she momentarily came too, "this was way out there in Central City!" As Laburnum gave an incredibly tight little laugh, not only had Central City seemed like an outrageous place to meet this phantom mother, but was she also having trouble giving this very private and sacred experience to her new landlord.

One was going through a range of conflicting feelings. Particularly as she had aroused my old instinctive ache to really want to care and help this woman, who had undergone more adversity than her share. Though, as usual, was my compassion ahead of me? This woman was from the world of women one hadn't allowed himself to know; though instinctively, he moved her hand between his, "Laburnum?"

She shook her head, refusing what she knew was my over-concern, and as her hair swung forward, and she gave it that odd little hand toss, suggesting its luxuriance again, she said normally, "I'm okay, Algernon." Retrieving this image of her more tangible, black-eyed mother sitting opposite her in the diner's booth, she said, "All I understood was, it was imperative I listen to my mother. And why wouldn't I, who else was interested in me? My instinct was—*I must not let her go!* My good parent's concern for me was my only hope of getting along in my job, or getting along anywhere or with anyone, and I can't tell you how much her words embraced and consoled. How often I've referred to her phrases, which bound around me like a huge soft shawl; and the amazing thing was, as she spoke she became—seemed—substantial." Some more conventional part of Laburnum knew that I wouldn't entirely swallow all this, but sensing that my intensity was turned to her, knowing without looking that my legs were doubled up so one knee supported my arm and my chin, she did glance up to see that I was looking down thoughtfully and was honestly wanting all she could tell me. "Mom coaxed me to read up on what was going on out there in Central City and the Indian lore before Europeans."

I was mostly listening as Laburnum continuing to bare what was so quintessentially this most unspoken and secret self, but heavens, hadn't she already pulled off veil after veil? Wasn't it mainly that I was unused to this kind of talk? Unused because of her gender? I'd experienced Telford's extraordinary core secrets—God, hadn't I? That time we'd believed to be fatally trapped in the corner of a collapsed building that was continuing to collapse—Telford, a man! Telford's inmost thinking absolutely scorching, though should it have been? Then, hadn't there also been hints of special secrets back with one's mother's innuendoes.

"That historic rush for gold," Laburnum was keeping on, "my mystery mom had been encouraging my love of history!"

"Ah yes," I murmured, as I coughed myself free of my own need for contemplation. Politely, I re-connected to my loquacious companion, seeing her supernatural 'mother' advising Laburnum to get into history—which had been the seed of the 'civilizations' studies she was delving. I realized, understanding it, just as her voluptuous voice had lost its variants, because unconsciously she had been distancing to stay with this rare experience of her mother.

Lost to Laburnum's emotionally super-charged story, I couldn't put words to how profoundly I was being affected by her 'lowly' soul-unlocking. Womanly Laburnum certainly was, though she hadn't shed a tear! Rather she held herself unnaturally taut, the tapering fingers of her left hand in mine, activated by an irregular nerve. This return of hers to her impressive spirit-visit had risked anything else it might upturn, I saw; and as she struggled to complete her story, I knew a difference to her presence here beside me and saw that my overview of her was needing to be changed. She was no longer the paranormal oddity in wonky glasses seen around the estate. Next to him this new Laburnum was a more sophisticated, intense, fully-lived woman, of maturity and well-focused intellect, because she had willfully squared with her miserable fates and all that had plummeted her into her 'civilization' studies here at Runditz's. One hoped that this remarkable woman, having told so much that was indecently intimate, may have risked it because she found him more than usually companionable? This woman with her carelessly gaping shirt. *Watch it, Algernon old fruit, be wary of all you're getting into—you've some way to go to become 'your own man in retirement', running a profitable winery.*

Aware she had moved her hand from mine, I saw it was because she needed to quash a tear or two from her eyes, though she wasn't into an all-out cry. More she was mustering some strength. "I've talked far too much."

"I'm very grateful to you for confiding in me, Laburnum."

Reinforced, she nodded. "My mother's 'visit' was so impacting, I badly wanted to know more about it." She relaxed. "And there you have it! That's how I became involved with the sixth sense, Algernon."

"Truly, I'm glad to know much more about you."

"I have never doubted that mother-experience, though I was being shown that I needed to comprehend it. To verify it, I think." Laburnum paused, looking tired, and as she slackened her position more and finished, "There, that's it! Anything else is just morbid stuff."

"Though you got your degrees?"

"Well, yes, that's where the rest of my parents' money went. And, should you want to know, my dancing attracted a gentle sweet guy out west there, and we got married. He was called up for Vietnam and not long afterwards was sent home in a body bag."

"I'm so very sorry, Laburnum."

Lost to how easily someone's horror became the most incidental that fate could deal to others, as Laburnum stared trance-like past him, till saying, "Well," which she said again, as she shook her head. "Well, as you know my fortunes changed. Hans and Eva put up with my eccentric pursuits… no, not right—they truly encouraged them. You must know that couple's hell-ridden story? To me

Hans and Eva's lavishing kindness made them more than extraordinary people. I hadn't been making it with most people."

"Naturally, you'd lost everyone close to you."

"Yes." Replacing her hand in mine, where my comforting was so helpful that once more she held back a yearning to truly weep.

What would one do if she did get into an all-out weeping? Desperately sorry as I was for her, her tears would demand an instinctive response, and I'd have to dig some out–what? Dig out biological instinct? Because for all that Laburnum was so courageously telling me, I couldn't believe I'd be equipped.

For Laburnum, though it was all past trauma, it could still upset; and she obviously didn't want to put one through what she wasn't handling. I had genuinely involved with her most metaphysical experience, that even to her had sometimes seemed beyond reality and over-dramatic. But sitting beside me, her story had emerged so easily, which I had accepted. Had this made her wonder what more there was to know about one's own worldly remoteness and one's understanding, as I was her landlord?! Given to these thoughts sitting so close to her that the warmth of her breath spread a wealth of contentment through one, though wasn't her own subliminal nudge from her well-practiced independence telling her that she should be treading more slowly with one's curiosity?

Tenderly stroking the back of her ringed fingers, I was looking down past the elaborate pattern of her skirt. *Her skirt!* Shame for any thought that clothing could even enter my head after this woman's moving history. With all this spirituality she had confided in me, trusted me with! One felt contemptible for even noticing her appearance! Her clothes! Though it wasn't in one to ignore disarranged garments, for a fellow who had always been made so mercilessly aware of 'appropriate' gear, Laburnum's outfits—peasant or country-artistic—were attractive enough and well-thought-out; though like her skewed shirt-buttoning, it simply didn't occur to her to put them on with care! Truthfully, I knew that her appearance shouldn't matter because more importantly, she had chosen to answer my question about that midnight paranormal meet, and to me it was this area of *herself* that was changing her.

One felt a tug of admiration that she could give her private story so fully and vividly. My meager experience of this woman, who had societally fought so much of her way, had led me to appreciate the strength she had to have developed. Though, could I be being too bowled over by Laburnum's traumatic youth, her young widowhood? One's compassion, again! After all, women in vast droves had undergone catastrophic suffering, which he had known of in bouts, more than theoretically. Using my rank, I had done my share of rousing the high commissioner into more action for those saddest of women, much as my empathy had struggled in me to aid them far more; but as other urgencies followed, they'd had to be noted as numbers and visitations if I was to spread myself through the over-filled immediacies of the next day. Laburnum, though having also been alone, was surprising him by demonstrating a good deal of her 'lowlier new insight'.

Although this woman had amazingly trusted me, I would keep my head. I had no doubt of the legitimacy of her story, which continually fitted in with Laburnum and her driven great quest. Yet to keep a fair balance, one saw one must keep seeing it from all aspects.

As a man who had loved his freedom from that life-wrecking succubus—that one still wouldn't elevate with the word 'wife'—undoubtedly, this had given me an abnormal appreciation of my freedom.

If I was to understand more about women like Laburnum, I would need plenty of time and loads of peaceful lake-watching to honestly get to know my reactions. Getting to know this past of Laburnum's, so essentially of America as well as of this particular woman, which still wouldn't part from that voluptuous voice of hers and its secret overgrown tendrils that could do a job of curling about one's intestines… de-oxygenating them, re-energizing them? *Though how could one forget her careless dressing?* Again, it was still his wretched compassion that drove all he did and saw, and this time it had driven him to dive headfirst into the poignant intricacies of this attractive woman's spiritual past.

It took some moments before I could come up with what I believed was an appropriately conversational remark, then, "During World War II, Laburnum, I knew spiritualists that under dire circumstances made telepathic contact with those they loved back home. Do you think it's when attachments have been exceptional like that, that the extrasensory operates? My observation was that these tragic connections gave their bereaved kin some incentive for hanging onto their own mortality."

"I'd like to know more about that sometime, Algernon. Yes, I'm sure dire situations play a part or cause them."

"How much is desperation, and how much a consequence of grief? Perhaps we'll come up with more about this." After some moments, we looked at one another and having been so filled with what had not been of our lovely tangible surroundings, we both eased into properly seeing one another and smiled. I said, "You've had to work limitlessly to overcome all that. It's especially generous of you to tell it me; and if ever one over-steps with insensitive questions, because there'll be a time I may ask more, I trust you'll stop me!" And as her landlord again, "But for now, this has made you tired, and you've missed your afternoon nap. One can't be the cause of setting back your recovery."

Giving an extremely long relieved exhale, Laburnum said, "I'm glad you know it now though, Algernon; though—I have to say—yes, getting into my sad story with you wasn't… it wasn't thoughtful of me. I shouldn't have emptied it out on you. You've obviously been around so much during all your spectacular years."

"Your American growing up and maturing is new for me. Yes, I've been with some horrible situations from within that machinery of government reinforcement."

"On this scale though?"

"Not one-to-one though. Right," given skeptically. "Even so, I've greatly needed to know much more about the fuller range of individual human experience."

"I've talked much… too much, Algernon."

"No."

"After you'd asked how I'd become clairvoyant, as you were already so greatly a part of here at Runditz's, I didn't want you to have the wrong idea of my night meets—that's all! And you should know too that I'm perfectly capable of shutting myself off if I choose not to answer a question!" Nodding while looking harder at the iconic designs of both the rings on Laburnum's youthful fingers. "Everyone should take care who they give their most personal stories to, don't you think? Transcending events are our personal treasure trove."

Looking around this little valley, then back to studying her rings, I said, "Yes, sooner or later you find out what's most precious." And needing to temper her regrets, "You're a good friend, Laburnum, and deserve equal honesty." Though becoming diffident again, I turned to look as if I was studying Paycock still paddling the stream as timidly, I said, "One prefers that this isn't for general consumption, but as you've been so forthright in allowing me to know your remarkable American story, Laburnum, I'd like to offer you this for you to think over. One hadn't noticed this happening until recently, but when one is with women, maybe you can tell me, is it possible that one might become 'bewildered'?"

"*Bewildered*?" Her peals of voluptuous laughter again, "I should say you do!"

"What do you mean, I do!" I said dumbfounding. "You're supposed to think that a retired European ex-diplomat knows all there is to know about the world, and all that's in it!"

Laburnum's hand gave that familiar push back to her hair as she struggled to become serious. "We all thought you fabulously worldly when you first came here, you know. You may have guessed that behind your back we referred to you as 'His Lordship'."

"No need, one prefers not to use one's title!" A little snort came from Laburnum! "Though one hopes that your first impression wasn't all wrong?"

"You've retired into entirely different days for a man knowing women, Algernon, which you must be discovering. But, hey, you've shared tables with princes and presidents, how could you not be worldly? Though as you're insinuating, for all of that, areas of humanity do get missed. It could be that your close experiences with women or with one specific woman," glancing him with that checking look of hers, her eyes shining outstandingly, "or some relationship that may not have allowed you into the depths of each other's gender."

My look back at her must have showed I wasn't sure one was hearing her correctly—but then on reflex, I had no doubt. "By the shoes of St. Peter, one will have to watch out for that blasted sixth sense of yours, Laburnum!"

Her laughter wouldn't stop. "Promise! I promise I'll never use anything I 'see' of you adversely, Algernon! Please believe me, I just *would not!*" Then in a restlessness that made her change her good leg's position. "Oh shame, Algernon! I hate to be the one to put an end to this unforgettable ride, particularly when I've done all the talking, but I must admit you're right; I am feeling a twinge or two. Could we have more of your miracle machine?"

"'Miracle's' a bit."

"Believe me, it's nothing less when you can't walk properly!"

Recalling that I'd been the one to successfully 'see' that Laburnum would appreciate my 'Gadabout', I re-lived this satisfaction again while starting up the machine. The purring engine alerted Paycock, and he paddled out of the stream. The setter came out tail-wagging, mouth-dripping, and muddy-pawed to bounce over and sit happily obedient, expecting Laburnum to produce her pocketed treat, which she couldn't deny him. Then knowing she was tiring, one drove Laburnum around the outside boundaries of the vineyard tracks, jubilant with our exhaustively fuller knowledge of one another.

Heading south, we came out on the path we had seen Rafferty home on that dark night. As the ride stayed steady, after Laburnum's little zap at one's 'bewilderment' with women, I'd needed to remind myself of one's higher esteem from one's former world; and that Thadd and various secretaries had often assured me that one was a fascinating conversationalist with 'resourcefulness and delightful masculine charm'. One had rarely doubted that one's company was much sought after because it had been born from one's mother's chamber music and other refinements which had ever since kept him checking for a good Prom or a La Scala opera, occasionally an art exhibit. 'Bewildered' as he might occasionally become, as a cultivated man, I was certainly not dead to at least this elevated level in women. Though it would have to be another time I'd think more about this because we'd come to the bramble areas with odd ruts and to keep the ride smooth, one had to lower the 'Gadabout' to a crawl. Driving was necessarily important with Laburnum—she would be bound to tense for the rock Rafferty had stumbled on. Though coming near, it showed easily in the semi-sunlight; and as one gave it a wide berth, Laburnum and I exchanged victorious smiles!

In sight of the barns, with the picnic table groups back at work, the lawn area looked subdued where I parked 'Gadabout' to the side of the visitors' cars. Laburnum didn't rush to get out. Instead, she was into a fatigued gaze at the sky and remained sitting. Looking up too I saw what she did—a flock of sea-gulls gliding in equally measured distances, typical of this time of day; their random pattern stunning against a sky of blinding cerulean. Multi-glides as the gulls descended well out over mid-lake, the shadows beneath their bodies and wings outdone by their gilded sunlit luminosity and whiteness. An inspired ritual, with the birds' wild-whiteness picking up distanced dabs of sun-braised cloud that could be mistaken for crocheted lace.

Putting a hand out to help his slower, more special new friend to get out, "Come on, Laburnum, no one's at the table; you don't have to perform!" She gladly accepted my arm, with an 'I'll get back at you' smile; as observing her descending, I saw how much she had run out of steam. Guiding her and her dragging great leg into her apartment, she dropped down on her sofa heavily. "Best if you lie down."

"Yes, I will. But, oh, it's such a damned effort!"

"How about if one lifts the weighted leg?"

"I would appreciate it. Ge-ently though." Lifting her cast with exacting care as she rested back, I placed a cushion under her knee. "Comfortable? Another cushion? What about a drink? Lemonade?"

"Would you mind? Pour one for yourself, Algernon, Sally-Anne keeps the glasses in the left cupboard, over the sink." Coming back with two full glasses, they both relished its cool nippiness. Sitting across from Laburnum's legs, I observed her childlike foot that had tossed its sandal off onto the carpet. Like her finely tapered fingers, this tawny foot was disproportionately delicate and small, irresistibly ornamented with gold anklet and toe ring.

"Don't look at my awful table-legs, Algernon. Father had them too. Nothing I can do about them."

"You don't need to with fine feet and hands like yours—topping!"

"*Topp-?* Ha, nice of you."

"Here, let me put your glass down," I was watching it lean in her hand. "Thank you for a prized afternoon, Laburnum. But no more talk now. Just sleep."

Leaving Laburnum for what I hoped would be pleasant dreams after their enlightening exchange that continued on in one.

Back at the house, energized by one's unexpected afternoon, I automatically grabbed gloves for returning to the row after Mel's down in the lower vineyard.

Feeling a shrill sensation of—*what?—personal renewal? Fulfilling information?* Knowing a good deal more now about my scholarly neighbor, one was into a happiness I was sure had also been expanded from deep within one's 'Supreme Habitat'. As if on a prescribed aphrodisiac, stepping along breezily, every stride exhilarated and purposeful, one got there all too quickly, with one's good strong tenor swinging fully into some favorite Handel. "The trumpet shall sou-oun-da da da sound. And the dea-ead shall be raised, be rai-ai-aised, be rai-ai-ais-ed, be raised incor*rupt*ible!"

"Hey, man, oh man!" came from Mel behind me, "Get some beat into it, and you'd make a peso or two!"

Smiling, one finished this glorious aria and got down to work.

Maintaining Hans's manual method of weed killing, I stooped beside some boisterous leaf growth aware that after one's lengthy sit on the 'Gadabout', my unused joints were taking a while to move—though damn it, one wasn't *that* old! Pushing it, I soon engrossed with this non-chemical weed-killing appreciated by lakeside residents for keeping beautiful Lake Seneca clean. Yet with so little rain, some weeds had welded into any cement-dry earth till forearms and shoulder muscles felt the environmentalist cost! Coming to several yards of fewer unwanted plants, I moved along faster before confronting a missed outrageous waist-high thistle and tugged at it, glad that my gloves were leather. Urging it, the too healthy prickly plant roots finally let go of its anarchist soil, as did the next yanked growth of young nettle and plantains. I left these strewn in the path for 'pick-up' while noticing that actions had brought on a warm, freshly glowing overall thought—*how easily I could relax on this piece of land that was passionately becoming 'home', and all that came with it. Which was greatly needed after his enjoyable but heady afternoon.*

While working, I wondered much this afternoon's session with Laburnum had added to my knowledge of lowliness.

Her sad story, and her genuine dramatic telling of it, hadn't let me evaluate how 'lowly' it had been, but wasn't one getting nearer to comprehending 'lowliness'?? After all, what *was* 'lowliness'? Human qualities certainly, though how distinct from former one's of one's own? *Couldn't there be more to defining of what 'lowliness' really was? After all, lowliness, my old, duck-billed-throw-out. God what a name! There'd been some reason I'd so easily become attracted to this elusive attribute.* But Laburnum's story was an example of how much I'd needed to compare the Cholmondley-Rute investments one's own parents had used for raising me to manhood, next to Laburnum's pitiful struggle for her trust money, and all she had financially suffered for keeping body and soul together—making her 'lowliness' unquestioned. *Yet thinking about it, old conniver, adulthood wasn't only more easily attained with money.* There was all that awarded expertise in stocks and bonds, or in great teachers at luminary schools—

major names and qualities to more significant insights, counseling. When these were all there at the press of a button, *how could one deny that professional supporters didn't encourage or even shape one's more valuable propensities?*

Oh listen to you, Algernon, you old leg-before-wicket! Though wonderful how well that 'lowliness' example got put together! Poor old Einstein would have gloried to have had a mind as plastic as that. Glory be, there's no doubt you're getting somewhere with this crucial understanding of how much of the world has lived more variously. Encouragement, old thing, you're certainly on your way!

Just then Mel broke through his self-lauding, "'Pick-up' is my job today if you're wondering." Mel's islands-tinged statement came from closer behind him in the vines.

One nodded knowing it was Mel's turn. As a change Mel, Reb, and myself quite welcomed this tractor-trailer run.

"Your 'Gadabout's' driving okay, Algernon?" Mel asked.

"Cracking well, I'd say!"

"Crack?"

"Though one would like to know what you think of its ride sometime, Mel. I think it has some natural compulsion, but you know machinery."

"Sure, give her a run." Mel was known to take a spin out on his jet ski after work. He kept it at the Henderson's cottage because Hans had disliked its noise and pollutions.

As one continued pulling and tossing weeds, Mel informed, "The motorcycle group were in here again."

"Any trouble?"

"Wanting to picnic! They'd brought their grocery bag."

"You got rid of them?

"Threatened the sheriff, but they'll be back."

"Hmmm, maybe not," contemplating this. Further along the row I asked Mel, "You get into shooting here, in the fall?"

"Hunting? As summer cools, I'll be rubbing up my bow, giving my gun a decent clean."

"Pheasant, is it? Quail?"

"You're lucky to find either. More likely wild turkey, deer later."

"Do you ever think about the wonderful shooting you'd had down in the Dominican Republic?"

"Wing-shooting birds? They've clamped down on the big stuff now—manatees, big cats. Pay enough though, and you'll get what you want."

"You miss that?"

"Not much." Each man had a similar turn of thought, "Hans?"

"Yes, by the way Mel, how did you meet Hans?"

"Huh! You haven't heard that story? Both getting naturalized. I'd wanted to live here, get to know the States, find out if its streets were paved with green backs—and I needed a job."

"It's come up to expectations?"

"Sure! Damn good-looking American babes over here! Inheriting droopy old Bruno! Got a cute modern apartment. Sure, yes, it's cool here! You've seen Laburnum's apartment—mine's even nicer; you'll have to come see it. I like outside work, and you know how it is. There's always vine replacement, row re-wiring, house maintenance, inside or out there's something. Few days are the same, and you've seen you get to know everyone—crews from town, like those guys over there too!" He said this nodding to a couple from town headed for signing out on his clipboard. "Great folks! Yep, even disagreeing, they're grown-up about it. I'll take that!"

I'd hoped Mel would say more about leaving the country he'd been brought up in and coming here, for more 'lowlier' immigration insight. But nothing else was forthcoming as one worked on to the row's end. The afternoon was ending, and I kept on finishing my row in front of Mel, who soon called loudly, "Pick-up time, Algernon!" Most of the hired crew from town had already signed out.

"Two more posts! I'll have them pulled by the time you get the tractor," one let Mel know.

Mel nodded and kept walking. I was staying fascinated by my 'lowliness' comprehension. I'd had a hesitant moment or two when I'd had to accept that plenty of money and excellent ready support was what had put Thaddeus, Hockney, and myself and all our other old sports—on the road to success.

Returning to Laburnum's 'lowliness', *was I right, was ample money and excellent support the key to getting higher up the scale than if you're hard up and 'lowly'? Too simplified?* I saw immediately, because family status played a large role in one's acceptance. One's own superior hyphenated family name had never hurt! And there was a good deal in just its expectation. A prominent family name and its contacts obviously fanned your aspirations, got you on the way to where you wanted to go.

Knocking and going into Laburnum's to get Paycock for his afternoon walk, Laburnum was awake, still lying on the sofa where I'd left her, poring over the Persepolis book beneath her turned on lamp. "Finding material you didn't know?" one asked indicating her book.

"It's a wonder of excellent photos, Algernon! I can ponder a choice one for an age."

Nodding, "Each of these golden ages, Laburnum," I asked, "what are you really looking for in them?

Her thoughtful look up at me let me know how much one's question had already been thought about. Her gaze narrowed. "It's not just that it replaces what was tyrannical, though that's where I'll start. Maybe when a benevolent system takes strong humanitarian steps to make practical improvements? What do you think?"

"Rewards rather than penalties?"

"If the rewards spread security."

"Won't it always come down to money?"

"It didn't with the Egyptians, or with the art exchanges of Bali or ancient China."

"Value systems then?"

"That generate and expand of themselves."

"A tall order, Laburnum. You might say, like the idea behind the freedom of this new world—which debatably has yet to create a golden age as an idea."

"Come on, Algernon, for refugees escaping persecution, this freedom is golden."

I agreed, though at that moment one was being distracted as hand was being overly licked by Paycock.

"Look, keep on with your book, I'm being told I have a dog duty. Let's keep looking at this far-reaching question of what answers the 'golden eras' can come up with."

Once outside instead of leashing Paycock, we two 'chaps' sprinted down to the lake, where I whisked off my clothes down to one's bikini and waded out to swim fast. Needing this cooling off, Paycock swam ahead as he usually did; and after I had got in some hearty crawl and backstroking, I returned to shore. Up on the dock toweling off, little chills of good health pleased one along with my tanned skin's radiance on this darkening late day. Paycock had gone slender with his drenched fur dragging at him as he lumbered out of the water, till giving his full-bodied hearty shake. From dear old nanny's stubborn insistence, one remembered to dry each of my toes before wriggling on one's shoes while listening to a jet-skier going out especially slowly—before the line of buoy-markers protecting swimmers and kayakers.

Tugging on my shirt's reluctance over my still damp skin, in the sultry evening heat one gave a whistle to Paycock, and together we ambled back. Higher up on the hill, one waited for Paycock to complete another of his interminable urinations as I gave it to him male to male that he really didn't have to make such an MGM production of relieving himself. Waiting for him anyway, I turned to look northwards, hearing Mel's accelerating jet-ski, and saw the wide incised curve of his wake as he roared off far out, breaking up the lake's glassy smoothness that still mirrored the late day's soft pink clouds. Without another boat in sight, Mel's colossal paintbrush had created a broad uninterrupted pewter arc—could Mel be giving vent to harbored frustrations? Smiling to myself, I wondered if his great pewter arc could be because of some ‘damn good-looking American babe’.

Chapter 14
The Viticulturist

Laburnum had exchanged her crutch for a walking stick having had her cast removed. Pleased with this improvement, she leashed up Paycock for a cautious walk along Han's gravel 'avenue' for getting used to her insecure freedom. With her return to more normalcy, Paycock wanted her to run him and gave her a sharp jerk. "Pay-*COCK!*" Laburnum yelled suddenly, having to slow before a customer's hood of his screeching car. Shrugging to the driver, she repeated her apologies through her opened window, loudly explaining to the woman who sympathized with Laburnum. Giving Paycock a yank, Laburnum delivered a great deal of her disgust to him as she pulled him sideways to wait by a tree because that car was being followed by another—their friends, it looked like. Letting Paycock know that his disgraceful behavior had headed him for solitary confinement, her dearest pet got the message; and once the cars had passed, she and Paycock, ashamed with his head down, slowly continued up the road. Soon though, another car filled with wine-lovers followed their friends and the passengers happily waved to one another and Laburnum. She waved back because Paycock had quietened, but her pulling and yanking him had made her arms ache; and when cars didn't slow down during the summer's dryness, a dense sprawl of irritating dust followed them that made her hurriedly find tissues to cover her nose and eyes.

One had been watching my recovering good friend through the dust dispersal as I hurried towards Laburnum whisking at the dust irritation, remarking, "Not the best place for you."

"Paycock has been very badly behaved," she replied, "Wrong place. Next time I'll take another route." A third car was coming in faster than was thoughtful as Laburnum grabbed my offered arm, and I guided her back by another maple tree. The driver and his passengers passed them, all waving and smiling; and I waved back before giving them the bounced flat-hand 'slow-down' signal. When the driver got to another speed sign, he did slow down, but then…yet another car! *What a day!* Though this one was a familiar deep blue and going so slowly he would not cause a dust cloud, and they knew it was Hans.

Coming to a near stop beside them, Hans rolled down his window. "Good news! I come to tell it to you," Hans called. "Sigmund, he phoned! Algernon, he much want you to know he will be back here on Friday! Yes, Laburnum!" Holding up four fingers, "Four more days!" Algernon and Laburnum smirked at Hans' typical use of stressing with his long fingers, as their German winemaker's news much relieved them, though Hans hadn't completely stepped on the brakes; and to hear what else he had to tell them, one had to keep up a half run as Laburnum gave up and followed, ambling. "Sigmund, his father! His health, it much improved!" Hans called. "Now Sigmund he can return to our winery again! Free now, he want back here!"

Limping along behind, Laburnum called to me, "Everything's okay? Sigmund's fiancée is okay too?"

Algernon passed Laburnum's concern on to Hans as she caught them up. "Static too much, Laburnum, connect not good!" Hans explained. "Couldn't get all that he said, but he tell us Friday. It may not all have been good."

Peering out of his car window, Hans checked back at Laburnum's long skirt and called, "The leg, it good improvement, Laburnum?" Laburnum nodded smiling. At 80 years, Hans' leg pain had reduced him to permanently lessened activity. Laburnum greatly appreciated that at her age, her leg could get better, and she would soon walk much faster. As Hans turned to them in his car, Algernon saw that Sigmund's news had enlivened Hans' tanned face and observed that the gleam to his eyes had become foxy again. *Sigmund's returning?* Living at his cousin's, Hans' worn body got plenty of resting time, and he didn't worry each work phase here as he'd used to. Though the pleased elderly vintner did call out, "Algernon? Is Mel out there for to spread the manure?" Ha, so what had to be done here all through the summer still stirred up old Hans! Algernon assured him that Mel and Garrett were shoveling large trailer loads of rich compost and manure on the vine roots. "Reb and Mel, Algernon, they need to hustle. Get it on before it rain! You two to come to porch?" Hans asked nodding to the private end of the tasting porch. Then giving his two-finger salute, he 'sped' up his car, "We talk there."

"Just ask Mel, Hans," One shouted after him and murmured to Laburnum, "Ha, what's the good! You know he'll look for himself anyway! Though Reb and Mel will let him know that we're not only on time, but that each vineyard is farther along than it was last year." Obviously, Hans had not heard him. But Laburnum agreed, smiling with the fondness they each had for Hans. "He doesn't need to blow a fuse; this weather is holding, and we've been putting in good long days."

Laburnum had tired because of her 'dislocating' dog and giving Algernon the leash, she took his arm. Knowing a good deal more about her since their Gadabout trip, one enjoyed her annoyed but needful affection. She was dragging as I helped her along and steadied her up the porch steps to make their way to Hans at their end table. The three settled, and this time I made sure Hans could hear, "Hans, each vineyard is in great shape, the fellows each say so. We're well along, you've no need to be worrying!" Hans used that evasive look and was deliberately slow to respond, as I kept on, "Look, you read a lot, and you know how helpful a good book can be. I'm going to find you a fine one on special Victorian houses. Anyway, whatever you complain about, you should know that you're looking insultingly healthy!" I very much wanted to keep my old friend's stress eased, as again Hans found other reasons to be concerned about the higher vineyards and parried this with Laburnum, until even Hans looked a little bashful as he really knew he was just re-living old habits.

"Have to discuss room for Sigmund, Algernon," Hans shrewdly changed the subject. "He paid to me small rent for north bedroom. That may not suit your plans. No reason you to do the same, and I no idea what Sigmund he prefer. He knows there're Sylvia's and other beds."

"I'm sure he'll have thought about it, Hans; and if he wants, there's a room here. Your same arrangement is fine with me if that's what Sigmund wants. He and I will work a deal that's convenient for each of us. He's intending to stay in the States now?"

"He want very much to come back here. Always he want to stay in America for plenty years; and now his father's winery goes well again, he concentrate on here."

Finally, they got down to Sigmund's return completely changing all they'd planned of their group-tasting idea, as some of the excitement of Hans' news gave way to concern for Reb and Mel being let down.

A low-keyed excitement had settled over the Runditz Winery. Reb had been getting his Lincoln repaired, and like Mel, both their good-natures had withstood their tasting jobs disappointment because by Friday morning, they and everyone else, knew that Sigmund was about to return from Germany.

Sigmund had kept his dilapidated car in a garage behind Sylvia's Inn, but as the muffler to his rumbling Volvo heralded his arrival, Sigmund, amused with its racket confidently drove up to the porch. Flocking out to welcome him back, Hans, Mel, Garrett, Laburnum, Sally-Anne, and myself, all chuckling at Sigmund's old rattletrap till he turned off his noisy car; and we watched our viticulturist disembark from his motley vehicle. I was surprised by this man of Runditz wine-making repute as he strode up the steps so obviously self-assured, using his engaging smile and his joyous irresistible warmth to greet and embrace each employee. One hadn't expected Sigmund to be as good-looking or as personable and well-turned out—understated jacket, collarless shirt, and de rigueur Italian trousers! Unlike the image I'd formed of Sigmund from Hans, his viticulturist threw out one's preconceived idea of their wine-maker as a quiet dedicated country gentleman type, as one stood back giving way to the fulfillment of this reunion while wondering—*is Sigmund ever going to acknowledge one as his new Runditz employer?*

Bypassed by this thrall of greeting, one continued to respectfully stand back, and I leaned against a porch pillar—one may as well watch this exuberance play out—studying this strikingly fine-looking new employee walking with such a proprietary awareness of his status here. Though, seeing him being so excitedly received, one barely noticed that a distinct melody had started in one's head until it so insistently drummed at me, and I needed to identify it. Giving this tune all my attention, one immediately knew it was. *That wonderful heroic and rapturous grand entrance of Lohengrin in his show-stopping swan-drawn boat! No doubting that's what it was, with all its lofty Wagnerian chords. Unforgettably, a noble welcoming for the great knight in armor of such silver brightness it caused eye-tingling spars. All appropriate enough. But—oh God—* one realized, *Sigmund was another German, and this one Wagnerian besides!* Though simultaneously, it occurred to me, *okay, Algernon, old sprout, with a metaphor like 'Lohengrin's entrance', you're certainly a long way off from being provincial yet.*

This most apt melody and its magnanimous chords kept on in one until one noticed that across the porch Hans had stood to lean his cane and was trying to wave to Sigmund! His good arm was gesturing as he called for Sigmund to acknowledge me, though his calls were being lost in so much joviality.

Signaling Reb to get Hans to sit down, I strode out to stoutly offer my hand to this new wine-maker—beating out Reb to his introduction. As Sigmund turned to mildly take one's hand to shake while saying a few right things, his more affable smile continued, "Then you know where my family is located?" et cetera.

"One knows that region," I answered having toured where Sigmund's family estate was in Southern Germany, as one kept Sigmund's off-hand query turned to me.

"South of the Mosel, *ja*," Sigmund clarified, "Riesling country." As one nodded recalling it, Sigmund looked back over his shoulder to make full use of his entrancing continental charm to release his *Liebe Schwan* as he renewed pleasantries with Mel, while rudely continuing past one as he assured everyone that he was settling back here. "…at least for eternity."

Certainly, Sigmund had the fine facial structure that could fascinate in movie close-ups with his swarthy complexion that decades ago one associated with German POWs—a thought one hastily banished! Refined as Sigmund's rural rearing appeared to be, his polish didn't quite put him in league with the Germans I had known at his country's consulate general; but all who were observing

Sigmund's innuendoes, and his meaningful winks or glances could tell that the winery and its employees had better prepare for some new stimulation!

Sigmund moved to Hans, "Hans, I have already told you that my father's health deterioration was misdiagnosed, praises be! As soon as his pleurisy cleared up, he broke out of his doldrums, like a chick breaking through its shell! Good that I was there though, changes had to be made. The manager, not a good man, not at all, and an old family friend, which is worse. *Ja*, our grandfather is even, you know the complication?" Delivered mainly to Hans, though slightly to me. "Anyhow, a reliable Belgian has taken over. I say 'reliable', because not only are his credentials impeccable, but he *knows* wines! You understand what I mean by 'knows'?' Sigmund's fingers tapped his strong brow repeatedly in that same irritating Germanic habit of assuming everyone too inadequate to catch his meaning. "And he takes time working with employees that have been there for generations! Sometimes that is good, though I got it all much improved in no time; and now, if I say it myself, it is excellent and progressive again! Even Father believes this Belgian is the right manager. I have no doubt that under him the winery will continue to be in good productive working order." One listened to Sigmund explaining all Hans wanted to know.

Unlike Hans, Sigmund had learned his English at so young an age, he scarcely had an accent. One also observed that Laburnum listened attentively to the handsome returned viticulturist, as did Mel, and there was no doubt Sigmund was thoroughly enjoying this role of the 'prodigal returned'. Garrett, never a person to stay still for long, had crept further along the porch to lean on its shingled wall, legs splayed before him. As a man whose mind worked best while physically active, one could tell he was preparing to slip off to the production center or to shovel another trailer load of manure. Sigmund had acknowledged Garrett anyway and was laughing now as he talked bottling with Mel. Nor did Sigmund forget Bruno and Paycock, who pretended to be asleep at Hans's feet while they cocked ears for possible worldly scintillation.

Finally one discussed the Runditz filtration process with Sigmund, though one's winery owner's confidence hovered as I considered it still formative. Later, as we all sat with exchanges surfacing from past underlying relationships, being left out again, I wondered how much there was to know about what had once gone on here. Laburnum, having presented to Sigmund her leg's slow recovery, found that Sigmund already knew about it in a letter from Hans, so she had sat back to become unusually quiet. I could only apprehensively guess how much Laburnum had been Sigmund's most special friend as one continued to study my winemaker's display of fulgurous charm. *Could Sigmund and Laburnum have meant a good deal to one another back when Sigmund had first dazzled this little Runditz Winery family with his wines' knowledge, using his then-fresh continental glitter? It was hard to believe there hadn't been a friendship of some significance between a single good-looking winemaker and the comely clairvoyant scholar.*

A car had rolled in. It was Sylvia, who was not about to lose out on Sigmund's welcoming 'home'! Though as she came up on the porch holding a covered dish, Sigmund did little more than give her a nod, till one realized that their more ostentatious meeting up must have been when Sigmund had retrieved his car from Sylvia's.

Uppermost, Sigmund's return was being met with great relief for his skills' excellence in wine-making, though with this came a new restlessness to the Runditz Winery atmosphere that concerned me. Much as Sigmund was needed here, could my concern be because I'd rarely been upstaged by another man? During one's conflict-negotiating, summit disputes didn't have much chance of being resolved if they weren't also being just as smoothly practiced by their team. Romantic ideals had stayed well-contained—it being needful that romantic staff difficulties got rapidly worked out. Though here, watching Sigmund, *Oh come on, Algernon old fellow, a Cholmondley-Rute doesn't get jealous!* With all one's getting into 'lowliness' though, could I be into an area I hadn't met? *Oh for heaven's sake, surely I was well beyond anything that was grossly without form or was crass.* Although, there had been that time.

That damned aggravating night in an infamous city's smelly slum district, when in the roomful of shapely feminine rentals, colleague Telford had nabbed the only desirable 'ill-reputed woman'!

Being palmed off with the least attractive *fille de joie*, one had refused to open one's eyes to her depravity and treating her badly, one bitterly made rough use of her and got off. Quickly tugging on one's clothes, that had included a disguising flower-pot hat and fake beard—Shame! *For all the angels above, Algernon!* And still soured that the only whore I'd wanted was wriggling away under Telford, one staggered out to sneak through back alleyways and side-streets and eventually slip in through the embassy's trade entrance.

Could this incident haunting me now because I recalled that Laburnum had asked Hans about Sigmund's fiancée?

Innocent enough, unless this saintly Saxon-charmer planned to return to take Laburnum over where he'd left off? A thought that actually stabbed a chest pain in one.

God, I reproached myself—after all, nothing between Laburnum and I had been addressed, so why see all this as so gross and painful? Was one having to understand that in this lower societal level, the subjective 'I' could throw one into a range of human conditions that included jealousy of this most despicably commonest kind? Oh, most omnisciently thoughtless Lord!

Obviously, there was no way one could directly ask Laburnum for her feelings about this man—this—this German exhibitionist! Being a diplomat and British, one believed that the etiquette would have to be—a decently candid woman in a situation like this must feel obliged to let him know her past. After all, Laburnum certainly wasn't a woman to be diffident. This would make it be up to her, wouldn't it? And surely, she could guess how much one needed to know what Sigmund with all his radiant impressiveness meant to her? Wouldn't that be truly honest and acceptable in relating to a decent woman? *Then, for that matter, what did he really know about women—any women? Though no overreacting, Algernon*! One's friendship even with Jasmine, for example, or overseas office staff, had naturally neutered to being professionally hands-off. Sex had to be regulated to a function one kept fiercely separate and only to oneself. Even humorous insinuations could only be made to worldly men such as Thaddeus or Telford.

Later one was alone reading the newspaper in the parlor and behold, there appeared the great white knight off the swan boat himself! Scarcely glancing at one, Sigmund remained standing until with business-like formality he asked his new employer if he might rent a room from one. One had no objection; and in this detached manner, we set up a renting arrangement that suited each of us. With this decided, Sigmund told me that he'd planned to follow Hans into town and pick up some personal belongings. Politely, I got up to see Sigmund off to his car. After Sigmund's percussive car had left, one did what one usually did on afternoons and took the opportunity to visit Laburnum. In no time, I was softly knocking on her door. After Paycock's dutiful bark, Laburnum's "Come i-in!" sounded surprisingly vibrant, though *what if Laburnum had hoped I'd been the Saxon scintillator?* One strode in anyway, "Is this a good time?"

"Ah good!" Seeing it was me, her smile seemed to broaden, "I was banking on your afternoon visit, Algernon!" In relief, one sort of hiccoughed twice. "I wanted to ask you, is your 'Gadabout' free?"

Assimilating what her question could truly mean, one looked hard and lengthily at Laburnum. Looking again, to be sure I'd heard correctly, glory hallelujah! Laburnum was whole-heartedly taking one up on one's swimming invitation! Laughing far too heartily, turning to go, I staggered; then grinning boyishly replied, "I'll see to it, it is! You'll be getting on your swimsuit?" Laburnum raised her correctly buttoned shirt to show him she already had on her bright zigzag-striped swimsuit. Calming my excitement, though out came that squeaky voice of mine, "Just a jiff! I'll get on mine and meet you at the miracle machine." Rampant delighted smiles continued from Laburnum! *Had Paycock smiled too?*

Getting shorts and shirt on over my bikini, in my elation I almost felt what it might be like to have been born an American as one exuberantly 'whistled' a distinctive tune of this country—as owner of the Runditz Estate, one tried 'Home, home on the range'. My whistling was unclear, but the tune came through. After all, one lived here now and would start to use their funny words like 'sled' for a 'sledge', 'robe' for 'dressing-gown', 'alumin-um' for 'aluminium', 'underpants' for 'knickers', which seemed so strange that when in doubt, one never failed to check my handy new Webster's.

With this wonderful hope for retrieving our promising liaison, I still breathily whistled this Americana as one climbed off the pulled-up Gadabout for aiding Laburnum. Instead, she insisted on climbing onto his vehicle again by herself, having handed him two striped towels. Watching her, one went from foot to foot, trying to accept her insistence that independence was her female recovery's due—though when she wobbled, the gentlemanliness in one's hand quickly steadied her. Paycock's tail was wagging in windmill-like anticipation of a lovely long exploring swim with Laburnum too this time, and off we set. Parking by Hans' old dock, we walked along it, Laburnum trying not to limp as she didn't waste a moment pulling off her shirt. One helped her unfasten her skirt, which she let drop; and one pretended not to observe her firmness that showed off her clear oak-hued skin, and the bright zigzags of her swim suit's creasing or stretching around her appetizingly ample curves.

Tentatively putting a foot on the steel ladder, Laburnum turned to me, "Look Algernon, it's sturdy! Still bolted through the dock!" Pleased, she carefully climbed down to stand on the first underwater rung; and with both hands on the ladder, gave it a stern shake, "Look, quite safe!" Thrilled, she let herself farther into the cool deeper lake. Without much wind the last two days, the water was fairly clear, though it was best left undisturbed as excessive mud brought down by the creeks from rain had unpleasantly deepened the silt on the lake's bottom. Awaiting Laburnum getting all the way in, one watched her cautious backing into the water, noticing that she wore a swim suit that could only belong to this witch-woman. One of her bursting shoulder straps was fastened with a large safety pin—a pin that had had been there long enough to rust! I more fully understood that Laburnum was not a woman to be excited by domesticity!

Neither Laburnum's fixed up swim suit nor her nicely contained weight affected her enjoyment once she was in and floating on her back, tentatively letting her head back to indulge in the water's cool freshness. Abandoning to the wonderment of her body's fast-changing temperature, her head raised as she joyously laughed to one while thrashing her good leg and cautiously testing her recovering leg. When Laburnum's laughter coincided with one getting down to my bikini, one felt uneasy—even though in several of the world's most splendid resorts, one's physique had been remarked on as especially elegant.

Laburnum though was varying her actions, turning over to do a slow well-formed crawl; her wet hair falling in points around her shoulders. Giving her a second glance, I was assured of my fabulous swimming partner's intense enjoyment and saw that her laughter had nothing to do with one's European bikini. Paycock obediently sat waiting beside me at the end of the dock. Given the command, he and I both dove off and swam out in fevered circles. Ecstatic with Lake Seneca's waters oozing one's hot body, merged with Laburnum's accepting my invitation to swim instead of hanging around for the excitement of the winery's hottest returned male. And another plus—after all her leg's slow recovery, she had entered the water with ease! Along with the weather and the water's perfection, this day was constantly pouring out lovely assets, like an over-flowing cornucopia! *So this was what 'being with a woman' could be! Oh, at last overtime worked great, Lord!*

Swimming close to Laburnum, I asked "You aren't tiring?"

"Ooh-ho, not possible!" *This was a day of all days!*

All the same, as we continued swimming out, one wondered, *had Laburnum looked all right?*

Suddenly, Laburnum became breathless and flailed! *"TREAD WATER!"* I yelled hurriedly swimming to her. She panicked, but in moments my arm was diagonally across her bosom. "Don't tighten up, Laburnum! Loosen, Go *LOOSE!* You're quite all right, I'm holding you! Loosen this arm too, you'll be absolutely safe, and one will swim you in." Her frown became a grimace because she was a superb swimmer, and her helplessness frightened her. I kept repeating this instruction as she breathlessly panted, trying not to panic; then as the rhythm of one's words got through, she gave in and trusted me—completely—loosening cooperatively. I *needed her to lie so dependently on one as, she simply floated, which I explained again into her water-filled ear while giving sharp propelling kicks to one's strong one-armed strokes for swimming us both in.* With her cooperation, I'd no difficulty recalling my old life-saving technique, boosted by the pleasure of Laburnum's giving in to me and the wonderful feel of her body. Getting her along easily, even with one's orgiastic arm tight across her glorious bosom—*elate only, old Casanova!*

Accompanied by Paycock's concerned snorts, one swam Laburnum safely back to the ladder, where she put out a hand to pull herself up till she stood safely on a lowest rung. One averted one's eyes as I helped her up from behind, and we paused for letting her strengthen to slowly climb further up on the dock. Once she was on the dock, she dropped into a flaccid sitting position; her hands locking around her knees as breathlessly she thanked me before letting her soaked head fall exhaustedly onto her knees. Following her onto the dock as Paycock too continued swimming into shore.

Watching her get back her breath, my hand naturally consoled 'the poor thing's' back as I sat beside my greatly shaken, dripping swimming partner. *With a reputation here at Runditz's for doing a lengthy stylish crawl, her disappointment had to be horrible. But she is all right—she'd made it!* I too needed to calm one's over-exertion. We both just sat awhile resting, pensively staring down, fixing to the water's clearing around the ladder, till into one's viewing came—just below her swim suit line—a white band of something around Laburnum's nearest thigh! *What could this be?* It made one feel awkward. "Laburnum?" I softly started, "I hesitate to tell you this, but I think your swim suit lining is coming apart."

This brought her to, "Where?" Out shot the poor dear's offense as one nodded to her upper thigh, "Oh that!" She exclaimed as feeble laughter got the better of her! "No, that's my panty-girdle! I put it on under my swim suit—I didn't want you seeing how much weight I'd gained!" She said this laughing weakly at her clever trick backfiring, till I laughed too. "Please don't expect me to care too much about such things, Algernon," as her head fell against one's shoulder. "Listen, thanks again," and getting her head more comfortable, "Algernon, I know I got carried away and swam out too far, but I couldn't believe—I'd—I've never had difficulty *swimming!*"

"Your swimming form is excellent, Laburnum, I'd been watching you. Obviously, you're usually a first-rate swimmer."

Regaining her breath, "Thanks. But Algernon. I have to tell you. Until I panicked, that had been one of the most esthetically perfect of all swims." Looking at one another, we exchanged happier recovery exclamations. "Sweltering inside so much this summer, I couldn't do justice to getting into that lovely water! I'll always thank you for this wonderful dip and for your neatest way of life-saving me! It's, now I'm sure I've got this one right, 'It's a calm sea that doesn't always make a good sailor'?" Getting back more normalcy, she asked, "How's that?! Appropriate, isn't it? You must appreciate its shortness. My decision lately, or was it yours, that I'd do better with smaller proverbs?"

"Shorter is better, decidedly," I encouraged, not caring that it had been one's idea because as always, I'd held my breath awaiting another of her embarrassing *'I'm sure I've got this one right'.*

"You're a hell of a strong swimmer, Algernon!"

"We learned swimming early in school. No one can go far on that merry old island before they're at a seaside." My hand still very gently rubbed her back, though the poor dear had got herself through her worst post-panic.

Toasting ourselves in the sun's steady heat, each breathing the air's freshness more calmly after our unplanned additional exercise in the unruffled water. On this blindingly hot afternoon, we noted the appealing bristle to our skin as it sun-dried; and it didn't take us long to get warmed through and for Laburnum to start to feel more herself. She talked up one's rescuing technique while Paycock having thoroughly muddied around the shore's edge, decided that he too could dry off best up on the dock. In an inebriated run along the planks, he stopped stock still behind Laburnum and gave his lake-filled fur a body-long wriggling shake that caused loud objections from both of us drying off!

Mainly warmed through, we both forced a few stern words on him; it was too perfect a recovery afternoon to make more of Paycock's misdemeanor. Miffed, Paycock stayed some paces along the dock, willfully refusing to share his delicious Canidae smell of steaming compost-wet fur by keeping this treat all to himself. An incident he would report to his best dog friends for proving he could stand up to Algernon.

Lazily and sumptuously warmed, Laburnum restarted their conversation. "Algernon, I'm sure you'll get a good new wine now Sigmund is back." One agreed, though I was slow to, but was most glad his 'poor dear' was feeling up to bringing up this subject of Sigmund, and he hoped she would further enlighten him.

With nothing more forthcoming though, I finally remarked, "Sigmund certainly is a dazzler! Laburnum, how smoothly did this place run when he was here before?"

"Both Sylvie and I went through being over-smitten—gorgeous new man, et cetera. Though we don't brag about it as it didn't amount to much, but," she giggled, "she and I had some laughs over it, because we knew that neither of us were what Sigmund was after; and as you might imagine, he'd needed to look farther afield. When he did, he found himself a glamorous Dutch woman over at a Cayuga Lake Winery. This was good for them both as she was well up on wines! The curious thing is Sigmund is supposed to be engaged to a woman back in Germany, though I know she had refused to come to the States, so I don't know how that was left. Yes, Sigmund is handsome and knows it, but it's difficult not to have an entanglement or two during harvest time when we're all seeing so much of one another."

"You've managed to maintain your independence?"

"Other than Hans, you mean? Yes."

"Ha-*ans?* Laburnum! Am I hearing correctly?"

She smiled. "He wasn't always as old, you know! I'm sure I told you that he and Eva helped me a great deal when I first came here. We all worked full days together until Eva got sick; and when she died, naturally, losing his one and only Eva of that former Germany, and that unimaginable escaping to the States, Hans fell apart. He might have seen me as the person who had known Eva almost as well as he had—in this country, anyway. Eva was an intriguing lovely woman who didn't hesitate to say what bothered her until she was very ill. I think, or hope, I had been some compensation to Hans. Our little affair was a comfort to me too, because," Laburnum suddenly chuckled recalling her bond with Eva, "long after the Runditzs had come to the States, Eva became fascinated with Attila and the early Huns! She said it helped bridge the gap to her home country. I guess if you're German, it's not so unusual to want a connection to it besides its recent history. And Hans was so passionate about his rebuilding here, and the skills of the men he hired, that when Eva was under orders to rest, he reluctantly approved of our being Attila-nuts! You know back when the amount of work on this house looked formidable, Hans deserved a great deal of credit for all he'd kept going. I'm sure you've heard more about all this than you want to, Algernon, but it was Eva's insistence on research that gave his fine restoration its authenticity. A habit that had got deep into Hans's brain by the time she couldn't work. What greater gift could a wife give her husband than a high standard for that building that they both loved? I know they thought of it like that."

"No, I can't think of a greater gift. But you, Laburnum, with Hans, you'd ignored a sizeable age difference?" *Wasn't this a very personal question? Then, weren't such questions beginning to lose some of their extreme privacy?*

"I was eternally grateful that Hans and Eva took me in as family, so age wasn't what mattered. They advised me tirelessly and were always kind. You appreciate just ordinary kindness like that when you haven't known it for years. Which is why I'm greatly appreciating your kindness too, Algernon." She said this looking past me at the steaming Paycock snoozing away as she nodded her continuing appreciation. "Hans' vision for the house and winery affected us all, but you know all that. He just doggedly worked through lack of help and his own miserable allergies and arthritic pain. He was exceptional; there wasn't anyone who came here who didn't catch into his envisioning for this place. Many just wanted in on the excitement. Wine-lovers bought liberally; they were often Germans too that liked his wines, helping out a fellow countryman—well, words aren't enough, are they, for that brotherhood that fled Nazism? But it wasn't just Hans' fellow Germans that came; there were many appreciative people around here too. There seemed to be some magic to how much his imagination for the place appealed. Reb's mother, for instance, and her young Reb. Later Sylvie, Garrett, and the many skilled workers, and local youth; and if a larger crew was needed, they hauled along family members. Hans managed to pay each a little money."

"He was very fortunate to have you as a lover-helpmate."

"I never think of it as anything but my good fortune."

Laburnum's easy openness about her and Hans was balm to my secret plausibility of my eventually becoming her lover? Though was that really how I thought? It was dealing with Sigmund's charm that caused one an occasional tightness through the belly. The probability of Sigmund's liaison with a past Laburnum bothered me, it drew a pall over this heavenly little estate. Because surely Sigmund must have had some interest in Laburnum's studies, or with the magnanimity of her 'civilizations' quest. And why, he wondered, was he himself feeling its effect this personally? Ha, it hadn't been the Hans-Laburnum liaison that had given him a belly-ache! Though it was easier to be more sophisticated about that natural annulment. However swashbuckling Hans had once been, and however caring he still might be of Laburnum, one's deep affection for one's 'wine guru', and their shared love of the 'Supreme Habitat', was intractable. Yet lingering on these past intertwinements, becoming aware of all the twists and unveilings that thrilled and depressed *lowlier* human passions—yes, 'lowlier' ones—one sighed lengthily, realizing how easily men and women slid into complex doomed passions. *Complications that protocol or personnel had known how to discreetly settle, only too well—hadn't they Algernon, old sport?*

That evening one sat in my study near the door window view of the lake—that place that always brought one solace. Taking down the 'Hans's album' off the shelf that documented this house's massive restoration, I got comfortable in the upholstered chair and gazed at the excellent opening photo of this sad shockingly ruined showplace as Hans and Eva had originally come across it. Dwelling again on its obstinately remaining corbels, its collapsed skewed fallen cupola, only distinguishable between jagged weathered planks, broken branches and overgrowths of wild vines and other underbrush, until it looked like that walled protection of the 'Beast's' mansion of Grimm's'.

Each of Hans' restoration phases had been carefully recorded with captions, and slowly turning the pages, one sought photos of Laburnum and Hans as they'd looked back then. Hans' blonde wife Eva too, and Fritz—their rugged first winemaker. Also, Reb's much-admired mother was in with them, and he presumed other local people that Laburnum may have mentioned were immersed in work on this hopelessly ruined Victorian villa. *Some pages along in this house's extraordinary emergence, there would be Sigmund.*

Recalling much of what Reb had told me on that first day he'd shown one over this house, using a magnifying glass for details, I saw it was Reb more than anyone besides Hans and Eva who had most profoundly known this house's metamorphosis. Here was a very young Reb with a re-worked porch pillar capitol on planked saw-horses that a very upright, arms-akimbo Hans was giving directions to. Distinctively Hans, with that dominant brow and straight spine. It had to be the blonde Eva at the distant front door, identifiable by part of the wooden acanthus leaves screen. On another page an inside shot of an earlier, certainly handsome and apparently agile Hans removing plaster and lathe with another man—Garrett? Hans had turned to grin at the photographer, carpenter's apron, and its tools slung askew as he'd bent to select from stacks of new lathe, and on to much other documentation of Hans' envisioning being applied by skilled friends and employees.

Neither Laburnum nor Sigmund had been here during these earlier stages. In Laburnum's case, she had come soon afterwards to pick up on Hans and Eva's audacious goals that then grew in various directions into far more than could ever be recorded in this album. Laburnum had darker hair, though otherwise was not too different. One studied these photos right through to this house's present developed magnificence. The whole effect of this album was of a mirage arising out of story-book rusticity, the last pages changing to proud professional shots of the crisply painted mansion splendiferous in all its present subtle Victorian colors.

Transfixed by everything of these lives that had reconstructed one's incredible Supreme Habitat, I closed the book on the resplendent edifice, having to accept that no amount of staring these earlier times into reality could answer my haunting questions about Laburnum and most notably Sigmund. There were photos of Fritz, Hans' first German winemaker. Only one later shot of Sigmund—no doubt it was Sigmund with those arrogantly held shoulders. Though did it really matter how strong Laburnum's attraction to him had been? *How much should I know of Laburnum's private feelings for Sigmund?* One was fond of her, and really didn't mind Sigmund as much now having seen possibilities in him that might become the assets Hans had known. *Good Lord, even if Laburnum had been Sigmund's lover, what was to be done about it?*

Though look Algernon, what was all this mania saying? Burrowing these habitat's photos, these inhabitants all entangled him to the core! *What had one been doing? Come on, Algernon, you nosey old Peeping Tom, what's happened to that reliable, old conditioning of standing away from any situation for seeing what part one plays in it?*

Point taken, don't you know! Righty-ho!

Very well!

Whatever had once interacted between these valuable people here, that one adored now more than his own family—*had they really needed this much studying?* Admittedly, I'd had an agapeic interest in Laburnum, which one may eventually find could be there with Sigmund too—were these the reasons one was after insights into *their* history? Or could I be trying to adopt a more historic view of my own secret Supreme Habitat's pathology to blend into the magnificence of Hans' epic story? *And another important question—was one's over-involving with this album and these special people here contributing to one losing one's worldliness? More honestly, could it be that I, Algernon, like it or not, was on my way to becoming 'provincial'? Beatified parliaments preserve one!*

At least as worrying too was this fervent private question that so often bugged him, *was I yet again trying to comprehend how one could have built my enchanted Supreme Habitat during those interminably boring Moscow staff meetings, while in actuality the exact edifice had been lovingly materialized over here in this country? Wasn't it always this incomprehensible metaphysical experience that one's inebriation kept stumbling upon?*

Losing one's 'worldliness', this wonderfully valuable part of him could be what was casting him into this annoying 'provincialism'. Dearest Lord, high up there as You are, one had tried one's utmost to confront all this, surely as much as any immigrated British male. Though in one's case as an immigrant, one's aristocratic lineage and a certain amount of wealth should have triggered one into more... But...

NO! There must not. There cannot be any provincialism!

Worldliness was an intrinsically desirable part of all he'd ever known. Provincialism must NOT be!

It didn't make sense that the many years of one's worldly high-level vocation couldn't at least have held one together through this... this 'challenge' from Sigmund to one's libido? *If that was what it was.*

Even with Laburnum's kind concern, if I didn't hold on to my finely developed worldliness, it might mean I'd have to do some damned heavy traveling again! Go find another dream diversion somewhere. Far away from here. But *where*, for the sake of all incinerated martyrs? Be off in a safari hat, like Hemingway up in African mountain peaks? Or like Jacques Cocteau become a marine diver and walk about in flippers, exploring unknown marine life deep in the Med?

All I could put together was that one's impalpable slide away from worldliness was to do with my Supreme Habitat's abduction of him. It's seducing him by emulating my priceless boyhood's happiness! That once-in-a-lifetime unforgettable rapture. Closing Hans' album, I stared out at the lake. How had I ever let one's personal management slide like this into such enveloping arbitrariness? What was it? Was his Cholmondley-Rute spine made of coconut milk? After all, wasn't he at least gaining some bearings from within all this new 'lowliness'?

Unless Sigmund?

Giving up I sighed and left the study to take the curved stairs, tread by each wide-wedged tread, one's lengthy lower legs alternately pushing to get my weight to rise. Before my bedroom's wash-basin, I rinsed off my face several times in cold water, aware of its pleasant coolness as I checked my fatigued sculpted features in the mirror. Shoving my feet down inside the bedclothes, I reached for *The Sound and the Fury*. If one lost oneself in that ruined old wealth of Faulkner's hierarchical family in their crumbling antebellum mansion, and on through the woven intensities of its various inhabitants, once that fabulous southern chorale deafened one again, maybe I would find resolutions to one's own nagging questions.

Chapter 15
The Birthday Party

Having shoveled manure with Mel and Garrett, I removed my messed boots at the porch door and stood them among others on the rubber trays. Cleaning up in the study washroom, one was intrigued with the laughter coming from the women in the kitchen. Needing a cool drink, I went in to find Sylvia, Laburnum, and Sally-Anne whispering and giggling as they dealt with dishes and utensils spread over both counters for tonight's birthday feast. I caught the name 'Sigmund'.

"What's going on?" I asked offering them ice-water and setting up four glasses,

Laughing incredulously, Sylvia glanced at Laburnum and Sally-Anne before telling him, "Sigmund's Dutch wine-making woman has a new handsome hunk lover, Algernon! I mean some huge muscular weight-lifter that sent Sigmund packing!" And as I didn't react, "The brute threatened to mash Sigmund to hamburger if he showed his blank-blank-ing face over there again," she explained. Then Sylvia's amused expression dropped, and instead a look of real worry for Sigmund changed her. "It's too bad! Though Sigmund shouldn't have expected a woman to hang around waiting for him without an understanding. I'm right, there wasn't one?"

"I'm not sure," Laburnum said more intent on digging out the eye of a potato.

"I don't think there was," Sally-Anne agreed.

"Wouldn't Mel know?" one asked.

"Why would he?" Sylvia asked.

"Being another single, you mean?" Laburnum said. "God, there's a different smell in here since you came in, Algernon. Though," taking her glass, "thanks for the ice-water."

"It's the manure on my jeans. Don't despise manure; look at its results on that first vineyard by the highroad, and you'll see how nourishing it can be. The vines are thick with large grape bunches and good-sized dark green leaves. See that and you'll agree manure really has quite a piquant fragrance."

"Mm-m—organic dolmathes," Sylvia was getting taste images.

Sally-Anne had spooned her steaming chopped orange peel, pine nuts and cranberries into a porcelain bowl and was covering it and making a space for it in the refrigerator. Drying her washed cooking utensils, trimly, prettily, she picked up her possessions and got ready to go, smiling at each of them. "Back later with the rolls, you people."

"Laburnum and I'll be here," Sylvia called to her as she tossed her freshly chopped herbs over two frying pans mounded with her sausage, apple, and walnut stuffing; she kept turning it with a bamboo spatula.

Tempted, Laburnum leaned to sniff and watch Sylvia sprinkling the water, "Wow, now that really does have 'quite a piquant fragrance'!" mimicking one so wickedly that Sylvia's strident hoot sent her arm flailing to knock a wooden cutting board to the floor. Laburnum smirked up at me, as I mock-clipped her one. Sylvia and Laburnum's peals screeched at one's 'offense'. Even at my expense, I adored the merriment of these lively American women. "All right, my jeans may not reek of Jean Patou or your stuffing's aroma, Sylvia, but a significant manure smell can make a wonderfully pleasant statement!"

With my 'significant manure smell' seeming to match Sylvia's stuffing, the women suggested some unappetizing dishes more specially for me tonight!

Sylvia gave a long sigh, "Though back to Sigmund, you two. Seriously, you know; now he's on the loose again, I bet there're women in town locking their doors."

"How did you hear about Sigmund and the Dutch woman?"

"Oh Algernon, you should've been there! Last night, madder 'n hell, Sigmund stopped at the inn demanding a stiff drink!" Sylvia explained. "And I'll tell you, no one at our bar missed one snarling word of Sigmund's story, which the guys kept asking him more about, so it got added to! By the time S.P. Martin came in, that Dutch woman's new muscle-man had broken three of Sigmund's ribs, knocked out his front teeth, and left him unconscious."

"God, did Sigmund look that beaten up, Sylvie?"

"No-o, Laburnum, you know Sigmund! Though here's something crazy—have you ever noticed that when Sigmund gets really mad, his eyes go a different color? I mean his gray irises turned purple!"

"Come on, Sylvie!"

"You watch next time!"

"Careful! You'll make him self-conscious."

"Aw, you can't make Sigmund self-conscious. Not when he's as mad as that, you can't."

"It's too bad Sigmund doesn't get along better with Mel," Laburnum observed. "You've seen Mel going off to a dance? He's irresistible driving away in his convertible all bathed and pomaded up!" She made big eyes as her brows raised, conveying how impressive Mel could look dressed to kill—I laughed as I took this in.

"So, here was Sigmund back, womanless again. Wouldn't you think the two guys would hit it off? They used to; didn't they, Laburnum? When they were both on the lookout for women."

"'American babes '."

"Babes, yes! And they both love looking stylish!" Sylvia mentioned. "Maybe you know this, Algernon, but our special Mel has to watch it if he likes a woman. There're still people out in these sticks that only see his skin color. Mind, he's smart, he goes with friends."

"Oh that's oldie-goldie stuff, Sylvie, no one thinks like that anymore."

"Uh-huh," Sylvia's dubious expression turned on Laburnum, "though agreed, it should be…"

"Mel could handle any prejudice without it getting to fists," one backed him.

"Because of his martial arts you mean? He could, yes. And since we're gossiping, do you think Mel has his eye on Sally-Anne?" Though Sally-Anne's car had long since taken off, Laburnum had hushed her melodic voice.

"So what's that situation?" Like them, low-voiced, one used this chance. "Sally-Anne has a husband?"

"I'm sure it's fine, Algernon. It's just that Newt is away so much, there's not the closeness they'd like, but the money is good."

"Oh, it's always the money!"

"You don't think some extra money is worth a bit of missing one another, Sylvie? I bet Sally-Anne and Newt talk it over," Laburnum said.

"Yep, but like Sigmund, it's got to be hard keeping up an intimate relationship at a distance. I never understand how it's done!" Sylvia was awed as she turned, "Algernon," she was struggling to keep one of the chickens up-ended, "would you mind helping keep this bird upright a minute—if your hands are clean? Let's see…"

"I may smell of manure, Sylvia, but I *always* wash my hands!"

"Okay, you're fine!" One held each plump chicken securely by its parted legs for Sylvia to stuff and keep the mix in place with bread crusts. "All I know about a long-distance relationship is, if Reb and I don't see a whole lot of one another, we get imagining all the unholy crap that the other's up to. Not good! I found this out when he took off to build a garage at his cousin's for a whole week. Guess I'm not the woman to partner some commercial fisherman that's out at sea for months."

"Unless he brought you lovely fresh haddock and cod?" Laburnum asked provocatively smacking her lips.

"Delicious crab and lobsters?" One added, as Sylvia shook her head.

"Not even if he was the spitting image of Robert-effin' Redford!" She said laughing as she stood back to survey their preparations. "Okay you two, now everything's set okay, and I'm taking off. Laburnum, you've got the flowers and the crazy table stuff?"

"Don't worry, there's enough in there to make Hans look 20 years younger!"

"Good! Back at 5:30," Sylvia left giving them her little-girl wave.

One looked around, then picking up a peeler from Laburnum's counter, "Very well. Hand me that turnip."

Looking at him wonderingly, Laburnum slowly picked up a turnip but held onto it, "No, you've done your work," she decided, though as he kept assertively reaching for it, she gave it to him. He eyed her for her changed mind before giving the turnip long virile peels. "Okay," she said, "then as you insist, I'll tackle the runner beans." I sat on Sylvia's tall stool as we got peeling, chopping, and tossing the vegetables into the large steamer. "You're tired, Algernon?"

"A bath will set me up."

We worked our vegetables, both enjoying the serenity. Peacefulness like this with the windows open lent us the wholeness of the vineyard's affecting silence. I'd noticed before that this soul-lulling background surfaced more when Laburnum was with me here. Neither of us felt compelled to break it, but then Laburnum did. "Do you miss feasts from back where you were brought up, Algernon? Have I got it right, you're not unusually fond of your family?"

Laburnum's insouciant question made one wary that I could be about to be offended again, as my virile peels came down doubly hard on one's turnip, till… "Oof!" The blade snagged my thumb. It was nothing, but Laburnum fussed, which disguised one's concern at being left with her intimate questioning. Fascinating woman and all the rest, but *though, what really was my apprehension?*

Her mind-reading? Her being a woman? *Lord, one surely wasn't afraid of her—was I? Oh come on, Algernon, why would I be?* And what a good thing one wasn't, I agreed with myself. She was a woman, like hosts of women, though certain other women could? *Okay, could what? Rise above the hoi polloi to verbally claw his meniscus – God, was that the right word? Such a vulgarism?* Even so, one tried not to be physically over-concerned by Laburnum's nearness and didn't believe. But then recollecting her amazing openness as she'd given that account of her own paranormal story on their first Gadabout trip, one mortally reproached oneself.

"Do I miss feasts?" In an all-out effort, I finally echoed her and coughed discreetly. "There was a time I did, but at home much of all that's changed. I always miss Christmas traditions and favorite country walks. Over the years though, on whatever part of the globe one was, if I was invited to a foreign colleague's home, I simply moved in on his family holiday, particularly when it was exotic. There was a pleasure to digging deeper into other cultures through their celebrations, which also nicely avoided getting oneself lumped in as the traditional British ex-pat that hung around the mission, moaning over missed traditions. Except when it was brutally cold—the winters in Moscow had taken some getting used to…" *Off he'd got. Such familiarity—I'll show her!* "Though one bought a fine beaver hat; and as there was so much to see, I walked a lot. But yes, one still gets a pang or two for sticky pudding, and having one's teeth electrocuted on a thruppenny bit; and I miss other meaningfully hot, spicy atmospheres too—which might mean that someday I'll need to gypsy to a favorite city or two, though it won't be soon. Rushing away can't be high on my list with all one's learning."

"You're well past the misery of homesickness then? I've hesitated to ask what 'home' was for you." I took my time lunging for the larger knife to chop off a turnip top while gathering one's wits as she asked, "Am I prying too much?"

Oh, wasn't she?

Though as forgiveness had been a rudimentary part of one's diplomatic training, one did owe her. "These days my father isn't the most enjoyable person to be around. Actually, Father never was." Soap opera stuff to keep her quiet. "My older brother has inherited the estate—older brothers are usually trained to take over from an early age—and on holidays, aunts, uncles, and that preposterous group from *Downtown Abbey*, knowing the 'Tatler' photographer was to be present, all gather around Gillie and his children."

"But without any reason to stay, you went off into the big wide world?"

"Buzzing all over a good deal of it, yes, as along with one's be-medaled castigating old uncles. I was greatly looking forward to settling down in some hidden away little place, like this. Do you know, Laburnum," one hesitated, "this move here is the first independent decision one has ever made! Shameful, isn't it?"

Laburnum nodded thoughtfully. "Though you must have made many highly responsible decisions?"

"Because of one's succubus, you mean, or one's work?"

"Sorry, I hadn't meant to probe, but if you've lived here some while like me, you can't help but be struck by a very unusual person buying this estate—suddenly, an amazingly suave and sophisticated landlord! It's hard not to be intrigued."

"Thank you! Do I really seem that different from other people?"

"Oh, you know you are! Cosmopolitan, aristocratic! What I'd meant to ask you was about your decision-making in general."

Clearing my throat, and again, attempting to broaden this conversation, one's voice came out too high. "In conflict resolution, I certainly made more than my share of decisions. Personal decisions though? One should explain, Laburnum, then…" Out it came—damnation! Drama class 101! "…no man enjoys being cuckolded."

"Oh, awful!"

"Not thought of as so awful, as Father had arranged one's marriage."

"Arra-anged?! You don't mean?"

"An arrangement that was highly endorsed! Obligated members of his club, relatives in line for an inheritance, certain freaky *Downtown Abbey* kin rarely ever seen—anyone the old brute out-maneuvered—'filial affection' wasn't a phrase Father knew. 'Love' being one that caused him to tremble and vomit. One's marriage was merely a business arrangement for Father to add a valuable chunk of adjoining territory to the manor's estate."

"Does an 'arrangement' like that ever work?"

"Not in my parents' case, either. Mother made some sensible decisions for me, but the old man badgered and threatened her till he'd beaten her down, then did exactly what he'd wanted. This went on till she became ill and simply faded from life." Laburnum shook her head, disgusted. "The next generation, my brother's children, won't be the same; and most old families are far less medieval."

"Feudal?"

"In Father's case, you're precisely right." Laburnum was muttering thanks to some former western-civ reviewing, as one tried to keep the ball more firmly in one's hot hands. "Father's means of accomplishment was through swaggering threats or utter frigidity. Just his quick tight hand-grip demonstrated he hadn't a dram of God-awful caring warmth. To him, pleasantness only displayed *naïveté* or an inferior intelligence!"

"So you bided your time by escaping to those fabulous places that the government sent you?"

"It was either that or becoming a drone under Father on the estate." One finished cubing another turnip and took up another. "Only poor families loved their children over there, Laburnum. The attitude of families like mine was, send the noisy little bastards away from here if we're to keep our nice peaceful home, for God's sake. Boarding school will straighten them out, corporal punishment does a splendid job of snuffing lively spirits, along with uncouth manners or a too fertile imagination. Find any excuse and send them packing! Or take them to the colonies where a mass of servants will keep them from misbehaving."

Laburnum was thoughtful. "But Britain, it has produced such brilliant writers?"

"Many didn't stay—D.H. Lawrence, Huxley, Lawrence Durrell."

"Though Virginia Woolf?"

"She did stay, valiantly, and tried to make changes for women. Though much as my mother admired her, Mom could only air this opinion in private."

"Many women's opinions were silenced, yes, and I don't mean to get all that going. Though with your interest in literature, I'm curious, Algernon, what books do you read here?"

"Faulkner and more Faulkner! That Yoknapatawpha writer is unlike any other."

"No-o-o!" Laburnum was amazed. "I'd have thought Fitzgerald more your British sensibility."

"He is, but! Don't ask difficult questions, Laburnum! Over here, it just has to be Faulkner! I'm, let's just say, I'm in constant admiration!" and stuck with Laburnum's skeptical glance, "All right, more specifically? Action of Faulkner's within an incident scatters time, yet the incident is encased in time! He creates a completeness that's stunningly beautiful as well as resonantly identifiable!"

"Ha, you'd expect Americans to love Faulkner, Algernon, and I do, but an Englishman! Faulkner's people and places suck you into them, as you say, but you haven't found them too earthy? Those characters, their very bones, are out of that ancient southern soil, there's generations of sultriness to those hunted woods. I was about to say that even Faulkner's wit is American, but I don't think that's right. But you being so English, yet loving Faulkner! You're full of surprises!"

"That soil – yes, it's his rich earthiness that fires me off on some lingering Mississippi track! Could it be that settling here in this countryside one falls into an earthier literary phase? After all, I love working down in the vine rows with all the various smells—did you know that those smells change with each section of the day? Hans knows it! There are so many atmospheres that lead one further into that growing world!" Uncomfortably, one wondered if I wasn't allowing too much of oneself through to his female neighbor as I took up the last turnip. "Laburnum, you don't know that during a good deal of my career, I couldn't wait to get earth under my finger-nails." *Watch it, Algernon, you ancient softie!* "That's it!" *Next you'll be telling her things you'd wished you hadn't.* "Yes, I'd longed to really dirty up my hands! Just that."

With Laburnum's supportive responses, one observed that I was indeed talking about myself; and not only that, but only too readily—horrors! Good Lord, I might start spouting about how while overseas I'd vividly day-dreamed owning a 'Supreme Habitat' for one's mother's special antiques! Embellished with a cupola, a south-facing porch, majestic corbels, and all its vivid wonderful details in some peaceful countryside spot.

Luckily though, instinctively, I'd hesitated to say more. Though admittedly, I knew that part of the reason I'd stopped speaking was, one was too unsure how one's 'Supreme Habitat' had all happened to one and was not ready to talk about it.

Laburnum had gone all out decorating for Hans' birthday evening, its colorfulness being her creative contribution the Runditz family expected. Standing on a chair, humming pleasurably, she wound multi-colored streamers together to swag over the sideboard, tilting her head back to assess the blend of colors as she attached them to lamp chains and plant hooks. Having come downstairs, one stood watching her, prepared to aid her when she wobbled; one watched until she had me help and instructed one on curling puffs of narrow ribbon to attach to the ends of a shadowed gold 'Happy Birthday' banner! One could reach it standing and fastened it across the wall over the sideboard. It surprised one how exhilarated I became watching Laburnum's lavish dining-room decorating. When she held out a bronze table cloth of Sally-Anne's to me, I took the other side, glad to help spread it over the table, in with the winery's tradition; and also I helped set out her prepared short bowls of peach-colored roses. We finished by scattering miniscule metallic 'Happy Birthdays' in silver and deep blue around the flowers.

Thrilled with the aims behind all this effort, it was like being back as a boy when Mother made festive little treat days. With Laburnum, everyone's assumption was that lots of color, effort, and beautifully cooked food could be counted on to foment a festive mood! Hans had insisted he would only come on condition there were no presents. Sylvia, Reb, and Laburnum had found several funny little gifts and labeled each 'No Present' and disguised them in brown paper to stash insignificantly behind a side table in a carrier bag. On top of this table was a large arum lily that Laburnum had dug up and potted that she had previously planned to give Hans as he appreciated her vigorous lily patch that went back to Eva's time. Everyone was uplifted and all cleaned up, so their ruddy complexions were at their best above crisp summer shirts or the women's cheerful light summer dresses, skirts, and blouses.

Finishing touches were made to the table, Laburnum and I lighting the dozen or so candles as Sylvia, Mel, and Sally-Anne dished up the meal. All conveniently just in time with Reb bringing in Hans. The group flocked about their honored guest, embracing him till he feigned objecting! Showering him with more birthday wishes anyway, till Reb guided the beaming birthday man to the table's honored end chair, and all sat, hungry for the wonderful smelling roasted chickens and their tantalizing stuffing, gravy, and side dishes. Though noticeably, one chair was empty.

"Sigmund, he not coming?" Hans' smile dropped to disappointment.

"He told me that all-hell wouldn't keep him from missing your big day," Sally-Anne informed Hans as she set a mounded dish of mashed potatoes garnished with chopped parsley on the table.

"Right, he said he wouldn't miss it if the sexiest woman in New York State stripped in front of him and begged him for a date!"

"He'll be here Hans, don't worry," Sylvia assured him, as one hopefully agreed.

"Hans?" Laburnum called along the table to him, "Ha-*ans?*" she repeated getting his attention, "Do you know that I attended your 70th birthday, and now here it is, your 80th? It beats me why you haven't added a single wrinkle."

Hans roared with laughter, which aptly made him look younger. "Don't hold your breath waiting for my 90th!" Then he turned to Reb, who had done a tidy job of carving the chickens and was passing along large platefuls before sitting. "Reb, you may not remember it, but your mother, she was here on my 60th and my 50th; and we had chicken that was almost as good as this. No! No, no, it was not chicken."

"Grilled lake trout—I helped catch'em, Nollie and me pulled'em in."

"Lake trout!" Hans repeated in bedazzled amazement. "Yes, Reb, big beauties!" Holding his forehead, Hans tried to stop laughing at his next thought. "I never forget it your mother, she had those fishes on a large plate…" Reb loudly guffawed along with Hans, "…she was talking and—and the fish they slip off the plate… spla-a-at!"

"On the floor, yes! I was just a kid, but nothing was to happen to our fish!"

"Your mom, she get large spatula and bend to scoop them onto plate again, and do you know? They tasted better than ever!"

"Fell skin side downwards?" Sylvia asked.

"My Lan', I couldn't tell you that! All I know is that those dandy fish had the best taste!"

"I've heard of planked fish," Sylvia joked.

"Reb and Sylvia, you were here on my 70th, Laburnum too, as she say."

"You remember what we ate then, Hans?" Laburnum asked him.

Hans went into a solemn think. "Eva—Eva… she made big bratwurst meal, special." Hans' memories had jogged Reb, Sylvia, and Laburnum back to when Laburnum's apartment had just been completed; and as Mel reminded them, later he joined the winery, and they feasted when they'd finished an apartment for him above Laburnum's too.

Mel recalled, "We finished up my kitchen closets and took our wine to the picnic tables to fiesta on guacamole and burritos!" As these past outstanding celebrations filled out, Reb made other comments as he re-filled the wine glasses.

Laburnum lyrically recollected another memorable celebration of Hans' on the Runditzs' wedding anniversary. "Eva put on a Strauss record in the parlor and turned it up so it came through the open windows."

"*Ja, ja*, Eva and me, we polka on porch! Much joy! We polka all evening."

"Like dolls, you two, going around and 'round!"

"It wonderful, *ja*! But you know, everyone, this is being rude to Algernon, who was not here then."

Thoroughly amused, I raised my glass, "Here's to those fabulous celebrations! Don't stop them, please! Look at you! You're all happily enjoying those good old times! Do keep them coming; it's wonderful getting to know them."

Hans was right; it had been rudeness to leave one person out—not done in the best circles—though I had dismissed any rankling 'rudeness' because the enthusiasm for all this prior camaraderie was so intriguing. After the tight sedateness of all I had experienced of family feasting, with his father's hatred of 'unnecessary expenditures' at the manor, eaten in near silence, or abroad when one was so loaded with societal obligations that any real 'R and R' couldn't be.

Though these Runditz 'good times' eventually ran down, and Sylvia stood to carry out some gathered dishes. "Time to clear the plates." Passing me, Sylvia whispered in one's ear, "Keep Hans talking!"

Nodding to Laburnum passing, one also whispered, "Time for the 'No Presents'." With this agreed to, on Laburnum went for the carrier bag and put it on Hans's lap. Seeing they were presents, Hans' objecting hands raised, and he pulled an awesome face, but he was much too happy tonight to make a real fuss. Laburnum coaxed, "You must look at them, Hans; they're just the 'No Presents' you wanted! Comic little nothings."

"Better find out what they are, Hans," Reb confirmed, "they took some searching for."

Laburnum encouraged Hans, who played at being reluctant till she helped him unwrap a present. It was a row of pretty fruit-shaped marzipan, the kind he adored and with an "Oh-ho-o!" smiling his wide show of still good teeth, he slipped the marzipan in his breast pocket to keep just for himself, heartening all who loved him! He was delighted too with another 'No Present', a tiny pewter bell, in the shape of a wine bottle that actually rang. I went to sit on the birthday man's other side and take over helping him unwrap, I asked him about his very first bottle of Runditz vinifera—Hans had to think. "I don't admit to my first effort, Algernon—it was not good. I thought it stupendous back then, but later when we make much better wine, I tell that the first bottle he had not tasted good." At this point Sigmund arrived, and Hans looked up much relieved, "A-a-ah, Sigmund!"

The conversation went quiet as Sigmund starkly wished Hans, "Many Happy Returns," then nonchalantly went to take the last clean plate on the sideboard and fill it with what was left in the dishes. Carrying it to the chair awaiting him, he arrogantly lifted his leg over its back in a show of over-casual behavior he'd decided befitted the distinction of the Runditz wine-maker. Laburnum, sitting next to him, ignored his showmanship to ask, "You have a room in town, Sigmund, or are you staying here?"

"Always you ask the most direct questions, Laburnum. You must have German blood. Well, since it matters to you."

"It doesn't really, just making conversation."

"I will stay here, by special arrangement with Mister Cholmondley-Rute."

Having overheard, I repeated, "Algernon."

"Should you also be about to ask me why it took so long for me to get here."

"I'd have stopped at that."

"I would assure you that it is the business of one person only, so I would not have told you!" This got a mild laugh in the general effort to include the late guest and overlook his rudeness. "Hans," he called loudly along the table, "It cannot be that you are four score years! You look younger than Algernon!"

"Hans is celebrating his '80th', Sigmund!" Sylvia imposed, astounded. "We all know Hans is youthful-looking, but there's no way you can say Algernon looks 80!"

"Appearances change with incentive, Sylvia," Sigmund defended. "With Algernon's management here, his manly assets get encouraged, so he does not need to worry. It might be that I look older than I am today, because my 'manly assets' don't seem to have the appeal to the women I'd like them to have. Why, I do not understand! I give them the same ingenious bull, so its merciless discrimination that it doesn't work."

"You'rc trying too hard, relax," Sylvia suggested.

One explained to Hans what Sigmund was saying further along the table and repeated Sylvia's reasoning. "Yes," Hans agreed, "Sigmund, forget trying! It will happen when it will."

"I wish I was better at letting it. Unlike you, Hans, I'm no longer a spring chicken."

Sally-Anne brought in Hans' favorite dessert, the pecan pie Sylvia had made him, with one beautiful tall candle sparkling above its middle. Hans was urged to make a wish as he blew it out. "I know what I'd wish for," Sigmund said.

"It may not be the same as Hans' wish," Laburnum guessed.

"You're right." Astonishing all, as Sigmund rarely admitted anyone else had a worthwhile opinion. "Look at Hans! Maybe I've a few years yet for 'letting it happen when it will'! Who knows, maybe the perfect 'she' will bump into me. I don't know where—at a convenience store maybe?"

"When she asks you to how to pump gas!"

"Or she could need to know the way to another winery."

Hans called, "Get Mel onto it, Sigmund, he always has dates." Surprisingly, Sigmund raised his brows and exchanged a fraternal glance with Mel.

Later Hans became tired, and the party reluctantly drew to a close as everyone knew it had to with Hans needing to leave with me as pre-arranged. Hans called to Laburnum, who had gone for the lily she had potted for him. Seeing she had, Hans followed her, “Listen, my dear Laburnum, that beautiful arum lily. I appreciate all that goes with him, but I wish you would keep him. I no good with indoor plants.”

“What about Bernice?” Hans flatly shook his head at involving his relative until Laburnum agreed to keep it.

Hans was helped to gather his presents as Reb, Sylvia, and Mel got the leftovers put away. They cleared the table and got its decorations mainly re-packaged as turns were taken at scrubbing the scraped cookware in the kitchen before the dishwasher was turned on. After final hugs and clever well-wishes, I took Hans home in my sensational sports car, which Hans said made him look like ‘a Hollywood big-vig’. Reb and Sylvia were the next to take off, followed by Sally-Anne and Garrett’s cars. Slowly, the evening’s contentment that had drenched the Supreme Habitat’s walls to its mystic core also yawned, with even Sigmund announcing he was in bad need of sleep. Reb dried the last baking dish, and Mel fixed the coffee for the morning before returning to his apartment as the birthday boy and his revelers made their happy goodnights. With the place suddenly emptied, Laburnum decided to get her large potted arum lily out of my way.

Carrying the lily in the huge flower-pot to her apartment, it became so heavy she wished she hadn’t watered it so well. Finding it too much, she let the rejected thing slide down her onto the cement, till standing over it; she determined that she had better just get it there and picked it up again.

About to turn off my headlights, one couldn’t believe that one was seeing Laburnum spotlighted struggling to get her absurdly huge potted plant through her apartment door! Aghast one jumped out, enraging as one watched her turn sideways to battle the flower and that over-healthy mass of greenery under her apartments’ outside light while fumbling through it for her door’s handle till that huge shoulder bag of hers dropped to the ground.

The gentleman in one rushed to her, though one’s words refused to match one’s chivalrous action, “WHAT are you doing, you wretched nincompoop?! With all the MUSCLE POWER AROUND here, WHY HAVEN’T YOU?”

“You’re *yelling* at me, Algernon!”

Lord, one *WAS YELLING! A significant ex-diplomat letting go? This wasn’t him?! What in hell’s name was happening? One must have sunk far lowlier than I would.*

Laburnum and I each had the pot hard-gripped as our bodies simultaneously squeezed to get the rotund container and its mass of overgrown foliage unjammed from her opened door, as each of our legs entangled in her handbag till we got royally stuck between the plant, one another, and the door jamb. One's freer hand wildly groped for the light switch—*on the wrong wall!* Making Laburnum's damn laughter lose control as each of us forced our way while spurting the plant beyond us through the door, she and I became bodily trapped to one another as we each maintained a bionic grip on the pot. To Laburnum, this opposed obstinacy in the semi-dark was so hysterical that all she could gasp was, "Wro-ong-! Wrong w-a-all!"

"Then *YOU* let go!" I commanded, "Why in?! GIVE it to me! Damn it, madam, it must weigh as much as you do!"

"Oh hell, Algernon, I'd almost got it! Look, either you take the fucking thing or turn around and turn the light switch ON—ON THE OPPOSITE WALL-! Hey, you're *hurting* me!"

"I'm hurting you-ou, you bloody nuisance! Oops, Paycock!"

"Damn it, don't think I'll forget what you've just called me."

"There're more apt descriptions," one muttered yanking to keep the entire plant and pot. Though... *relief!* One had dragged Laburnum and it through the door while she stayed clinging to her pot's side. "Only a mindless old gasket would choose such a gargantuan pot! Look, as I've got a purchase on the blasted thing, why don't you?"

She did—*let go.*

"O-o-oh Ch-rist!" Each trusting that the other held it, the pot and its contents clattered to the entrance tiles. *"GOD! Oh-oh! Oh Laburnum, my dearest, my darling, are you hurt?"* As the apartment door slammed too behind us; and she groaned but more with the hilarity of the situation as we were both trying not to skid on the wrecked plant's foliage in the dark among jags of smashed earthenware and chunks of slimy earth. Laburnum's laughter tripped a perfect down scale as she bent to grope for her precious lily, though, instead,

one's empty hands clutched her upper arms, *"Poor dear, oh you poor darling! Are you all right?"*

Suddenly, one was holding Laburnum so compassionately, so drastically, that the seriousness of one's grip drowned her laughter, and she simply stood, like a gaussed mine-sweeper paramagnetized so her hair scrubbed one's chin. Pausing from this emoting, I removed her tresses from my face and with greatest tenderness guided her out from the broken pot till...

"Not NOW, Paycock, damn you!" as one's lips caressed Laburnum's forehead, and I removed my knees from her dog while continuing to press one's untamable lips rivetingly on hers. Though oh—

Damnation! One had offended Paycock! Making dearest Laburnum instinctively pull from me.

It was one's philanthropy—one's misused inbred refinement—that was suddenly redeemed by one's reserve gentility; and while self-upbraiding, the heat to one's finger-tips painfully restrained one's groping beneath her shirt.

But by the windows' thin outside light, she must have been seeing one anew as her landlord. As one's tall shadowy normal elegance that one's mirror had always reflected stood before her halted by powerful masculine shock waves that drew on her so relentlessly, that in one pounce we each bound the other into an abundance of euphoric limb-wrappings.

If there was ever to be any more of this wonder-delirium, one must demand a softening of oneself—extract some gentleness from one's rusted romantic fathoms. With some effort, this was managed; and at last one indulged in those magnificent breast wobblings I'd so often ached to give appreciation to. One's rapt hands followed the hot fleshy curves known to be beneath the swollen zigzags of her swim suit; and even tightly packaged as we were one to another, we tumbled onto the sofa, away from the plant pot's sharp scummy jags.

Rents from yanked or ripped garments as one pinned this flesh-warm plentiful chunk of womanhood beneath me, and she bestowed on me her sultry permission. "Ye-es-oh, ye-es!" as in a gale of amazed instinct, she helped one tear off my bikini; and with her tiny feet locked behind one's buttocks, she yanked one into a more vulcanizing embrace.

My work-toughened arms brute held her, while one whispered in lulling tones, "Laburnum, oh my beloved sorceress! Cunning woman that you really are!" While one's marbleized phallus jostled to its predestination, till one let go, "Oh, oh, GO-o-od!!!"

"How would you like it, my gallant swain?" She forced her steadier confidence.

He: Dear Lord! Hot zigzagged gluteus maximus—rusty pinned bosom strap—spirals of psychedelic lake reflections! Moonlit diamonds screaming at one from the lake's other shore—peace doves dropping weighted olive saplings. Sutpen's forlorn decaying mansion—its southern portico. Oh help me, William Faulkner! *Absalom Absalom! Algernon, Algernon!*

She: Her knees splaying rapturously to practice that same timeless ancient act known to the early-kingdom Egyptians, the orderly ancient Persians, the hyperventilating Aztecs in their weak mountain air, nobles and servants alike, all performing this intuited marvel of a biological common denominator to all civilizations.

Chapter 16
Algernon in Love

With my scholarly lover just steps away next door, on this beautiful sunshiny day, only contentment resonated one's splendiferously rich voice! Being an aristocrat, naturally, one accepted that one's wishes would be fulfilled. Then being British besides, all one had to do was to let my inherent self-discipline wave its wand! *Oh ye gods, can life actually be like this?!*

Reb was beside me helping to replace weak vineyard posts—and asked, "That an exultance noise, Alg'non, or is it ridding frustration?"

"It's Mahler's First. The orchestration continues on in my head."

"Tried an aspirin?"

"I'm perfectly all right, Reb. Haven't you had a tune in your head that wouldn't go away?"

"Do I!" he expostulated. "Lately, I can't get ridda 'Happy Birthday to Yew'."

"It bothers you?"

"Never liked it. A heavy-metal greeting woulda bin better!" Using both arms, Reb swung the sledgehammer high over his head and brought it down exactly on the post with his 'Happy Birthday-a-*YEW!*' This last word yelled as he knocked the post further into the ground. Eyeing it for being level, "There's another," he passed it.

When Sylvia drove in later, Garrett took over Reb's sledgehammering. Garrett and Algernon soon had any tagged poles replaced in the lower-east vineyard before still 'soloing'; one couldn't wait to see Sylvia and left the finishing up to Garrett as I scurried up to the house, becoming aware of dismissive little chills percolating one's happiness! Earlier that morning, I had phoned Sylvia to ask her if she would pick me up a potted arum lily I'd ordered from the florist and bring it with her when she drove here to have her noon sandwich with Reb. Going up the steps one's back felt cooler away from the vineyard's burning sunlight. The shady porch's clamminess was balm to one's spine, as I noticed that Sylvia, as dependable as always, had left a healthy new lily outside my study door.

Showered and changed after the long morning's work, one took up this new lily couched in frilly ribbon and cellophane, and although one's exuberance was overflowing since our love night of rabid hyper-cultivation, now one was about to meet my 'love' in the coldness of day, I grew absurdly timid! But images of her smooth olive skin soon got the better of me, and I took up the lily and ordered oneself to get over there and gently tap on her door. Receiving her shameless, "Come on i-i-n, Algernon," Sounding as sultry as a black-widow spider mid-catch, one ecstatically obeyed. Seeing the lily he was holding, she exclaimed – "Oh-ho-o!" Coming closer to admire it though, she stopped and laughed incredulously as she watched me put this symbol of our mythic night on her coffee table, "Oh my dearest! We must've been thinking alike, Algernon! I was in town this morning and found just the pot for our poor sick lily."

"You bought a pot to replace the poor?" *Why was I dumbly repeating what she'd just said?*

Nodding, her black eyes flashing white from her smile creased lids, "It has the most appropriate relief! You'll be surprised—*wait*—let me get it!" While she went off for it, one braced for what an 'appropriate relief' for their bomb-test's love night might be. Photos of erotic sculptures from Pompeii? Famous artists' porno sketches? But back she came holding an ornamented beige pot with a relief of fine Irish setters chasing one another around its rim that Paycock might have modeled for. Whew! One breathed more easily.

Loaded with our new roles, each now into in this defibrillating new relationship as we remained standing apart admiring one's lovely new lily side by side, with the beige 'Paycock-pot' on Laburnum's coffee table. Our timid-lovers' smiles brimmed with the amazing new sexual highs later life could bring. Daring direct looks at one another, we stood so physically aroused that our auras visibly echoed our rippled illuminated contours. Laburnum, unrelentingly smiling as she stumbled out her thanks for the new lily. More boldly, she came over to properly greet one; her silky hands sliding behind one's hips to pull me against her while deploying an ambling kiss on my lips that teemed, and even screamed, with more prospective thrills.

One remained exciting against her theme-park bosom. The lily had been such a ridiculously lowly price for being rewarded by so much of Laburnum's physical treasury. It was more than being given the key to Bluebeard's private room as one furtively dabbed at—*oh God, no, not drool*! But Laburnum's arms tightened around one anyway, as on this new plane of mutually advanced acceptance, we kissed like pile drivers, our desires working toward an effulgent follow-up as one's finger-tips slid under—*oops—that couldn't be a voice at the door?*

Unmistakably though, it was a sophisticated, playful voice. "Guess who it can b-e-ee-?"

Oh no, not Sigmund?

One's excitement was like a sky rocket fallen foul of its track to be doused in a pond.

Maddened, Laburnum abruptly went to the door to barely open it a crack. "Go away, Sigmund, I'm very busy!" But laughing too much to hear her, all Sigmund had to do was give the door one hard shove and he entered, grabbing her retracting arm—*until he saw me!* Flinging Laburnum away, Sigmund shot an angry look at her, then at me, then the florist's lily on the table, the lily pot, before in utter dejection he emitted ghastly expiring sounds and flopped back onto Laburnum's scarlet sofa. His quivering hand running over his damp forehead. "Chr-rist in a typhoon!"

"Other people do have lives too, you know?"

"Not you to-o, Labby!"

"You and I are 'friends only', Sigmund; you know that. We don't even write one another." And waving her hand to include Algernon, "We're all your good friends."

"Oh to hell with you, Mother Mary, there're times when a man needs more than friends."

"Friends can be the backbone for holding each day together, Sigmund," came one's brusque pseudo-righteousness.

"Till—as Hans advised you last evening, Sigmund, some bigger change comes about," Laburnum tempered.

Laburnum's and my incinerating embraces had been so cruelly clonked, I was actually feeling lower stomach pain. I'd seen myself so far along on Laburnum's amour wavelength, I'd been prepared for outlandish pleasures—but oh Great Thor—now one's most loving woman and I would have to drum up patience, and possibly even 'compassion', as she too stood so wholly struck with indecision we both undulated—she moved forward toward Sigmund, and myself backwards, the two of us waving about indecisively, like hill-top grasses.

It was Laburnum who finally made a floundering effort. "I'll… I'll get us herbal tea."

"Te-e-ea?" Sigmund mocked.

"Look, Sigmund," one stated, "Give me your gentleman's honor you'll stay respectful of Laburnum, and I'll fetch you the pacifying kind of beverage you want."

"Need."

"Kind of you, Algernon," Laburnum said for Sigmund. And as one passed her, "Return quickly," she softly begged giving one a dire private glance. Then to Sigmund, "As friends, the three of us will talk this out!" Vitally pained, one nodded, wishing this pedantic, well-groomed priapic well off the face of the earth as one sprinted faster than I'd believed I could across to one's house because it occurred to me… *God, how safe was my beloved Laburnum with that concussive-brained lecher?* Damning Sigmund and his abominable timing, I suddenly felt like… like that disgusting, squeezed-out old bunch of solar tea bags rotting away in Laburnum's large vineyards jar that I couldn't stand. This Sigmund of Hans might be an expert at wine making, but as one tore at one's desk drawer to grab my first aid flask, I knew that Sigmund's insensitivity to others was most likely intentionally rogue! Though admittedly, the louse did have women problems. Scurrying, one returned to find Sigmund with his eyes closed lying back on Laburnum's scarlet sofa with my own dearest darling leaning over him into some downright talking. One was determined to get this whole situation straightened out, just as Laburnum was trying to, as one nudged the flask against Sigmund's upper arm.

"I appreciate it, Algernon, thanks," Laburnum said for Sigmund. Then speaking to the upturned flask covering Sigmund's face, "As I was just saying, Algernon, Sigmund you've always appreciated women, but apparently, there's more than appreciation behind these recent affairs."

Sigmund swung his legs down to sit up and take longer swigs from one's flask; the back of his hand wiping his mouth as he raised his anguished head, "Can't you two te-ell? I'm flat on my damned ba-ack!" His voice gushing high as this last word jack-knifed with him tossing his head, his damp forelock with it, his eyes rolling to the ceiling to madly drum it.

"More clearly, Sigmund?" one requested.

"Oh da-amn you, da-a-amn you!" Laburnum and I refrained from even shrugging, as not bothering to object, Sigmund held tears back in a pitifully elongated exhale. In his unbearable frustration, he kept up quick little hopeless head turns from side to side, before saying, "She and I were to *MAR*-rrry!"

"The Dutch woman? Her name, Sigmund?"

"Waleva! Oh my God, how long was I away from here, Labby? Three months was all, no more. My heart still tells me she only loves me."

"She wrote she agreed to marry you?" Laburnum probed skeptically.

"We talked by phone every other day. It was all settled, our new shared days! They meant everything to her too! Then I came back over here and phoned, and she would not even *SEE* me! What would you have done? After—it was all so unlike her! So after I saw you that night," he glanced at me, "I drove over to make her see me, and, oh—you know the rest! The man is an uncivilized brute. A perverted wild boar would make her a better lover. Terrible!"

"Before Waleva," Laburnum calmly pushed her probe, "weren't you to marry a German woman?"

"Oh mercy, Labby! But you see, really I knew that was over. I kept waiting for her, but no, no, she would not consider coming here with me, not even for limited years."

"I'm very sorry, Sigmund."

"Not all a surprise. She was close to her mother, who was dying."

"Her mother has died?"

"Still not, no. Though that may not have been all the reason."

"No?" one queried.

"I'm not viewed as good husband material." Truly hearing what he was saying, Sigmund smiled wryly.

"Why, Sigmund? You're a steady worker. Your father has vineyards. Hans met him, didn't he?"

"It's not my father the woman was to marry."

"No, but believe me, pleasant in-laws make all the difference!" One's sudden deep voice had boomed this out so abruptly, unexpectedly, it made Sigmund's head turn uneasily, because neither Laburnum nor he could take one's emotionally charged statement lightly.

"You're married?" Sigmund's head turned to ask one.

Very interested, Laburnum turned too. One ambled to her desk-table to rear-end against it. "You're European, Sigmund, and not my age, but you know old European families. My father arranged my high-profile marriage to a woman I'd barely met."

"*Terrible!* For business reasons, I suppose? Oof… fathers."

"Yes," as one held onto center stage, "valuable land was to have been annexed to the Cholmondley-Rute's estate and tying the knot with Francesca was to settle it. Father not only didn't get the land, but I happened to walk in on my wife with her lout lover in our bed."

"*Your* bed?"

Nodding, as one wondered what in all blazes I was doing saying this!

For all one's sudden gaucheness though, one was turning the tables on Sigmund's pitiful romances as one kept up this motivation. "In our case, it wasn't so unpredictable," one blathered on. "We hadn't known one another and our opinions, tastes, any semblance of what a decent marriage could be were oceans apart! It was a debasing experience; and to keep the press from damaging our families, they bribed us to remain together."

"Francesca?" Laburnum asked, "Your wife—she had relatives on fine French estates?"

"And for that I thank her, yes. Though," hesitating one scratched at an itch in one's ear—*dear God, I'd got myself in so stupidly deep, spieling on about one's youth, like a phobic 20-year-old*—as the eyes of Sigmund and Laburnum stayed on me, like two plugged toilet reamers. One scratched one's ear again. "Though it hadn't been Francesca who introduced me to fine wines, Laburnum."

"No-o?" Laburnum interrupted bent with curiosity as she and Sigmund studied me.

After another head-scratching hesitation, one continued, till out came one's Golden Globe Award for Drama, "No, the wine connoisseur was my mother!" Amazingly, un-self-consciously, one let out this fiercely personal matter that one had never spoken of as I struggled to get a better hold on what was actually dropping from one's lips, which – oh God – was still keeping on—of its own accord? "I used to go up to her little library for an hour after meals; and while we shared an excellent bottle, she'd talk to me—on school holidays, I was nine." Sigmund and Laburnum lapped this up. *dearest Lord, for heaven's sake, what was this blasted 'lowliness' doing to one? I'd just given away one's dearest mother's most holy secret! He had dishonored his poor, most blessed, and most beloved mother! What an unmitigated unredeemable cad! A son of such historic lineage, loyalty should be automatic, yet where had his loyalty gone? What an unrefined immoral sort of rotten crook one really must be!*

Laburnum kept softly repeating, "Nine."

Fallen into those far-reaching, most extraordinary days, there was no exit—one was forever cloaked in that immortal love of one's mother and her tireless guidance of one onto an open-minded and 'compassionate' path. "Certainly, it had been more Mother's escape than I'd understood," I continued, "because soon after those mind-rending summer holidays, my beloved angel mother died."

Sigmund looked straight at me, "Algernon, that's most sad. I'm so very sorry.

One's poignant story had successfully swiveled us away from the drama of Sigmund's blighted romances to send all three of us into escalating separate thoughts. Laburnum, rocked by her landlord's initial blurt, seeming incongruous; and oneself, having diffidently played with my ear again before rear-ending her desk more so, had also shown her that much of me was still greatly appalled at giving out this personal, highly classified information. I'd have been shot at dawn if it had been classified Service information I'd so liberally given away. Though some aberrant power I'd had to obey made me continue telling my story so tentatively and caressingly about one's lost parent that Laburnum swallowed one's every intimate syllable.

One's love and admiration of my mother when one was a boy made one believe that if there were to be more of those fine guided wine times with one's beloved parent, one owed keeping our *tête-à-têtes* strictly to oneself—an exclusivity that was uniquely the second son's, and only his, not inheritor Gillie's—which until today one had honored on pain of death. Beside her little library's fire, lit even in summer, the coziness of her airless hideaway had profoundly connected me to her higher-minded, lonely expectation of one. Even when she needed one to be charitable about Father and Gilmore's disgraceful attacks on her, I'd only appreciated the immensity of her generosity as I'd grown older.

Wandering back from Laburnum's desk, the knots to one's gastro-intestinal threatened a grossly uncouth misdemeanor as one willfully sat solidly on the sofa's arm beside my lover. I was glad, just 'glad' at this point, of her consoling little hand creeping my forearm; though inwardly, one remained self-morally crushed. Only to friends like Thaddeus had one ever spoken of Mother's early demise; and even then, only as a statistic. The appearance of personal tribulations during one's education and my diplomatic career were considered weaknesses of character, infra dig, which was why one's expounding about himself to Laburnum and Sigmund now both awed and broke one, yet it had still surprised that one's emotion-loaded words had actually fallen quite crisply from one's lips. Particularly to a woman. One's initial objective with Sigmund had been to show him what else could truly shatter a man and so broaden Sigmund's painful women experiences, bump him off his stories, and get him well out of Laburnum's and one's relationship. Though by strange chance, this effort had led one to see how much more honestly I needed to comprehend my own story!

Laburnum broke our lengthy introspection, "When you were away in Germany, Sigmund, you wrote to Hans?"

"Hans has always been good to me. As you knew, when I was here, it was a relief to speak German with him. I know that Hans and Eva were kind to you too, Labby. They were exceptional people—Hans still is. Yes, Hans and I always wrote one another. We were good friends. I… I still don't understand why could he not have let me know how bad his legs had become. Couldn't he have written me he'd had a fall?"

"He wanted you to return."

"Before I left," Sigmund continued, "Hans had been able-bodied, masses of energy."

"A fall affects so much of you when you're older, you know, Sigmund; you're forced to come to terms with all its results," Laburnum reminded him. "For Hans, it was the turning point; he finally had to admit that his legs could not get better, and that he was suffering far too much from them. Though you know Hans, he hated having to make that life-shaking decision, and why wouldn't he—it meant selling up all he'd loved creating and going off somewhere. Though, Sigmund, couldn't you have guessed any of this?"

Sigmund shook his head. "After some weeks of not hearing from him, I wondered what could be wrong."

"No one else wrote you?" one asked.

Sigmund shook his head. "Hans only wrote *after* he'd sold to you, Algernon. *Sold* this place, just like that!" Awed, Sigmund clicked forefinger to thumb. "Excuse me saying it please, but this winery here, Hans? I didn't know who or what to expect! Finally, damn it all, I decided not to care—my own life-changes were going on."

The enormity of Hans' un-communicated decision had been so hopelessly unacceptable to Sigmund, he stayed turned to the window, shrugging helplessly as he sat on making defeated little blinks.

"Then it must have been a jolt," Laburnum empathized. "But Sigmund, wasn't it the greatest good luck for all of us that it was Algernon who came along?"

Dubiously nodding through his utter dejection, Sigmund turned back to Laburnum. Crossing and uncrossing his arms, he said, "Ha, please forgive me, I see I've been very rude! To you too, Algernon. Why? Because I could not see the Runditz Winery being run by anyone but Hans! Not complimentary of me, I know, I know, and naïve, but for me, not for you, Labby, you had seen Hans wasn't doing well, but when I was here he'd still been so energetic!" Sighing, Sigmund was trying to adjust. "No, one cannot say enough about all he did creating this wonderful place. Though I know it isn't politic to be saying this in front of you, Algernon."

"On the contrary, everywhere I turn on this estate, I overwhelm with what Hans and Eva meticulously restored—out in the production center, their vineyards, the avenue of trees coming in—all that Hans built, planted, and ideally managed. No Sigmund, feel free; its best you express your thoughts. I assumed your loyalty to Hans, particularly as he had known your country and its vineyards. Actually, I see there's a great deal more to understand about you, Sigmund."

"Thank you! You may not believe it, Algernon, but I am not always this flighty."

Laburnum stood up and said, "Sigmund, I remember very well how dedicated you could be when your instincts and expertise were fired up together for creating some extraordinary wine, and," but gesturing with her shoulders, she let him fill out the rest of what she was saying. "Now, I'm really going to make that herbal tea."

"A cup for me too please, Laburnum," one needed it.

We men sat listening to the friendly sounds of Laburnum's tea-making in the kitchen, as our better general understanding of one another let each add observations.

"You and Labby had plans when I barged in on you, Algernon?"

"Yes." Raising one's voice so Laburnum would hear. "I'd hoped Paycock would need a walk down to the lake, Laburnum?"

"We'll have our tea, and I'd love to, Algernon!" Laburnum called back. Hearing his name, Paycock got up and went to give Algernon's hand some subservient licks. Just licks, after all he was 'only a dog'.

The day was its most hot and humid when Laburnum and I tucked both our rolled towels beneath our arms to trundle off down the rough footpath in sandals and swim suits; she making comments about our unhappy wine-maker. One answered sullenly, as my instinct was to try to forget our disorganized afternoon. For me, like that derelict 'Doctor Foster who stepped in a puddle up to his muddle, on his way to Gloucester', the lake's blueness ahead looked unbelievably tempting. A blueness that anticipated being in cooler water for dousing the humidity trickling necks and underarms and the entire afternoon.

Before getting to the dock, she asked, "Had you ever told anyone that secret of yours and your mother's, Algernon?"

"Never! Never before, no. Though as we're here now, let's just swim."

On the dock, kicking off her shoes, Laburnum got right into backing down the ladder. Standing on a rung with the water at her knees, she tried to adjust the rusty safety pin keeping her shoulder strap attached to her zigzag swim suit, muttering, "Must get Mel to fix this."

"Mel? Why, what would he use a stapler? Are needles and thread so hard to come by?"

"Mel's so self-sufficient, he keeps them."

"Useful."

"I'll bother him till they come up with a fabric-mending glue."

"Oh-ho, how many women enjoy such slovenly appeal?"

Grinning she replied, "Okay, I'll admit I'm a slut!" laughing back at me as she cautiously lowered her whole body into the refreshing water. With her weak leg noticeably stronger, she didn't waste time getting used to the water's bracing coolness.

Paycock and I dived or plunged in ahead of her off the dock's end and were enjoying a slow wallow in the rippling lake floating on our backs to serenely watch the clear sky as we cooled down. Once Laburnum had ridded her overheating, she made sure she wouldn't exhaust this time and turned to swim back and climb up on the dock. Once one too had swum around and got cooled, I joined her to drip off and watch Paycock happily swimming out deep in circles.

Side by side, sitting with our legs dangling, one was aware of the patchy temperature changes to one's skin, as Laburnum smiled and said, "On a hot day like this, I love just sitting to drip off !" Flipping her wet hair back, as she watched Paycock paddling in to explore the shallows, before she spoke tentatively, "I suspect you don't generally tell people that you'd learned to discriminate about fine wines at your mother's knee, Algernon?"

"Damn right."

"It must not have been easy telling Sigmund and myself about your wonderful mother either?"

Laughing uneasily at being brought back into this personal openness again, even though this time I'd been the one to get it going. "Returning to school, Mother was the only person besides Nanny I missed dreadfully, Laburnum; and, needless to say, much more so after she died." Hoping that would satisfy Laburnum though, "It saddens me that so few people knew how fine that reclusive mind of hers really was. As a student, she'd been lured by the distinctive arts of Egypt and Italy and paid them a few visits. Egyptian animal sculptures and drawings were her special love, and she succeeded in intriguing me with a good deal of what they meant. I adored her illustrated books, as we, or she, decided what qualities made that night's wine distinctive."

"Your belligerent father allowed this?"

"Father probably thought Nanny was in charge of putting me to bed. It was understood that Mother's library—off by itself up its little spiral staircase—was her private section of the manor, and she saw to it that what she did up there didn't get gossiped about."

"Your mother would have been the one to have fought your father's arranged marriage?"

"Oh yes! You should've heard her over the placement of an antique table or a painting. She'd put up an incredible battle with Father and Brother Gilmore, who were really only battling her for entertainment!"

"Awful!"

"She was constant about that. For years if she didn't like what they did, she'd stalwartly oppose them! Though if Mother started to tackle Father's dislike of me, or more importantly, his bizarre household policies, she'd receive more humiliating disparagement and facetious scorn than she could tolerate. Their jokes at her expense were noisy and shameless. Mother owned two fine Constables and an extraordinary Turner, and it pained her that these artists got called 'mealy-mouthed psychotics' or worse! Father never missed a chance to banish all artists as 'pointy-headed imbeciles'."

"Unfortunately, your father is not alone in his ignorance. There're people who boast they hate artists. It's a defense that becomes a vogue."

"I'll debate you on that one sometime."

"I'll look forward to it! The only way I make sense of the artist-non-artist debate is by going back to Schopenhauer."

"Ah, I should have guessed you'd go in for Schopenhauer!"

Determined to only keep what was worthwhile between us, Laburnum's solemn glance at me cooled one's flippancy. Continuing, in her teacher's tone, "Your mother's artistic appreciations would certainly have been from 'Idea'."

"Oh, already we're into 'Will and Idea'?"

"Same with many of our most admired artists whose over-beating hearts caused their most history-making work from their hearts, nerves, and their most alembic cores, rather than through mental mechanics. Unhappily, this is likely to fade during this much more 'Will' monopolized era, which is innovation."

"Surely, 'innovation' would come under 'Idea'?"

"Not if it's creating for a practical demand. Not if it is out of material substances—like making a more competitive furnace or a smaller radio for more marketable appeal. Fine art has a singular advantage—it springs from the unknown core's intangible depths, from a deeper human condition."

"You've obviously dwelt on this."

"Yes, but watch out for this human condition; it may well be a drastic cry."

"A *crie de coeur*?"

"If you prefer!"

Unable to take Laburnum's artistic perceptions more seriously, though one's laugh had awe in it! "No, sadly, in Father's case, you'd be right. He was so zeroed-in on business, he took a pride in his artistic inadequacies, which made finer people keep their distance. Although, strangely, it was usually assumed by people who didn't know him that Father *was* personable!" Both tittered. "A school friend of mine came to stay at the manor once, and he hadn't been around Father's belligerence for a half hour before he phoned his parents to come and fetch him! Not that I minded being alone, I could roam off places, which suited Father. You know, Laburnum, with all that so far behind me now, whatever one's parent's attitudes and opinions were back then, they all do conveniently flow into an acceptable past."

"'Flow into an acceptable past'!" Laburnum echoed admiringly. "What a vivid description of being young!" One agreed that that's what it was while looking far out at Paycock still swimming; and far beyond the blissful dog to way out on the lake, where the haze of the day's humidity had settled, like frayed chiffon, to curtain off just a far section of the opposite shore—some fine air-water-temperature oddity.

Turning abruptly, one audaciously checked Laburnum over, "One tries to live within the confines of the situation one finds oneself in, doesn't one? Though looking at whom I'm sitting next to now, so ripe and tempting in her bathing suit, why would I ever wish my story to have been different?"

"Oh 'one' can't imagine!" She grinned mischievously.

"A nice hefty shove is what you need."

"Aw, not you—not with a gentleman's conscience like yours!"

"That's what you think? Wouldn't a genuine gentleman have gallantly picked up an attractive woman's smashed-potted lily last night?" one asked smiling. "By the way, your swim suit? No wonder undergarment glamorizing your fine shape today?"

"To hell with a few pounds! For you it's the genuine article or nothing!"

"Should you be saying that when you know you're looking as tempting as a fresh spring water cooler in a steaming gymnasium?" She smiled, though given to sudden tiredness, she lay back on the dock, first on her elbow, then lying out flat on her back as I leaned to place a thrilled kiss on her well-fleshed shoulder. "Or as tempting as a delicious organic melon," looking down, "or two." She cuffed one's arm that I caught and leaned to walk my finger-tips along her forearm. "Damn it, there's not enough privacy here—who do I speak to about this place?"

"Algernon, I love hearing you say that, but are you watching? Look back this way," she twisted her head on the dock planks to look northwards, where two silent bass boats followed one another around the cliff. The fishermen sat high up above the water, getting broad views looking for bass. They were about to pass us close. Seeing them, I quickly kissed my lover anyway, and anyway she kissed me back! "Don't worry," she tautly whispered, "we- *will!*" I'd needed this assurance as one of the boats gave a witty honk, and the fishermen called over some over-friendly comments! When the fishermen had passed, with Laburnum's need to drowse, I put my towel under her head more comfortably and sat beside her, amazing at the renewing stillness.

For all that had come about since Sigmund's knock on the door, and having been shaken by it, this was still the kind of happiness one wanted taking one over!

What was 'happiness'?

Surely, it had to do with his amazing sensation of being ultra-alive beside his radiant and beautiful new lover? Though this wasn't completely new—he'd been variously 'happy' before—recently discovering his very own 'Supreme Habitat'. Though that was an enigmatic strain of euphoric 'happy'—a proprietary kind—which wasn't the same as this novelty of being with this flesh-thrilling, recovered witch-wonder-woman, whom he loved and knew now that she loved one!

This unleashed happiness from that 'lowlier' fulfillment was still very much unknown to him! Though it was an 'unknown' that in some subliminal way he had *always* been seeking. A little like his profoundly desired Moscow reveries that must have manifested his Supreme Habitat. Couldn't this untypical and desirable woman have been just as deep down inside him too? Unconsciously, as a much needed matched and completing companion? And for far longer than he could put a time to?

Back at Laburnum's apartment, I leaned against the counter, watching my lover produce a cooked bone from the fridge that Paycock expectantly 'sat' for. The salivating dog 'stayed' as Laburnum commended him for his excellent swimming and his politeness shaking off while staying on the shore. Getting her dog's eyed understanding, she allowed him his bone on the floor tiles. Taking the pizza out of the freezer, I keenly observed my most fabulous swimming partner's little runnels of lake water still finding paths down her shapely brown calves to wet the floor, till unable to wait any more, I went behind her to pull down her damp swim suit's shoulder straps, as we both laughed and turned to check we were both headed for the bedroom.

Turning her to me, her black eyes were more ignited than falling sparks from a log's sap igniting as we lost no time in resuming our earlier embraces, made more intriguing by the dampness of exercise-warmed flesh pressing flesh. Our fumbling hands wrenched at my wretchedly well-fitted bikini as neither gave a thought to the unattended thawing pizza, or the lettuce, tomatoes et cetera awaiting being picked. Instead, our released arms and legs wormed tendril-like among her sheets and pillows, ratifying our physical compositions, readied for action, and making all that captivated be the sheer luxury of passionate undiluted love-making. Flat on one's back, one's loins- now a model for the Washington monument, as my unrestrained fingertips could at last appreciate the beautiful mounds of my beloved's 'genuine article'. I was about to say something sweetly flattering in her ear when her hydraulic kiss stopped me because our undulatings rose to a pre-combustible heat. Not bearing more, one rolled onto her as one's substratum fiercely conjoined us, and sanctifying words gasped or spluttered to replay our lily-night's coital frenzy—made more feverish this night not being ankle-deep in the smashed slimy plant. Although mid-action, I did do a mental stop when her melodious voice pronounced the word 'Bo'.

"Bo?" being her lover, one queried.

Coming to from such cataclysmic loving, it took some moments before she recovered to courteously murmur, "Thanking you kindly, good sir!"

"No, on the contrary, one insists on thanking you, my 'faery queen'."

"Oh no, the thanks should go to you for your massive doses of healing help, including this last 24 hours, naturally."

"No, no thanks, one absolutely insists! For a Briton, it was nothing more than philanthropy!" Wickedly, one read her dimly lit outdone maddened facial response, "And one feels one has some right to ask—who, madame, is 'Bo'?"

"'Bo'? Oh… 'wulf'. 'Beowulf', I'm reading him again. And you said something about fairies too, you know? Though I didn't think you were really consumed with those corporeal beings."

"Then what did your crystal ball show?" Laburnum's new lover asked in fear and trepidation.

"That your difficulty is that you really love Paycock and instead need to hug my gorgeous red-setter."

"Oh then my game's up! As a dog-lover, I honestly have to admit that Paycock is superb!"

Slant-wise through the open bedroom door, the sparse kitchen-light rinsed one's relaxed muscles, contouring one's long lean body that crazily reminded my lover of a position of Paycock's. "You're still thinking about getting a dog?"

"Depending on how lonely one becomes."

"You've been lonely here?"

"Not in the least," one gave a squeeze to her nearest breast. I liked her defined Roman nose, its glowing translucence in this semi-light, and the winsome smell of lake-weed in her nearest hair strands. "I must say that this has been most pleasant, and far more than I'd dared to expect after our first night's intergalactic." She agreed with me nodding. "Laburnum, seriously now, how are we going to manage all this happiness?"

"It was Sigmund, Algernon! We'd better thank him for interrupting."

"Abominable timing, but later yes, fantastic compensation!" One rolled away from her. "God, I'm ravenous."

"I'll only take that hint if you'll get up and help me." Reluctantly agreeing, I kissed the tip of her glowingly translucent Roman nose as she switched on the bed lamp, and she, tearing at her strewn clothing dumped on the rug, rustled out her large yellow marigold knickers. One thought it appropriate that Laburnum would wear underwear with one leg's elastic tight under one buttock, and the other elastic having been broken long since gaping over her other olive gluteus maximus.

"You're studying my panties? Marigolds are cheerful and lovely, aren't they?"

"The disparate fit's pretty entrancing too."

"I knew you'd be to refined to notice! It's best you understand, Algernon, I've more to do than mend clothes. Here, pull on this big shirt of mine. You can hold the flashlight, and I'll pick the salad."

One had just become nicely relaxed into melted marshmallow. "We don't *need* a salad."

"We do if we're to do more of this."

Such inhibitions to our developing relationship were dissolving quickly, and it amazed us what excuses we could come up with each day to seek the other out. More amazing still was that charged with brilliant and adoring smiles and achingly-caressing hands, each immediately stopped whatever she or I was doing. As lovers when in one's house Laburnum and I preferred being alone, and on one such evening after Sigmund had gone off on the town with Mel, I phoned Laburnum to come up to my bedroom and see my 'etchings', as one musingly termed my mother's fine miniatures. I'd had them framed in delicate gold, so they looked perfect against the tiny gold-dotted wallpaper Laburnum had researched long ago with Eva Runditz especially for this niche.

Laburnum was fascinated with each of Mother's tiny landscapes, adoring all she saw, while one's hand gently ran the contour of her waist—that she wished was more shapely. Though knowing that these beautiful little paintings were not my only objective, as with our wonderful body titillations we each sought unending delights for 'spoiling' one another all so marvelous now the Sigmund question was resolved, and our adoring actions were devoid of emotional setbacks. This was especially so when we sprung from my brass springs sleigh bed to replay our wonder-love midair—emulating turns we'd seen performed in *Cirque de Soleil* by aerial artistes. When we'd used up our internal spark plugs so much exercise soon had us craving canned Norwegian sardines on toast. More lethargically, yet still while plonking exchanged kisses, we pulled on jeans and shirt for me, and a dazzling gem-colored muumuu for her and kept up our kissing as together we dropped down the stairs. Deciding we wouldn't let it matter if Sigmund and Mel returned from their night out and laughed when these two fellows happened to return, loudly expounding about their evening; and just as planned, one simply opened another couple of cans of sardines, and our foursome relished our good health in the late night feast.

One very early morning, Laburnum was positive she 'saw' that one was in great need of a decent loving start to the day. To catch me before I was lured into the lower vineyard, she slipped over in her robe sans underwear. Barging in on one's early morning ablutions, she answered my unasked question, "Don't be concerned about how often we do it, beloved seducer," ignoring one's dripping face as I elatedly helped her remove my fresh bikini. "I'm making up for decades of chastity, and you are too!"

Their only unsuccessful effort at getting private time away from everyone was when one drove Laburnum to a cozy country spot and parked. Whatever our re-positioning, some Lamborghini lever or knob plugged her ribs or pained my shoulder or squashed her thigh; and as this released the emergency, one quickly got my foot on the brake which took care of our experiment. After this botched effort, we agreed to limit our mutual body appreciations to the splendiferous bouncy brass bed springs of one's lovable sleigh bed. Again, we thrilled with cartwheeling mid-air with our forefingers entwined. Addicted to these athletic body merges, when one ultimately plunged her fantastic hips, for me Laburnum's marvelous physique truly transformed what 'home' could really mean—which was a surprise because it was even more euphoric than brilliantly reversing the Lamborghini into an unbelievably tight parking slot.

One rainy day, when the winery employees hung around the coffee pot in one's kitchen, our sudden amour got furtively resorted to at her apartment on her scarlet sofa. Breathlessly spent, we held one another from falling off as we dozed or slept against the other's well-formed chest before being tormented by food pangs. In the kitchen, Laburnum's *naïveté* surfaced through the rocket-powered uplift of our days. "Algernon, do you think this alliance of ours is being noticed by our Runditz group?" She asked this as she changed my selection of white sandwich bread to multi-grain.

"You don't think they've already talked up some suitable grand meal?"

"After all our discretion? Although, yes I know, late-night feasting—Sigmund and Mel." Laburnum had also caught more than a few innuendoes from Sylvia.

"Does it matter? It's ours and marvelous! How easily one forgets that all that strengthening the body gets swimming and working the fields needs the balance of an uncorrupted, completely contrasting appreciation! Look how perfectly it's given us a new lease on good health! You've quite forgotten your poor leg! Companionship too, though I'd always presumed ours was exceptional."

"Long talks, good friendship—though with a wo-*oman* for you, Algernon!" Laburnum loved this tease.

"As you know, dearest temptress, I admit I had missed knowing women as friends, and certainly none that began to compare to you. Not to say that one is incredibly innocent, because I'm not, but loving and being loved by the woman whose companionship one most enjoy—we-e-ll!" One was at a loss for words, "Dear, dear, expressing such things is bound to turn your head!" Laburnum's eyes gleamed as she agreed that she might enjoy having her head turned! "I'm assuming there're other aspects in it for you too, my charming vampire?" I asked, "Though, will they be enough?"

Laburnum demonstrated her agreement with such a suctioning kiss, then put the bread knife down as he worried he would be turned into a mortician's corpse. "Yes," she replied. "All this would be more than enough! Put it this way, it beats the wildest of solitary dreams, Algernon!" Overloaded with bliss, one nuzzled and kissed her shoulder exhaling a languorously fulfilled sigh as one reached around her back to change the bread back to white for one's egg salad sandwich. "You never fail to do things that make me think, you know?"

Chapter 17
Dog Time

Finally, Rowley asked, "All right, now what's going on with Algernon and Laburnum, Paycock? Should we be preparing for her having infants for Great Canine's sake? Notice I said 'infants', not 'puppies'."

"And would *their* infants pop out speaking arched?"

"If their offspring is around Algernon, it'll talk like him, Bruno. Though are you sure Laburnum can procreate, Paycock? I'd heard *sapiens* have a limited infant-bearing age?"

"They must not think so the way they keep jumping one another. It must be that some *sapiens* are a bit different. Did you know that Algernon and Laburnum do cartwheels in the air over his bed before they rut?"

"Farmer Henderson says that too much rutting causes dementia. Mind, I don't think he's too crazy for any frontal-sagittal with Mrs. Henderson anymore. Paycock, do Algernon and Laburnum have other pursuits besides those gymnastics?" Rowley asked in his classy snout-lifted style.

"Great hair balls, yes, they don't just sit around and fall for TV snake oil ads! There's all the activities going on here—wine-making, picking, de-stemming, pressing the must," Bruno explained to Rowley as he was from a crop farm.

"What about Laburnum; is she still picking?"

"Not much. But you know she's smart, being paranormal she gets plenty of psychic work. That was what she was doing that night she broke her leg up in the woods up past your place; and my howls came over nicely operatic, you remember Rowley?"

Rowley grunted. "What's she psyching?"

"You haven't heard? There's this kid, a son of her friend, and it's really disgruntling—his father's kidnapped him," Paycock said frowning.

"That's very disharmonious!" Rowley exclaimed. "Then we should help her."

"Oh you're talking about *that*!" Bruno said knowingly. "Though Paycock, you haven't told her yet?" Bruno asked.

"Told her? Who? As a good friend, shouldn't I be in on it?" Rowley anxiously leaned forward.

"Well, Rowley, Bruno, and I have a little astral cabal going," Paycock explained.

"A secret psyching of your own?"

"Good enough. Though as you are our good friend, we'll tell you." Hushing his voice, "We *know* where—the—kid—is!"

"Congratulations!" Rowley was so intrigued, his ear ends curled. "It's healthy for dogs to exercise our talents," he was all for his good friends' cabal. "So, what did you find out?"

After receiving Bruno's agreeing nod, Paycock became the spokes-dog, "Now promise. It's secret." Getting Rowley's eager affirmation, Paycock activated his most impressive pointing posture, "Okay, Rowley, there's this elderly *sapien* woman in the next town. She's so old, her meals have to come on wheels; and you know where she lives? Her house is slam next to that huge blank wall we all use as a favorite *pissoir* beside the grocery store. Yes, we three know it, it's that great sunshiny brick wall with such stupendous aromas that… well, you've heard of that Chanel person over in Paris who sells those astronomically expensive perfumes? Chanel's planning to bottle that wall's fragrances! It's the most highly valued dog's leg-lifting spot in this state, and—you know it—it's that big blank wall that hides most of this elderly woman's backyard; and it's so overgrown, you can't tell that there's an old shed in it! The poor rocking old biddy can't walk without a frame, so she hasn't been near her shed for years. The house on her other side's foreclosed, no one lives there. It's a perfect hide-out, right in town under residents' noses, but no one thinks of looking there! The boy's dad keeps the kid gagged and bound in that shed; and we hope that after dark, he shoves some crackers and water to that poor battered kid."

"Laburnum can't get the boy imaged?" Rowley asked. Paycock shook his head. "It might be because the boy was hidden other places before that?"

"Before this buried shed? I bet he was!" Bruno reiterated.

"We all know that if there were other places the kid had been hidden, those places could have inducted Laburnum's magnetic waves," Paycock added.

"Yes, that would throw her off all right," Rowley agreed. "Can't you help, Laburnum?" he questioned Paycock.

"It doesn't work too well giving *sapiens* hints, Rowley. Laburnum gets this glossy country magazine which has a photo of an old country shed on its front cover, much like the one the boy's imprisoned in, and I've pulled it out on the floor; and when Laburnum's looking at me if she isn't admiring me too much, I pound my paw on it over and over, but she just *doesn't get it!* Then I lick the shed dark; two times I licked just the shed dark, so it stood out, and I pounded it with my pastern. Another time I scratched it with my nails, but even then. Well, I don't know, maybe there's a chance she could be catching on it's the *shed* she should be looking for."

“Shockingly insensitive with the poor kid there starved and suffering,” Rowley’s snout went even higher when he was disgusted.

“Unconscionable!” Paycock stressed.

“So that’s what Laburnum and her friends are divining! Has she any maps?” Rowley wondered.

“Not that I can find.”

“Mel has a New York State atlas,” Bruno said.

“Keeping Laburnum picturing the shed’s best,” Rowley believed.

“Algernon likes maps!” Paycock remembered. “He used to tour our state in that hilarious two-seater that dogs mustn’t ride in—he-he!”

“You go to his house, Paycock. Don’t you know where he keeps his road maps?”

“I’ve some idea.”

“Even so, how would you get the map to Laburnum?”

“Ye-es. We could help her if we used our Calming Cores?”

All three dogs agreed. Sitting upright, deeply immersed in this quandary with their heads fallen forward, so that to anyone seeing them, it looked as if some pretty glinting object had to be lying between them in the muddied grass. All were horrified by the torture of a young *sapien* taken from his mother and bound so rigid so he couldn’t lift his leg; and as he was gagged, he couldn’t call for help. It was so contrary to Canidae beliefs that the three dogs just sat grieving for the poor boy.

Bruno said, “Normal *sapiens* have chemical elements inserted in them for good sense and politeness, but that kid’s father must have been so grotesquely incident-altered that any good chemicals he’d started off with got removed by pollutant poisoning.”

“That’s why *sapiens*, and even dogs too, need observant friends,” Paycock had said aloud what was being mulled over in both the other dogs’ minds.

“Because it might be so subtle it doesn’t greatly affect some creature’s warped behavior. Canines are fortunate to receive impulses from unusual psychic changes,” Bruno said. Looking at one another, Paycock and Rowley were slow to nod their agreements. Bruno’s longer experience was often helpful as heads down again, they contemplated this as he said, “Augh, just thinking about it makes me hydro, hydro.”

“Hydro-phobic, Bruno, just say ‘hydrophobic’.”

Bruno had his paw raised again, and the other two turned to give him their full listening attention. “When I used to belong to Hans, one day long ago,” without answering Paycock, Bruno used his most senior mode as he went back some years. “It was while Hans was getting his flu shot, and I was waiting outside the clinic for him. I was just standing there quite happily when some big ugly dog came up and pushed and shoved me hard, then he said repulsive and insulting things about my mother."

"You'd met a dog with no cultivation or refinement, Bruno! Horrible! So what did you do?"

"There was another far nicer boxer waiting with me; and without saying a word, we looked at one another and he and I got either side of this ignorant scum dog; and before he did any more harm, we forced him into an alley around the corner."

"And then?"

"We put this pitifully badly raised creature through what we'd learned in pedagogue classes about negotiating."

"Very good! That scum dog badly needed your help. He must have been grateful?"

"The boxer and I gave him the important attributes, until this bad dog admitted that his uncontrol needed help and understanding."

"Using that scene he'd just made of shoving and pushing me, we acted it out putting him in the attack position, as I took defense. When he'd begun to get the idea, we swopped and let him become defense, and I pretended to be attack. He quickly caught on to what it was all about. He was a bright enough dog and deserved to learn a lot more."

"You handled it admirably, Bruno! Now that gauche dog will teach all his friends about negotiating. I hope he was appreciative?"

"Oh, he certainly was. He kept thanking the other dog and myself over and over."

"So he should have, unpleasantness like his might have led to a dangerous fight."

"But you got him so well-behaved, Bruno, he'll be a lot more pleasant to everyone and smile," Paycock complimented.

"Well-bred dogs love to maintain our rules and good instincts," Rowley observed. "Your clueing him in was sensible, Bruno, and he'll grow into a much more respected dog now; and he'll always remember you and that good boxer dog."

"That was a genuine contribution to our Canidae creed, Bruno—congratulations!"

"Commendable, Bruno!"

"Meritorious!" Paycock said; and after another heady pause, he suggested, "Have we finished with that heavier creed topic of Bruno's for today, good friends? Rowley? That's all right, Bruno?"

When they had nothing more to add to this discussion of their Canidae obligations, they got their loaded contemplation pauses completed.

"What an excellent example of our ancestral creed demonstrating to *sapiens* how beautifully 'cooperation' works," Paycock got this going, "and aren't we fortunate? Look at us three here! A Bassett hound, an English setter, and a– a mi– Mix?"

"You can call me a Mix, Paycock," Rowley assured him. "I'm proud to have a mother and a father from different breeds. But as you see, in appearance, I'm more my father's collie, which I'm perfectly happy with."

"You don't mind being called 'Mix'?"

"It's my actuality."

Paycock and Bruno thought this courageous of Rowley—they knew how much he'd always aspired to being in the Westminster, which as everyone knows has obsolete discrimination rules about entrants having to be pedigree.

"Henderson keeps me caged because he knows I'm valuable. Only you two good friends know I dig under its fence to come here."

"Take us three differing breeds, sitting here together with inherently different upbringings and opinions, as mature Canidae we know that however viral our differences, they can *always be bargained.* Since puppyhood we've known that bargaining is wisdom-building, it clears out painful belly aches and mental debris, like grudges, and argumentative personas, because as beasts we are innately noble! We know that losing control and injuring one another must never happen because our civilizing creed doesn't allow it. Aren't we the most magnanimous and admired of all living creatures?"

"Shapely Hocks, yes, all that mass injuring *sapiens* do is regressively mindless!" Paycock affirmed. "Though I'll tell you this—Algernon's the exception. His opinions don't get stuck in a rut. He's more 'cooperative' because he was brought up with dogs—he calls them 'hounds'." Paycock took the opportunity to keep his friends on 'cooperating', and the blissful fluid flow and denser tranquility it causes.

"Thanks to those legendary Egyptian dog gods, Canidae are bred to understand that if we lowered our standards like *sapiens*, dogs could not advance-think —not throughout the whole world! So listen, wouldn't it be outrageous to be a *sapien* officially ordered not to travel some roads because there was bloodshed going on? Wouldn't being banned from certain streets where dogs were fighting to death be freedom limiting as well as undemocratic?"

Paycock's friends agreed, though they were readier to move off serious topics. "What do you have stored, Paycock?"

"We need something relaxing, Paycock. Make it entertaining."

Paycock nodded, then coughed as he prepared to use his voice lyrically. With one hand, he gave a gracious wave as he said slowly and romantically, "'It droppeth as the gentle rain from heaven upon the place beneath'."

"Senseless!" came Rowley's interruption.

“No, it’s not senseless,” Paycock alleged. “When Algernon and Laburnum saw an actor using it on TV, it made so much sense, their eyes swam, and they went pale.”

“Of course, it would have to ‘droppeth’ on some place beneath. Rain doesn’t drop upwards,” Bruno said logically. Always his sharpest after they’d reviewed.

“Except that with Shakespeare, the rain can go any way it wants.” Paycock pointed out.

“With Longfellow it would, but not Shakespeare,” Rowley was sure. “There would have been some ‘Hey nonny nonnies’ if it had been Shakespeare.”

“It’s not Longfellow either, Rowley,” Bruno enlightened. “Longfellow has more Gitche Gumee. Mel sings Longfellow–” mimicking his owner, “‘Forth along the Gitche Gumee, on the shining Big-Sea-Water’.”

“That just shows how few quotes *sapiens* need to appear intellectual socially,” was Rowley’s disgruntled comment.

“Though Rowley, I really like, ‘droppeth as the gentle rain’,” Paycock added, staring off at what his mind’s eye saw, “Its beat is like rain hitting the windows at night, and it quivers like a taut bass drum that soothes me off to sleep.” ‘Hearing’ the rain’s rhythm, Paycock kept on turning his head to its beat.

“I prefer poems about animals. There’s a fantasy one about ‘a cow jumping over the moon’.”

“Good. Do you know it?” Bruno asked. “A cow poem might be more embraceable.”

“Yes.” Rowley’s back paw scratched his head behind his ear before he shook it. “It’s something about ‘The little dog l-laughed’!” But instantly, this poetic line sent Rowley and the other dogs into bellowing fits of laughter! They laughed so hard, they fell backwards onto the grass and rolled till they gagged, drooled, and had to take brisk stand-up shakes! Nothing could be more screamingly funny than a *sapien* trying to imagine that ‘the little dog laughed’! A dog could whip-snap his head laughing about a *sapien* working his brains moldy making it convincing. Bruno, with his long, not-too-agile body, rocked back and forth like a boat on rolling waves, which made Rowley and Paycock guffaw more still, till they had do other double-rolls and sideway stretches as the trickles rolled from Rowley’s eyes. “Shakespeare can ‘droppeth the rain’, but he would never have made ‘a little d-dog l-l’!”

The vision of a *sapien,* pen in hand, straining his every last sub-neuron, so affected the engrossed Rowley, it was too much for him to get the word out; and he went on bumping his rump with laughter till rolling again and finally giving a giant sigh—his front paws clutched at his aching belly.

“It wouldn’t have been Longfellow either,” Paycock informed.

"No, it couldn't have been Henry Wadsworth Longfellow," Bruno had the writer's full name memorized from the cover of Mel's 'Hiawatha'. Paycock accepted him as the Longfellow expert.

Rowley sat up; his paw still dabbing laughter tears from his cheeks.

"Let's forget the cow poem. We'd better help Laburnum find that kid before anything more happens to him."

"Quite right," Paycock and Bruno agreed. "We've got to get that suffering child out of his misery. That's our top priority job."

The threesome nodded enthusiastically.

It was a wonderful time of year with yellow leaves sauntering the air, and the little thuds of hazel nuts dropping. The three devoted friends adored this cooling season, when they would no longer sit smelling of sweated fur with fat, lolled tongues out panting. And the zinc-hued branches above them promised a long, cuddlesome winter before shadowy fireplaces, where tummies would always be warm. Being good dogs what an overwhelming amount there was to hungrily anticipate as they settled down to Laburnum's problem by preparing to get into their wonderful Calming Cores.

Chapter 18
Harvest Time

Determined to scrupulously get to know all areas of one's winery, early that first morning of harvesting, I went to the vineyard track to be beside Mel and met two brothers who had motor-biked from town. Also the Durham family's teen-age girl and her mother that had picked for Hans, then several friendly younger men and women that arrived together in a wildly painted van. An older couple followed, a single man Laburnum knew, who asked after Hans, two college student friends of Sylvia's, a part-time aide from the hospital who was also a dog trainer that Sally-Anne had passed the word to that the Runditz grape-picking started today. Surprisingly too along came Rafferty. One hadn't expected Rafferty, but in his appropriate cut-offs, here he was.

Before this oncoming harvesting call, Sigmund, Mel, and oneself had tied hundreds of metallic-colored streamers to the vine wires to scare off great flocks of fruit-hungry birds ready to swoop down from the long lines of electricity wires. Besides the threatening birds, readiness for certain grapes kept being avidly checked; and on this early fall morning, having tied on hundreds more flashing streamers, still the voluptuous beauty of the grapes' ripening stages thrillingly pulsed one.

This momentum boosted one's sights for this first grape-picking that to oneself I named a 'Cholmondley-Rute Harvest'—the name Hans and I had agreed 'Runditz Winery' should be changed to next year. Heightening this momentum, at a Grape-Growers Association meeting, one had been auspiciously wished well for this first harvest. Actually, with all this impetus heightening, one's anxiety for unforeseen weather change became much too like the stressful hours of awaiting each tormenting report on a vote for an ominous Brussels multi-national treaty! *Oh for Bacchus' sake, Algernon!*

Getting warmed up picking, I tossed my Fair Isle jersey over an end post at the mid-morning break. Returning to one's row, one of the motor-bike brothers caught one's accent, "I say, righty-ho, Gov'nor!" he mimicked me getting some snickers.

"Ah how nice, that you're from England too?" I pretended to inquire.

"Huh? You thought I was?" the complimented youth replied and turning to his brother, "See Jim, I'd got it down good!"

"One didn't catch from which area though?" one still conversed.

"Gotta get more cultivation into it, Al," his brother whittled at their situation.

"Forgetting the 'Rs' and stressing the 'Ts'," one suggested.

"So that's how you speak BBC?" Laburnum had overheard as she came over to join us with Sylvia, Reb, and Sigmund following.

"How to speak?" Sylvia hadn't caught Laburnum's question.

Walking across from one another, going back along our rows, one turned to the mimic, "You know there's a foolproof way of identifying an Englishman? If he's alone and clumsily knocks over a chair and says, 'Oh I say, I'm so sorry?' You can bet your dollar where he's from!"

"A dead giveaway?" the mimic guy asked as one was being appreciated. Then the youth caught on, "Naw, he'd never say that, not if he was by himself."

"Just a joke, Al," his brother-protector helped him.

The call for pickers had gone out when Sigmund and I announced that the time to pick the smaller Marechal Foch grape was *now.* Laburnum too had stopped her studies and got out her own clippers or 'secateurs', as one correctly called them. Cautiously standing on a chair, she had got down her straw hat from high in a closet; and in the Runditz gardening barrow box, she placed the huge jar of the solar tea she'd made that I couldn't stand, adding throw-away cups for all. Joining a group that were signing in on a clipboard with Mel, we all listened to his directions for which rows to go to. Each row was piled high with empty baskets at its beginning. I was three rows ahead of Laburnum, which was best as we both preferred keeping our liaison low-keyed.

This day was gray, clouded, not too threatening, but humid, warm, and impressively still under a far out lingering morning fog, in a stillness that was breathtaking! A vineyard hum came from those getting together again as both new and former pickers geared up for bringing in this vineyard's abundance of fruit. The filling of a basket took on individual rhythms, the numbers of baskets often competitive. Paid by the hour, how many hours each picker worked was their choice, giving further enjoyment to snipping off the fat juicy grape bunches out in this moist freshest air. Environmentally a change for those aware of a couple of crows into some guttural altercations till remarks were passed on how antagonistic the crows' cawing sounded, and the baskets got filled as Mel resupplied from the trailer. As the sun rose higher, it noticeably pushed through the fog and the temperature rose; and well into one's repetitive movement, I took a moment to stretch away any stiffness. Arms straight up, stretch then hold, the same again still reaching but bent; this relief making one feel unusually replete with my optimism for this harvest still soaring high above the debating crows.

Once again, one knew I'd been exceptionally favored to have 'discovered' this little winery, and with one's gorgeous new 'lover' nearby—for 'lover' was what Laburnum was now—promoted from 'a neighbor relationship'! I knew how turbulently we needed one another, and how much we'd awed at the 'reality' that had caused all this to so wondrously fall into place. One may never know what cunning enchantment had been in this air so fortuitously coating what one breathed—giddyingly pregnant thoughts! Though—*ugh!* Yanking back my razor-sharp sheers, I'd come close to clipping my forefinger.

While on this harvesting high, sophisticated wine labels kept frequenting one's imagination. Removing my long-sleeved shirt, I joined other warmed up pickers as some striking labels came to mind so tastefully impressive, one knew I'd feel a kick every time some old chum raved about it!

Some pickers had known Hans as the German who had fled the Nazis with his wife and done the splendiferous job of restoring his derelict house, and others knew him for his winery. Like Hans, one affably conversed with pickers, though I was a different employer to work for. Hans had long depended on residents for their skills and was keen to add to his knowledge about their families, careers, or pursuits. As the newcomer-owner, however well-intentioned, one was at a disadvantage without those former ties. Being a British islander without relatives here and having spent much of one's life as a societal diplomat, one wasn't the easiest man to get to know. This was unfair because knowing of anyone's adverse situation, one would be unusually ready to help.

Both Hans and one's presence in the fields had a tempering effect on excessively eased communication, which kept the pickers' interest narrowed to how expertly they were grape picking. As everyone worked, it became understood that the more experienced older man with the shock of steel gray hair who picked alone far along a row was getting in plenty of hours. He was furtively watched or admired as his nimble fingers used a swift exacting cut above each grape bunch for dropping it so strategically, it stayed on his basket's mounded grapes, and he'd quickly lead with yet another filled basket.

By lunch time, walking along my own row, I was pleased that several rows had been picked clean. Up the tractor track for sandwiches where Mel, Reb, Sylvia, Laburnum, and Rafferty were already munching at the picnic table, I found a place at their table's end next to Laburnum and sat to listen to the conversation between Laburnum and Rafferty while watching the younger crew at the farthest picnic table get to know who each of them knew. On Laburnum's other side, Rafferty was saying something about an article he was to bring her about the discovery by divers of a glass pyramid, believed to have been part of an ancient civilization off the coast of Florida. "Earlier than what you're delving, but it's an ancient site that had humungous technical knowledge, all the same." Laburnum replied that yes, she would enjoy reading it, although she believed that with underwater finds cropping up throughout the world's oceans and lakes, a good deal could be getting left to misinterpretation. This didn't deter Rafferty, who was convinced that other civilizations had reached greater heights even in science than the superpower efforts of the present 1990s. Intriguing with this conversation as Laburnum cursorily talked with Rafferty, frequently smiling at him as if she really wasn't in the mood to be seriously drawn into his opinions. After Rafferty had left though, Laburnum and I finished our fruit as she asked for one's thinking on underwater discoveries.

"Exciting, when the discovery can be seen or photograph-proofed."

"What about this fanaticism of our poet's that before its calamitous end there had been a more technically advanced civilization than our own?"

"You're thinking of Globekli Tepe? It's just one of many buried mysteries."

"Globekli Tepe—though over 9000 years old."

"I'll have to look more up on that one, Laburnum, but given that there's mind-boggling evidence, I would agree with you that much as there have been other mind-dazzling discoveries, it's hard to accept that every ancient find is from a former, more highly advanced civilization. Though unlike you," glancing her mischievously, "I wouldn't fatalistically close my mind." One was bringing up their 'fatalism' opposition again as I let a smirk curve my lips.

"Interesting, but I'm inclined to stick with what can be verified."

One stood needing to get back to the rhythms of his picking, as did Laburnum. "More of this another time?" She agreed. "You didn't overdo the standing, I hope?" Laburnum assured him she hadn't; then calling Paycock, she left to go in and rest on her sofa with 'Beowulf.'

Later I too cooled off with my newspapers in the parlor. Apart from one's mailed *Guardian* and *The Economist* for keeping up with the troubled areas of world news in depth, particularly ones I'd known, one looked through the local paper too to see what businesses were offering. Many were Mennonite, reputedly excellent at their various skills, as we may eventually need good masons if Reb, Sigmund, Mel, and oneself planned to extend the production center's cellar; and it would pay to know who advertised. Pleasantly tired sitting with one's Guinness in this restful tall-windowed room, one was hearing movements within the house. *Sigmund coming in the back way from the production barn?*

"You are the-*ere?*" Sigmund's dulcet interrogative. Coming in where I could see him, making his 'Oh-there-you-are!' face. "We've some good pickers, Algernon! I'm always relieved when we don't have the odd one that doesn't have a clue."

"Picking's simple enough, isn't it?"

"Some don't get it."

"Slower?"

"And mess up the vine."

"A little kindly attention would set that right, surely?"

"Yes, though being held up's a nuisance."

"I hadn't realized we were so fortunate!" Cocking one's head, "Wine and beer is in the refrigerator."

Sigmund went to get a tall thirst quencher of cold water and returned to sit opposite me. This elegant little parlor had become an end-of-day's meeting spot after we'd had all we'd wanted of the outdoors. Sigmund raised his head to say, "Of course, they won't all be back tomorrow, but we can be pleased if most return. Anyway, the harvest's just beginning; word will get around."

Nodding, I'd given up on the newspaper, "I've been making observations, Sigmund. I hope it's not unwise of me to ask, but it looks as if you and Mel are working together all right?"

Sigmund laughed loudly. "Oh, you're so convolutedly British, Algernon!" Catching the footstool between his feet, Sigmund positioned it to get his legs comfortably out dead straight. Putting down his glass, he rubbed his boyishly shrewd damp face. "You couldn't know that there had been a time Mel and I had been close?"

"You might remember that I'd been given the opposite notion."

"That was only if we were both after the same. Well, far be it for me to bore you with more of my sappy Hollywood romances! Though come to think of it, I shouldn't say Hollywood, their movies always end up happy-happy!" And as an aside, "It's no wonder Labby used to call me 'Short-fused Sigmund'!" he related laughing. "Blame 'women'! It's always those Jezebels, never our pitiful strategies! Though your mentioning Mel and me, for two Scorpios, Algernon, similar consciences, each ahead of what the other was doing. Labby once put it this way, 'Dionysus gifted Mel and me with wine-making souls just for making us compete'!"

"Hmmm," I groaned barely amused.

It took a moment before Sigmund went on. "Look, I'm sorry I don't mean to always make insinuations, but even if you don't trust me, you must know from Labby that nothing significant ever happened between us. Should it matter." One was finding aspects of Sigmund I'd begun to like. Then Sigmund, remembering he was reputed to elegantly tease, bantered on, "Look, Algernon, I admired her, that's all. She was nice to be around, and she was pleased I was helpful to Hans." This I could believe recalling the Hans-Laburnum affair. "But I see that even my past mundane observations irk you, so I must be more sensitive. Truly, I mean to be, because I see that as a woman, Labby has plenty of significance for you. I think that with my own women frustrations overwhelming me these days, I would be behaving a lot more reasonably to you if I'd understood your feelings."

Finding Sigmund's 'straight' talk too deviously personal, one didn't respond. One had no obligation to rummage Laburnum's and my fragile newly developing attachment; though after some moments, one's head fell forward and almost involuntarily, I gave a nod, that Sigmund had the grace to accept meant that Laburnum did indeed mean a great deal to me, but just as Sigmund and I had reached this slim basis of understanding, Sylvia 'Hullo'ed' through the back way.

Ending this arbitrariness, one stood, asking Sigmund, "You're here for supper?"

Supper was to be in an hour, and Sigmund assured me he would be here, "Showered, changed, and my promise—I'll be on my best party manners, no more zapping!"

"It really isn't a party, Sigmund." Catching at what was being discussed, Sylvia called through. "It's a hefty supper for grape pickers, but it'll be good—if Reb has left us plenty," as she went back to the cauldron she had on the stove, I went in to her. Making room next to several boxes of linguini, she filleted baguettes to spread with squeezed garlic and whipped butter. "Sally-Anne is to bring her fresh Caesar salad."

"Nice of you to let Laburnum take a night off, Sylvia."

"I knew she'd be tired, putting in most of a day."

Mel had come in with a large flat box and informed them, "Laburnum is doing fine. I've just stuck my head around her door. She's curled up on her sofa reading and says she'll be here."

Sylvia looked at the box suspiciously, "Me-el-? Is that from that new bakery?"

"Surprise! You have to guess?"

"It had better go with my spaghetti."

"Better than anything."

"No-o-o, you didn't find tiramisu!" came Sylvia's hopeful intrigue. Mel gave her a knowing nudge. Tiramisu was hard to find as he teasingly opened the box's lid and both laughed. Over appetizing exclamations, they breathed in the custard and brandy fragrances of the delectable-looking dessert already cut into squares.

"How's that for a first harvesting day's treat!"

"You knew my most secret favorite," Sylvia gushed giving Mel a peck on the cheek.

An hour later, all were changed or at least cleaned up, Sigmund noticeably so in an emerald German T-shirt—his dank hair formally combed. Sylvia, light on her feet as always, brought in the great bowl of spaghetti, then its sauce and meatballs separately to place on the sideboard's flamed trivets, beside stacked plates ready to take before sitting down. Sally-Anne placed her large salad bowl beside Sylvia's; and when Sylvia put the hot pads in one's hands, I knew to go for the garlic bread to put on the bread board beside its serrated knife. Sigmund and Sally-Anne took plates, but before I took mine, I looked across the room and pressing hand to temple, I said, "Sylvia, I'll just make sure Laburnum hasn't fallen asleep."

"She told me she'd be here. Hans is to come too. But we all know Hans can't always make it on time."

"Righty-ho. Back in a tick." Seeing Laburnum's lights on, I walked briskly to the barn, knocked and went in. Not finding Laburnum in the living-room, one cooed, "Laburnum, my turtle dove," heading for her bedroom, but one's voice trailed catching sight of a note on the coffee table with my name in large letters across it. I did an unpleasant double-take and unfolding the notepaper read, "Algernon, don't let Sylvie wait supper for me. I'll be back soon to join you. Nothing to worry about, please do *NOT* follow me – L." Re-reading her sophisticated hand, one was sure her sudden move was because of the kidnapped boy.

Double concerns hit one… Laburnum was not to be out walking alone at night, it had only been the last time she had broken her leg. Then in dismissing her wish not to be followed, instinctively I knew she was making a mistake, and I needed to go after her. Probably she'd been thinking about Sylvia's dinner, and I was too—damn her! Though I knew I'd have to drive to that woodlands meeting place. Devilled demons… how much of her fine good sense did Laburnum use? As Tillie knew about Laburnum's broken leg, it didn't seem likely they would be where they'd met before. Better still I'd take a chance and hurry on foot to check past Rafferty's place? Tapping the end of her note against one's thumb, one's good mood had plummeted to sickening. Yet I hadn't heard her motor-bike—walking, she couldn't have got far.

Plan: Back to supper—Sylvia should know this situation. Heading to one's house, Mel was coming out of the front door. Taking in one's frown, he asked, "Aw don't say it! Bet Tillie called?"

I nodded handing Mel Laburnum's note, who took it under the porch light. "We've no idea where she is, and she doesn't want us following her."

As Mel's knuckles struck Laburnum's note, Reb drove in with Hans. Mel and I hurried to the Lincoln to show the note to Reb and Hans.

"Shit on her!" Reb said getting out. "Not meaning Laburnum, Alg'non, but that damn Tillie!"

Sickening worked at the pit of one's stomach. How much of this occult work had been going on while Laburnum's health had been recovering so well one wondered, while bending to temper an abdominal spasm that thankfully didn't continue?

"Must be they know more?" Mel said to Reb's nodded certainty. We stood expecting Reb or Hans to fill us in, but Hans wasn't hearing and Reb knew less than Mel, plus Sylvia's supper was getting cold.

It was Sylvia who pushed open the screen door and came out on the porch. "What's up? Ah-ha, I'll make one guess!" She called out. "Any idea where? We can nuke platefuls, you guys."

"Keep us plenty," Reb called, and signaling she'd heard him, she went back in to Sigmund and Sally-Anne.

The three fellows decided on the footpath past Rafferty's first, all annoyed but anxious. About to cross the lawn, Hans called, and they turned back to him. "Nasty business," guessing at the Tillie story as he struggled to get out of the car holding his cane, and Reb ran to him. "The story has its mystery, and all of that, but it is too powerful! And you know, Laburnum, remember she isn't the deciding one," Hans stressed this statement as he directed a meaningful look at me.

There were mumbled agreements as Mel and I left Hans to work up a good pace across the lawn. Into a good stride, one's annoyed anxiety toyed with Hans' 'Laburnum isn't the deciding one'. Hans' opinion did not sit well with me. Why? Because I just couldn't agree! I knew what Hans was saying, but… No, Hans, what Laburnum's done had been up to her! She'd had the choice! Though even while arguing Laburnum's move to myself, I knew a bombardment of what Hans' opposing insights would be. Finally, one's relentless sense of fairness made me admit that only a few people had as much affinity with the occult that Laburnum had—there was a chance Hans was right. If she'd received a persuasive enough phone call from Tillie to meet her, her concern for the kidnapped boy could have outweighed any choice of her own.

Having sent Hans in to Sylvia, Reb jogged to catch up Mel and myself. It was uphill on this track, and the earlier nights made seeing tricky. Sylvia's good meal was being missed, but if like that last time, Laburnum was hurt? This fear kept us moving fast with little to add to what we knew or could guess at, we hoped to hell our trek's direction would find her. "Hadn't you better return?" I asked Reb.

"First things first. Sylvie will save some."

Having hiked to the highway, we awaited a tractor-trailer's noisy high speed, lit up like Christmas with quadruple lights front and back. Once across the road, we spread out across the gravel lane and moved higher on the hill, where we could see more, and walking was easier. Leaving the oncoming dark over the lake behind us, ahead remnants of nacreous cloud reflected the sun is having already set. Despite my awful concern, one had the wit to recognize Rafferty's orange jacket slung on a garden chair in a front yard. I'd seen Rafferty take it off grape-picking and was sure this must be his single man's cottage.

"Yep, Rafferty's," Mel confirmed. "I'll ask; you two keep going."

"Give a yell," Reb meant if Rafferty knew anything.

"Oh, you'll hear me!"

Without missing a step, Reb and I kept on up high on the ridge till seeing a promising wooded area ahead of us—wind-blown till self-contained, its trees taller toward its center as if molded by an inverted bowl. As one's hopes grew, I was thankful that this walking kept down one's stomach pain. Though it hadn't calmed my suffocating concern that a woman I now greatly cared about could fall into more unimagined adversity. This was a price one hadn't been prepared for. Having allowed in feelings, *which was a large part of lowliness- oh right, feelings were in with lowliness, all right! Feelings like these for his best woman-friend, such feelings that were basic to humanity too.* Basic, because even national conflicts got going out of uncontrolled feelings. *The kind of feelings his adult life had managed to float above, other than compassion, that he was experiencing more of now. In one's past, one must have floated above a crater of unfelt feelings with so much left mystifyingly unknown*—that other than his mother's death and the war, he had drastically missed out on or only seen through the blur of protective statistics, *that if he hadn't met Laburnum, he would have gone on dumbing down with it to infinity. All in all, wasn't this simply meaning that he might be dearly loving Laburnum??*

Which could be why the terror of how she might be when they found her caused these abdominal pains and flashes of former feelings. *Lowlier feelings? His mother hysterically fighting his father's command to have one's pony shot. Oh horrors! That ever-indelible childhood scene—Mother's God-awful screams as his father ordered Horace to ram her into her car and drive her somewhere; while Nanny, her long-nailed fingers paralyzing her grip on one's ear, roughly shoving me up to my room, then—that piercing shot, all their eternal non-erasable screams incising into eternity!*

Surely, his despair for this surprise move of Laburnum's was much like his mother's, and his own trauma back then. That pony scene had been his boyhood's most devastating personal experience, excluding war's massive gory removals, though this diverting look backwards? It wasn't helping! Pulling myself together, we'd reached the woods, and using a foot-worn path, moved through clean-trunked trees devoid of underbrush till straight into denser penumbra. Just the kind of woodland I believed Laburnum's group might be attracted to, as catching Reb's warning, one raised my step over a fallen forked branch, shuddering that so near to dark Laburnum wouldn't have seen it.

"PayCO-OCK!" Reb had the sense to shout a couple of times. I called too while peering along a path of broken twigs flattened by former use. We kept walking, Reb and I calling, "Pa-ayCOCK! LabURN-UM!"

Mel's breathless call behind us caught us up, "Rafferty didn't think she'd come this way."

With our calls unanswered, Reb and I agreed Rafferty could be right, and we all stopped. One advised, "Look, you two, go get your supper. I'll drive and check where we found her the last time."

"No, you get in to Sylvia, Reb. Algernon and I'll shoot up there," Mel changed his plan

"Aw hell, then it had better be in my car!"

"Ha, you're enough to send one to a second-hand car dealer!" one lamely quipped.

"Get a good one, make it a Lincoln!"

It was easier walking down the hill, except we were headed into the blacker eastern darkness shrouding the lake again, and after re-crossing the empty highway and finding our track again, we avoided stubbing feet on embedded stones and brushing brambles, often at face height as we held them back from one another. Ever mindful of Sylvia's spaghetti dinner, we kept up a good retracing pace; then in front of them bounced, out of the darkness, Paycock!

"Oh, Paycock!!!" One greeted relieved, hopeful. "Here, boy, *HERE,* Paycock!" They made out the dog turning to exuberantly wag his entire body at me. "You tell us then, good boy."

Mel spoke, "No need, Algernon, look!" A rustling came from left of us as Laburnum walked toward us out from an unseen path as coolly as a displaced phantom. In this southern most area of the same woods. We slowed at the sight of her. Not just at her, but at what we could tell of her demeanor, till Mel asked, "You okay?"

She too stopped—no reply.

Did she even know us, as she silently looked our way? Hopefully I wondered if trying to see through this darkness had slowed her reaction, but all we got from her when she finally replied, peculiarly soft, dutiful, was that yes, she was all right! And as much as we could see of her dimmed in her long loose clothes, she might be. "Fine," she said, "I'm fine," repeating this for them detachedly. Spoken as if saying anything just then confounded her. To their mix of attitudes, she said, "Though I'd thought—"

"Ye-es?" One dared her.

"Course if we'd met up an hour ago, it would've been a whole lot easier!" Mel got in facetiously.

Having made this initial contact, in their mixed tensions, the four turned mutely to head back to the house. I was feeling great relief, though Laburnum's distancing pained me, so I lavished Paycock with anxious pats and caresses.

"Might've drawn us a map," Mel called back to her walking beside Reb. "What's down that way?"

"Just woods. Oh- you're here, Algernon," her voice wholly indifferent.

"Going to tell us what happened, then?" Mel asked her, as I stayed back, calming her dog.

"Law enforcements are to officially use our help," her usually beautiful voice was joyless. "They wouldn't, you remember? Didn't want us in with them."

"You've their blessing?"

"They won't impede. We'll work deeper at our regional area, where we believe."

"They took the kid to?"

"The father abducted him." Walking on, she said pitifully, mechanically, "It looks like I've messed your evening. I'd had to hurry—" then irritated, "I did write you not to follow."

"S'okay, s'okay! So all that's happened is we just got in a good hike for whetting our appetites."

"It wasn't what I'd have chosen either, Reb." We were back at the house, and Reb and Mel lost no time going in for supper.

Left on the front porch alone with me, Laburnum lamely attempted, "I guess I've caused."

"YES!" Burst my pent-up worry. "Why? Damn it! You could've phoned, let me in on it for God's sake!"

"Algernon! *Don't...* please!"

"Some indication, Laburnum, we've been close."

"I did my best."

"But we're..."

"All right. It would've been nicer of me; though, should there have been an obligation?"

She couldn't have hurt me more if she'd slapped my cheek. Never had Laburnum and he jarred this profoundly. Despairing, one's hand slid to hold my forehead before I dropped onto a porch chair—All right—*'should there have been an obligation?'* After some fraught moments, I looked lengthily at her through this night's dark until my head involuntarily tilted back. Once again I was seeing her as that mystical witch-woman of our first vineyards meeting, which helped me re-find some tenderness. "No, no obligation," one replied in fairness, "no, I'm just so bloody relieved!"

"Yes, I guess I know you are," she said through what one was at last seeing was her unutterable exhaustion. "I do see that if it had been you who had rushed off."

"YES!"

She sat down too, slumping with all she and the meet had expended, trying not to give in to terrible all-in exhaustion. One knew that Laburnum expected exhaustion, and meteorite-like, it had already dropped over her to encase her insides as she'd told him it often had after progressive meets. One could see she was fighting inner inertia, and that it was so leaden in her, there were other depths to her. Depths one hadn't known that he'd had to turn away from. Studying along the porch to her lit apartment, its normalcy of appearance was consoling, and at last was one's steadier fair-mindedness re-emerging?

This paranormal incident of Tillie and Laburnum's had apparently gripped his beloved woman inhumanely. After all, she had been using that full and innately protected otherness, her supra-human self, so the Laburnum he knew could no longer receive—*and why wouldn't it grip her?* The warm, loving, erudite Laburnum was lost to the clutch of this 'power', as Hans had correctly described, while he, her lover, was being kept at bay!

Then oh Lord, what did he really know about this woman, or about any independent vital woman? And how much was any woman or any-person justified in inflating their pursuits till they barred off those most dear? The two sat on too divided to speak, hearing only the thumped isolating of their own drenching thoughts. To herself, she could be vainly spreading out all her evening meet to really see what I was pushing in on. And I, knowing I was being barred from her, was so viscerally in need of this woman's completing connection, it pained being barred from her, though to what degree? Too entombed in our separate hurt to put out a hand, or to in any way put flesh to the other's distasteful flesh, each looked beyond the other or just away.

Finally, giving a long melancholy sigh, Laburnum arose. A specter of her former self as she floated, rather than walked, her draped body appearing to be above the porch's floor as she rolled around to the lake side chairs, where she sat again, which incidentally was where I usually wandered too for confronting one's state of mind. Dragging oneself I followed her, and both of us looked out at *a most miraculous sight!*

At just this moment a blood-red full moon was rising from the opposite misty horizon!

Struck to our fragmented cores, we each stared out at this hazed, startlingly spectacular intruder!!

Oblate with birth, in moments this moon's redness segued into orange, changing yet again as, it cleansed our initial ire. As both man and woman, we were digesting its bold rise as if the earth's revolving had paused for it to glorify to its sensational amber. For moments, as we consumed this magnificence that phenomenally eclipsed our churned distress, this upstaging orb discarded its horizon's bed—callously casting it off to leave it. Speechlessly studying this moon, both I and this woman were realizing the power of our inexpressibly buried affinity while watching it mature to a solid whiteness, where it flaunted its suspension within the night's purest ultramarine as it tossed its silvered smithereens onto the rippled blackness of the festively unheeding Lake Seneca!

Fixated to this all-reigning harvest moon, Laburnum's and my divisiveness had weakened until finally she found the strength to say, "I hadn't intended to hurt you, Algernon."

"It's all right though, isn't it?"

Her hand went to tentatively lie on one's forearm, where I knew she felt for its glossy silken hairs she'd known from drying off beside me down on the dock. Though tonight, that was it. As she said, "I've known independence forever, I think," and I knew that she simply knew one's silky arm hairs as if they were alone out in space.

"It's easy to forget that forever was back when one kept hoping to God it would change." As she retrieved her hand, he risked adding, "Though Laburnum, it was only after the last meet that you had fallen and had badly broken your leg."

The moon had dipped their faces in molten silver, tinting what had been familiar till their features appeared different. With her hair tucked behind an ear as she lifted her head, I saw that beneath her cheeks were shadows that couldn't glisten like the rest of her face. This blaze of a silver moon was bringing us each a profound solace that had the possibility of forgiveness in with it, even as Laburnum nodded to one's testy reminder of her broken leg.

Recalling that I'd been looking out for her, I saw that the Tillie incident tonight had brought on this suddenness of change. She said, "Understand, Algernon, when Tillie phoned, she's rarely demanding by the way, but on the phone she couldn't say all of why she needed me—see there was tonight's 'in conjunction' opportunity."

"Wouldn't I have understood that?"

Hesitating before she leaned to lay her head on my shoulder and closed her eyes, even to the reassuring moon that silver-coated more of her body, she said, "Planning will be easier from now on."

Planning?! Good Grecian Gods! Hadn't I been a veteran of infinite military planning of every detail in overwhelming situations?!

Though what in hell's name was missing from one's pathetically wounded heart that stopped one from sensibly being pragmatic about this 'planning' of his lover's? Something within him certainly caused one's wariness in this elusive roulette game of loving Laburnum, and one wasn't sure what that was. Though what one did know was that a considerable amount of moon-watching lay ahead for me out here. "Do you suppose we're in a bind?" I murmured. Her answer was silence. Then out from nowhere, one's non-sequitur. "If we're trying to forget all this, Laburnum, and I am, I had started out to you this evening wanting to tell you something, though nothing too world shattering, just an interesting little coincidence." There was more directness to her look up at me. "You helped me get my boxes of books from home onto my study shelves." She made a scarcely audible affirmation. "Last night I took up my Egyptian kingdoms' book and started to read it when a couple of notes I'd made while out there dropped out."

"Yes?"

"You might like to browse them. That's all."

"They're about?" she asked through shoulder-drooping tiredness.

"Egypt's soaring into the wider world. In fact, its golden era was dependent on the ingenious planning of its armies, their successfully worked out soldiering, et cetera."

"Yes, yes, oh I would like to, Algernon—like to read them. Brilliantly conceived—during the middle kingdom." Laburnum's heavy eyelids were closing over her sporadic thought or two pushing through her dire need to sleep when the latch sounded on the screen door.

"Ah, this is where you two are!" Sylvia said cheerily. "I'll bring you each your platefuls. Trust me, they'll help." The latch clicked after her.

"Algernon," Laburnum begged me after Sylvia left, "Please, listen, I very badly *have* to sleep."

Her blatant stating her physical condition surprised me! Sated by one's own pain due her lack of trust, one hadn't given a thought to the cost of her other powers! "So sorry, Laburnum! I'll walk you back."

"No," as she stood. "You stay for Sylvie, I'll be fine."

"Wait," one said. In less than a minute, I was back from Sylvia. "Here my dearest, hold my arm, we shouldn't have sat here so long."

"Oh but that mo-oon!" We were both wordless with appreciation, and as we walked, "The Egyptian notes—please, don't forget them. Yes, their armies set precedents, though let's not talk any more tonight."

"No, my darling Laburnum, we won't." She overbalanced then, and my arm quickly went around her to pull her to me in extraordinary sensations of her preciousness—wonderful, hot, and over-aweing—as she, within my firmer hold on her, abandoned to him, curving her torso to my hip for walking to my step. "I'm going to put you to bed, my dearest, and one will promise to leave you to sleep. Proof of my love, because sleep is what you must have. Sleep till noon, or till you're hungry."

"Thank you, Algernon," as a shred of the Laburnum he had admired looked back at him.

Guiding her into her apartment and through the living-room, she stumbled again, more than once, and had to lean all her weight on him. By her bed, he helped her unbutton her shirt but whatever they were working out as lovers, it was utterly mandatory he restrain to a more pure companionship this night as she kicked off her shoes, so close to being asleep, she fell against him again. "Off with this too," his arms went around the precious body he profoundly loved, in ways he was yet to understand.

Down she flopped onto the bed he'd only just opened in time. Lying on her side, her bosom flopped toward the mattress as he gathered up light covers to lovingly tuck around her; and once again, he sat to watch her already closed eyes twitch into some health-giving sleep. Turning off her bed lamp, I kissed her and sat to be sure she had dropped into the abyss of deeper sleep that had been aching to possess her.

Though I didn't sit for long. Paycock came in to lick one's hand and remind me that however much humans could hold off eating, dogs very decidedly could not. Going to fill Paycock's bowl, I watched the beautiful setter gulp down his chow, as I realized that I too was hungry. I hoped that Sylvia still had a plateful of her 'hefty supper' left that I could heat up. Because while eating it, one would think out the next day's routine; and for normalizing one's thoughts, I would work at what all this evening had meant.

Chapter 19
Conflict

Back in the kitchen, Sylvia and Reb were wrapping food to find spaces for another dish or two in the refrigerator or the dishwasher. Sally-Anne had just left.

"Your plate is in the microwave, Algernon. On top's Laburnum's."

"No need for Laburnum's; the sandman has already visited."

"You're sure?" Reb asked derisively. "Think we can count on a quiet night?"

After agreeing with him, I asked, "Reb, do those meets always take so much out of her?"

"Out of all of us, y'mean?"

"Hey, don't forget Laburnum put in a couple of days picking, Reb." Sylvia defended her friend.

"Each of us have to care what we plan."

"Aw, I can't believe you guys don't get the biggest kick out of gallivanting all over the woods! I check your faces when you come back," Sylvia flirtatiously countered.

Sigmund came from the dining-room, having cleared the table of a few spoons and forks. Seeing them in his hand, Sylvia held the dishwasher open for him to drop them into the cutlery slots. "She's okay, Algernon?" One noted that for once, Sigmund didn't refer to Laburnum as 'Labby'.

"Laburnum is asleep, Sigmund, she'll be fine."

"I would've come and directed your posse, but it looked as if you'd manage! Best I stayed to entertain Hans and Sylvia. The spaghetti is even better just made, I ate exceedingly well!"

"I'm sure it's still delicious, though after all you'd planned and cooked, Sylvia, it was a shame we couldn't have all eaten together."

"That's why the joint efforts. Sally-Anne and I don't let it get to us if the meal has to be in shifts. One thing she and I make sure of, it's so yummy it will eventually all get eaten. Look, if you'll hand me Laburnum's plate there, Algernon, I'll save it. Yours will be hot now. Here," giving me the hot pads for unloading it. Thanking her, I'd always appreciated being one of the team. Sylvia said, "I'm staying upstairs with Reb tonight, Algernon, okay?"

"In the cupola?"

"That's our crow's nest." Reb gave Sylvia a hurry-up slap.

"Is that bed enough?"

"It's a three-quarter old antique, and it has a great feather mattress. You should try it sometime, Algernon; you get lost in it, it's so soft!"

"It's *so-oft,* Algernon. Not like your brass bed's springs, he-he!"

Chuckling, Sylvia and Reb eyed one another, recalling Algernon's sleigh bed with the heavy double box springs. "Reb and I love a soft bed, and Reb hon, I'm about ready to tuck in up there."

"You two will love it tonight; the full moon is ablaze."

"Should've known, just right for paranormals! Sylvie, come on, you first. Better bulldoze you up the two flights, u-up with you!" With affectionate shoves, Sylvia's backside got slapped and pushed as she pretended Reb was being too much. "Night, all!"

"Thanks for all your thoughtfulness, Sylvia, and for not freezing mine," I said getting my plate as I nodded them goodnight.

Their voices and feet could be heard high up climbing the stairs.

Taking a beer from the refrigerator, I set myself up at the kitchen table, noticing that Sigmund had grabbed a can and had companionably straddled a chair back to front. This was fine, although one was hoping for some time to oneself.

"The Aurores are coming on fast, Algernon." Getting the early varieties of grapes in was on Sigmund's mind, and he had plenty to say about the De Chaunacs that he had given special care to the year before. "The Vignoles will be about right if we don't have torrents."

As I ate, I made an effort to listen to him, agreeing as I knew most of Sigmund's field observations. Lately though I had to admit that this fellow was more creditably the wine-maker Hans had so admiringly led one to believe he'd be, and it was a help to everyone that this Saxon lover was getting his 'women troubles' under control. With these important later stages of the grapes taking our attentions, I greatly hoped that Sigmund and my stickier first relationship would keep on smoothing. This would be easier too when everyone's objective was the sheer work of bringing in the harvest before birds or fungus got it, but tonight one was having to work at keeping one's mind on what Sigmund was saying. After our evening of chasing Laburnum, and one really did need to finish my dinner alone. I liked Sigmund more now, but one's earlier disagreements with him made it harder to take in more of Sigmund's comments. Finally I told him, "Sigmund, I'd like to talk more, but after this evening's mess-up, I'm really needing to."

"Say no more, Algernon!" Sigmund butted in. "Enough has been said for tonight, anyway; and we'll both be out there at it again in the morning. Besides, you're looking tired." After this Sigmund decided that he was feeling the day's work anyway, and agreeably we wished each other goodnight.

This unpleasant Laburnum situation had been hanging on inside one like some wretched flag bound too tight around its pole to show what it stood for. Like my bound flag, I was miserable that my friendship with Laburnum was no longer what she could be knowing too. Having finished my plateful, as the house went quiet, I tried to relax against the back of my chair with the remains of my wine and get back to this sadly disrupted evening. I really knew that Laburnum was not ready to put what she and I could be meaning to one another any higher on her list—which was a great disappointment—too often I had been the one waiting for her-! *Ha, so much for one's serious attempt at wooing, Algernon, you ancient run-over Romeo!*

Yet one also really knew that this clairvoyance of Laburnum's was too dynamic a part of her for it to be any other way, *damn it.* Though if she and the police did find the kidnapped boy, if it should all change, wouldn't I regret not having been patient? I'd known her occult power after arriving back from England when she'd 'seen' his returning hour and made sure that Sylvia welcomed one back. Laburnum didn't arbitrarily use her clairvoyance.

Still this current kidnapped boy situation was taking a good deal out of her, and for how long would this be? She was doing all she could for this boy's sake, which was certainly commendable; though as her lover, was I always to keep uppermost that finding this child was *her* obsession and *her* priority? Her *only* priority? Surely, discovering our man-woman appeal was extraordinarily opportune too? How often did such an appeal happen? Though with her exhaustion tonight, he was having to re-think what was going to help this situation. By giving their friendship a pause, for instance, would that be enough? Is that what *he'd* want?

All right. *In his straightest and most honest fairness, here was the trouble.*

Could one ever overlook the stupendous physical excitement Laburnum could give one? Quite a jolting excitement with her hotly inquisitive glances stomping up at him. In this, she had been the apotheosis of womanhood I'd always strongly hoped I'd meet!

Laburnum apparently couldn't know how greatly this gender attraction, along with her individual personal attraction, meant to *me*. One's proudly conservative blue-blooded family were out of an over-disciplined lineage she couldn't possibly understand. One's father and Gilmore too had weathered bare-buttocks flogging at prep school—his father during that earlier time of suppressed notoriety when some of the Eton hierarchy had notoriously sexually abused their students. Conditioned by this demon history, one had seen that in an age of competitive empire spreading, the world needed to be organized by outstandingly brilliant men, which had made men the dynamic, the superior sex.

Although in one's case, the secret little têtes-à-têtes with Mother had eventually shown one that there were possible reasons to be secretly skeptical of these exalted masculine beliefs; but since there was no place for disloyalty, I too had put in my share of falsely agreeing with Thaddeus, Telford et cetera.

One had barely got a start on re-forming what his mother's intellectual views were on inequality. *Her...* 'Men is abominable ignorance of women!' Which he'd shamefully complicated in the Foreign Service when he'd joined other bachelors for sexually misusing women. *More deeply he had known that this decision had not been in with either his mother's or his own true ideals* – One had found this to be so when on occasions an overseas couple demonstrated how greatly a mate could make life infinitely happier! Though a beautiful woman with his own interests had been exceedingly hard to find, let alone get to know. Laburnum having become his ideal, yet—*oh awful! Here he was undoubtedly more greatly valuing her again than she did him.*

Most fairly, he knew that if he was to get back Laburnum's full attention, he would have to make sure her clairvoyance in looking for the kidnapped boy had better hurry up and do its work. Though, damn it, surely tonight he had not been all wrong in letting her know how little her not caring about one had hurt?? *If our caring had been mutual, shouldn't she have seen how horribly it pained me she didn't give a damn? But had she even noticed that I'd hurt?* Laburnum wasn't a person to be deliberately unfair—recalling that she had done everything she could to relieve my anxiety, she had not had romantic inclinations toward Sigmund. During this reviewing, *one was well aware that I had plenty of work ahead—not only in one's own life but in persuading one's 'amorist' to know and understand him.* Loosening, he slid his chair further back from this pleasantly familiar kitchen table they all so often enjoyed.

I had not expected to sleep well that night and didn't. The next morning, I worked on a row by myself, direly hoping that Laburnum's lengthy sleep would move us back into the full loveliness of our earlier routine. Yanking at a rogue plantain, abruptly my arms didn't seem strong, and I became unforgivably tired—not even Mel's good coffee had given one a good enough lift. Was it going to take a morning like this threaded with doubts about Laburnum's and one's earlier wonderful friendship for me to admit *my* own lack of inner verve? Most mornings I was energetically ready to sing out to the faster-paced clouds, the compositionally lit and shaded vine leaves, or I'd assess the day's weather differences caressing my face, or—I'd take such moments of immediacy to toss around up there with Laburnum. Though there was none of this. Where was one's reliable old spirit? Wasn't one dreadfully lacking in one's usual *'bounce,'* for want of a better word? Could I ever admit that I was chronically missing her??

Tired and desperately needing to physically be with her, on the noon break I gave up and went up to Laburnum's. Beside her bed, just as I'd expected, his exhausted woman was still enviably off in her deep dreams! Sleeping so lengthily, one couldn't be sure what her awaking mood might be, but stealthily letting myself down on her bed, when her bed clothes moved I leaned to kiss her fantastic Roman nose. Absorbing her night-warmth, her woman's sleep-smell, her arms lazily moving from her dreams to uncannily reach to wrap around me! *Though why should she be the one to have everything she wanted?* Lifting her bed-clothes, I jammed my socked feet along her torso and legs for getting in beside her as any worries about what her response might be vanished when her warm arms sleepily tightened about me.

Getting comfortable, I whispered croakily, "All last night I was having to think about *her* far too much—some woman kept me up."

Suddenly looking at him with a surprising star-brightness illuminating her sleep-ridden eyes, Laburnum asked, "She couldn't have been a witch-woman?"

"Must've been. But how in all Hades could a nice British islander like me get caught in a weirdo web like hers?"

"That didn't have had anything to do with a smashed arum lily?"

"It might have. Tell me more, I'm getting sleepy."

"You will come through all this a far better man," came her strong statement.

"Is that what pro Encouragers say, or is it witch-talk?"

"It'll slide you into a better sleep so that when you're wakeful again; we can do some proper talking."

"*One,* will do the talking."

Just this much of being with one another was allowing us to sample some promise of a possible newer companionship, though I was still too mixed up and exhausted until at last in her arms some mystical furnace burned me incredibly molten, so I fell asleep.

While succumbed to this cuddled recharging sleep, later, she slipped from my arms to go to pull the curtain around inside her tub and let plenty of warm shower spray her to greater wakefulness. Aware of her bodily absence, I roused, got up and rinsed off my face at her kitchen sink and went to wait for her on her sofa. When she came out, I was filled with so much we'd have to work out, yet one's strident longing for her had one taking in every nuance of her blue polka-dotted wrap, her nimble tapering fingers tying her belt, her damp hair ends fallen into fairy-tale points. Being lightly tanned when she came to sit close to me, it didn't help my gathering disagreements that she looked indescribably moist and lovely—waxen, near to unreal!

Dewily much more awake, she told me, "Coffee will be ready in a few minutes."

"You could have it with your tiramisu? You saw I brought it over?"

Nodding, "Thanks, I will. It would be a shame to spoil all that good sleep, Algernon, so I'm going to skip the fields today."

"What with your Tillie trouble and your overreacting lover?"

"Not you, Algernon, not at *all* you! Though as you saw, finding this kid is taking a hell of a lot of effort."

"Excusable, when you'd put in a good day in the fields."

"I had, yes. Oh, *hold on!* The coffee!" Unlike her wraith-like look last night, the light of this bright mid-day reassuringly prove that beneath her sky-blue, white-dotted silk robe was that solid flesh woman one was so needing to love again. Much more her old self now, she left him to go and pour their mugs full of her wonderful-smelling beverage and bring them in. "As I've upset you all though, I shouldn't sound so helpless; if you're short-handed, I could help."

"Not a chance, we only hire experts!" She slapped him with her handy rolled-up newspaper. "And no, you'll be glad to know that fortunately we're not short!"

She nodded, and guessing at what he was needing to know, she said, "I can't say much about Tillie Algernon, you know that that way works best. But with law enforcement cooperating at last, we owe the boy."

"Look…" gathering one's wits, "Look, I am interested in all you're doing, Laburnum," one stopped her, "but much as the Tillie-kidnapped-boy is necessarily taking most of your thought, at the same time it shouldn't be forgotten that you and I are living out this man-woman myth?"

She turned from him, stricken. Then finally, voraciously, "Okay, there's no denying your masculinity, Algernon; and yes, besides being a good kind of witch, I must say that in all honesty I'm glad that you also see me as a woman."

"Then hell, Laburnum, isn't that a lot to deal with right there?!"

"Al-*gerno*-on?" That awesome pleading little whine, so impossibly hers.

"All right," I coaxed, I'll concede that just now as a man and woman, you aren't free, are you? Free to notice what's happening to us? To me?" I said this, then leaned back from her, collecting myself as a soft newer feeling was infusing my eyes that caused Laburnum to see what I was working to hang onto. Softly one said, "You may not know this, Laburnum, but I have always coveted the hope that there could be a day when I might find some of that 'love and loyalty' paradise that's triggered all sorts of wondrousness in certain coupled friends of mine. Late as I seem to be getting to it. Though my 'coveted hope' is nothing new, and I may not have spoken much of its possibility, but believe me it has always been close by."

Looking back at him with that rifle-shot look of hers, she repeated, "'All sorts of wondrousness'?"

"Don't make fun of me, Laburnum."

She stared down at the coffee she was stirring. "I know I must seem obsessed to you, Algernon, which I am. I feel horrible that what I do affects Sylvie and the guys, I wish for all their sakes it didn't. Poor Sylvie and Sally-Anne, it's bad enough just preparing a large meal."

“I’m glad to hear you understand that,” I’d pushed in on her again, pleased that our eased former sensibleness disclosed this hint of returning; but even as she spoke in that cavernous voice with its distinguishably varied releases that were no one’s but hers, one needed to patiently loll back into the depths of her cozy sofa for awaiting getting a start on all that truly needed to be discussed. Sipping her rousing coffee, she was struggling more now for any least contentment, though I… I still only kept seeing how a much more contentment between us there *could* be.

In that manner, Laburnum had of suddenly expanding her mood, she stated, “You’re right, Algernon, I’m very fortunate everyone understands how imperative Tillie’s call was last evening, they’re all exceptional friends to care about our tragically abused boy, but I’d like you to know,” she sat forward to him more intimately; the silky polka-dotted fullness snuggling the tawny curves of her still moist bosom and its glittering little gold chain, “It’s often without warning that this ‘gift’ of mine makes me ‘see’ so potently.”

Butting in again, “*I don’t know* enough about all of that, but there’s also a vast amount that somehow, someday, you’ll need to know about me.”

Her deep breath, “That I’d dearly like to know, Algernon, my dearest.” *Words he’d so desperately needed to hear last night.*

“Very well.” I sorted loading with better hope. Because of course, in this instance getting at her occult revelations while they were still vivid might make a clearer way for his more long-term loaded thoughts that could only wait—*for a while.* Taking another tack, “Last evening, Laburnum, after you’d left, Hans said that you’d ‘had’ to go to the meet, meaning it had not been your choice. I hadn’t ascribed to his way of thinking, or I hadn’t after reading your note and first knowing you’d taken off again. I just—damn well couldn’t!

“Naturally, Algernon, as we’ve grown to mean a lot to one another, and you must have worried I’d break more bones. Have I been too much of a handful for you lately?”

“Yes, you know you have, which makes me realize what comes of loving a chimerical brand of woman!” I looked up at her from my coffee as it amused me to say this.

“Kindly put. Yes, I mean that. I’m not your average woman, which I don’t mind, so thank you. Though eventually, you might want to lessen that description of me!”

“‘Chimerical’?” I mused sipping my coffee still feeling that like my metaphorized flag bound so tight around its pole, there was much that was still not coming clear.

Oh come on, Algernon, you’re a Cambridge man?! What is it that’s so unclear? Was one going to worry that now Tillie and she were both allowed into the official investigation, through stumbling ineptitude I could lose Laburnum?

It was especially hard for me to settle for Laburnum's version of last night's occult evening, because no way around it, *she simply had not included me!* Not by acknowledging our disagreement, nor even that there had been those supra-extraordinary moments when both of us had fixed to that spectacularly wondrous harvest moon! Such a bizarre and transcending alliance, yet had she intentionally left my reactions out?

Why was it that at times being in America only seemed to be so bloody difficult?

My concern hadn't escaped her. "Searching for a kidnapped child is unusual, Algernon. But on occasions, psychic imagery like that can be so defiant, it's all I can do to keep with them," she continued, as her neat fine fingers flipped the air. Then, "Tell me something," she asked me more breezily, "back when you'd first heard I had this gift, what did you think?"

"Talking of before I'd purchased this estate? Sylvia had warned me that a witch lived in this apartment. She didn't warn me nearly enough! She referred to you as a 'white witch'."

"You were smart to listen to Sylvia, Algernon, she's a remarkable woman," And off Laburnum went again, "She not only knows how to run a successful inn and make our good friend Reb a very happy man, but she has no half-measures; she fully devotes to what she takes on." I nodded that I knew. "I know what Sylvie was saying to you, though a 'white witch' isn't what I'd call myself as I don't practice wicca. I tried to once, but it takes too much effort." Looking at me till impertinently, capriciously, she deliberately changed her voice to fake mine, "'One' would have to give it hefty chunks of time!" Caustically smiling, more to herself, "We each distill what we want to for shaping our happiness, don't we, Algernon? What other way can we become generous if we don't fulfill our self-possessing natures?"

As these weren't the answers my sleepless night's perturbed questions had been about, I realized this might not be the day to keep at one's more important questions. Nodding, as I toyed with this, wondering if I might achieve more if I completely gave in and really listened to her, but after some shattering moments—oh—as one suddenly loudly asked her, "Is it because you yourself have an affinity with the loneliness of this boy?"

"Oh-ho! Interesting! Are you asking what would have happened if instead of me some other medium had received the kidnapped message? Hmm, I'll have to think about that." She tried to lay her head against my shoulder, but as her damp hair from the shower wet my neck, she pulled forward again.

I continued, "As you 'see' an incident sometimes, though as you say, not every time, I would think it would matter that what's incoming was welcomed."

She appeared to be fascinated with how woven into her occult life I had become! Nodding slowly, as wide-eyed with intrigue she took my hand, "What

I do understand is that on a specific need, like Tillie's phone call yesterday, while I'm listening to all she's describing, another mode, an uninvited one, completely takes me over. This is no exaggeration, Algernon, as it can be surprising, but it always becomes another sphere." *Was this Laburnum's clumsy way of trying to reach for more of my cooled friendship-?* Though again, it was on *her* terms, as she lifted my hand to hold onto my fingers, emitting little exclamations that made me hope that at least some of what I'd been trying to tell her had been getting through!

"Then all right. I will need to know more about your occult gift if we're to get back onto a more trustful footing."

"'Trustful'? Are you meaning you'd like me to explain any unexpected decisions?"

"Is that asking so much?"

"Time can be a factor," she said leaning from me. "Last night, Fergie needed Tillie and myself because she'd had clear new images of our boy and was sure we could." She stopped. "Algernon! I can become so entangled in what she tells me, that honestly, a stampede of wild buffalo wouldn't stop me from doing what she'd asked me to do."

As she pleaded for more understanding, I was back again feeling like that poor old bound flag of mine, so tight around its pole there was no distinguishing how it looked, or what it stood for. Or whether I was up against such unwanted feelings that weren't abrasive enough for me to get them over to my lover? *Though I did comprehend that I still knew next to nothing about chasing a certain woman, and whether in doing so, I should have to forfeit my own self-esteem? Particularly with me still new to this country.*

Finally, Laburnum caught on to some of what one's Englishness was, and through moistened eyes, she shook her head. "All right," she said sounding conclusive, "If I make sure you know everything, then when Tillie calls," This statement of hers greatly relieved me, I had to have sat visibly deflating. "Then, Algernon, with this agreed to, don't you suppose? With all we have, couldn't we make a bigger effort at trying?"

"Oh Laburnum! Can't you tell how much I've been trying?" I said and letting this sink in.

On this instant, she seemed beautiful to me again, and our looks at one another became silent but strongly insistent, as if each was momentarily seeing the other as another unfamiliar person?! We both held to this strange exchange until our eyes disclosed our more separate apprehensions, and there was a rigidity building into these newly apprehensive looks one to another. The looks themselves containing renewed and changed knowledge, though neither of us had much of its awareness just then as to why we'd each given up expressing with words. Though through this mutual eye-locking, we were each understanding that there had to be more for it to be extraordinarily long-lasting. Intrigued with this impasse to one another's verbally expressed thought, we slid into at last becoming more languorous; and with nowhere else to go, our looks took on a metaphysical turn that let each of us see more of this otherness. *From eons ago, in a prior, even in some Neolithic form. Of an ancientness in which we'd known no differences.*

With many yawns and far more satisfying sighs, each separately stretching from the boundaries of this shared otherness, to badly—*what?* Make little inarticulate gestures that some re-thinking was in the air?

Lifting her head and her hand, she smiled as she un-self-consciously resorted to that banal feminine push to her hair! With a little laugh, she said, "Wow!" Then adding, "From all that one lives, one of course does learn a thing or two!" Given with such a change to insolence, it snapped the eeriness from our 'communication' to instead make her bodily so irresistible to me again that my stern fingers took her coffee cup from her hand to put on the table. Wanting to get beneath her well-sashed robe, my desire's voltage pressed her full-bodied against the sofa's back, as my hands wrangled and entangled in all her polka-dotted silk. Not getting anywhere, I groaned louder, like the grinding to a calamitous halt of an unmaintained bulldozer!

Realizing what maddened me—*oh shocking*—but she couldn't help but laugh! "Here!" She straightened to unknot her wrap, "Good grief, I'd been so totally safe when you were down there picking!"

Mutual sensuality rewarded thrillingly again, as despite Paycock's snarled annoyance I dragged her back to her bedroom. Laburnum pretended that she was not safe at all as I more fully and lovingly seduced her 'more than she'd long since remembered'. Finally pulling from my continuing embraces, she slumped across the bed. "Oh de-ear! Oh m-y-y!" Though she still giggled, "How will you ever make a dedicated vintner?"

"Not to worry, there're brilliant vintners of every description!"

"Okay, Algernon, but just now we shouldn't be getting too carried away with so much of this body stuff. You know last night, you really got me going back into those ancient Egyptian armies again?"

"Yes? By the way, I brought you my notes. They're on your desk."

"My *de-eESK,*" one of her needling aviary squawks as she attempted to rise.

"As for this 'body stuff'," I blocked her from rising with kisses inspired by the lit canons during the 1812 overture, "a lot may depend on how one rates it."

"You mean, ratings like 'four star'?"

"Four is all it goes up to?"

She lurched from my locked grip. "Oh look, I need to see those notes, Algernon! You know I'm back filling out my Egyptian study."

"The notes can wait to be with you, Laburnum, I can't," my octopus arms kept yanking her.

"The planning behind those armies though, Algernon? In the night I was recalling, wasn't it Truman who was into similar soldiering with his 'universal training?' After men get called up to serve, their home, their jobs had to be retrieved, just like the Egyptian system."

"Like the military systems of other countries too, certainly, which isn't what we're talking about right now! Though, oh yes then, all right, yes it *was* Truman!" I agreed detachedly. "As president, Truman was looking for what would be compensatory and fair for reserve-soldiering. Just as it had ideally been considered for thousands of years and still is. So, what does that tell us about us or about your golden ages, you hopeless-to-woo woman?"

"Please, Algernon, you're bruising my boobs."

"We know that powerful armies were a great part of their planning; after all, with it the middle kingdom's secured 500 fantastic years of peace and prosperity!"

"Yes, 500! We can't be contemptuous of that."

"And my Egyptian recollection is that it was the Pharaoh who was the big cheese director, witch-woman, never the army chiefs."

"Sensible, wasn't it, as it happens? Much later, powerful military forces were Roosevelt's big worry too. Algernon, don't you think that the Egyptians had it pretty well-balanced?"

As I lounged beside her on her piled bed pillows, resigned to being stuck with this discussion replacing any further lusting, I turned from my wooing to cautiously bring up another ongoing thought I'd had while picking down in the field. Pulling over a third pillow to sit straighter and get my arm around her shoulders, I asked more seriously, "All right, Laburnum, here's my most arcane thought—You are listening? All your studies mean a great deal to you, and working with Tillie is apparently crucially important to you, too; though tell me, how do you manage to move from your scholarly civilizations research to being entranced with Tillie's current personal problems up in the woods? Tillie's situation is vastly different, and it's ongoing? Do you see these two major pursuits of yours helping one another?"

"Ouch!" Her look of intrigued surprise. "Funny, I've been asking myself that same question. You're sharp all right, Algernon! Look though, wouldn't you prefer to rest? Okay, then, it could be that my occult work does have an effect on my studies." Then throwing up those neat tapering finger-tips of hers, "Oh, but I don't know! My hunch is that they're not *un-helpful* to one another."

"Not *unhelpful,*" I repeated kissing her arm. "You do understand that I'm trying to know you better, don't you, my frightfully elusive beloved? In with your great 'golden eras' quest, you're anxious to find out how a particularly unusual advanced nation became secured in great lengths of enduring peace?" I was toying with a strand of her still damp hair, "Laburnum, another question, and please forgive this sudden change of subject."

"Uh-oh!"

"After what you've told me about losing your parents, then—forgive this—but you said that because of Vietnam you lost your husband too. Then there was your struggle to find people you could relate to. I'm trying to get an overview to all this, my dearest."

"Yes, Algernon, so what're you saying?"

"That if it was tragedy that triggered this 'Great Civilizations' quest of yours, couldn't you have been hunting for a system where at least husbands didn't go off and get killed? By finding out how military defense and attack had been successfully dealt with during what we call 'the golden eras'."

Without turning to him, she slowly nodded and said, "That's so, yes."

"Then keep at it, Laburnum, my darling!" I leaned to kiss her and her strand of hair. "A book like that would provoke widespread thinking for and against! It was only after World War II and Vietnam there was any public furor against the draft, remember, or what is now the pretense that there isn't one."

"Yes, yes."

"Even if a book like yours gets looked at with suspicion by military leaders, or politicians, you'll be honestly stirring up more about what non-war could be. What could truly be secure peace?"

"It would be nice to think so, although I can't worry about a book's wider effect."

"Ha, your fatalism?"

"It all badly needs airing, so right, I'm trying to keep my 'fatalism' out of it. I don't have the faith in our leaders and diplomats that you do, Algernon, other than you yourself, as it's hard to believe that everyone responsible for national conflicts has your integrity. By the way, now, are we getting along any better again?"

Accepting her compliment, I answered her with a strong nod. "How much of this book have you written?"

"Just areas of several golden eras, nothing's put together. I'm holding off till I have a stronger hold on its theme."

"Is there anything I could do to help you? Maybe if I read those sections?"

"If you really wanted to. Though you may prefer to wait until the theme is more coherent."

"I'll be over tomorrow afternoon. And anyway we've more to talk about with your clairvoyance."

"Algernon," she knew what he was referring to, "understand if Tillie suddenly needs me again, I'll be sure to let you know."

"Laburnum, you're making me feel quite respected."

Chapter 20
The Letter

Mel and I moved our pickers up to the Aurores nearer the highway, as Sigmund took over finishing the Marechal Foch harvest. We had been lucky, each new day of good weather had added to the long spell of dry coolness, with our town group returning to mostly put in a full eight hours. At the wine production center, Sigmund and Reb received the tractor loads of filled baskets to press and process their juices into Hans' great pride—the ceiling-high redwood barrels. All was going well!

With so much satisfaction, it was no hardship to stay out late with Reb or Mel in the fields, where one mulled over Laburnum's and my clairvoyance conversation. It still played on in one as one became sure that Laburnum only saw me as *what?* 'Unuseful' to her? Thank God she had stated she wouldn't run off again without telling one, but how good was her promise; I'd only known this woman for a few weeks? I could still be bending too much of my valuable self—and as tiredness got to me, *was this fair or best?* More justly hadn't I better look out more for myself? I knew that *those embraces of hers* could be *debilitating!? Disabling?* For a Cholmondley-Rute of historically admired position in Europe, and not to boast but both one's own humanitarianism and internationalism had been well-known and even celebrated over there—which Laburnum did *not* know. Nor that throughout one's career, my expertise 'at bat' as they'd say, in heading one's team had reputedly been heroic.

These characteristics were a large part of oneself as the unassuming Algernon Cholmondley-Rute second son; and if my desire to metamorphose to become more proletariat was dimming one's overall esteem, then maybe I was taking on too much by locking-in so hard with this witch-woman? Insights for lowliness were certainly commendable and good, but ha –! Why forget I'd been written up in outstanding editorials and followed about by 'Tattler' photographers for all the gifted tooth-fairies! And why 'followed about'? Because I too had known my share of rare and remarkable experiences, that apparently Laburnum knew nothing about. Experiences that simply couldn't be expurgated from memory on an eye's-blink! Mind, all this was so well-known, I shouldn't have to describe it to her! One wasn't the kind of man who wrote out all I'd done in enormous letters and got them lit it up on highway billboards! Though surely, some smatterings of one's illustrious past should have been echoing? I saw I would have to get much more of this thoroughly worked out with Laburnum, before getting to know more of her—*what was that I'd just said then? Was getting to know more of her what I'd really meant?*

One's once acclaimed status and all I'd meritoriously earned buffeted around in me again walking back up the hill to the house, and going in the front way—to a slight commotion?! I was met by Sally-Anne hurrying to me as she loudly called, "Regi*STERED!*" Looking at what she held around her clutched long-handled pan and duster. *Uh-oh! A letter with several Elizabeth the second stamps!* "I was about to bring it down to you, Algernon," she added apologetically.

Just as I'd most dreaded, there was Father's threatening scrawl! Father, who rarely wrote, as I moaned and shook my head, tempted to burn the letter unopened. Instead one thanked Sally-Anne through one's muttered contempt, "Eternal damnation."

Look Algernon, it has to be read!

Taking this repugnant mail into the parlor with me, where I looked at its stamps, then stood the blasted thing on a chair and looked at it again! *Algernon, for God's sake, just read it!*

Tearing open the envelope, I sank into my favorite chair as my eyes ate up the vicious message. *Oh dear Lord! Because he was 'dying', one's demented crank of a parent was 'ordering' one home! Yet this was in my father's hand! He'd been well enough to write this vomit!*

Inevitable descriptions in his child-like cursive—blood clots in his legs, emphysema had bent him double, and his doctors pronounced his bladder infection too far gone to be worth-medicating! One just knew that the troublesome old cutthroat was up to something during one's exquisite harvest, one was too well-aware of Father's bloated realities though I wasn't going to have any of Father's old dictatorial stuff during this much-worked-for harvest time, for Saint Harpo Marx's sake! Father had dealt with village harvests, he knew what harvest time's entailed. What could he be thinking on this fair and thrilling earth, that could possibly make one even consider taking his 'command' seriously?

One'*s sole reaction was to not on any account let one's father get his way!*

With all the ever-dazzling opportunities flowing from my enchanted Supreme Habitat here, I'd be a fool if I didn't protect this place till death. One also cursed that this day's Laburnum concerns were also fighting one's father's orders to return home; but top of the list, I truly believed that at long last, one was profoundly involved with a fabulously reciprocating woman—it would be hopeless to expect my father to comprehend how imperatively I needed to pursue one's clairvoyant Laburnum. But I'd better keep remembering how that battling old parent had treated one's angel of a mother during his own marriage. And another thought, *it would be madness now to leave Laburnum here now, with Sigmund just returned from Germany and restless.* And hadn't I nicely just got the hang of keeping all the grape types variously ripening along with one's brilliant team that in full swing now couldn't do enough to get it all in and bottled. *No, it was here, right here at Runditz's that with some care all these finest assets, and everything he and all who had been working with him had hoped for, were getting in with every grape!*

Though, no matter!

Suddenly, his contemplating was immaterial because his answer for his father was simply a gigantically resounding, NO-O!

NO, not this time, you merciless torturer from the Bloody Tower!

Because just getting to know the complex Laburnum was to take one's best thinking.

In truth, no woman would ever mean this much to him. Laburnum may not be aware of it, but with Tillie's zeroing in on the location of the kidnapped boy, Laburnum would badly need me—he'd seen her exhaustion during these immensely committed meets, and he owed keeping her from wearing herself out. Especially with the police unhappy about 'mediums'. This meant that before Laburnum and Tillie handed their findings in at the station, they would have to be absolutely positive about their trance conclusions—no doubts. Which would be up to him to help them make sure. However, inattentive Laburnum had been, there were more reasons she must have his fullest care and thoughtfulness now. *After all, think Algernon, she'd dropped her studies to grape pick? No, he owed her and Paycock staying right here with this splendid harvest.*

Laburnum was expecting me for walking Paycock, and now I had this decision about Father soundly and irrevocably decided, one would amble along beside her and enjoy this lingering good weather as she would. By this afternoon's end, I would be thoroughly observing the bird activity and plants closing down again. By scorning my parent's 'urgent demand', I was sure that as my dearest woman had far too much else on her mind to bother with it, like me she would see through this 'dying' trap of his father's.

Conversationally, in just mentioning this letter from my father, I was surprised that my lover's clairvoyance read one differently when her response came unexpectedly. Instead of consolingly agreeing with me, she asked irritating questions concerning the urgency of my father's request! Outrageously, especially when she conventionally reminded me, "He is your *father,* you know, Algernon."

"Lab*UR*-num!" Stopping dead in one's tracks, her name burst from me like a ship's torpedo.

"Oh!"

"You would have to know my hoodlum father to understand that he's the most tyrannical of criminal parents."

"O-oh sorry! I am *sorry,* right—yes!"

One wondered what she had been thinking? During this most promising harvest, why in all souped-up multi-cultivation was she muttering about being 'sorry' for not endorsing his decision to ignore his demented father?

Though she hadn't!

Why to heavens wasn't Laburnum sensing his dreaded father during this season's heavy work and all their overloaded efforts that had led up to this harvesting? Which she knew as well as I! Why in Satan's name was she taking this righteous school teacher's stance? *Then... or was it him?* Shouldn't I have just dealt with that letter myself without mentioning it to her? *It was only because this damn woman beside him was unusual in her thinking and had a physical attractiveness that sometimes compensated—although he still had times like this when he wished she'd run back to her sisters stirring their cauldron on 'the blasted heath'.* Which made one wonder if there could be a good deal more about accommodating this mood-driven female that I should know! "For God's sake, Laburnum!" I said aloud, "one just can't keep on."

"But what if your father is mentally losing it?" she overrode me.

I shrugged. "He's always been a brute."

She walked ahead of me a few steps with her head down before quickly turning to me, "Oh look, Algernon, I'm sorry! I'm forgetting that this was the man who forced you into his sleazy business deal of a marriage. He must have been a crapping beast! God, what infamy!" Angry with herself, Laburnum was at a loss for words. "Awful of me, Algernon, I do regret what I said! I've been so loaded with this Tillie business! Though honestly, the trouble is, even if your father is a predatory monster, parental influence lies so deep within us, we don't immediately comprehend how much we're altered by it. This doesn't always emerge while they're living, you know?"

Smothering one's hurt, I dug again for one's innate fairness, painful as this was. But cooling, it did make sense that as Laburnum had lost both her parents in adolescence and been forced to fight for survival—she might see him as lucky to have any sort of father. Answering her more reasonably, "All right, with Mother's early death, I know a bit about all that too, my good woman!" *Oh God, was I becoming patronizing too, now?* "I don't excuse myself, but I am 60-years-old, and I've only lived the life my deranged father planned for me!" It also occurred to me that if there was ever to be a time Laburnum was to meet my family, it would depend on how candidly I informed her about them now. "As you know Laburnum, my own choices were always soundly walloped. I'm sorry if this sounds callous to your finer principles," *Augh, was I adding in bitterness now?* "Though my instinct says, over here in America I'm completely away from that parental despot, and it is high time I learned to say 'No' to such a contentious old piranha!" *Oh Lord, were we already falling into more of last night's miserable disagreements?*

Luckily, images slid back to me of all that had gone so wonderfully right since purchasing one's Supreme Habitat, and this helped me adjust, so finally I put a lightly uncommitting hand on her shoulder before taking a pause or two and reducing one's baritone to a whisper. "I don't suppose you know how greatly I've craved the enlightenment that you, Hans, and this place have given me, Laburnum? I mean, your benevolent humanitarian enlightenment?! I can't find words for all those conversations and insights I'd been longing for; and with my final breath, I shall defend this chance to love this most peaceable of all havens," and sneaking her a quick look, "and even *you*!"

Here we were with remnants of this 'at odds' atmosphere from the last evening enclosing us again, like sticky rain. We walked on, Laburnum feeling more approbation for me even though I stubbornly refused to see if there could be any truth to Father's 'dying'. Assimilating my offense, she saw more clearly that her own personal reasons for greatly valuing her parents had made her jump to judge mine in an entirely different situation. "You're right, Algernon! Yes, for heaven's sake, don't listen to me, you are so-o right!"

Gratefully, I nodded as she more sympathetically took my hand, and Paycock diverted us by bounding over to lick our entwined fingers. We both patted him, and I threw him a stick that sent him burrowing the hedge and made both of us smile as he came out with a quizzical tall-eyed look at us through comical burrs crowning his head and the stick threading his muddied jaw.

Walking on down the hill, I sighed more contentedly. "Laburnum, you did notice it was *'I'* that needed you and this place, and not the diplomat's 'one'? I hope you've noticed that it's 'I' much more now, and much as I know you hate my overdoing compliments, you should know that I am grateful for your translations."

"You're just justifying being a person, Algernon. There's no need to."

"Which is why I want you to see, that with this much at stake, I can't let that parental blackguard keep me from you and all that our winery's bringing in." Emitting a dry laugh, I said, "I'll risk being outrageously honest with you and tell you that you have generated another strain of humanism in me so, my every fiber is saying, STAY here! *Stay here* at Runditz's with you."

"You're giving me too much credit and regarding your father. Yes, I do see you may need to put up a super-aggressive defense! When you were growing up, he must have been insane to prevent you from making your own choices. Not allowing you the freedom to independently develop your own special character? He must've been nuts! Then all that anachronistic business of forcing you to ignore your feelings and marry his bought-off slut! What a corruption of his privileged position! It's hard to envision what it must have been like having a powerful crazy-man like that for father." Listening to her at this moment, I adored Laburnum for her more realistic view, although admittedly I felt rather tossed around. "Though Algernon, I must tell you that the scope of what you've done, all you've recently chosen to undertake since coming here makes you a most intriguing man on many levels!" Laburnum quickly looked away, her usual impertinence gone as her hand pushed back her 'extravagant' hair—for once, was she shy?

It soothed one to more agreeably have this woman's personal support again! I'd been longing for her dependable kindliness, her boosts. Assets that had most impressionably been lavished on one long ago from my mother. Walking by the barely rippling lake, I mused that I no longer felt any lack of charity for turning down my Mafioso father, as adamantly I decided I would boldly put it to him on paper. *Mentally, one wrote, I will not be coming to you, Father! There—simply and soundly. There could be no mistake!*

With Laburnum and I each thinking so much about my father, it was natural for me to stay on for the 'white-witch's' offer of supper. Reb and Sylvia were at the inn dealing with a load of fall leaf sight-seers, and Mel and Sigmund were off with friends. Hungrily, we scanned Laburnum's refrigerator and decided on an omelet. I cut up broccoli flowerets, a red pepper, and shredded the cheese, as she poured the beaten eggs into her large skillet and skillfully changed the burner's temperature for keeping it firming slowly. As she always did, she poured the wine she kept chilled for me.

Having planned separate evenings, after our consoling good meal, I left to return to my study and read. Regretfully, I'd finished *The Sound and the Fury*, and by way of a non-fictional change before getting to my newest Faulkner purchase, I tried to finish a book I'd been reading of my mother's about the building of the Egyptian pyramids, though tonight it wouldn't grip me… tormenting me was Father's injuring letter. Finally, unwisely, I pulled the dastardly pages from the air mail envelope and flattened them on top of my book for re-reading Father's bitter words.

Just holding this letter got my father's arrogant 'infallibility' bristling in me—why didn't he just leave me alone like most fathers did their sons? One hated fitting myself into my father's bestowed role for me as the dutifully obliged black sheep, when it was so immensely hard to endow that old hypocrite with any traditional kind of kinship. I was ashamed I didn't have it in me to just neatly deal with one's father. After all, on one's last visit we had quite enjoyed trotting off together to Corfe Castle. I should be niftier at dealing with our opposed lives.

Though how to deal with comments like, 'never having found out how those adjuncts between your legs could affect you in business or marriage—ha-ha!' Dear God! Had the old duffer written such tripe for his own perverted entertainment, or was he losing it as he watched life slipping out of him? And would any of that alter if one did do as he'd commanded and returned to England? Anyway, how much should all this matter when Father had Gillie, Jasmine, and Maudie to buck him up?

Sigmund had stopped by one's study to cheerily tell me about two gorgeous women staying at Sylvia's that Mel and he were getting to know. Sigmund could be an uplifting diversion, but as soon as he'd gone up to bed, with umpteen excuses for doing so, one returned to dodging Father's poisonous epistle until one had a blistering headache. Unable to sleep, at 1:30 a.m., there was only one thing to do—allowing for the time change. I risked Father being awake early over there as I returned down to the study, took up the phone and dialed the long distance overseas Cholmondley-Rute number. Maudie's voice identified the residence. "Maudie? Algernon. Is anyone up?"

"M'lady, sir. Your father too, by the God-awful racket! Here, I'll get—*hold on.*"

I listened to loud unidentifiable sounds and distanced shouts during a long pause before Gilmore's clipped voice came on, "A bit early in the day, don't you think, Algernon?"

"Is Father really sick, Gilmore? What does his doctor say?"

"Oh Father, so that's it! Actually, it's still more of the same, what do you expect at 90? Have you any idea what you chickened out on here, by the way, brother mine? More likely I'm sure you have! Father is on medication for his legs—blood clots. It's helping, but he doesn't walk, as you know. Why this untypical concern? You can be sure the will won't be changed if that's."

"Gilmore, he's written me he's dying."

"Well, he is. We all are, aren't we, nothing new there! Ha-haa haaa!" Gilmore's laugh could be the lonely mid-lake call of a loon.

"Of emphysema, Gillie? Advanced bladder infection?"

"A bit of each actually, I believe. Though look, if you want the clinical jargon, Jasmine sees more of him—she's just come downstairs." His voice turned away, "Algernon, Jazzy."

Jasmine greeted him. "Jasmine dear, how are you?" Jasmine sounded to be her normal apprehensively warm self, thank goodness; and as she graciously asked about his 'grape harvest', one told her, "We've full days and are dependent on the weather, but so far so good. Jasmine, you may know I've received a letter from Father."

"I knew he'd been going to write you."

“He says he’s dying. We’re only just getting the grapes in, and he’s insisting I come over now.” Algernon caught her chuckle. The pathetic woman apparently didn’t understand the full reach of his father’s letter. He tried again, “Ostensibly, he’s far gone with emphysema, leg blood clots, and a bladder infection that’s so diseased the doctor won’t prescribe.”

“To be fair, he has a bit of all of those, though as you can probably hear him shouting at Maudie, none of them diminish his voice! Lately though, he’s been insisting you should give Gilmore a proper rest, Alge’non, and Gillie certainly needs one.”

“Just to get this clear, Jasmine, Father is *not* dying?”

“He certainly is not, listen to him up there! He’s still amazingly in charge. Alge’non, I’m sure you understand what I’m saying.”

“Then it won’t change anything if I don’t make an emergency return?”

“Surely you can hear that?! No, pitifully, it’s all just the same! No emergency.”

“Jasmine, you know wine-making? This being my first harvest, it would be far better if I came over when we’re through picking and bottling. By the way, thank you for the Indian tea.”

“Quite right—about the harvest then, quite right! Come when you are free of it, Alge’non, even then it would be a tremendous help. Thought you’d appreciate that tea.”

We signed off affectionately, and one sat back much relieved, though angered that even 3000 miles away his father could stir up so much avoidable distress. Getting up I went to look over at Laburnum’s, but as expected, her lights weren’t on. I longed to tell her that Father’s letter was just his over-inflated boredom, because anyone who could shout out his every distinguishable word from the manor’s upstairs and have it come across the Atlantic over the downstairs phone was likely to live longer than Methuselah. Plodding back up a few stairs for some sleep when *the phone rang!* Rushing back down to it in the study, hoping it was Laburnum, he cooed, “Hull-oo, my turtle-dove.”

“Can’t you speak grown-up?” His father’s shriek was strident in his ear. “Listen, you blasted nymphomaniac, don’t you understand there’s a conspiracy going on here? The doctor, your brother, everyone’s denying I’m disintegrating right before their stupid dilating eyes.”

“Father, look, it’s two in the morning here, and by the way, a nympho–”

“For once in your life can’t you show the teeniest concern for your dying parent? Quit acting as if you’ve never got on a plane. I’m imprisoned here and having *TO TRUST YOU, IDIOT, THOUGH YOU’VE GOT YOURSELF OFF IN STORAGE IN SOME PUKEY PLACE!”*

“Stop shouting, Father, or I’ll hang up. *I’M HANG*ing up, Father.”

"NO! DON'T!" A prickly breathiness as each of us worked at calming. "Look, I will say this, at least you had the guts to run away from the dim-wittedness in this place, and you may even have had moments when your eyes were more open than others here. Now listen, I'm a dying man."

"You're *not* dying!"

"If you don't want me to get another lawyer and change."

"Just don't expect me over there during this grape harvest, Father!" One almost shouted. "Afterwards, I'll come over as soon as I can."

"You sound as if you're losing it."

"*I'm* losing it?"

"It's a wonder you ever kept a job!"

Not waiting for any more of Father's senility, I tried not to slam down the receiver.

Agitated, I paced the downstairs rooms. Paced them again. *It was monstrous I still let my father tweak me like this—'your eyes were more open than others here'! Fathers!* Ha, why did that credo of D.H. Lawrence's hit him right now of all times? Procreation was the central fire for keeping humankind viable—*yet how could one's ungovernably dyspeptic father ever have dropped seeds into one's poor sweetest mother for making one jot of difference in helping along that 'fire of humankind'! Never, not his weasel-brained mongoose of a father.*

Oh Algernon, how one used to agonize if Father didn't notice that his prestigious newspaper's op ed had praised one's role in a certain conflict-resolving? Or mentioned one's much coveted royally presented awards! Even that time he'd accepted investiture from Her Majesty with all due pomp in the palace ballroom, though all he'd received from his parent were pejorative comments about the imbecilic mistakes that only an enthroned *woman* could make.

Sadly, one knew that his pitifully power-ridden human beast of a father was really a deeply angry man who needed pitying. Anything in his father that had been inherently decent, kind, or compassionate had been kicked a mile down under the Cholmondley-Rute's famed Elizabethan herb garden eons ago, so what was a son to expect? His father's exaggerations at any opportunity only added to his vile baseness. I had been six years old when one's Cholmondley-Rute grandfather had expired, causing one's father to wallow in his inherited village and farms that he inspected, riding to them on his fine stallion as he'd spiraled himself up as a feudal lord of the manor. With his over-confidence frothing, Father supposed he was making sure the capitalist obligation of estate wealth was being kept in 'honorably shrewd hands'! *Did Father or Gilmore have a clue how much they had contemptuously dynamited their ancestral privileges? Tragic, because had his grandfather's estate been humanely managed, even using their clumsy antiquated system, it could have continued to produce quite reasonably.*

What didn't occur to one as my anger tore on at one's father was that it had been one's own privileged Eton and Cambridge schooling that had prompted this savoir faire for criticizing his parent. Schooling that had developed and broadened his mind to a scathing dagger sharpness as long as he kept himself clear of the Cholmondley-Rute fold as much as possible. As one had been on the boards of various famous institutes and systems, corporative as well as governmental, one had seen how happy and successful employees became when they were treated equally and had a say in handling the profits; and by the Runditz Winery's excellent results, he knew that Hans' fair-minded principles were what had proved so successful here too.

Understandably, after my father's cock-up command letter, one spent a good chunk of the night cooling down as I tried to focus and re-focus on my new Faulkner book *As I Lay Dying*, before being taken off under the giant wing-span of a huge predatory bird for a very few hours of tormented ogre-nested sleep.

Chapter 21
Father

After the following day of picking, one felt unusually fatigued and kept adding more hot water to keep soaking in one's bath. This was unlike me, though I knew my changed mood was related to one's preposterous father. Trying to ignore one's irrevocable blood-kinship wouldn't entirely stop me from concerning about my parent. *God knows why?!* This on top of the day's intermittent sprinkling from the ever-darkening clouds that finally burst to make the pickers go home when they had yet to get to the Vignoles—*though one would watch this worrying, one mustn't land up a neurotic vintner like Hans.*

One's much-practiced Zen for over-stressing had never let me down, even on that legendary time in Stockholm when he'd waited out each globally significant vote on a massive arms treaty. Having managed that, surely, one could summon up the resources for keeping cool during these small peaceful happier wine-making phases? One's present worries were leagues away from being internationally consequential. *You can do it, you wrung-out old thing!*

Though, actually, there was more to it than that, recalling his other mind-wrenching worry—*Laburnum's commitment to Tillie and the kidnapped boy.* Needing to keep a keen watch on his belle amorist, this too was best relieved by continuing this soak in the good hot water. These concerns had been pricking one's poor 60-year-old muscles, like jabbing locust thorns, though as one's torso hit cooler air rising from the water for turning off the hot faucet—air that was quite jolting and *about time too! After all, one had always thoroughly disliked feebleness, my own especially, and I despised whining complainers! Inexcusable!* I wasn't suffering from some God-awful disease for all the good-looking wives of Henry the eighth, so why this white flag act?

As one's Supreme Habitat had bestowed so much that was favorable on me, all I had to do was oversee the winery's agenda for keeping the harvest moving along. One was a Cholmondley-Rute after all and perfectly capable of dealing with the field activities and the production center's fruit-pressing—not forgetting keeping a watch on Sigmund; though updating, Sigmund was becoming more reliable.

Reaching to unplug the water, I fixed to the water's defiant swirl-sucking into a tight silver circle for going down the drain to take all one's wretched feebleness with it. Up till now, there had been lots of the most desirable weather—a lovely graceful fading off of summer. For weeks, one and everyone else had been appreciatively attuned to the reliably good days, amazing with yet another one; though today had not been typical—a coming seasonal weather change? Shuddering from chilliness, I again reproached myself. Foremost, if we were to get all we needed done here, I would just have to royally forget my overbearing harebrained father! Surgically *cut-him-from-mind-!* Stepping out of the bath more determinedly, I wrapped my dripping body in one of Sally-Anne's huge fluffy towels and rubbed it against my wetness, as I hurried back to my room and closed the bedroom door behind me with my foot as an old childhood phrase returned, *Between the toes, Algernon!* How could one ever forget Nanny's high, two-noted sensible words recalled as bending to do my toes, one's armoire door had swung open and its mirror happened to reflect this rear-view bending position with startling completeness.

Intrigued with one's body so concussively naked, this nude, lean, older man's physique reflected *what? He hadn't sat on a bag of pinot noir must, surely?* Though what should he expect? Hardly the cummerbund and dress sword view of a formally announced Cholmondley-Rute! But what most drastically shook him was the thought that this was the body that had attracted his liebe Laburnum! Wondering if it looked better from another angle, I quickly spun around checking it again, but beyond the scarcity of fat covering my lithe, rock-like muscles, I'd had to admit there was an oncoming slight droop or two. *Oh for pity's sake, Algernon!*

All right!

But this worrying about one's body must surely mean he was heading for provincialism? Oh heavens, such *nonsense!* I'd been endowed with admirable height, and no one could deny that standing straight one's tallness had attraction, because one had never accepted the word 'lanky' as a self-description. Nor had I resorted to that hollow-chested Tiny Tim posture some tall men crumpled into. Anyway, as I pulled on my bikini briefs, one really knew that Laburnum wouldn't let the kind of love she and I were experiencing bog down because of a couple of minor wrinkles—*which-was-all-they-were!* Nothing imitating a fossilized, moldy old prune, and almost no age spots! Laburnum was not ungenerous, I reminded myself, and as long as my body moved well—*forget humility for a moment*—I'd better keep remembering that it was one's agility, spurred by my sparkling, endorsing intelligence and one's splendid hyphenated lineage, that had mattered universally. In this way, one got one's self-esteem restored before going over to *her*, as one took up the little branch of beautiful glossy black berries I had plucked for her from a hedge.

The moment I'd walked to where I could see Laburnum's head in her apartment's window, I cataclysmically felt all of one's old self returned! Including that deliciously loaded cerebrally by-passed ache to be with her that most often overwhelmed me! Yes, here it was again! That sickly anti-intellectual ache filling one, like a hot air balloon, till one's stride quite overbalanced, and I had to consciously compensate its yawing. Affecting me too, because one was aware that it was Laburnum's and his maturity and refinement that had put us far beyond mere common infatuation. Or it certainly was for me, as no woman one had remotely known came up to this witch-woman! Recharging again with electronically painful flashes for his enchantress' lustful touch, I gallantly knocked and entered her apartment; and as my thinking proved sound, I chuckled with relief because looking up from her desk-end of the table, one's comely lover smiled at one so winningly, so utterly astonishingly, that another paining lower down inner whorl intoxicated me, making one have to turn from her! Standing she accepted the berry branch with a hotly promising kiss and stood it in a tall glass. "*Al-l-*gernon," she bathed him in that opulence of low vocal warmth variation, "My dear, what a lousy night you'd had after your father rang."

"Huh? Well, right, yes—you've certainly called that one!"

"That bad?"

"It's settled, so don't let's waste our breath talking about it, Laburnum. Not now anyway. I'm much more concerned about your Tillie plan."

"Oh!" Her happy expression grew dull. *Disappointed? Had one broached this subject too fast?* "Yes, well, I'm to go to her house tomorrow afternoon."

"Her *house,* Laburnum? Not meeting in a woods?"

"Tillie has a stomach virus and can't go anywhere. Poor Tillie, it's unavoidable, but it's using time. Today she's stuffing herself with cheese and Imodium sandwiches to make sure she'll be fine by tomorrow. Fergie, our other medium friend, is to come, so along with some preparatory phone calls to one another, we three won't be losing our hold on the boy."

"Tillie's house, it is then, Laburnum?"

"A bit far to walk, about ten miles."

"I'll drive you. Be assured I'll wait."

"It's to be clear tomorrow, Algernon, good motor-bike weather."

"Should it rain, do let me?"

"Algernon, this is my business, my darling man. Tillie, Fergie, and I will get all this done right, I know we will. As they say, 'It's a bad workman that, *oh-oh*—that's easily parted'?" Algernon forced himself not to bend double! "All right, you wretch, then what is it?"

Controlling, one said, "It's either 'A fool and his money are easily parted', or, and this is more likely what you were after, 'It's a bad workman that blames his tools'!"

“Yes, that’s the parody! Damn it, how come you remember them? I meant it’s going to be up to us to go very carefully dealing with this kidnap situation.”

I was still smiling. “There, dearest, did you listen to yourself then? You just descriptively summarized your situation so I understood it perfectly, so why are you bothering to memorize those ancient folk sayings?”

“Because when they’re right, they’re so succinct and picturesque.”

“Unless they’re only half recalled?”

“Then they won’t be, you rude man! Just you wait, I’ll study them up and quote them to you verbatim.”

“Oh, I’ll wait all right! But go back to what you were telling me.”

“Yes,” and slowly, putting her hand on one’s arm. “Tomorrow, Algernon, let me go to Tillie’s my way, my dear one; then I’ll be better off for bringing our best efforts back to you. How’s that?”

One nodded, “You’ll know where to find me should you change your mind.”

“You keep on with your formidable job of getting in the grapes and checking all that’s going on with crushing and de-stemming. That’s a lot to get right, my suave cavalier.” Laburnum’s endearments had the joyful effect of sizzling within me before dropping to nestle so low in one’s groin, one had to slip one’s arm around her pretty shoulders to give her impassioned squeezes. Then one bent one’s head and pressed one’s lips on her full ones.

Adjusting one’s hugging position to his most beloved, I wondered to myself *– dear heavens, why that low mood in the bath? Shameful! Great flocks of people have courageously pulled themselves through all kinds of tragedies in this teaming multifarious world, plus I’d had the good luck to have been led on a wonderful supernatural trail since that fine spring touring evening, when I’d so incidentally steered Lamborghini in at Sylvia’s inn. Great Willikins, how unappreciative could one be?*

With his chest against Laburnum’s spongy voluptuousness, one felt the magnificence of this uncorrupted procreative love that can exist between a man and a woman of finely developed sensibilities! Ours was a love cut far above those sex escapades I’d needed long ago for avoiding a second spurious marriage; and as Laburnum sweetly pulled from him to take the berries and glass pot off for water, one could only stand dumbfounded at how surreal their actual connecting was! A connection that was expanding—like—like a precious rock mineral enlarging while being uncovered by a stonecutter’s chisel. *Galloping Guinness, Algernon, how was that for a sophisticated analogy?*

“Algernon?” Laburnum called to him coming back.

“Mmm.” One was still into my analogy.

“Listen! You are listening, Algernon?” She had my full attention! “Food! I got brave and made us a casserole! It’s an eggplant-parmesan kind of dish with hamburger, ricotta, and bread cubes.”

"Why, why you sweetest little wagtail! Ha, the right name for you, wagtail."

"I can't think why," Laburnum feigned doubt with one's quirky mood.

"Listen, most entrancing of all women, and that includes that most tantalizing of Trojan females with a face that launched more ships than Onassis has in all his shipyards! There! With all your studies of the Grecian years, you can't dislike that?"

"Playfully like this once in a while, then, yes, that's lovely!" she said leaning to receive another full kiss on her smiling lips. "Though it will depend on your reason for saying it!"

"Nothing too abstruse, Laburnum dear, I simply meant it straight from my percussive heart and always will. I'm that kind of a man."

"There's more I get to know about you every day."

"There quite well could be, yes. Look, I've a question. Actually, it's a favor to ask you, and please, don't answer straightaway." She had been about to sit down, but caught by the importance of one's tone, she hovered. "In a week or two, would you come to England with me? I would see that you're comfortable at an inn, or there's a hotel just a couple of miles from the manor. One wouldn't ask you to stay with one's family. Though if you could put up with my beastly relatives for just one meal, I'd be everlastingly grateful. Once would do it. By the way, there're beautiful river walks."

Laburnum's mute unsmiling response slowed one down. She had ambled over to sit on the sofa, and her sitting position made her appear to be mesmerizing with the sleeping Paycock. Which one saw was because Laburnum was having a hard time taking in one's invitation—much as she appreciated and was even intrigued with me, her landlord inviting her to come with him to one's 'mystery' home, the actuality of suddenly having to leave here must have hit her till she could only sit breathing noisily. Finally, she announced that she was half-way through organizing her voluminous notes, so one's sudden invitation shook her! Then on she went to the super-good organizing concepts that had been emerging lately, because of oneself, but also—also—there was meeting one's family?! She'd always prided herself she could meet anyone, anywhere so she didn't believe it was just that one's relatives were high-born. But this and dealing with dearest Paycock, and much else for leaving here struck at her distressingly—yet it was very kind of one to ask her, very kind!

She was looking up at one's most desperate waiting. *Had I been I counting the milliseconds?* "I'm thrilled you've asked me, Algernon," she finally replied, "and thank you, it's a lovely idea."

"A-ah, thank God! Just as I'd."

"*Though,*" said so loudly it stopped me from saying more, "quite honestly, it's really *not* a good idea!" This unexpected stronger statement made one turn all one's consummately well-dressed elegance to her. "Not for either of us just now, Algernon. It would be a big interruption to my work and, think about it, with the guys just getting to know your way of harvesting?"

"But my dear, arrangements can be made—one has to have some personal space?" One soothed.

"Then you aren't listening to what I know," and in her voluptuous voice she made stabbing appeals for one to look carefully at this apex to all their grape growing. "By ignoring the timing just now, Algernon, after how hard you've worked with Sigmund, Mel, and everyone." She went on forcefully as one, deciding to be polite, made an immense effort not to say more as one forced one's self to sit and hear her out and try to understand why in belligerent blazes she couldn't be more accommodating.

It pained me that she hadn't relished our flying off together to advance our mutual appreciation; and quite frankly, one wasn't used to being turned down. Outside of Washington D.C., his 'Cholmondley-Rute' name may have lacked clout over here, though—*oh my God! Wasn't being incognito what I'd so direly yearned to have? Having plunged my elegant hands deep into this soil to truly get to know what lowliness was all about, had I buried myself here till not giving a thought to the lack of recognition of one's famed family name?* And now, for all the heat from light-headed Lucifer, *was she still keeping on about her need to stay here?* Having courteously heard out her opposition, it struck one—*wasn't she being rather insufferable?* Unpleasantly arrogant, in fact? He hadn't ever thought of Laburnum as a repugnant, middle-aged female termagant, but out came my arresting shout, "Lab-URNum!"

Though compelled to continue emptying out how totally impractical his sudden invitation was, Laburnum continued clarifying her views; and as she spoke her more forceful feelings caused her to emotionally stumble, to take weird pauses. "In this peak of—wine—wine-making! Algernon, it's... it's your presence that makes all—all the difference—as you must know. Hans... Hans used to say it's the decisions made during harvesting that... that make the wine. Not only that, but—but you and I, Algernon? Our marvelously fulfilling days here! I can honestly say I've never enjoyed days as much, since—since that night I—I dropped the arum lily!" One smiled as she was even being discreet as to which of them had dropped that plant. "And as you must know how much I love my little apartment-home and all that being here means with you, Paycock, and our very good friends."

"For the solstice's sake, Laburnum, I'm talking about taking off for two weeks. One, if you'd prefer?" I studied her. Maybe this wonky-eared fortune-teller was provincial after all?

"Friends here understand my reclusiveness," she picked up on his thought. "You know, I'd figured I had everything worked out for my kinky independence here, until, oh... *did you say for one week?*" But before I'd answered, she gave me a sly grin as she finished, “From some unknown planet in walked Sir Algernon Cholmondley-Rute, hot from his fabulous travels to the world’s ‘greatest civilizations’ that *I happened to be studying!*” Given shrilly with a taut little laugh. “Which as you know is what I do?” Giving this last statement with such pitiful insistence that one’s initial favor of her got replaced by her pathetic need of assurance that one did indeed know what she did. “Thank you then! And—oh what an uplift! A landlord who knew so much about what I’d endlessly been digging at!”

Even my frustration to my loud shout of her name had barely got through to her! Yet here she was waving her hands around as helplessly as a frightened penguin on an ocean-headed ice floe before she flopped back against the other end of the sofa. “Oh Algernon, I don’t suppose you know how much I’ve adored walking with you and Paycock?”

Perhaps she wasn’t altogether such a yanky-twit. Getting up, the bottled frustration in me making one need to move, I paced back and forth before determinedly going to crouch beside her, chin to knee, to get her to look at me, “*LISTEN* to me, my darling! Or rather, could you let me understand? It is the Tillie business?”

Turning to him, “That has to be in with it. But if you’re talking about going in a week or two, Tillie and I could have our sixth sense data narrowed. Though, no-o, it’s not all the Tillie business, there’s more than that. It’s the timing for many reasons, and oh Algernon! *Crossing that ocean again-?!* You think of getting on a plane the way other people push a shopping cart, but I’ve been away from all that for years, you know?” And as her pleading held me, “Algernon, have you talked about this trip to Hans?”

One sat back again near her. “I’ve told you that my family is batty?”

“Yes, I know.”

“It’s your research then? A week or two would hold you up?”

By opposing my invitation, Laburnum had certainly flabbergasted me. Such opposition was also a different attitude from all one had been used to during one’s ‘elitist years’, as Laburnum dubbed them; although, one may have thrust having her fly off with one to England too soon?

Another significant question—could her harvesting advice be in with one’s own more deeply subliminal desire to stay here one’s self? Certainly, she was right about one item, indeed there was a good deal to talk over! If as she believed it was essential I stay here, then the first thing I’d need to do was to put an irreversible stop to one’s ultra-gastronomic father’s constantly derailing me. In retirement, over here having fully embraced one’s winery responsibilities, I was at last living my own free choices. *Every stage of grape-picking now needed crucial observing and re-assessing; and although any thought of travel evoked nostalgic pangs, I might also be truly finding out how much I’d integrated with the processes of growing grapes, as I knew there was much to be done here before the final ice wine grapes were pressed and bottled.*

Eventually, after Laburnum and I had agreed that there was much more between us to disentangle, we also knew that if this was to be done with any enjoyment, it would be best to get a good night's sleep first. With little more to add, we cordially left one another with a frosty kiss.

Keeping on my jacket this cooler night, one returned to sit out on the porch and observe the darkness thickening over the lake, which might cool one's stewing over the witch's unexpected reaction. It had not been at all what I'd planned or wished—though being fair, I could glimpse bits of merit to her arguments. Back that time her leg had been so slow to heal, I'd been longing to make a better change for her and sweep her off on a trip—though that was back then. So why her obstreperousness to his well-thought-out planning now? What was causing these fall-outs with this lady lately? *Where did the fault lie? Without a doubt, hadn't he really known?*

The real source once again was his ruddy father raising such a bloody unnecessary rumpus even over here in America. It was always his damned overreacting troublemaker father!

In this earlier night's moonless dark, like fake diamond brilliants, planets, hung by silken threads to ornament the cosmos, an odd one or two brazenly beaming across the placid lake. A blackest of nights, its piercing stars and smudged galaxies doing little to lighten the firmament. During the day now as the summer's activities got through, there were fewer boats or water skiers; and in this pre-moon jet blackness, cottages had noticeably closed up—the number of far shore lights having greatly lessened. The lake's oncoming seasonal quietness was instead bringing on another atmosphere. One was becoming isolated here with one's Supreme Habitat and its dearest family! As one sat steeped in all that this place so richly meant to one, steeping so long that one's dispute with Laburnum would keep rolling back to one. It irked that his compromising with her each time may very well *not* have been what *I'd* wanted. And could it be keeping one mentally 'small' headed for becoming 'provincial'? But… *O-oh-!*

A soft brushing movement was interrupting one's thoughts.

Looking down, in front of me, on the lowest step to the vineyards, in the beam of light from one's study window, a magnificent, large, healthy raccoon sniffed the treads for crumbs as he precisely picked up a single crumb between his long elegant fingers to delicately nibble at it! Not hearing me, the lovely animal sat up on his hind legs to become a huge ball of near transparent clear furriness before he targeted me with his tall luminous comprehending black eyes from within his bandit's mask! As this fine animal took in that one was an unknown quantity of furtive manhood, the beautiful creature abruptly turned and ran off down the path and through the vines, his ring-tail lax behind him. One was so thrilled, I wished that Laburnum—though no, of course—if Paycock or Bruno had been here, the beautiful raccoon would not have visited! I wondered if this fine creature had made other secret night visits that no one knew about. I hadn't heard anything about a raccoon from Mel or Reb, but pleased to have seen this stealthy night visitor, I vowed to keep a quiet watch out for my furry, tall-eyed, bandit friend.

The next evening as Laburnum and I walked Paycock down to the lake, having immovably decided that it was to be 'No' to his father. Off-handedly one remarked about Father to one's belle amorist, "I should never have let that scheming old rogue get to me, Laburnum! Augh, how ridiculous!"

"This is not the first discussion we've had about your father, you know, Algernon," Laburnum gently reminded me. "I understand that working all areas of your own winery is a vast change from your former urbanity and all your conscientiously higher objectives. Contrasts must continually confront you, but why do they, do you think? Is it from your habit of travel, or could you be in need of more input in handling your father?"

"That's the question I can't quite answer, Laburnum my sweet, because, alas, the enjoyment of traveling and what to do about Father won't disengage."

"Then you'll eventually plan this trip because you need to journey or out of a necessity to obey your father?"

"I very much need to be with you, as I thought you knew—damn it, you shrewd little wagtail, you're tricking me into making compliments! Though much as the habit of travel draws me, nothing should tear me away from you and all the peace and nature of this heaven-sent place! Though, no more of this!" as one on strode ahead of her, "We've said it all anyway."

"Ah, then you are handling it!" she called after one.

Walking ahead of her in a fog of mystification that I'd once again permitted one's father, brother et al, to so unforgivably get to me! The annoyance kept on in me as I walked, nudging one's mind into how completely his family had always done exactly what they'd wanted to! Gilmore and Father having decided every last item to do with the manor, even if they had been long-term considerations—blast them both! Putting in that unnecessary second pond, complete with baby sharks, then the balustrade and that new incongruous statue of Jack-the-Ripper. Then another fountain—but never a word to him! *After all, one was an inheritor too!* Also, they'd built that unsightly high wooden fence down along the river, of all places! Which was not only ridiculous but profligate! Ostensibly for keeping out prying fishermen, that had quickly made another path around it anyway! Gilmore and Jasmine had reaped ample entertaining projects and benefits, and now, as one's father's illnesses worsened, Father's belligerence sadly had to also be their fate. Sorry as one was for all of them—wasn't this how the hierarchical game played out?

Father would never have got away with his constantly bellowed insults if he'd been born to lesser means. Inadequate, as Algernon was perceived to be by his family, one did have a historic connection to them, and on occasions quite understood their freaky miseries. Yet he was never permitted to be more than the ignored second son 'rotting away among fermenting grapes in an American winery'—as his father had worded it in his letter.

Laburnum had caught up with him and threaded her arm through mine as I turned to her, remindful, "This is sinful, my love. We've come this far down to the lake, and all I know about yesterday's meeting at Tillie's house is that you motor-cycled there and back without a sprinkle."

"There was even a minute's sunlight!"

"So, what else can you tell me about that afternoon, my manipulating little bird?"

"You make me feel as if I've escaped from an aviary, Algernon! Well, all right. Tillie, Fergie, and I did make some headway! We've got leads to get somewhere specific at last, and that's all I'll tell you. Tillie believes we've already achieved all we need to, and she's ready to hand our findings in to the police, but Fergie and I are holding off; we're sure there's more we can come up with." Laburnum said this standing on the dock looking out at the lake. "Algernon? Would you like to sit here a few minutes, and we could let Paycock have a swim?"

"Sheltered here by that pounding westerly wind, yes! We'll sit and watch those gusts coming over the trees to make those great color changes out there on the trout grounds."

Sitting on the warmed wood, we fascinated with the changing teal-greens and silver grays from the wind thrusting down on the far out deeper water. The shadowed crescents of the wind rippled from them to merge with the larger lake's reflected milk-blue sky. Laburnum, though, stared into the clear water directly beneath us. Observing its depth, as she described Tillie's pretty little house, till she stopped abruptly.

"Is it bad luck to tell more?" One asked.

"It's best to have the whole story completed first, Algernon dear, as you know. Yes, I guess it is superstition. Because I've always worked this way, I worry that anyone else getting in on it could spoil it. Do you mind very much?"

"Not as long as you're quite all right, I don't. I'm not one to ascribe too much to luck or superstition."

"That may change," she said enigmatically from her other knowledge. "Along with that worry of yours about becoming 'provincial'."

“Aha, clever of you, as that is what I still keep pondering! Though why tell you what you already ‘know’?”

With Laburnum not wanting to tell me more about Tillie, I looked out; and prompted by the serenity of the lake’s late changes, quite arbitrarily I offered her my current irrelevant personal thought. “Laburnum, one must have had some unaccountable ancient streak in one’s Cholmondley-Rute ancestry—or else why do I always have such unremitting humanitarian concerns?” Receiving a thoughtful, though dubiously agreeing hum from my lover. “Even as a boy I had always valued this knack, or insight, which was another reason I got away from the manor. Ha, just words like ‘sanctions’ sent the Father-Gilmore duo off cackling and adding ludicrous aberrations,” I filled out. “As you know once well-honed, eventually this personal quirk found its usefulness on the Foreign Service’s international scale.”

“Awful! As your ‘knack’ as you call it was really a unique talent for the overview you’ve developed.”

“Yes, and it served one well preparing for crucial resolutions, and Laburnum, I’d like you to know that I made it my job to keep that humanitarian effort as benevolent as possible.” Her more brown-eyed interest, “getting to know you and other people here up close! This was new for me and eye-opening on a daringly personal scale. It may even have helped one over the distress of letting go of diplomatic service glitz! Actually, I’m not even minding too much if I do become *somewhat* ‘provincial’—if that’s what one calls it.”

This word ‘provincial’ always struck one, because to me it meant—*well what? Did it have a different meaning here now in America? One wouldn’t use the word ‘lowly’ as it could offend Laburnum, though ‘provincial’ lately had included certain unforgettable moments.* “For instance, a day ago when I’d walked to a lower vineyard, I’d come to complete stop before some arresting little nature sights! Those shiny black berries I’d picked for you, and also in the early morning’s low sunlight a perfectly circular cobweb stretched over several sumac ‘candles’ glinting jewel-like with dew. This humblest of sights had pierced my most curious sensitivities with more heralding than a fanfare of umpteen military bugles! As did some sunlit purple bramble arches beyond it, till I began to awe that one could be this easily stupefied into chronic admiration for such simple sights! Sights that an urbane colleague of mine, like Thaddeus, would have scorned. And adding to these wondrously simple little sights, there had been the pleasantly familiar sounds of the tractor mixing in, then Mel and Sigmund’s enthused comments and happy laughter floating over to one as they talked up some sensational American chicks! All these had startled one into the conspicuousness of these mundane sights and sounds that had hotly transmuted into the freshest of vast new pleasures! Pleasures one would have formerly bypassed.”

Telling this to Laburnum, we idly contemplated this 'provinciality', she supporting my observations as one's 'general new loosening'. "I've noticed this with you around our guys too, Algernon. You'd been so detached when you first came here—necessarily, of course, you'd needed to be wary." I took up her hand to brush her fingers with a sticky kiss as I still had a caramel in my mouth I'd been sucking since nabbing it from Laburnum's bowl. "You've not as much of that British 'stickiness' now, except if you will keep kissing me after eating my caramels! I've been meaning to ask you. Do you think that your re-settling here is moving along as you'd hoped?"

Again, his witch-woman was personally slipping him into improved views of himself, as we watched Paycock swimming fast after being thrown a driftwood stick. The dog found it and brought it to the dock, where he obediently shook off at the far end before padding along with it to present it to me; and due his politeness, he received a treat from one's pocket.

Later that afternoon, I took a book over that Laburnum had been wanting. "Algernon, do you like liverwurst?" I'm making a liverwurst and lettuce sandwich." As I followed her, Paycock got up and went to the door. "Yes, I'd love it. Does Paycock need to go out?"

"He's just been out. Sometimes he stands like that when he's looking for Bruno." Just as Laburnum said this, they realized that Paycock had gone out, and moments later he returned with Bruno. Both dogs came in the kitchen to sit unusually formally beside one another and seemed to be getting set to just watch Laburnum and myself! With one's appreciation of liverwurst, both dogs and I looked on as Laburnum slurped the meat slices, mayonnaise, mustard, and lettuce on rye bread for me too. Laburnum and I took our plates and napkins to sit in the living-room, and she brought in a beer for me and a glass of milk for herself as the dogs followed us in, and we all four settled.

As we sat over our meal, thoughtfully, I asked, "Laburnum, may I tell you my very personal thoughts while one was working down among the grapevines?" The dogs' heads both turned, and they appeared to listen extra-carefully. "I say, Laburnum, they aren't hungry, are they?"

"Paycock just had a bone—it's over there by his basket. You were saying?"

Since Laburnum had refused my invitation to one's U.K. family, she seemed to be making a bigger effort to be interested in me—though I couldn't get over the dogs' untypical interest in her and myself! Paycock was now sitting bolt upright, with his head held back, hunting poised as he slowly let his eyes *close*! "Laburnum, have you seen him doing this before?"

She snickered, "He's even got Bruno trying to sit straight now too, look! No, I'm not sure what's got into them." For a long bodied, short-legged hound, Bruno's stiff formal position looked uncomfortable, particularly when, just like

Paycock, he slowly closed his eyes! "Don't pay any attention, Algernon, dogs have their own secret games. You were saying?"

I had come over to Laburnum's to make a suggestion, though, "Just *look* at these dogs! Beloved, have you seen them do this kind of thing before?"

"Paycock went a bit like this once—it's something of their own they've got going, but I don't think it's anything unhealthy." Laburnum waved their strange behavior aside as if there wasn't anything she didn't profoundly know about the dogs.

"Laburnum," One re-started, "once you have the Egyptian chapter refined, would you read it to me?" I was hoping that this would more thoroughly test her genuine wish for me to know her feelings about my joining with her, *as it was what I too, also deeply believed,* I really wanted to work with her; and *apprehensively, I awaited her answer.* Not having completed a year of retirement, I could easily use old contacts for further information should I want to, and I'd begun to really like the idea of burrowing the 'golden ages' and getting into a more cosmopolitanism, more of the worldliness, I read about in newspapers again. "Laburnum, you're into humanitarian causes that we could all do to know more about, I'd like to offer you whatever you think I could do that might help." This began to look like a step forward in our better relationship; though—*were both the closed-eyed dogs into a low hum?*

Laburnum looked skeptically at me, "You must have some idea what an enormous amount of work this'll be, Algernon. Are you sure this is what you want?"

Nodding. "As long as you'd want me in on your work."

"Wow!" she exclaimed before becoming more thoughtful.

I said, "Though we'd better consider all sides of us working together, Laburnum. You and I know we can't always be harmonious." *Was a stronger, low-singing sound coming from Paycock?* "This enormous quest of yours is a deep personal involvement that's had you in its grip for months."

"Years."

"Years, yes. It's your magnum opus. Which is why you may prefer not to have me in on it."

"I don't think I've kept it to myself for any vain reason, Algernon. Until you came there hadn't been anyone around here remotely interested in these golden ages. Naturally, if you're willing to be free with your travels and all you know, it would be a wonderful opportunity, and having your company wouldn't be all that bad!" She smiled and added, "Though I'd want a heavy hand in what we're to make of it all."

"It's *your* fabulous quest, Laburnum, you'd have to be the decision-maker-director. Though you'd need to be aware of the times the winery will be all I can think about."

She nodded, "No difficulty. We all know what happens to grapes."

"You might want to think harder about this, Laburnum. It's all been yours. The decision doesn't have to be now, we can talk about it again—it may change more than we expect."

Looking at him, she said, "I can't think of anyone who could get in on what I'm doing, or who I'd like to have working with me as much as yourself."

Hmmm. "You know..." I was wanting to say more about my own appropriateness. "...throughout my years, there hasn't been a time I've not had my eyes wide open for the improvement of human situations."

"Ha, oh yes!" giving a little laugh. "I know how violent your optimism is, ha ha! Which is why I see through you twisting our talks on golden ages to make them fit your upbeat philosophy!" Given with a sparkling glance at me, "And Algernon, let me warn you, I'll take you to task because whatever you tell me, it might be that you'd been very lucky as a diplomat having come from your influential family and background."

"Now, *wait!*" one's enormous offence.

"Well, shouldn't I say it? It worries me that some of those highly responsible 'improvements' of humanitarian situations chanced to come from colleagues that were covering for your personal diffidence."

"L*aBUR*-num!" I yelled.

"I'd heard you weren't so suave that day you'd returned from England." *From Sylvia, I guessed... and she didn't need to say more.*

"Good Lord, Laburnum, look at what I was coping with back then! One's major property purchase in another country, I'd just left my difficult family and was getting myself used to the whole idea of immigrating! Diffident I may have been, but that was under those circumstances which, if you think about it, was *not* characteristic of me?"

"Shouldn't we be trying for complete honesty?"

Lord above! What was this spectacularly ignorant monster female trying to do to me?

Was she embracing some pathological ignorance from someone's misdirected social comment? Which given by this loose cannon wombat was grossly insulting! One's spine was sizzling to upright! This mealy-mouthed aging tart presumed she was so empowered with all aspects of Freudian psychology, but whatever she'd heard about my return from the U.K., whatever her over-ripe dramatic interpretation had made of it, she was completely wronging my truer character—why? For hurtfully maligning one? But my self-worth refused to let her get away with this blatantly imagined fable, whatever it may inevitably cost me. "Listen, Laburnum! I thought you'd know a good deal of what I'd once done from Hans, and that much had been accomplished through step by step intense foreign policy decisions! Though apparently, you're drawing a blank!" Gulping, as I'd had to take a breath. *Knowing one's defense was at the price of losing her friendship, yet I owed myself making it clear to this cocotte that her doltish unintelligence had come down squarely on one's sorely abused fairness to oneself.* "Damn it, woman, teams of us were buried up to our sinuses in overloads of highly secret international data," my hand drew down my poor buzzing face, not once, but again, as objecting Laburnum moaned. Dear God, this witch-woman's pitiful vulgarity could be so personally injurious, one needed to barrel over her pleas. Voraciously, I defended, "I doubt you have any idea what it took to set up Nixon's Helsinki Arms Limitation Treaty." *She may have been trying to say something—maybe the word, 'SALT'? Well, this time it ruddy well wasn't her turn!* "Yes, I'm talking about SALT One! And all those hard-nosed modifyings of London's demands and the high commissioner's! For that most far-reaching, beautifully engineered set of agreements—which you'll recall were being made between arch-enemy superpowers! Few believed it could be done, hope was lame for it at best; but at that time we were having to live with those continent-destroying weapons so, what could be our choice? Imperatively, agreements had to be reached. You'll never know how stratospheric our hopes were for limiting ICBM's with a major superpower accord, I don't suppose—but try to think about it? We were constructing this globally intense, prospectively useful foundation! An unprecedented first meant for being built upon. Try to envision the endlessness of constantly disrupted preparations, then the clobbering anti-climax when a trusted major source proved useless. Or just as bad—was miscommunicated. I doubt you can imagine the deadening effect of such resounding defeats, but even so, ultimately, *we did get it done, and it did go through!*" I leaned back to slow down considerably. "Have a heart, wagtail, don't always dwell on what SALT 1 or what any of our work *didn't* do. Bales full of wrong-headed opposition had already been axing us for all that, and keep in mind – that that treaty reduced the number of land and sea-based launchers for nuclear missile heads; and even though both the Soviets and the US had the right to withdraw, yet remember—*neither did!* A stupendous step too because as you really know, it *did* set the groundwork in place for SALT 2," one finished with a shake of one's head. "So now you know!"

"*A-l-*gernon!" Her objecting lament had been trying to get through. "What you and other brilliant diplomats did was little short of miraculous."

"It was a *titanic,* Laburnum!" It had not been one's wish to get into this kind of a description of what I had contributed, but hadn't his hard-earned past work given one any distinction to this fleece-head? Is that what this witch was up to as she had driven him to spell it out? "Though damn it, this isn't what..." Shaking my head again, till I said more inaudibly, "...this isn't even what I'd come over to you to talk to about."

"Sorry, Algernon."

We each solemnly folded into breathy separate-nesses.

We'd hit knowledge limitations yet again; and at this moment, each of us needed to secure within our own scattering thoughts.

Talking like this to a woman was not easy for me. Gathering my struggling battered wits, I wasn't willing to stick around anymore of Laburnum's troglodytic foreign policies; and as one noticed Paycock and Bruno opening their eyes and getting up to leave, I decided that any more talking with this North American pussy's mind so closed would only be counter-productive. The dogs had it right. Leaving her possibly miffed and confused, I only paused to turn and murmur, "See you tomorrow."

It took countless times of one's steady walking back and forth around my porch's two sides for me to more usefully respond to Laburnum's remorseless over-tease. Though she'd had shown so little interest in him in where I'd lived or in my family. Probably she'd intended to just 'tease'. Though I was not wrong in judging her inflammatory remarks to be based on ignorance. After all, international diplomacy had not been her vocation, though why in blazes had she jumped to such venal conclusions?

Oh, Algernon, for God's sake, what have you got yourself into now??

Badly needing to remedy this injury she'd dealt one, I helped to rebalance by reviewing one's rock-solid compassion for saving fate's helpless victims. That belabored compassion of mine that had been so obvious since back rebuffing my colleagues lampooning one as the 'Hopeless Emancipator'. The truth was that out on a mission, once philosophically behind a major consequential move, I'd simply dismissed departmental precepts and all their bureaucracy, even if it meant bitter exchanges with Whitehall! Thaddeus never stopped scolding for what he called 'letting down the team', but to me, the function of a team and all its red tape meant nothing if we missed the opposition's underlying purposes.

Well-known for this 'obstinacy', one had little trouble holding onto one's singular fight, as it had attained one praise from some surprising heads of state—though rarely from those heads above one's own! It was out of those former times that one's greater understanding of compassion on Foreign Service levels had found any like-thinking as it had helped create relieved futures for tragic large blocks of humanity. *'Compassion'... what a multi-leveled entity and much else, it actually was!*

On the next afternoon, Laburnum and I walked Paycock down to the lake together anyway! Rather silently.

The reason I'd decided to was, because I really saw that this witch-woman's more kind intention was to personally and entertainingly slip me into more innovative views of myself—which was not going to be likely again today! As we both watched Paycock swim after his thrown branch to find it and bring back to the dock, where he obediently shook off at the far end before bringing it along to present it to me. *God, did even this dog have more savoire-faire than his erratic owner?!* Diving after the stick again, the setter got vexed looking among the ripples he'd caused, comically swinging his head from side to side. Before calling Paycock in after several more 'fetches' that Laburnum and I mutely watched for the solace it lent to our on-edge unshared introspections, till with nightfall coming, we walked back up the hill. We had each agreed to go to our separate lodgings tonight, to read for me and get back to working the Egyptians for her. I saw Laburnum to her door, where confirming this loose return to our companionship, one kissed her cheek more platonically than two presidents celebrating an unpopular photo op, as I truly wished her to have a good night. Laburnum accepted this cooled kiss as a step towards our mending friendship, knowing very well that her 'over-tease' of what I had spent my career attaining had been extremely unwise.

Too tired to read for long, I fell asleep early; and although alone in my own big bed, I slept well until about 1:00 a.m. when one awoke with a start—a sudden dreaded certainty that my father was truly dying had awakened me! Such dreaded urgency had hit me with a stabbing ache down my temple that fortunately relieved almost immediately, though it remained intractably urgent that my father was taking his final breaths. Jumping out of bed, I paced myself into reasoning that this state of my father's could be nothing more than the fertility of nighttime imagination, and all that had lately gnawed my mind—though this did nothing to stop this ice-cold certainty of one's father's demise reiterating in me, like a striking dinner gong. Finally, the chills within this certainty sent me downstairs to the study to use the phone for rattling up some former airline contacts.

Leaving the study, I heard Sigmund in the kitchen busily opening and closing several cabinet doors. Back from a date, all Sigmund could think about was the taste of canned pork and beans as he was missing the cans closet one opened it for the merry lover to hand him a can. Opening it, Sigmund ladled the beans into a cereal bowl to microwave, as one got his attention, "Sigmund, I need to make a trip to England."

"When will that be?"

"Tonight."

"Something is wrong?"

"My father."

"O-oh fathers! I am most sorry, Algernon."

Not taking time to explain I agreed, nodding. "I've a flight out of Rochester, but it kills me to leave when we're mid-processing. Would you get hold of

Hans?" Agreeing to do so, Sigmund looked ready to do anything to help me. "It's just for a couple of days?"

"Hans, Mel, and I will keep it going, Algernon, trust us. You know you may have worries enough over there. We know what to do, so do not be concerned. Believe it or not, we ran the place once without Hans for a couple of days, so please, no worrying about it." Sigmund spoke altruistically and assuredly before shoving a steaming forkful of beans in his mouth and reacting to them being too hot.

"I'll write what I'm doing for Laburnum. I don't want to wake her; she has the Tillie problem about to erupt."

"One of us will talk with her tomorrow. She'll use the time you're gone at her desk, you know that."

Sitting over my sudden plan as Sigmund munched away, one watched him. Tipping a few of Sigmund's hot beans onto a left-out saucer, I took a spoon and joined him as he assured me that there were enough capable people here to keep up the picking pace and pressing. Sigmund soon got up to clear the table. With my wine-maker so helpfully concerned tonight, I was glad of him; and before leaving him, I went upstairs for my passport and quickly packed a hold-all and pulled on better clothes. Grabbing my light tweed jacket, I took these down to my study. At my desk, I wrote, 'My dearest Laburnum, you needed your sleep with the Tillie case climaxing. I'll explain my acute haste to you by phone tomorrow and be back in a couple of days to find out how your Tillie-time went. Loving one another as we really do, I know you'll understand my sudden haste, my darling. Please keep that place warm in your heart for me while I'm away. You know mine will be at white-heat burning for you, dearest wagtail. Kiss kiss, Algernon.'

Taking my bag, I crept across to Laburnum's darkened apartment. Neither Paycock nor Bruno heard me, or didn't bother waking with footsteps they knew, and I slid my letter to her under her door and crept to my car. In low gear with my bag on the seat beside me, I drove out and headed for Rochester, in time to make the Rochester-Toronto flight without a Toronto lay-over. Up in the skies, I accustomed to every nuance of one's competing feelings, getting them in order, a habit I'd always had while flying; and in six hours I was in Gatwick, hauling my carried-on bag along the moving corridor. Quickly through the short British passport line, and I hired a car—annoyed that there wasn't much choice as usual, I conscientiously kept to the left and drove out to the family manor as fast as one dared to through the brightness and traffic jingle of mid-day London.

Barging in, the manor's household looked to be in disarray. Through the Great Hall, I could see Gilmore standing in the dining-room, fine plate in hand lapping food up into his mouth. But it wasn't Gilmore I needed to see. Maudie, who was carrying a large bundle of towels across the Great Hall, peered over them; and as if expecting me, she shouted, “Hurry, Sir Algernon, y’father can’t last!” Horace too was the most agitated I’d seen him, unnecessarily pressing himself against the wall halfway up the broad Bloody Tower staircase to let me rush by, as Jasmine came out along the landing from Father’s bedroom, wringing her hands to get the blood of King Duncan off them, till seeing me, “Oh-! We weren’t expecting *you,* Algernon!”

Striding past her to the clay figure of one’s diminished parent sunken into the white sheet and pillow, I bent to get my head close to my father’s pronounced face—his wizened body. The odor was nauseating as Father’s head turned slightly to me, and mercifully, his expression faintly changed, as if recognizing his second son. “Snot-bottom?” one of Father’s old names for one as a boy, spoken so weakly it was barely audible. “I wanted...” But his wheezing and grimacing disclosed that Father was indeed suffering horrible pain, “...wanted. It wasn’t fair... to include...” Through a prickly wheeze-wheeze, “to... include your mother... in with us. She’d said, Ha…” wheeze... wheeze... “You could be quite bright.” Rattled rasping gaps between these pained words that almost had his laughter in with them? Except that his father’s face screwed up each time with pain before he dropped into noisier rattling.

“That’s all right, I really knew that, Father,” I soothed unaware of Jasmine coming beside the bed.

“There’s some—ach—” His wheezing was so erratic I held my breath as if this would keep one’s father going, but... wheeze... wheeze...

“Yes, Father?”

“Something more Snotsy,” he was drooling bubbles, “Listening?”

“I am, Father.”

“Life—is—a bloody bugger.”

With these most apropos words from my father, I sat staring into the draining face. Stared more still, till a hand came around my shoulders to go to my father’s pulse, and I fixed to my parent’s time on earth finally being spent before the hand went to each of Father’s eyes to lower his lids. Father’s lifeless head had barely slipped sideways as I stared at the death relieving this scary old tyrant when amazingly; at the last, he had been righting just one of his old wrongs. Father’s only scrap of parental decency! Standing, I saw that the owner of this hand was their elderly family doctor, who must have drifted in with Jasmine and Gilmore.

“Horace!” Jasmine called sternly turning toward the groan at the bedroom door, “It’s all right; he’s gone to paradise.”

Nodding, Horace muttered, “Bloody best thing.”

Jasmine spoke to Maudie as she came in, “It’ll be quieter here now than under the ocean, Maudie.”

Bottled with how close I’d been to missing my father’s death, I turned away to let the doctor, Maudie, and Jasmine close in on their expired patient. As if nothing different had come about, Gilmore authoritatively beckoned me away from our parent's body to meet him as we walked out of the bedroom. In his usual bullying tones, he said, "We didn't expect you, you know? It would've helped to know you were over here?"

"I won't be staying, Gilmore."

"You'll have to *stay*."

Needing some moments to myself, I stopped on the landing to lean against the banisters and look down at the Great Hall of my enchanted young boyhood, scarcely aware that Gilmore was not only waiting, but with his eyes glazed, was impatiently tapping his foot. But I couldn't move from one's last parent now being beyond what must have been horrendous human suffering; as instead, the young boy in this now parentless man looked down at the lower story's mural with its faded armored knights' torsos torqued mid-battle. Writhing bodies and limbs, a blood-covered foot, that had long ago piqued my childish curiosity, but looking down at them all today, they appeared to be nothing more than faded decaying paint. One's mother had hated their goriness, and after this significant family event with his father's last phrases replaying in one's head, those walls of familiar old battles looked absurdly innocuous. Father's last phrases kept replaying in one, till his death mingled one's awe that only hours ago back in the U.S., one's night time's agonizing head pain, along with its forceful command, must have actually been a telepathic message! How else to explain my compulsion to just get here? Could there be any doubt that this had been an extraordinary messaging, and why had it been from of all people, one's father? What an indestructibly hidden connection one must have had to the damnable old miscreant!

"I'm counting on you for the funeral," Gilmore said; his eyes agitating toward the dining-room downstairs with its left lunch that their father's death had had the audacity to interrupt. Gilmore's brittle authority brought one too. "Don't make a big show of it for all our sakes, Algie." Gillie's stern tilt to his head, demanding one hurry along the landing to him to take the staircase down.

Sitting at the dining-room table as one's brother removed the silver dish lid and helped himself to another heaping plateful of Maudie's bubble and squeak, I too, absently helped myself, using the only other plate. "It's to be private, a family-only affair. At Father's age, his friends had mostly died off."

"He'd had friends?"

"One, a vegetable." And leaning back importantly. "Father will land up in the Grecian temple vault the day after tomorrow. I expect you to be there."

"I doubt I'll even stay the night, Gillie. I've walked out on a great deal that's unfinished back in New York State."

Jasmine had come down; and going over to the table, she lifted the lid of the emptied silver dish as Gilmore informed her, "Algernon ate yours, Jasmine. Have Maudie make more."

"We'd no word from you, Algernon. We weren't ready for you."

"I just came, Jasmine."

"Poor Father, all that suffering, it was horrible," one nodded disinclined to mentally meet her comments. "He was so brave his last few days. Gillie and I wanted to cry."

"Thank God he popped off before that snarling beast of a vicar got to him." As usual, Gilmore's thinking was practical.

"You mean Reverend Pigott, Gillie? Not such a beast really—a bit heavy with the social niceties is all."

"Heavy at snagging a damn large chunk for his rotting church windows."

"Community churches desperately need repairs."

"Not from us. We've our own chapel."

"How would you know? You haven't been in our chapel or the village church since the children were christened!" She turned to me. "As you're here for a week or two, Algernon, when they've got it ready, you'll be in the Guy Fawkes bedroom."

Having already had enough of my brother and sister-in-law after experiencing the exhausting fullness of every last moment of one's father, it amazed me how abruptly my years of attachment to the manor and my family were dissolving. Quickly, I assured Jasmine, "I'll not be staying, Jasmine. I've a great deal to get back to."

"Coffee and brandy it is then, in the greater living-room." Then she suddenly let go, "I'll go and tell Maudie, as the fornicating bell is broken, Gillie; and maybe I can get Maudie to make me some toast." Off Jasmine trotted.

"If you're so unconscionable, you'll avoid Father's final send-off, Algernon; you'll also miss old Becksley's reading of the will, though no doubt you've always known what you're to receive. It's a tragedy decent lumps will go out of the country."

"A large chunk will stay at Lloyds."

"Investing? God, you're not marrying again or anything of that sort, are you?"

"I've certainly got the ideal woman, should it go that the way."

"Well, don't let's go on about it. Wouldn't have gone down with Father, you know. Didn't believe you were man enough—he he!" Gillie's crackled two-note rent the air at his father's offensive joke.

I wondered if our father had believed Gilmore 'man enough' too; but as his brother and Jasmine had so many offspring, one's slim thought quickly moved on. “Gillie, you must have noticed that neither Father nor I cared what each other did.”

Another- “He he!”

After coffee and brandy with Jasmine, two of their adult daughters arrived, eager for news of their grandfather. Good-looking like Jasmine, these women were quite striking; though both spoke with such kapok-stuffed noses, it was hard to understand what they said. I was delighted to see them again, but as Gillie and Jasmine abruptly adopted something akin to abject grief before their daughters, I made my virtually ignored goodbyes. Going to the kitchen, I thanked Maudie and Horace for all the hysteria they’d put up with and promised to look in on the household in a few weeks. Both longtime retainers came outside with me to wave me off in my rental car. Overflowing with relief and loaded with much larger un-contemplated thoughts, I drove to the airport hotel and ordered a comfortable suite.

One foot pushed off the heel of the other pigskin loafer, and both thumped to the floor before I flopped across the dusky gold, satin comforter. Pulling the phone onto the bed, I dialed my overseas ‘beloved’, unsure how she would be. On hearing the warmth and sincerity of her sultry alto, immediately I indulged in the love back in it again as it spiraled around my viscera, like an over-fertilized clematis vine. I felt quite weak as I kept Laburnum talking for that magic balm to her voice massaging my careening inner roots with the oil of extra-virginated olives. “Oh, Laburnum, my sweetest darling, just let me keep hearing the wonderful love in your mellifluous voice that’s all for me-! That cradling distinguished voice of yours! *I need it,* oh God, my sugar-plum, you can’t know how much I *need* it!”

“My love, *o-o-oh* my wonder-love!” Was she needing to swallow? “You got there in time, my chivalrous Algernon? I’m so thrilled for you, my wunder-liebkin!”

“You’ve been zeroed in on me?”

“Not till I awoke this morning, then yes, I knew it before reading your letter. And listen, my lover-legend, I owe you a humungous apology for being a drag on your earlier invitation for me to return to your father with you, Algernon. On that one, my clairvoyance completely broke down.”

“It was being heavily used for the kidnapped child, Laburnum! Believe me, I understood. What can you tell me about that boy?”

“Yes, marvelous news! *They’ve found him, Algernon! FOUND him, yes!* Using our directions, the police zeroed in on him, and they’ve got that bastard father behind bars. *Can you believe it?* The poor kid’s not in the best shape, but he’s to make it—he’s receiving special care in the hospital. Isn’t that the greatest? Everything went more smoothly than I’d hoped, though look that’s not for now. You’re returning?”

"I've a flight to Schiphol at 11:00 a.m. and another to get back to my car in Toronto; then I'll be driving to you on two wheels."

"Can't wait, my Sir Galahad!"

"Ah, I'm a venturing knight of the fabulous round table? We'll do more serious looking into that."

"Yes, let's! And Algernon, Hans wanted you to know he's checking Mel and Sigmund, Reb too. The guys think Hans was glad to be taken out of mothballs."

"Yes? Then I'll have to get him back more often."

"He'd love it. *Though wait!* He and I were talking, he really does love his long, slow reading days too now. They suit his limited movements, and he's getting down to the books he'd always wanted to read."

"Excellent! And sweet-maid-of-the-woodlands, I'm so happy that you, Tillie, and Fergie have had such great success! Happy that you'll be degage and free to tell it to me now too! You must know a lot more about what's worked, and I'll want to hear every tedious detail. All right, I should certainly be with you for supper. Give Paycock a cuddle for me and tell him he's not to get hyper-excited when we walk him, because you and I have a great deal to say to one another."

"Algernon, he did go peacefully? Not Paycock, I mean your father?"

"Yes, he did. But let's save all that for tomorrow, my darling."

"Oh, and in case you're in the mood for, though after all you've crushed into these last few hours you'll—Though no, I shouldn't."

"Stop teasing, Laburnum. Say it."

"I'll have on my black lace bra you admire so much!"

"Lord, I won't need a plane!"

"Come home safely, my valiant swain."

"First a bath, then some great dreams of black lace bursting over your gorgeous olive curves in a lovely, much-needed sleep. My darling, keep that most special place deep in you bubbling for me. Soon, very soon. Kiss-kiss, my gorgeous tawny mistress!"

Chapter 22
More Dog Perceptions

The three dogs smiled at one another as they shook off from their vigorous back-rollings. "Aren't we fortunate that our ancestral creed expects us to show *sapiens* how beautifully *cooperation* like this works?" Paycock asked. "Just look at us three! We're the best of affectionate friends, even though we're a Bassett Hound, an English Setter, and a mi—Mix?"

"Call me a Mix, Paycock," Rowley assured him. "I'm proud to have a mother and a father from different breeds. But as you see, in appearance, I'm more my Father's collie, which I'm perfectly happy with."

"You don't mind being called 'Mix'?"

"It's my actuality."

Paycock and Bruno thought this courageous of Rowley, because they knew he'd always dreamed of being in the Westminster, which as everyone knows has obsolete discrimination rules about entrants having to be pedigree.

"Henderson keeps me caged because he knows I'm valuable. Only you two good friends know I get under the fence for coming here, though I wish… my greatest wish is to go park-parading."

"Park-walking isn't really so great, Rowley," Paycock soothed. "Your owner gets schizoid wanting you to walk regulated in an agonizing posture; though if a male dog passes, Laburnum thinks I'm feeble if I don't bare my teeth and growl! So, I give her a jolting great tug so she flies off her feet—he-he, pretty comic! Then when it gets to snarling bites and drawing blood, it all changes because—*this is what you do*—you wink at your opponent so you can both act out some sinister barking before getting yanked; then, like the actors on the healing TV snake oil commercials, you fake loud groans and limp off."

"Masterful!" Rowley commented. "Does Laburnum get upset?"

"Oh Great White Worms, you should hear her! Though it's all show. With people around, she acts like she's spanking me; and to the other dog owner, she rattles off a flood of nonsense about my going without my chow and being sent to dog school! But you know why she doesn't starve me and lock me up? She just can't resist putting her feet on my nice warm belly under the table."

“That’s how it is, Rowley,” Bruno confirmed. Owners like to look as if they’re in charge, but it’s just an act. What Paycock’s described about winking and faking limps is exactly what happens—which is another good example of our subtle canine cooperation! You won’t find a park dog that resorts to true savagery because it’s not in our canine manifesto—our chromosomes wouldn’t let us; we just don’t believe in violence! And anyway, we’re too well choreographed in sensational performance.”

“Though if *sapiens* caught on to our faked performances, couldn’t it push along their cooperating?” Paycock asked.

“Whatever helps eliminate *sapien* savagery?”

“Right, Bruno!” Puffing out his chest, Paycock continued, “Now this beautiful morning, we need to keep our exceptional minds exercised for agility. You two good friends must already know about the South African Truth Commissions? *No-o?* Rowley? You and the Henderson woman must have heard about them?” Getting Rowley’s nod. “Is there any other example to beat that brilliant *sapien* resourcefulness?”

“It’s the best,” Rowley agreed. Paycock and Bruno respected Rowley’s knowledge of History because they knew that he and Mrs. Henderson watched the History Channel on their kitchen TV because Mrs. Henderson disliked the prohibitively expensive athletes that her husband and brother-in-law sat ogling on their living room’s big screen.

“Those commissions couldn’t be more instructive,” Bruno agreed.

“Ha, I know why you’re so hopeful, Bruno,” Paycock said recalling that Bruno and Mel had stopped by when Laburnum had that blockbuster South African TV program going, “The African continent’s government experiment? You remember?”

“That’s it!” Rowley had Paycock and Bruno cocking their ears provocatively. “The South Africans have a mandatory system with mandatory community service, so plenty of infrastructure gets accomplished—bridges, train crossings, perennial pot-holes.”

“Luckily we dogs have an instinct for knowing what South Africa achieved with their Truth and Reconciliation Commissions,” Bruno added. “In fact, I’d heard that Bishop Tutu got the idea from his dog.”

“*Bishop Tutu has a—?*”

Paycock explained, “I bet you’re right. *Their* unusually civilized South African leadership concentrates every effort on across-the-board healing.”

Bruno knew this, “Yes, Paycock. It’s their Truth and Reconciliation Commissions!” Helping Paycock explain, “Get the Henderson woman to get it on the History Channel again, Rowley. It’s when a killer is interrogated for days on end facing his victim’s families till he can’t stand what a torturing, grimacing, hate-loaded maniac he truly is and breaks down and confesses. This digs down to what's so *sapien*-raw that even multi-killers will beg for Kleenex. Everyone's had a family; it destroys even a serial murderer to face mothers and brothers he'd caused to grieve."

"Yes, *their* Truth and Reconciliation idea is silver-bright all right! Other countries' crime departments have been so amazed, *they* try to copy that South African world-shattering progress," Paycock continued. "Though the South Africans are so far ahead with all that over there, it startles our own progressive *sapiens* clean out of all their patent leather party shoes."

"Ha!"

Paycock's enthusiasm for this powerful new crime rehab system sent all three dogs' heads falling forward toward one another in an oiled unity of awed assimilation and contemplation. Incidentally, during this obsessing mental work, a mass of seagulls came off the lake low over the silent dogs in their random flying pattern, but not one dog's observation-instinct was diverted. Nor did they immediately hear Mel coming around the barn.

Fortunately, he called out, "Having a good time, you lucky Bow-wows!" Alarming all three dogs into automatic good canine postures for pleasing Mel. "Laburnum says you can be let off now and have some run-around fun-time, Paycock! So, you and great good doggie-woggie Bruno can get rid of some energy! Your pal Rowley too—here!" He unfastened them. "There you are—off and free! Okay, now get in some cool run-arounds!"

With all three dogs unleashed, they showed Mel their appreciation by bouncing and skipping in circles around him as they took him back to the production barn. When the dogs were alone again, they chased one another up and down the parking lot, until a visitor's pickup honked at them; then they ran around back behind the barn to their catalpa tree again to try out a good new stretching exercise Rowley knew. Standing on their back legs, they reached their fore-paws high up as far as they could on the catalpa bark, stretching their bodies to unbelievable long skinny lengths before relaxing down again to chase one another around the catalpa, hazelnut, and locust trees, catching at one another's tails and braying with laughter! It was a great game, till exhausted they fell down back where they always rested anyway.

"Not bad, Rowley, you've got unusually good foot springs."

"It's the collie in me. That's what gets me here faster than a chased fox."

"I like this spot here behind the barn best anyway," Bruno commented. "The higher twigs and branches way up there are compositionally more design-attractive."

As the word 'cooperative' had come up, Paycock took the opportunity to move their topic to a larger one to dig their back molars into, as he assumed a more philosophic posture. "Being dogs, we know that *'cooperating'* causes blissful fluids to flow and gives us plenty of tranquility. Take us three different breeds again, sitting here together with inherently different upbringings, opinions, and customs; but as mature Canidae, we know that however viral our differences, even if it takes all day, we can always get them comprehended." Sturdy agreements from Rowley and Bruno. "Since puppyhood, we've known that explaining and assimilating are the wisdom-builders that clear out mental debris, like grudges and argumentative personas. It's because as beasts we're innately noble! Our civilized standards prevent us from truly losing control and seriously injuring one another. Don't you two think we're the most magnanimously admired of all living creatures?"

"Shapely Hocks, yes! All that mass injuring that *sapiens* do—it's is so regressively mindless!" Bruno affirmed. "Thanks to those legendary Egyptian dog gods, Canidae are bred to understand that if we lowered our standards like that, we dogs would not advance-think! So listen, wouldn't it be outrageous to be a *sapien* officially ordered not to travel some roads because there was bloodshed there? Wouldn't being banned from certain streets, where dogs there were fighting to death, be freedom limiting and undemocratic? Argh, just thinking about it makes me hydro—hydro?"

"Hydro-phobic, Bruno, just say 'hydrophobic'."

"What you just said then." And looking up skywards, Bruno was diverted by the irresistible beauty of what his eyes were seeing just then. "Say, look how symmetrical that design is." The threesome sat raising their heads high to study what Bruno was seeing of the upper tree branches' elaborate composition.

Finally, as their necks started to ache, Rowley surprised his other two friends with an astounding remark. "Remembering we're wanting topics of substance for digging our teeth into, my good friends; well, in case you haven't heard, here's another incredibly amazing item."

"Tell us Rowley?"

Having studied what Bruno was seeing of the lovely upper trees' composition lines looking so striking against the pale sky, the dogs turned their heads right and left to rid their stiffness as Rowley finally got his friends' attention for an astounding remark, "Have you two ever heard that *sapiens* only collectively civilize after there's been an enormous war? Which shows us what mega-genius *sapien's* occasionally force out of themselves if *they* make a crucial all-out effort."

"*War?* You mean like a World War?"

Rowley nodded, "Yes, a war that went on in just about every country in the whole world. And here's what we need to think about—it was only after all that massive slaughter and the destruction of *sapiens,* cities, governments, animals, birds, homes, and spiders that nations' leaders tried out their good sense when *they* stopped competing! Hard to believe, isn't it? But instead of competing, *they* tried 'cooperating!' I know it sounds unbelievable, but after that massive World

War, even with many nations speaking different languages, with different heraldries, badges, and marching tunes, *they all got together!* Can you believe it?! And listen to this! *They created what they called a 'League'.* Don't look like that, Bruno, I know it's hard to believe, but historically, *sapiens* really did create this colossal meet-up! Together, these multinational-*sapiens* pledged that after such an annihilating world war that had ruined almost every family and every city and wonderful urinating place, they pledged that *they* would *never go to war again! That whatever provoked, they vowed they would talk it through to prevent one another from mass killings like that ever again. And do you know why?"*

"Because *they* at last realized that life was *their* most valuable gift?" Bruno butted in. "Which mattered more than being victorious."

"*They* couldn't have cooperated that much, Rowley," Paycock was disbelieving.

"You're sure?" Bruno wondered, too.

"Absolutely sure!" Rowley said this recalling more of the History program that had so greatly impressed he and Mrs. Henderson.

Bruno was thrilled with this History that he'd only remotely heard about. "Hurray! Good for them! Do you know any more about it, Rowley?"

"I do. After all that pledging to keep everlasting peace 'forever', some years later in some place where there had been no cooperation, a Second World War got started anyway. And would you believe it?"

"What? No, don't tell us! This next generation saw with *their* own eyes what massive killing could do—and get this! *They* cooperated again?"

"You mean after this second massive destruction of helpless lovely families, bumble-bees, and every kind of creature and ancient fabulously fragrant places?"

"Yes, you've guessed it! *They* passionately re-civilized a-all over again! Forming a better league, with many amendments this time, so it could never go wrong. You both know it, it's called 'The United Nations'. This was done in San Francisco."

Bruno and Paycock's ears perked high at this brilliant nutshell History that made such extraordinary sense, yet neither knew a lot about it. Listening to Rowley telling about this historic international meeting in California, they were still skeptical that such huge quantities of *sapien* multi-nationals could have cooperated this much, and the three dogs simply sat, jaws dropped, nodding their superabundant hopefulness as they lavished on more admiration! Westminster-inspired or not, Rowley could surely devastate with historical facts.

"*Their* trouble is," Rowley went on just as didactically, "after splendid cooperating, like those history book no-war pledges, it turned out to be *their* own nationalist politics that was *their* worst enemy. Wouldn't you think that after all the torture, mass burials, scarcity of food, and eternal rebuilding, that they'd?"

"Right! Having seen that it was *cooperation* that had very nearly made it."

"*Nearly.* Which would have kept killing safely and forever over with, permanently! Imagine! So very *nearly* it kept all evil-minded destructiveness *gone!*"

Nodding, Rowley agreed. "Rotten of *them,* when *they'd* seen what cooperating could have done! But all it took was just one politician with bubble-wrap between his ears to inflate his talking up of national interests."

"Yes, that could be all it takes! Just one-climbing-the-grand-ladder two-bit politician."

"That's what we've just said, Bruno," Paycock's groans heightened with each of Bruno's repeated remarks. "Get Mel to wash out those long ears of yours, good buddy."

"That's all it took—some over-eager dingbat political fiend hell-bent on promotion, to ignore *sapien* history's fantastic good sense! Ignoring all *their* hard work." Paycock got in, "Algernon says that corrupt powerful leaders will often compete for more territory, or *they'll* steal another nation's resources, or its shipping short cuts. It makes *their* ragweed-headed leaders come over big on the evening news and look more powerful."

"Forgetting that *they're* dishonorably ignoring their international pledging! Disgraceful! Shocking! And I bet that'll start the world-wide hate-volcanos erupting all over again," Paycock said shamefully.

"Easy to do if they're disloyal enough to conveniently forget their international pledges," Rowley agreed. Bruno had delayed them again, and this time it threw the three dogs into a lengthy dynamic ponder.

"Bruno, you really don't hear well now, do you?" Paycock was miffed at being interrupted again. "I was about to say that when international *sapiens* forget what *they* pledged, then the next step is—*they* take sides."

Not listening to Paycock, Bruno was keeping on. "Super-shocking! After all *their* homework and extra overtime making contracts and treaties till everyone everywhere was talking up that irreversible peace, and planning home additions."

"It's weird that after all that killing, *they* don't have more stable memories," Rowley commented. "You would think *they* could never forget losing family members, or those long terror nights of shrinking down in a shelter, like a chunk of meat waiting to be tenderized."

"Though it might take more patience than sapiens are able to develop. After all, I've heard Algernon say that to permanently cease-fire, *they'd* have to go on and on appeasing one side and then the other, then back to the first and."

"Wait! Laburnum told Sylvia that Algernon spent his career doing just that."

"That must have frustrated him right out of his Eurobikini," Bruno said. "Though it could be the reason he speaks arched!"

"That's what we're just saying, Bruno! Though I'll tell you this—Algernon is the exception. His opinions don't get stuck in a recording rut, like Farmer Henderson's. Algernon is more 'cooperative' because he was brought up with dogs—he calls them 'hounds'."

"Could be," Rowley then summed from his History program, "So that's what modern history is all about! Doesn't this mean that as long as nations keep their expensive forces armed up to the gills, *they're* bound to have to see that they work by *exercising* them?"

"With all they cost, you could be right, Bruno. Because we know that *sapien* hostilities have been going on since they were armed with pea-shooters riding around on mammoths—that's historically correct, isn't it Rowley?" Rowley and Paycock were into slow solemn head nods because after the masses of lives lost in World Wars I and II. Very sadly, they were realizing that *sapiens* were light years away from having the insights to become the real peace-prophets every living creature had secretly hoped they'd be in his throbbing little heart. Into this saddest of slumps, the three friends studied the muddied grass between them as they continued to groan and shake their heads.

Finally, Bruno summarized, "I'm afraid any excuse, and *they'll* go to war because, just as Paycock says, it's deep inside *their* reincarnating that *sapiens* need to be competitive. It's the DNA of their species. Their Milky Way human breeding can't help it. All we dogs can do is thank our fragrant paws that within the political differences of our beautiful Canidae creeds, we've long ago learned how to peaceably overcome political differences. Though listen, another major question, how do you two good friends think all this arming and debating will eventually end?" Bruno scratched his left ear, then suggested, "Listen, why couldn't we work at it the way we did with Laburnum's kidnapped boy?"

Paycock looked up brightly. "Yes, we could activate our rare Canidae brilliance and release our classified data for working hard from within our Canine Calming Cores? Oh yes, we could."

"And help shove perceptive *sapiens*—into a far more benevolent direction?"

"We'd better try to, Bruno, because you know that whatever *sapiens* come up with will certainly affect us."

The three dogs eagerly and desperately agreed, nodding their heads as they shared the same staring spot again, till Paycock said, "We've got to find subtle ways of attracting smart *sapiens* into our highly classified dog honesty and integrity, without—I said, *without*—giving away our most quintessentially sacred secrets. Let's respectfully remember, it has taken centuries of ancestrally hard philosophizing to develop our superior all-weather ideals that have long ago gone global. Though if *sapiens* would just get with it, *they'd* notice that we dogs have done the only legitimate civilizing since Jesus Christ Phd. did all he could. Though as I say, there's a Canidae encumbrance upon us to stay true to our quintessential canine philosophy. Our ideals are so incalculably valuable, they should only be hotly bargained for, never thoughtlessly just given away."

"Right. Even if we don't live as long as *they* do."

"I get what you're saying, Rowley."

"You're right—just giving away our sacred principles would be Canidae betrayal as we're leagues ahead in philosophic ideals and empathy, and there isn't a dog that doesn't value them." Paycock sighed with Bruno's repeated suggestion. "Our parents and grandparents always talked out their differences," Bruno went on anyway. "My mother told me that my grandmother and grandfather sat on the grass civilizing for a whole day and half the next, till they'd overcome a couple of cultural-breeding annoyances! It'll take eons for *sapiens* to catch up with that! Though it would be nice to think that maybe *they* would one day?"

With *sapiens* so intellectually blocked by competition, the three friends made space in their archival storage for maintaining all that they had just reviewed here by the catalpa tree behind the barn, because they knew that the power of whatever the next *sapien* international would be could have such an infinitely demoralizing and a dangerous effect, it could change the lives of every tiniest living creature. Paycock, as the spokesperson, had nothing more to add; though as a brilliant dog, he was still tense with what they were about to commit to. Getting into a better sitting position, he looked down then gave his warm furry belly some consoling lovely, long, gritty tongue licks. Rowley and Bruno watched Paycock using each lengthy lick to relax his tension, till they too felt a need for a nibbled haunch or a desperately scratched ear after this scariest of highest level Modern History and all else that could be impending.

Into their lying positions, the three dogs got down to batting off depression by allowing in the multiple fullness of this splendid autumn mid-day so generously warming them. As fraternal colleagues idolizing the 'civilizations' that Laburnum studied, it took time for their hot discussion to formally settle as each kept looking at the other two, till Bruno sat up and spoke. "We all deeply love our owners, but we're letting them and ourselves down if we don't squeeze out our best genius files and start helping them out till we hurt."

"Right," Paycock and Rowley were unanimous. "It'll mean straining ourselves and being prepared to revise argued contemplations. But keep in mind that Algernon and Laburnum are showing signs of wanting to do what *they* can too."

"They are?" Rowley asked.

"Laburnum is seeing how her historic golden eras came about. And Algernon has traveled to most of those world places and must know a thing or two."

"Good! Would it help them if we got some sizable meditation toccatas going?"

"For pushing them farther into more targeted benevolence?"

"Yes, that would be best, oh yes."

"Okay, then we'd better rest up. A critically urgent meditation toccata could take a lot out of us."

Quieter having made this decision, the three dogs slid rustically into the lusciousness of this time of year. Where they had removed most of the grass from the hardened earth, and the plentiful nuts drummed away on it, scintillating newer little dog tunes, these friends adored this cooling season. They no longer had to sit with lolling fat tongues, and there was the promise of the compositionally zinc-hued branches above them only bringing renewed beliefs in a long, cuddlesome winter before stacked fireplaces, where hot fur would always keep tummies warm. What an especially opulent planet this could be that they lived in, with this lovely long leisure together bringing new enlightenment to their toccata meditations, and all that could overwhelmingly surround them that they'd hungrily anticipate as they lulled into these immense files while especially enjoying each other as good-friend genius dogs.

In muted agreement, the threesome each gave long licks to their bellies for quick calming. They were also preparing their Canine Calming Cores to refresh their minds and give them their needed most outstanding canine integrity and equanimity.

Chapter 23
Happiness Pursued

Returning to my beloved woman and my enchanted Supreme Habitat, with much at the manor rearranged, I was also annoyingly slowed up by a couple of hitches—I'd had to kill 90 minutes at Heathrow for a later plane, then a thunder storm doused the QEW and Thruway, though knowing my dearest wagtail was waiting for me as back in my synergistic Lamborghini I drove fast, cautiously, and immaculately. Unwinding from that brief but unforgettably rattling trip montages of one's recent U.K. hours kept reframing in one's mind. Lingering on the pallor of my father's complexion, so pale it merged the sheet, then his heart-breaking frog-croaky wheeze; Father's stunning words, his life-draining face—all that to him had meant life!

As the storm subsided, I pushed my wonderfully erudite little sports car as fast as I dared till finally one came to *Aha!* The winery's tree-lined avenue and swung into it! Relieving, I deeply breathed in one's house's magnificently sculptured moldings yet again—as I would always. And there was Mel going to the porch from his apartment, but hearing my sports car he turned to affect a droll militant mega-salute!

Returning his greeting, though I was filled with new prospects for my enchantress till.

Oh yes, yes, and what else could be missing?!

Then at last there was—'*she*'*!*

Out ran his dearest darling, eagerly waving to him as she scurried along the porch and down the steps to bound across the grass to me, all smiles and blown kisses in her typical long skirt—though with a saffron shirt. *Saffron,* the exact color for my woman's gorgeous olive complexion, her intricate mix of dark and gray hair—*hold that picture!* My eyes wouldn't move from my lover as I peripherally caught Paycock sprinting along beside her, both coming straight to me as my love's fluttering outdid my tiredness! In both our exuberances, I could tell that there was no doubt our recent rougher misunderstandings were gone—over! Forgiven! Thank God!

Sylvia, Reb, and Hans followed Laburnum coming from the front door. Closer to me my beloved's laughter-creased eyes ignited white streaks to me as

I no longer cared who knew Laburnum and I were lovers; and slipping from my car we both rushed to be in one another's strangling arms. Straight solid kisses as we spun like tops between engorging exchanges of penetrating looks and joyous little bursts of laughter that ignored our witnesses' facetious or sexy comments—Sylvia's "Ooo-la la!", Hans' "Ayee, what more?"

Sigmund, coming from the production center, called out a more sophisticated welcome home, and Sylvia came over to give me a peck on my cheek around Laburnum, as she fired, "Lucky you made it, Algernon! Your sweetheart here was so dead sure you'd be back an hour ago, we made a super-delicious lasagna—you may know what over-baking does to pasta. If it had spoiled, believe me I'd have had to whack you with my dear old mum's favorite skillet!"

Relieved and thrilled as I countered these friendly zaps, one oozed yet another level of happiness?! Smiling down at my smile-wrecked Laburnum beneath my arm, I knew her to be a permanent part of myself at last; and in more gentle greetings, I also caught the consolations for one's emergency trip to England being thrust at one. *What a welcome! Better than rousing rows of a uniformed foreign military brass band on a carpeted parading ground! Never had one been given more genuine affection!* My cuddlesome Laburnum and I had become this moment's central figures, adored by our most special friends that had been filling in for me during one's emergency trip and had much more going on with me now than just the making of fine wines! As all of this was being sardonically watched over by one's sacramental Supreme Habitat!

Once we had all moved inside, Mel and Sigmund needed me to know all they'd accomplished while I'd been away. Sigmund apprised one of the lost order of new bottles, now received, unpacked, washed, and filled, which all melded in with the enticing cheesy lasagna being put beside the fluffy salad. Catching up with the amounts of new must filling our famed redwood barrels, Reb reported that two more of the vineyards were now picked clean. Sally-Anne put down her several home-mixed salad dressings and lavished another welcome home kiss on me as she asked me about my father.

Lured by the sausage and mozzarella fragrances, we each filled our plates and sat companionably family-style around the big table once again. Having opened the subject of his father, I more formerly thanked them and took the opportunity to explain, "Wonderful to come home to all this affection and all your cooperation—thank you! Truly, knowing you now, I hadn't felt I should worry. Yes, Sally-Anne, it was quite an amazing coincidence—my father died a few minutes after I arrived." This statement was met with quiet and awed condolences, and suspecting that Laburnum had already given them this news I kept it to, "Father and I may not have had an ideal relationship, but I was immensely pleased that we'd had that last chance to see one another." Mindfully returning to the sickly smelling bedroom I sensibly left Father's finale at that, keeping to myself that this had been the nearest I'd ever come to really knowing more about one's belligerent parent."

Talking cursorily about his trip, one again caught my good friends' culturally or familiarly more kindly convictions. Whatever the relationship of a father and son, it was assumed here that there had been much deeper attachment—as with Reb's, "When a parent is gone, you're only left with what went right."

Nodding, as Reb's comment inspired reflections on various other fathers, such as Sigmund's concerned exclamations, and Hans' overwhelmed introspection causing his head to slowly go from side to side. With these direct connections to these wonderful friends, I knew it was best to save the more detailed descriptions of Father's expiration for one's loving temptress. Reading my thoughts, Laburnum grasped my hand to delicately massage it, little caresses that brought shivers to one's physical actuality of being beside her here and reminded me of her seductive temptation beneath that saffron shirt.

Between jokes about how smoothly the winery's processing had continued without Algernon's 'hifalutin comments', stray condolences were still being given me till relievingly I was drawn into the winery's workings again by a discussion across the table between Hans and Reb, "Nah, Hans, I won't be sampling it. What do you say, Sigmund? Ninety days, isn't it?"

"Malolactic fermentation?"

"Can't miss it peaking, push it up a little," Hans insisted.

"That's right, Sigmund? Isn't that how we've done it?"

"Using a tight filter," Sigmund agreed.

"Make sure it's tight," Hans endorsed.

"And the extra-sterile final filtering," Mel reviewed to Reb, back on their previous fall methods.

"That's not my job normal times, and it'll get normal again all right now Alg'non is back!" Reb's unctuousness was delivered with his infectious grin that caused both light-hearted and doubtful agreements!

This flurry of expertise for the last grapes continued to be reviewed as I sipped the wine that was helping distance my recent sensation of stratospheric living hanging on in me. Awaiting relief from this unearthly lag, I kept myself with the men's thoughts on their current planning while keeping my communicative hand over Laburnum's warm sensitive fingers on the table to sense the blessed shapes of her occult wrought silver rings. Exchanging squelched smiles with my dearest wagtail, the weary immensity of all this happiness infused me as I listened and watched this valuable and dear group's comments and observations. How could I not feel sure I was listening to the formula for truly superior wine production, anticipating Mel, Sigmund, and Hans as I looked forward to being a fresher participator with them again tomorrow? Tonight, it was enough to be back on these wonderfully new transcended terms with Laburnum and enjoying her radiance that she had me back! Later, one would settle one's new parentless status over here more with her.

After the party had cleared away, they affectionately broke up to take Hans home. Refusing to let go of Laburnum's hand till she came with me, I wandered outside with them all to get my hold-all bag from my car as goodnights, embraces, and well-wishes sent Sylvia happily driving Hans off. Having waved to them and watched them go as without a word, Laburnum yanked me loaded with my bag toward her apartment.

Allowing Paycock to enter first, but as soon as Laburnum's apartment door was closed, there were only greatly understood sharp looks between us as in a 'jiff' the setter had been appeased with a juicy bone and I, roused to the reality of what had kept tempting one beneath that saffron shirt, found it already being removed! My garments were off too, like a gale force wind tearing sheets from a washing line, and I was bodily on top of her. Though with my fatigue and all that had been exceptional this last 48 hours, I couldn't believe that our mating would rise to more than 'barely satisfactory'—yet wondrously, desire was thrown into high voltage as some ineffable inner beat let loose in one's blood stream; and I recognized that inimitable love theme from Tristan and Isolde—its lilt pounding one's inner ears, spurring their ecstatic flesh-love to build to Wagner's glorious finale amid glittering many colored sprays splashed across the black skies, that more traditionally opened the Olympic Games! No maidenly tunnel-visioned academic here!

Getting back my breath, I held onto her as one rolled on one's back. Tired, thoroughly worn out, yet incongruously more oneself, I observed to Laburnum that not only had our fabulous love-making brought me drastically back into the chosen marvelous rusticity of this hemisphere, but without hesitating we had each sought all that we knew would thrill the other, and I loved it that she couldn't have participated so passionately if—*if what?* If she hadn't known plenty of prior experience!

She too rolled away from me on her back as she read him once more, "So you love me for the love-making I've known, Zaubermaus?"

"Yes, I do. And it's only fair that one asks—and you?"

Giving me a doubtful look, "If you'd been inexperienced, I'd have hated fearing that your libido was fragile. No, it's because you've known other women that I love you, Algernon."

Reflecting on this, I said, "A-ah, then as long as there's all this wonderful physicality between us, and our interests knit together so enticingly, marry me, witch-woman?"

"No, Algernon, I won't."

"Actually, I'd had a premonition you'd say that."

She gave me a look that told me I was being flippant. "I appreciate all we've got just as it is here with you and Paycock," she leaned over to pat her dog's head as he lay nearly asleep on the bedside rug. "Dearest, you know that my research is for a book. Being meticulously honest, I think that you also know that this is as valuable to me as you are. Am I taking a chance saying that?"

"The book is to be the baby that you and I are making."

"A spiritual creation of our own."

"Blending your extraordinary thinking and research, and what I can vouch for from my travels, and my personal distilled foreign policy dissatisfactions."

"Ah, yes—I've never had any kind of a baby, nor have you."

"Will this baby be enough?"

"En-*ough*?" she whined out this last syllable like a sick emu; her head turning to me in disbelief.

"It sounds too loose, though we both know that it will be up to us. Creating it will take a great deal of ourselves."

"This book-baby?"

"Naturally, the book. Though tell me, my darling, with me will you get enough loving?"

"What do you think?"

"There was a time I savored an assortment of pitiful women and didn't get to know any of them, but that was reaction to marital failure and having messed up one woman's life. Superficially, I'm not beyond admiring good-looking women—haven't you noticed? You wouldn't want me lacking in appreciation? It's silly talking about this anyway, since knowing you I've been so poignantly smitten that all I long for is to just be sitting beside you, like two wagtails."

"Perching together out on a limb."

"Chirping at the same view."

She laughed and rolled over full length onto one's lithe body to ardently embrace me. "It was lovely of you to want to share your life with me, my bon vivant; but if we stay as we are, won't you be happy? It's been too blissful to analyze more than that, hasn't it?"

"Ask me in a few weeks!" I said keeping my eyes closed. "Wow, one is exhausted. And we've a lot more to talk about."

"Not really," she said.

"There certainly is, but wagtail, you know what I want to hear? Your momentous 'Tillie story'! I'm jubilant it was so successful by the way. Now," one adjusted the pillows for both our heads.

"No, it's got to be your emergency trip first."

"No, Laburnum, you know that the poor kidnapped boy has to come first."

"Listen, Algernon, I can't tell you how guilty I feel about not going to England with you."

"Oh, I say that's a lot of frightful rot, Laburnum! You know I accepted your refusal as part of your Tillie situation. Now for heaven's sakes while I'm still wakeful, tell how the three of you focused on the boy's objects."

"Well, as you're tired then."

"Get to what matters, wagtail."

She nodded, "As we're trying to find someone specifically," Laburnum got into it, "just like last spring, remember, when I used your glasses to psyche the hour you'd arrive back in the States? Feeling a person's close possession, letting my finger-tips warm on the boy's miniature bulldozer till mentally engaging with it, stoked up my mental penetration. For me, this comes as a metaphysical blank and a strong 'knowing' that there's to be more. I'm not sure if this is how all clairvoyants work. Look, I can't explain it better, Algernon, because at this stage it moves into the intuitive."

"Beloved, this psyching is a lot to go through. You may say that the sixth sense is in anyone that chooses to develop it, but listening to you one sees that this development is much too considerable for just *anyone!*"

Abruptly, she started to laugh. "Not laughing at you, Algernon, but I must tell you something odd, my beloved, or I think it's funny! Tillie has got over her stomach virus by the way, but here's what was comic." Plumping her pillow to raise her head and shoulders higher. "That morning before we three were to have our meet, Mel was to go for groceries; and he checked to see if I wanted to hop in his truck with him. We've often done groceries together, and in the cooler weather we'd give Bruno a ride with this lazy old teddy-bear here," stretching her leg over the bed's side, she jiggled Paycock's head with little foot rubs. "Mel has the back seat of his pick-up cab set up for the dogs, and you'll have to see the two of them—they sit up and stare through the back windows at passersby, like solicitous royals! Going into town sure boosts their self-esteem! When we got to the grocery store, I only needed a few items, but Mel was getting stocked up, so I agreed to leash up our dogs and give them a town walk—good obedience training. We'd done this before, and they knew what to expect; and with both dogs behaving, I got them ready. But here's the odd thing. When we got past that huge blank brick wall outside by the grocery store, I'm sure you know it, both Bruno and Paycock decided that the wall was the only place to pee and insolently yanked me to stay there—both pulled and huffed at me till I gave in. Algernon, you know how long Paycock can keep up his urinating? Both dogs' back legs went up, but Paycock's faucet kept going long after Bruno's, and poor old Bruno has more reason to be a long time. When they'd finally finished, I guided them away, wanting to walk where I could see some roses and lovely color mums, but—I couldn't believe it—Paycock blatantly refused to move! He stood stock still, all 70 pounds of him! Then he sharply pulled and yanked, I thought his collar would come off! Then, get this, he even started to growl at ME-E! Hell's broken bells, did I scold him!"

"Paycock, you didn't?" I raised my head to look reproachfully at the setter. And as Laburnum too had used his name, Paycock sat up with his head sweetly tilted for listening. "But Algernon, Bruno was also pulling me back, and you know how solid he is now. They were so willful about this that rather than have all three of us getting over-emotional out there on the pavement, I gave in and followed them back to the brick wall, where they went through all this peeing performance again. Which wasn't so easy, was it, Paycock?" Over the bed clothes, Laburnum jabbed her toe in Paycock's neck, "You'd had to hold your lifted leg up for an age and pretend you'd turned on the hose when all you could really squeeze out was a drop or two, wasn't it?" As she said this, Paycock's head turned to continue listening to Laburnum, "And you know, they kept up this leg-lifting act till Mel came out."

"And then?"

"We all got in the pick-up and came back home."

"Oh Paycock, how could you misbehave so badly for our lovely Laburnum?" one leaned to ask him. "You've been beautifully bred, and you're from an excellent English Setter line. You knew perfectly well what was expected of you!" Paycock looked away at the kitchen with an offended snort. "Interesting, Laburnum! Though this didn't have anything to do with the Tillie-time?"

"That's the thing, Algernon. The more I thought about it, the more I was sure it *was* connected! It wasn't like Paycock to misbehave like that." Laburnum was looking directly down at Paycock. "Didn't I explain to you how much your bad behavior upset me, tricky hound?" Paycock stood and leaned to lick the rings on Laburnum's hand till she had to caress the sleek hair of his ear. "And listen, scoundrel dog, I kept wondering about your disobedience, or I did until I went to see Tillie and Fergie, and *then*—now listen to this, Algernon! At Tillie's, we'd no sooner got our psyching going, and... hallelujah! There it was as plain as could be on my metaphysical blank! *The brick wall!* Honest to goodness, just as Paycock and Bruno had been showing me! You'll think this is ridiculous, I know, I did too! But I'll tell you, my darling, something made me refuse to let my mental screen deviate from that brick wall, or rather, it turned into one very much like it; and Tillie and Fergie were apparently also tuning in on brick walls! And once the three of us had a good dense focus going, into our wall pictures came the old lady's neglected house with her wildly overgrown backyard near this wall. And behind this, barely seen under overgrown bushes, her beaten up old shed! That criminal father had been cunning all right because you couldn't see the shed from either side! Tillie, Fergie, and I had each received these separate versions of this brick wall close to the ruin of an old shed, where our poor kid lay bound and gagged! Finally, when we were all sure we had where the boy was, we were ready to phone the police and get that poor child out of there. Tillie made the call."

"And the child is all right?"

"Half-starved, barely conscious, but the doctors think they've got him in time."

"That's one for criminal history books, Laburnum, and congratulations!" As Laburnum laughed with satisfaction, she shook her head incredulously till one asked. "Have I got this right, wagtail? The dynamic was that you may never have pictured the boy's shed location if Paycock and Bruno hadn't insisted on unloading against that grocery store's side wall? Incredible! That brick wall!" As one reiterated one's last words in an awestruck whisper, Paycock had had enough and rolled over comfortably on his back. "It's astounding! Too astounding to just be a coincidence."

"Algernon, your eyelids are…"

"Ye-es," I agreed sleepily as we both respectfully watched Paycock. "Payco-ock, old fellow, what do you have to say about this?" But Paycock was into a lovely purging back roll as he twisted his head toward his hips first to his left, then to his right; his teeth glistening in the lamp light in a loosely drooled, spreading broad grin. Watching him, I said, "Excellent dog, Paycock! Clever and sagacious—corkingly well-bred!"

"It had to be a coincidence, Paycock, didn't it?" Laburnum asked him.

Rolling onto his forelegs, Paycock stood up, and ignoring us he walked out of the bedroom to his basket. Getting into his most desirable of curved positions with his head on his bent leg for inhaling the good clammy smell of his lower belly, he fell 'asleep' in moments.

Laburnum and I smiled at Paycock's theatrics. He was a beautifully shaped russet quadruped, and observing the fineness of his side-on head I wondered, "Laburnum, this notion we have that dogs have limited self-awareness, and they might be fine companions, but they're ridiculously lazy pets and have their place—You know it might need reassessing? It is possible they have abilities we *prefer* not to credit them with."

Laburnum looked at me with her eyes shining, "You're saying there's a chance we might be just catching on?"

"After your outlandish 'brick wall story', we would be foolish if we didn't take a more serious look at 'woman's best friend'. And Laburnum, listening to your fantastic story, here's what's even more important. You and I could reach for dogs' elusive abilities far more easily if the three of us could always be together."

"Don't let's talk about that now, Algernon. It's your turn to talk and you're getting tired, but please, I do want to hear about your trip."

My resigned look affected her, "Let's leave that till tomorrow, my love."

"Oh, then just tell me if your father died peacefully."

My head rolled back making what I knew to be my attractively pronounced jaw look sculpted and clean. "My father must have threatened God Himself, Laburnum, because that old rogue couldn't have died more peacefully."

"In detail tomorrow, please?"

"Let's go out to dinner somewhere nice tomorrow night; we've a lot to talk about. Answer me for God's sake, Laburnum, I'm falling asleep."

"Damn it, Algernon! Okay it's a date. Now go to sleep."

The next morning, having regained some energy after a sound sleep in my beloved's magical arms, I put in a couple of hours in the sunny processing center, catching up with the barrel production Mel and Sigmund had talked up at last night's supper before joining Reb's pickers over in the farthest north vineyard. Loading the stacked grape-filled crates this new weather-fresh day, Reb and I took turns rumbling them off by tractor along the slopes to Mel and Sigmund. With the students returned to school, fewer pickers came; but according to Sigmund, the 'regulars' were more 'expert'. I was extremely pleased I could fully feel all aspects of my mysterious Supreme Habitat and its winery; now one's instant trip to my father's demise had slid into days gone by, all with more of a sad satisfaction than distress. I was yet to observe any 'void'.

Quickly slipping back into the swing of grape-picking, it soothed my overstuffed mind to put in an immensely physical morning before going over to find Laburnum to walk Paycock. As Laburnum and I mutually longed to see more of one another, she gripped my hand following one along a narrow footpath along the lake shore we didn't usually take, it ended at an old disused abutment. Its dock had long since gone, but its sturdy weather-whitened platform boards were in a last splash of late sunlight that invited us to sit.

"It's so great that everything that Mel, Reb, Hans, and Sigmund kept going was how you'd have managed it, liebling, but can we get back to your father? You wouldn't let me ask last night, and I really do want to know."

Laburnum had changed in ways I was yet to recognize. No longer a yanky-twit, I'll keep on observing her for 'provincialism'. "More could keep coming out, Laburnum, you know how an event like that takes time?"

"No, I need your special trip better than that. Start with that night you got the phone call."

"Ah, after I'd left you at your apartment?" She nodded, as we grudgingly recalled it had been that stiff evening we had each agreed to work. "I'd tried to read, did read, then once I'd got to sleep Laburnum, a brutal head pain jolted me, it must have been in that night's early morning hours—and I mean it was *'brutal'!* In retrospect, I believe that this pain was when I was receiving my father's telepathic message, which was about as clear as his loud voice could be over the phone, though you'll tell me more about that."

Her look at me was fierce with interest as she butted in, "Yes, and as we've said, the sixth sense is there in all of us, Algernon."

"All right, but you believe that the sixth sense is in all of us."

"You believe it more than you know."

I conceded that this might be as I lifted my hand needing to say more to her, "All I knew was, it was a dire spiritual demand, and its message made it utterly clear that my father was desperate; and that I'd had to go to him immediately, then and there! I've thought a lot about this pain-message since, and I'm convinced that even if I had sternly rationalized that I had the right to my own judgment in preferring to stay here with you, my precious goddess, and to all I owed my wonderful habitat's vineyards, I doubt I could have done it as his message was so potent. But no matter, I yielded to this strange night-time communing, set up my flights, and simply took off to him." Laburnum's nodded approval stabbed at me. "As you know, most beauteous one, I arrived at exactly the time Father was drawing his final breaths," Abruptly, I stopped relating.

"You may prefer not to tell me more?" Shaking my head to her, I relaxed, loosened.

Vividly caught back to the manor, I didn't really need her gentle consideration and smiled. "Father might have been on his death-bed, Laburnum, but to the end he was the same! Though what had I expected? Naturally, he wouldn't have stopped believing me incompetent; in fact, he emphasized that this was how he still saw me—though, *did he?* I ask this because he annunciated quite clearly that he had '*not been honest*' when he had included my mother in with his lousy opinions of me! Imagine my astonishment! It was more astonishing still that he was seeing this as *his* sin, and he divulged that my mother had 'even believed me quite bright.' Laburnum and I exchanged looks of uncontemplated concern, aware that there was more to this that would eventually come out. "But here are his very last words to me, Laburnum. Having made sure I was listening, he looked straight at me and said, 'There's one thing more…' and as ardently as he could, one word at a time, he said, 'Life-is-a-bloody-bugger!'"

Looking at him, Laburnum's mouth hung open before she bent double! Descents of hysterical laughter embarrassed her, and she lowered her head into her hands while fumbling for a crumpled tissue from her pocket to dab at the laughter tears running her cheeks. Finally, she got out, "Great constellations, Algernon! Forgive such a serious moment seeming hilarious, but—what do you make of it?"

To Laburnum's bray of laughter, my telling of Father's private last words in that bedroom's rattling death scene sent us both unrestrainedly into my father's incongruously immortalized words, as our looks checked for one another's distaste. For myself, I was finally openly sharing its hidden, much-deserved humor with my ultimate amorist, which made the words of my father become more impressively meant and complete! I'd been longing to share this final bit of pantomime, and now it chronically caught our hilarity, as neither of us could bother with the parenting ignorance behind those wildly misplaced words! Ironically, I simply shook my head that it had taken that pitiful end of my father's tyrannical life for him to glimpse how he might have better used his years.

With my shoulders still shaking from this comedy, I repeated luxuriously, "'Life-is-a-bloody-bugger!' You know that 'bugger' in England is obscenely sexual!"

She smiled nodding, "Yes, Algernon, I do!"

"For my father's final words, they were an absurd choice, Laburnum, but how can I feel too sad? No one had as wholly directed his life as Father had, so who could he find to blame?"

The dying sunlight was barely edging the abutment's stringy whitened wood as we sat continuing to muse on my mercurial father more soberly, till Laburnum asked, "You think he could only express this through some death-facing enlightenment?"

"I'm sure of it," I agreed. Then pulling from Father's engrossment, "Laburnum, can you take a look this way for a minute? That can't be Mel?" Having turned to look beyond me, Laburnum assured me it surely was Mel as a fine red canoe skimmed nearer us very lightly, and I too saw plainly that it certainly was Mel with his back to us peacefully rowing. "Hullo-o!" we called. "That's a sedate means of coming along the water for you, Mel. A magnificent canoe, by the way."

"It's Nollie's. I kind of like it."

"I see why and your rowing looks timeless."

"Didn't I see you rowing out here a day ago, Mel?" Laburnum asked.

Mel's all-encompassing smile, "I don't always go in for speed. I'm thinking of buying it."

"It's a beauty, you should. By the way, Mel, I'm looking for a special place to eat tonight," I said. "Any thoughts?"

"There's a real cool restaurant south along the lake with the best steaks, and they do Mexican. Casual, if you want, I've jet-skied to it. Laburnum knows it." Laburnum said she'd been to this restaurant with Mel. It had to have been a favorite place of Mel's by his loose head stressed nods and his rubbery brows' flexes as he described a favorite entrée.

"It's not a long way?" One asked; after my U.K. trip, I didn't need too long a drive but both Laburnum and Mel assured me it wasn't far at all, and that I'd love it.

Chapter 24
The Internationalist

Laburnum wanted plenty of bathing time, so I went to the parlor and chose the love seat for catching up on my accumulated overseas newspapers. While in the U.K., Father's newspapers had kept me well up on world events. What I was mainly re-establishing here was this restful habit I'd got going before taking that trip, and now, here I was back again assimilating the pungency from the woodwork and plaster's dry ambiance of my 'American old' again! A pungency that over there I'd been struggling to recall.

It amazed me how fast the affection of my gorgeous Laburnum, our friends, and this place had steeped me so profoundly into it all once more! Possessing me right now was this room, that had often been shared with my house's other occupants. In this less active time of day, one's mightily cared-for fine Victorian house kept me from a foreign affairs article—because it was all striking me so penetratingly. The sun's cooling made this room especially pleasant with its stillness of sun-beams' quiet, which had so quickly and completely re-swallowed me. In this Supreme Habitat's elegant little parlor, one's meditative contentment let me see that since arriving here last night, so much had at least been. *Pleasant—no, with my beloved—an outright joy!*

This fascinated because it was just as I had planned it back in Moscow when I'd originally sketched its tall narrow windows on Cadney's wretched envelope! Just then my eyes incidentally rested on one of these windows as I looked up over my foreign affairs article. It was another tall slot looking out onto the still sunny exterior of porch and lawn views that had materialized with all its incredible splendor of narrowed-viewing, and that wouldn't stop whisking me into that *much recalled original Moscow sketch!!*

Gazing this window, how greatly I and time itself had moved on! Most eccentrically! After all, what could be lovelier than this coming evening and *escorting my queen to our jubilee dinner?!* A celebration with the woman I loved. *Oh God Algernon, don't start sounding like that treasonous old ruffian the duke of Windsor! Loving one's woman as, one decidedly does, was not one smidgen, like the Windsors, Algernon dear, because one had invested far more wisdom, masculine virility, cajolery, and much else into courting one's throbbingly beautiful Venus than ever that notorious duke had his ugly femme fatale. No, spiritually, Laburnum had been awaiting me here.* A thought that stirred one to push away the newspapers, stand up, to nip upstairs and get my bathing, grooming, and fastidious dressing taken care of.

Cleaned up for this most auspicious occasion, I donned a fine Scottish cravat that gave me a learned yet debonair-look mirrored above one's pewter Italian suit and crisp white shirt. After elatedly approving my fascinatingly still lithe appearance from different angles in my armoire's reflection, I went down to drive Lamborghini up beside Laburnum's apartment, and.

Oh! There she was in her best clothes!

Though jumping out to escort my fabulous lover… *hells bells, wasn't Laburnum earnestly talking to Paycock and Bruno!* Going to her, one heard her explaining to the dogs that, "No, we're *not* going for groceries!" Then more consolingly, "Look, we won't be far away," to her pet's pesky jumping up persistence. "*NO,* Paycock honeybun, you can*not* come with us! Tonight you're going to stay here with Uncle Mel!" But the dogs ignored her as they bounced up and down; Paycock flailing his arms as he danced on his back legs to enthusiastically lick her cheek while Bruno did his 'bouncing boat' rock beside her. "Oh, Paycock, you're being absurd! Dogs, do *STOP* this!"

Beside her, I reproached, "Paycock, you're not into more of that closed-eyed funny business, for heaven's sake!" though obviously Paycock wasn't

"Just a moment, Algernon!" Was Laburnum's only greeting to one as she disentangled herself, while pushing Paycock down, "Okay, now listen sweetheart-dog, it's our night out! Yes, Algernon and I want time to ourselves."

Catching Laburnum's vocally rising annoyance, Mel looked out of his upstairs window, "Oh wow! Just look at *you,* Laburnum!" Swinging his head in melodramatic disbelief. "And oh, look at Algernon! A handsome cravat too, wow! I hadn't realized this was such a significant dinner!" And as Paycock kept up his annoyance, still licking Laburnum's face and her shoving hand, then rubbing the back of his head along her arm, Bruno stopped his bouncing to slide his long body behind Laburnum's ground-length skirt—which Mel saw and called, "Be right down."

"What's got into you lately, Paycock? You're acting up! Or behaving strangely," one insisted, "Make Laburnum happy, Paycock! Mel is your obedience man tonight; show him what a finely mannered setter you can be." But whining pathetically, his forelegs still up on Laburnum's chest, Paycock's nose strayed all over Laburnum's chin and cheek till she and I had to shove him down.

This concerned Laburnum, as she crouched down to her dog; while Mel, retrieving their leashes, stood by. "Listen, honeybun dog, now *LISTEN!* Algernon and I are going to do some work together. Yes, we're going to work here each day, where you'll be too—big serious stuff—though right now, we need to go off by ourselves to make plans."

"No kidding?" Beside them Mel asked, intrigued.

Laburnum gave him a furtive wink, as her information very much intrigued Mel; and listening to his beloved owner, Paycock finally cooled and got down. "You'd be helping us if you and Bruno would behave nicely for Mel tonight." Paycock and Bruno both looked harder at Laburnum as their tails reduced to more somber swings, and each became calmer and just interested. "You help us—let Algernon and I go and have a good talk; then when I come back tonight, you and I will have a nice long discussion about all this by ourselves, Paycock, okay?" Paycock used his irresistible head tilt to her, making his eyes go charmingly tall. Then his head tilted even more with this promise of a good talk with Laburnum. Satisfied with the changes to each dog, Laburnum chucked them under their chins. "I'm sure now they're both going to be very good dogs," she pointedly let them know, as she addressed Mel.

With the dogs turned sweeter and submissive, Mel agreed they'd be fine, and was returning their leashes to their hooks as the dogs willingly followed him into Laburnum's apartment. "Hey, doggie-woggies, let's let these guys get going? How about some yummy chowie-wowie?" And lavishing more head pats on each dog, they went in with him for their supper.

"You know the dog chow closet, Mel?" Laburnum called after Mel. "And thanks!"

Having exuberantly looked forward to formally escorting my lover, I awaited my fabulous date getting free of dog-counseling, though now she needed to straighten her clothes.

"They'd had something in mind tonight," Laburnum muttered to me coming away.

"Unused to seeing us dressed up to go out?"

With the dogs settled at last, I brushed the dog hair off Laburnum's sleeve, then really looked at *her.* Nothing—not even the dratted dogs—was going to spoil our most special evening! Difficult as the dogs had been, Laburnum was pervading such radiance tonight in her hand-knit purple alpaca jacket, which I noticed was left open because a large ornamental button to the jacket missing! Though I loved her in that color anyway, especially with her crisp emerald shirt beneath it, which I gallantly praised. Laburnum's eyes twinkled, knowing what I was *not* praising, and graciously she accepted my discreet compliment, calling it her 'casual best for their Leibnizian occasion!'

"Leibnizian! Ah, the mathematical genius up there with Newton? Exactingly appropriate, my darling! Excellent, Laburnum," while helping her into his low passenger seat. As my exuberance returned, one feigned the hefty gesturing of a Lord Nelson favoring his gorgeous Lady Hamilton. Wrapping Laburnum's long skirt around her calves, then unbending, I let my elation continue as one's arm raised with exceeding grace high up over my head, till with courtly eighteenth century posturing, one swept my hand over Laburnum's door to snap it too! One finished by wittily leaning to bestow a slow romantic kiss on her readily receiving lips before getting in to drive to my lover's directions.

"Nice of you to wait on me, Algernon, but I am a strong healthy woman."

"I had noticed you were, wagtail, but the man in me wants to make you feel your femininity—currently all wrong?"

"That is what's current, but there's no right or wrong as long as you understand that your overdone gentility is a left-over from your illustrious career?"

"Certain habits from Foreign Service social occasions are hard to break, beloved." Gearing low up the avenue of trees, "And considering how civilizing they are, here's the dilemma—should one be rid of them?" I countered as my admiring glance took in her profile as driving her hair was blown back, making my marvel of a two-seater look ideally glamorous.

Arriving at the hilltop restaurant, I was out and around my car before my lover had her door handle figured. Wittily opening her car's door to her dubious approval, I made a slight bow. "Oh God, Algernon, all this nobility is gut-shaking! Oh, all right then, here, let me have your hand."

A group of diners were about to come out of the restaurant's entrance and to their amusement, I supposed, I held the glass door wide to dramatically gesture to my most important woman for her to go through before everyone else! Exaggeratedly I stood back to bestow another elegant court bow on them! Laughing at my overdoing it, Laburnum decided not to fuss further and boldly strode on through, as we both noticed that a couple of politely waiting diners hid their disbelieving looks to one another. I supposed they amused with one's ultra-suave manner, and what they might ignorantly see as one's outlandish cravat! Once inside, Laburnum and I were aware we were a source of entertainment to nearby tables of diners too, and catching my eye, Laburnum smiled her delighted approbation as she made it clear that she was glad I was a fine-looking if a quirky companion! Fully enjoying my beloved woman as she did myself, we didn't care that in this rural American restaurant I might be seen as an elegant oddity, as we ignored the heads turned for one's distinctively cultivated Etonian syllables when one loudly requested a window table well away from the bar.

Intent on the evening being this unforgettable pleasure for my most darling woman, we followed the manager as I swept an arm at the restaurant's broad view of Lake Seneca and its marina below the cliff as I asked, "How's this, my inamorata? Does it suit you, my sweet Schatz?"

Laburnum attended my staccato concern and my calling her 'Schatz'. "Perfectly!" she replied, thoroughly entertained.

Left to ourselves we took in our table's splendid view of the late day's last colors far across on the lake's opposite shore, though it was mostly hidden by a high cliff that covered the nearer launching site for this marina. Then we contented ourselves with the historic photos of steamboats from the barges era, all well displayed on the inside olive walls. A waiter who had been intriguing with our differences as customers came over to us. His discriminating drawn-down, thin-lipped smile was set off by his smart black tee and narrow black pants. Automatically, one ordered Laburnum's grape juice as well as my wine. Though apparently this had not been wise as one look from one's gorgeous 'inamorata' darkened both our moods and Laburnum let me know, "Regardless of civilities, Algernon my dear, I do prefer to make my own choices."

Poised pencil and notepad in hand, our waiter hopelessly tried to control a spasm of hilarity as he observed what a painful concession it was for the European in one to let the lady do her own ordering. Each time this waiter came over—with salads, or hot bread sticks—he struggled to control his exhilaration as Laburnum was caught by this man's greatly stifled amusement that once he was behind the kitchen's swing doors erupted into coloratura guffaws that Laburnum couldn't help but find unbearably funny!

Though aware that one caused amusement here, one was not a fool. To me other people's reactions to cosmopolitanism simply must not matter. *What may seem pseudo finesse in this Western New York State restaurant would not have been noted on the European diplomatic circuit that I never denied being from, and anyway it was innate for me to pervade the charm of one's earlier urbanity wherever one was. After all, didn't everyone exude evidences of their rearing, and how they'd spent the greater part of their lives? And as long as self-possession and shrewdness were in with this 'charm', wasn't this simply being who one was?* Though one realized it was less likely to be observed working down in the vineyards with Mel and Reb. But even there, to me, it couldn't be what mattered most.

Flapping out my serviette expectantly, one nonchalantly flexed out one's right hand to pleasurably observe that my fingernails had only scrubbed up to be *fairly* clean. Laburnum sat musing over my little vanity before bringing me around to our former conversation, "On your trip, Algernon dear, your father?" Sultrily she was getting me back to my promise to tell her more, making me instantly return to that extraordinary final scene I'd so recently lived with my father, "You must be experiencing enormous relief too?"

Stretching my head upwards trying for a suitable non-whistle, then giving up I turned to her, "To answer your question, Laburnum, how can I express the freedom it's brought me?! In fact, well," but attending our waiter, "though I was going to get to this after a glass of champagne—you really prefer not to imbibe, sugar-puff? Then just a single glass will do it, waiter. Yes, Laburnum, I wanted to tell you."

Laburnum fixed her gaze on me for keeping herself apart from our waiter's likely levity, before giving me that extracting expression of hers that turned her brown eyes onyx and in her lowest most beckoning tone, she encouraged. "Your father, chu-chu-? Do go on."

"Chu-chu! Good one there, Laburnum! Yes, though I was attempting to tell you something quite different before you so rudely interrupted."

"Sorry, Algernon."

"Look, I'll raise my hand like this when I'd like to talk. Though one will accept your apology as I know you will want to know my latest *'epiphany'* as we'll call it."

This arched reproach of mine couldn't dampen the festivity we both really felt being with one another, and as each caught the other's eye on this sprightly disagreement that neither needed on this our special night as we were spasmodically in danger of rolling on the floor with laughter.

"All right!" I refrained from laughing. "Now look, can we get back to being serious, Laburnum?" Her meek nod. "Yes, well, what I'd like to tell you—at this point this is only between us, fine? Good. You'll soon understand why, but you are the one who should be receiving it, as my head's been full of some of the most incredibly lucid thinking I've ever known." Giving her a nod before I returned to that scene when I left the manor, "It wasn't until driving back to London after Father's death that I saw why I've always been so riddled with optimism. Bear with me, wagtail, but remember, this has also been your big bone of contention- In that slow congested city traffic, my thoughts wandered over my decades of service to my country, and I saw that throughout all those years there was *a major factor—missing!* Yes, I know you'll remind me of that juggernaut of decency, empathy, brilliant efforts, determination, tolerance, intelligence, and more that came with my work—and you'd be right; but I'm saying that even with all that, overall, some much more rudimentary factor or entity had been *missing.* Then coming back here on the plane—the strangest of coincidences! The chap next to me got up, and on his seat he'd left a magazine opened at an article on China! I picked it up—*oh-ho, Laburnum!* How easy it is to forget the extraordinariness of certain great civilizations! I say this knowing that this is what you've spent much of your life bleating about," to her slow expressive head nods.

"Ah, so this is what you're getting at, Algernon—China?"

"You may guess that I'm talking about Confucius, Laburnum, other philosophers too before and after him." I awaited my lover's surer nod. "Confucius, Laburnum! By no means your usual historically eminent leader because he refused prophet status or being a leader. You remember he wanted to be known only as a conveyor of selected Chinese philosophies? Just that! But his genius was in gathering these philosophies into such an extraordinarily civilized order that the status quo wanted more!"

"His orderliness became the system."

My hand was raised and waggling. "The Chinese adored him for guiding them into this system that was not religious. And Laburnum, schuckiputzi."

"Schuckiputzi! Nice word! What does it mean?"

"It means you're a fine piece of horse flesh."

"No-o! Damn it, Algernon, it's some endearment."

"If you're going to keep interrupting my extraordinary story, it's going to have far more unmentionable meanings! I won't tell all this to you unless you stop so rudely interrupting."

"I only want to save you."

"Please, dearest, just bother to find out why this magazine article was of particular importance to *me.* This…" thumbing my chest, "this being the fellow that's to assist you with your monumental project. Listen—if we're to get along, Laburnum, we'll have to start sensing."

"Sensing? Damn it, 'sensing' we'll waste whole days."

As my head frustratedly waggled, "Listen, a jilted hyena couldn't be more uncouth."

"Un*CO-OUTH!*" she all but screamed.

"For all I know a hyena in that situation might maintain more politeness." My own imagery making it impossible for me not to join her laughing.

"You know with all your fine schooling, that's really hitting below the belt, Algernon!" Though she too was enjoying this banter, and as she figured her next strike, by chance our laser eyes locked to one another, and our locked looks froze until one admitted more soothingly, "Very well, you're correct, that's a word no decent man should call a woman."

"Uncouth?"

"No, a hyena!" Simultaneously in gusts of impromptu laughter, we both rocked! Her head plummeting as she held it with both hands, because it had hit the basket of bread sticks, till concerning I leaned to grab her left wrist and raising it saw that she was only into levity.

"All right, you win that round!" We were both surprised to find our waiter looking concerned, standing beside us again, "Is there anything I could bring you that might help, sir?" he asked. Laburnum's mouth was twisted into a half-smile.

Wiping my eyes with my palms, Laburnum answered for me. "It's nothing, waiter. Something my best friend here said that seemed enormously funny, that's all! I'm sure you've known unexpected humor?"

He agreed that he had, as he put our salads in front of us. "Your entrées will be ready shortly. They may help."

"Thanks, yes, they will!" She was pulling fresh tissues from her large bag, offering me a couple. Our waiter left, and she dried her own cheeks, giving a lengthy exhausted sigh. "All right, you irascible man, so tell me all about this unusual slant of yours… on, what? To do with Ancient China?"

"Darling, you must know I'm doing my utmost to talk about Confucius!" I'd brought us both back to it. "As we've said, you remember too that he wanted to be known as a conveyor of selected philosophies."

"Yes, you just said that."

"But his genius was that what he selected to put together made that immeasurably civilized doctrine that the status quo couldn't get enough of. Again—*as you know!* I'll remind you that the Chinese proletariat adored him for guiding them into this non-religious orderliness, and Laburnum beloved, I know this is reviewing for you, but I can't tell you how refreshing it was to re-discover Confucius's benevolent *humanitarian commitment,* and how even by today's standards it was immensely forthright and non-self-centered. His thinking and sayings were meant for the welfare of all! Making one wonder how much we have progressed as human beings? Read again how he encouraged meditation and self-knowledge. Wellness… it's as if his oratory was just being given and reported on! And it isn't so surprising that central to his educational system was that amazingly innovative civil service exam! An examination that any son could enter, and did, even though it was not an easy standard. Think about it—Classical Asian literature!"

"'Change'," Laburnum softly murmured this book title in an awed steadying tone.

"Yes, that wonder book that had taken umpteen generations of thinkers hundreds of years to produce. But, get this! Examinees had to bone up on music, pottery, poetry—all the arts, and if they passed, their hard work was rewarded by being honored to become a government official. You and I both knew all this once, but in recalling it again, it jolted my imagination to think of influential government officers being admired for their integrity and cultivation. Let alone…" as I ushered my gracious hand for Laburnum to complete.

"…honored to become government officials, they were expected to produce poetry of their own! A bit much, I've always thought!"

Like myself, Laburnum was also refreshed by some of these unique Confucian tenets as she nodded, a slight smile lingering her fine features as she let me rattle on. "With officers from his own state."

"Of Lu."

"Lu, yes," I confirmed. "You recall he was renowned too for his judicial system, which was so fair and effective it greatly reduced crime. Think of all his organized concern for the humane qualities of being! Just an extraordinary civilization!"

Laburnum was diving her bag for notepad and pen. "Ah wait, let me get that down! 'Humane qualities of being'."

We'd both known all this, but wasn't all our enthusiasm commending that same human progress that similarly been up there in the leaderships of a much more modern Dubchek or a Mandela?"

"Or Aung San Suu Kyi's earlier years?" Laburnum leaned back, snapping the lid on her pen. "Though come on, Algernon, prosperity played an enormous part?"

One's raised hand came down, "As the Silk Road opened up foreign trading…"

"…all across Asia. Yes, bringing in in other nations, goods, influences."

"Yet instead of Confucianism antagonizing merchant traders, these other nations intrigued with China's civic orderliness. Would any of us doubt that the Chinese hadn't been greatly admired for their skills in marketing? Influencing other nations—mustn't traders have been intrigued too with that Chinese boom making such a stunning statement, their economic growth producing it giving them a widespread respect. Then also appealing was that admired Chinese tolerance born of their education, and its incredible new objective of *classlessness!* Good Lord, in this master-slave epoch, for heaven's sake?! Societies then certainly weren't based on equality! Mustn't the Chinese people have been incredulous as they lapped up whatever came next of this new civility?"

"Satiated with expectation!? Do you think a wonder-system like this could still safely still be ahead for us?? Yes, there was a wealth to all those enriching humanities, though Algernon, not every great leader was as admired or was as kindly and paternalistic."

"Though Confucius worked hard at getting him to be. If the emperor didn't rise to being a model of cultivation and an esthetic leader, then another 'honorable man' was found that fitted this figurehead's perfection."

"After Confucius's system became powerful, he might have, yes! You're bringing it all to life for me again. All so crazy, when you think that Europe had yet to reach the dark ages!"

"And like you, Laburnum, one was left wondering why scholastically we've haven't looked a lot more closely at that extraordinarily enduring Chinese golden age. Got to know its causes, their success secrets."

"And that endurance you mentioned… Four hundred years?! And in which reign?"

"Han, Tang, Sung—500 years before Christ."

The waiter was putting iced bowls of fragrant fresh jumbo shrimp before each of us, momentarily baffling us after our heady discourse. The waiter, more sensitive now to us as different customers, lowered his head as he intrigued with our seriousness as Laburnum and I still kept consciously ignoring that our waiter might still be needing to give into hysterics as he'd refilled our water goblets at least twice. After he'd left, Laburnum, still immersed in my story, said incredulously, "A golden age that was eons ahead of Europe. You and I will have to allow a disproportionate amount of time for China, fritter-mouse."

"Fritter?"

"Bat."

"Hmm! Yes, I must say I was left wondering why there weren't more studies than Bertrand Russell's."

"There were."

"Then there's more for us to look up."

"Hmm, a golden age that was eons ahead of Europe! But all that aside a moment, my darling. By the way, that cravat makes you look extravagantly handsome tonight! But I've a far different question now, please?" Even though I relished her appreciation of my appearance, we mustn't let it divert us. "My question, Algernon—do you suppose it was more than a coincidence that the passenger beside you just happened to leave that impressive article on China?"

"I've wondered about that too. Anyway, as you say, all that fabulous demonstration by the Ancient Chinese was long before our 'Science age', and what's been carried away with all that a wealthy superpower stands for or was perceived to be. And also as you are quick to maintain, all that bled people's right to fully live their God-given unthreatened lives. We've lost sight of what unthreatened far finer living could be, I agree. It makes one wonder why after several hundreds of years of Confucian civilizing, it came to an almighty end without us learning that such civilizing needs the humanities highest prioritizing. But, Laburnum, if people like you and me don't do all we can to get back more of that well-reasoned humanism, you know that other negative build-ups could fill any voids with other propagandas that could balloon into more hatreds, more weaponry."

"Or Armageddon. Let's hope there are endless concerned hordes besides just you and me, Algernon. And Algernon, getting all this into place, keeping our overall objectivity, here's another very different thought, wouldn't we also need to consider the Rafferty implication?" She caught my frown. "At the risk of interrupting you, my toffee-head, the 'Rafferty question' is what he was talking about at our lunch picnic table. Could our constant progress be like other extraordinary civilizations that faded like the Romans, or that could have been stopped by an interplanetary disaster?"

Nodding, I added, "Rafferty had been saying that we could be racing along inventing and developing until some catastrophic event barely leaves evidences we were even here? Atlantis all over again? We'll have to keep our minds open. Other extraordinary civilizations leaving little evidence become a guess at what's happened. Though what do *you* think? Should the 'Rafferty question' be on our list?" One asked her, looking out at the night rolling in to smother our colorful lake and a great deal of our outside view. My agitated neuroses from these history scintillations caused me to jerkily look around the emptying room. One's glance steadied again, as I summarily asked her. "You don't you believe that all??

"If we don't want darker powers filling in where they can, we'd need the protection of well-reasoned humanism."

"Huh, a good deal of your or *our* quest efforts would have to be devoted to that." Then making an effort to sit straighter. "By the way, I'm very glad you like my cravat. It's from Edinburgh."

"Most tasteful, yes! Won't it depend on how well-constructed the humanitarian empowering is?"

"How far ahead of evil-mindedness?"

Just then before she got out her notepad again, I couldn't stop my compulsive guffaw because neglecting the food in her left-hand, Laburnum had dropped a dollop of shrimp cocktail sauce down her shirt and was quickly dipping her serviette into her water goblet to rub at the sauce spot, turning her emerald green shirt into an expanding brown blotch! "Oh, good Lord, wagtail! What a *disgusting* mess!"

"Accidents do happen," she curtly reminded me. "You've undoubtedly been given table etiquette since infancy."

"At the breast, actually. But surely, you must have picked- up?" As out came my strongest frustration whistle!

"Algernon, as you've pointed out, I've not had the social advantages you've been privileged to have had."

"Very well, then it will be up to me to give you lessons."

"I'm not sure I could stand."

"In the same way you helped Rafferty with your creative writing expertise?" She nodded slowly agreeing. "My only condition will be that you graduate outstandingly." My sturdy glance disclosed my quasi-seriousness and reluctantly again she nodded. "I was about to say – *if you will let me, wagtail*, that I'd very much like to help you make your studies into such a fine provocative book, that it can't be ignored. 'Fine' not only in content but in how it is written—and naturally that's *you!* You'll be the one writing it, so—*oh good Lord, Laburnum,* what *have you done to that poor blouse?*"

The blotch kept growing larger as she lamented, "Oh why didn't I choose a patterned shirt? If only you would stop your vulgar laughter…" *Rub, rub…* "Being messy is not funny, Algernon!"

"Very well!" I cooled even my dying to laugh. "What I'm trying to tell you—*oh God, now it's turned a Vandyke brown!* All right, now just listen to me, shrimp-sauce lady, will you please stop rubbing and listen to what I'm trying to tell you?" still squelching my amusement with her hopeless rubbing, I handed her my serviette, "If you'd pay attention to me instead of your blithering ineptness."

"*'Blithering'?*"

"Everything you've got thought out deserves all aspects of our best talents and most skillful knowledge." And as my suavity returned, which to myself I saw was with good reason. Because looking at this messed woman, really looking at my much more profound and complete lover, I sincerely loosened to her predicament, becoming more pliant—*compassionate?* Into this prompted pause, I comprehended that above Laburnum's fatuous rubbing, above her comely physique beneath her ruined blouse, I *was seeing that tantalizing face that I'd so helplessly kept remembering—kept loving, while in England, and I knew that regardless of her carelessness and her shameful proclivity for interrupting, she would always be my dream witch-woman! I also knew that my unique Laburnum's dynamic quest had been directly out of her skillfully delved intensely rare intellect. She was a scholarly woman, on a gargantuan hunt for what had made certain civilizations spectacularly and influentially luminous in unforgettable parts of the globe at various times when there was far less communication. Eras that had historically dominated, which she had brilliantly perceived were not being usefully appreciated, not applied. Not enough. Hers was a far-reaching cranky quest that as this article on China left on the plane was proving, studies like hers were profoundly needed. And with this quest of hers, wouldn't I also find out more of what had been so distressingly 'missing' during one's career in international conflicts?*

Studying her, she was uttering that *all* golden ages were tremendously valuable. As I watched her '*working*', watched this most extraordinary woman's continuing thoughts reflecting in her slightest of facial movements, while—she was still rubbing till obscurely a non sequitur—one's vivid image *of a crossing I'd made of the Aegean;* when from the boat's rail I'd been studying Mount Vesuvius rumbling into an eruption, and just like that magnificent Italian volcano, my most brilliant lover was also being stoked by so much that she knew was to be found in other great historic events. In her case, the outward flexing and fluctuating of her beautiful features were so subtly enlivened by her sorting thoughts or her affirmations being, re-considered? Each inconstancy minutely displaying till I reacted. "My darling, I won't pretend I'm not thrilled! It's going to be laborious for us but, I'll be working with you my most tuneful of warbling birds, with the bonus for me being—I'll at last be—truly getting at what has *been missing!*"

But my observations slowed.

Because I was also seeing how deeply and quickly I had entangled with this Runditz witch that had caused my own coveted independence to slide away from me. Recalling how fiercely my retirement plan had been to let go of everything to do with foreign affairs and diplomacy and shove them behind me forever! But more deeply conscientiously, this must not have been what I'd wanted!! Then this jolting article on Ancient China on the returning plane that proved that there was far more to know if I was to help Laburnum and articulate what had been so soundly *missing* during my career! This became devilishly lucid to me now as I saw just how much Laburnum's researching, gathering, and luring with her quest had grabbed at all that had once been deeply and compassionately meaningful within myself, and I'd become more desperate to unobtrusively do all I could to help this woman's wonder-quest! Not having completed a half year of retirement, I could easily use my old contacts should one need to, and this working with Laburnum would mean that in with the grape-growing, with my more worldly usefulness operating again, wouldn't I enliven my attributes again!!

Looking harder at my dearest Laburnum in the semi-dark, I asked, "Laburnum, once you've the Egyptian chapter refined, would you read it me?"

"Think very hard, liebermaus; seriously, for a moment—are you really and truly *sure*?"

"*Su-re?*" My choked laugh! "Though we'll both have to think carefully about every aspect of working together, because we're not *always* harmonious—or *you* aren't!" She threw her messed serviette at me.

"All right," I said catching it before it landed on my fine cravat, as I said. "Though it's *your* deep personal involvement, this tremendous quest of *yours* that's had you in its grip for months."

"Years."

"Right. Your research is never ending—it's your *magnum opus*."

"It is, yes. But I haven't kept it to myself for any vain reason. Rather, until you came there hadn't been anyone around here with a 'golden ages' interest, who could have seen what I was after. Naturally, if you can be free enough with your knowledge and traveling, then your expertise would be most valuable! Though I'd want a heavy hand in what we're to make of it all, but…"

"It's to be understood between us that you would do all the directing! Though you'd need to be aware of the times of the year the winery…"

"*Needs you?* Not a problem. I'd heartily welcome some good shake-ups to our eventual manuscript! We'll constantly reassess until everything about it completely suits, as this has been what keeps me awake nights."

"Part-time, it will have to be for me. And when we get going, even these might be more of me than you'll want?"

Laburnum's expression lightened as she laughed, though she didn't reply. Then darting into that sudden quickness of hers, she muttered away enthusiastically, while slumping in her chair, her tawny unselfconscious good-looks staring back at me. "Listen to us planning, Algernon. Isn't it hard not to be excited? You'll be using your foreign affairs again, your hands-on traveling? And with all that we agree is so ragingly fundamental, you'll have to get into my studies straightaway and with both feet."

"With your permission, that's exactly what I'd most like to do," and as our waiter came over, "Laburnum, my dear, would you care for dessert?" Laburnum shook her head, and instead the waiter and I settled up. Turning to her, "Should we get on our way, my darling?"

Helping Laburnum on with her jacket, we said goodnight to our waiter as he solicitously begged us to come again and ask for 'Sean', and we left the restaurant without further theatrics.

Pleased with our inspiring evening, we sat close in the Lamborghini as I drove languorously, not wanting our impressive dinner to end. "We'd better get Paycock in on our plans, beloved, before he gets miffed."

"He'll understand and be helpful."

"An evening to remember, my sweet-smelling inamorata! Ha, did you notice back there, it said that an 'overview' is coming up? Laburnum, I'm going to pull over. We'll see if that moon is come out." As she agreed, I pulled in with the car lights hitting a rustic fence and turned off the engine and lights—just as clouds moved one cloud after another to let a half-moon through that was especially bright. "What do you think? Does that moon have meaning?"

"There are to be clear bright days ahead for us?"

"Which we'll need," putting an arm around my hard-won enchantress, I turned her, "Look down this way, beloved, those lights—are *they not* Us?"

"The larger light is in front of my apartment, and the next is the production center. Yours diffuses behind that big beech tree." She snuggled against me, "Algernon, you are pleased with all this planning?"

"More than you are, probably! It's a wonderful way of thoroughly knowing. Well, more than we'll want to know of one another probably, while digging away at it all."

"Will you really be pleased?" Listening to Laburnum's reiterated question. "Look, dammit Algernon, you must have some idea what had been so impressively '*missing*' throughout your vocation?"

As I was seeing more of all that was actually happening to me, I had to laugh to myself, realizing that I had not only learned what more I needed to do besides get 'provincial' dirt under my fingernails, but with my beloved liebekinder, I was about to articulate what that increasing wrongness had been that had plagued me throughout my career. For the first time ever to anyone! With my lover's aptitude for pulling all we studied into an order, and as we were to do it within the mysterious auspices of the Supreme Habitat, all lit up down there, this brilliant woman nestling my arms would surely be a nymph sent down to me from some unexplored celestial orb!

Chapter 25
Epilogue

"Listen to me Algernon, you pisser," Laburnum cringed forward into the moonlight to speak more emphatically—her arms sliding from me, "Have you any idea what this missing is you keep talking about?"

In the clear half-moon's light, this 'pisser' got a start on my most major question. "I wondered if you'd ever ask!" Though I was pleased she had as I lounged back from Lamborghini's steering wheel, "Okay, so far, what is 'missing?' Though… *Warning, danger!* Prepare to bear with me Laburnum because you'll likely find it too 'poetic'." I'd expected her objecting, "Okay, okay, I'm starting!" Having got through to me, she slumped down again, letting her head rest on my shoulder. "Look, Laburnum, I'm saying it like this because what's missing comes at me in… in 'indecipherable colors'." Knowing she'd be frowning, I tempered, "That's the only way to describe it, my gorgeous woman, it's the way it's always been—and I'll tell you why. That first time I returned from England from financing the Runditz estate. Yes, after you'd intimately got to know my spectacles."

"For foretelling your arrival?"

"Yes, though do let me get on with it. Coming back through Toronto, I visited my colleague, Thadd. But all Thadd wanted to talk about was an ambassador's current effort… and, *Oh God, Laburnum!* On and on he went as if I wasn't understanding! *Till I just couldn't bear listening to him!* He sat there so smugly assured, just banging out all the usual reiterations we'd learned in our first year of diplomatic training. No turning them about to fit another country's situation, no attempt to understand an opposing country's perspectives. No far-reaching overall picture, just the traditional old formula because it had been decided that this was best for the west! So, that's what had to be! *I'm telling you I got really sick of hearing this, and think?* How could any foreign representative coming to us in dire need of stopping his country's damaging conflict, how could he drum up even the foggiest interest in what he was being told? What Thadd, my diplomat colleague, was saying was so loaded with offending ultimatums that they'd better damn well get along with the west! Laburnum, it was… Just do what we're telling you to do, we'll make it worth your while. Nothing else! Not a scrap of what could have objectively or practically cooled their raging conflict!"

"God!"

"Exactly, Laburnum-! Dear Lord, great chunks of what could have been sensibly offered, for helping were so obviously *missing!* It was hard to believe that the Foreign Service hadn't officially scrapped this obsolete kind of 'negotiating' a generation ago! And although I didn't know exactly what I knew to be *'missing' then, I see now that it was also the proportion of it that distressed."*

"The *'proportion?'* Then you knew?"

Levering my arm around her more comfortably. "Yes. Speaking as the retired Foreign Diplomat that of course I really am, I can tell you – If you'll let me, that yes, I had ideas about what was missing!" Pausing to realign one's back, to myself I saw that I was about to have this rarest of opportunities *to at last tell about my professionally prolonged diplomatic stranglehold, to my dearest Laburnum.* Which could give me a further understanding of what had so often outraged me throughout my overseas years. "So, all right—as you say, *what's missing then?* To begin with, if you're about to help out countries with injurious conflicts, forget the old definition of 'objectivity' because there's a need for some scrupulous change to its definition. Replace it by giving them the freedom to express all their complaints in absolute freedom! They should never need to worry about what will please the west, that Thadd so persistently and stalwartly insisted on, because there'll no longer be a western stance. Not threateningly, and not covertly, and nothing's to be set in cement. Thadd and I would have to generate a much different type of strength for keeping our own opinions or desires removed from all negotiating. That's what we'd represent. We'd have to develop the courage to not give favors or extras to one side, whatever intriguing bargains they pull from their pockets." Looking down at my most beautiful lover again in her soft moonlight glow, "...and yes, my darling if you're going to say that this could make diplomats like me nothing more than super-arbitrators, you'd be exactly right! We'd only be intent on extracting honest complaints from these opponents, getting their direst honesty for what was causing their collisions, riots, and worse. First by encouraging one side to tell all, then, and with just as much probing curiosity and concern, fully hearing out the other side. If they wanted, we'd toss a coin for who goes first? To be model arbitrators, we'd come to the table having cast out our own archaic opinions, which is a damn big job because there'll be endless twistings and proddings for our former 'understanding', but our newly trained immovability to only get at their direst and most honest complaints must never cave in or be taken advantage of." As I'd kept on explaining this, Laburnum had managed a bare nod or two. "The heavy work would be keeping each opponent digging out *only* their own *honesty* till they're convinced that with our arbitrating completely unbiased that they will reap improvements."

"You'd only be digging deeply into what each opponent's most desperate needs are?"

"Augh! *Damn it, you fiend!"* I exploded at Laburnum's interruption as my head swayed unbelievably. *One's emergency self-discipline, then Algernon?* "Listen, my love, I'd just got this whole thing going! All right. Then. Now hear me out, Laburnum, I'll raise my hand like this to remind you—*No interrupting."* Though my hand got stopped by Lamborghini's ceiling as my annoying lover smothered her laughter.

"Look, my dearest woman. Think of this, with the west out of the bargaining, there would soon be a new basic common communication between opposing foreign leaders, and our sole job would be to spoon-feed these into this direct purer new language."

"A-a-ah, Algernon! But just as anything is once it's become routine, inevitably it will bog down—then you'd have to fall back on heavy-handedness again—threats?"

"It won't all be easy, right. Surreptitious bargaining will inevitably sprout."

"Algernon, as arbitrators in such an unfamiliar system, would your job still be considered 'diplomacy'?"

My partially raised hand waved at her. "Oh Lord, give me a moment to just think, Laburnum!"

"All right, I'll shut up till you're through then. Go ahead, you excessively rude man."

"All right. Very well. You know that traditional diplomacy has always been heavily PR, wagtail. What's been *missing* were good-sized doses of patient diplomatic altruism for encouraging the opponents to truly dig out the guts of their conflict. It'll take lots of space. You know that the west is perceived to have infinitely armed strengths and resources, not to mention our fiercely applying them for our own interests. But with that great new strength of ours staying quietly obdurate, we'd be in a global position to afford generosity foreign policy-wise. We'd help with their dire complaints, by peaceably shuttling them back and forth for as long as it takes."

Laburnum turned and stared at me before expounding! "You are indefatigable, Algernon!! And l*ook, for God's sake, put that crapping hand DOWN!* Okay, now listening to what you've discovered about your *missing 'indecipherable colors'*—not so '*indecipherable'* by the way. All right, arbitrators like you would need to relinquish *every*thing from the past! All your training and experience. It would be re-training and no holding back! But you know very well that there would be powerful groups just waiting with enormously prepared means to block anything that even smells of losing western control?"

My nod was forceful. "It will appear that way, yes. And any innovation like this won't sound appealing to aspiring young diplomats either."

"For simply becoming a cog in this new ultra-redefined machinery? Though I agree it would be an extraordinary opportunity for improving humanitarianism?" Sitting straighter, Laburnum adjusted to her more mocking voice, "*Arbitrating? S*olely to bring peace between warring segments or countries?! Keeping a 'hands-off reputation?' Huh! Well, you're right—getting in on how appealing would that be! Though, Algernon, surely during all your career you must have done some of that?"

"But how could it ever lead to being official when the aims are anchored in immovable patriotic commitments, Laburnum? Whatever we did would be non-effective, and the conflict would continue or worsen."

"Then as you say it will have to be drastically dug at, my dearest, because formalizing it as a basis, we'll both need to do much heavier research. In fact, I have some of that already started. And we'd better remember that much of what we're finding out will be disrupting former holy fundaments. Listen, Algernon, you'd better get into what I'm discovering in my quest straightaway. Right now in fact, and with both feet. Because you need to realize that that's how it will be with anything we do in our studying?"

Lengthily I breathed out as we turned to each take a protracted look at one another. We were each wide open with all we'd got going! I saw this before my words came out to her, softly, and in immense relief as I said, "Thank you, Laburnum."

Having Laburnum's contented partnership, I'd felt some newer airing to my 'overly enriched mind!' *Her term.* Perhaps in retirement, *one was really learning what one truly needed besides 'provincial' dirt under one's finger nails?*

What an evening!

To my most beloved of women, *I had actually articulated what for me had been an epic missing wrongfulness, that had constantly pained me that so little that could be done when there was such massively grotesque suffering.* My attempt to convey it to my beloved Laburnum tonight had been a first. Now with my brilliant lover getting order to my sprawled thoughts, and also pulling at them, she and I would not only be activated into what humanitarianism could more authentically be, but personally I would be back into my more natural 'non-provincial' worldliness! While keeping abreast of the grape growing! All this had been from within the mysterious auspices of my Supreme Habitat, all lit up down there! Which made me wonder if this loving woman nestling my arms wasn't a nymph sent down to me by that celestial place! Though her sudden vehement kiss made me know more!

"Getting into it all with both feet! Yes, with your permission that's precisely what I want to do most, golubchik, which—even as we've said—could be an overriding relationship's test! We'll each have to develop mountains of patience." And as I eyed her, "Or working with a Libra Interruptus, I'll certainly have to." She kissed what must have been my moonlit twisted smile.

"We'll take notes on what works," her reply's soundness came over differently responsible. "As I'm the one having to accept all this. Let's get this straight, there'll be *no* juvenile rules—like waving your hand to speak."

"Then advise me, my pragmatic partner, how am I to complete some glittering new thought if you will keep changing it?"

"Talking of real thought only now? Not some critique of my table manners?"

"Talking of an exchange forum for the leaders of brutal conflicts—the way Jimmy and Roslyn Carter do at their center. Removing our own national, international, and personal interests so that arbitrators' strengths can keep developing once they get the feel of this new structuring."

"What a bone-headed realist you really are, Algernon!" Laburnum said, "Okay—*warning!* Isn't that how we do it now? Because I'm going to interrupt *you*!"

"Mon Dieu."

"Listen, you need to know this, and it is *my turn.* I badly need to tell you this! At this moment, I'm getting strong images of what I'd seen earlier today that was very significant! You'd better be listening? This was this afternoon when I'd been talking to Mel before going in to bathe."

"All right, what in hell's name? Please note that my hand is down."

"Algernon, all you've told me. You've got it so beautifully thought out, it's almost mystical, I'll admit. But look, and you'll see that what I've seen is important too if you truly think about it!"

"Go on, you moonstruck witch."

"Okay. Talking to Mel about taking over the dogs tonight, we were standing at the foot of his apartment's stairs. Mel had come back from tracking up in the woods with his gun. Taking off his jacket, he checked that his Winchester was unloaded and stood it against the stair wall."

"Yes?"

"…and Bruno and Paycock being intrigued with what we were saying—you know how they have been lately? Okay, you remember that bushel basket of apples Reb brought us? He'd left them on his stairs for Mel and me? Well, wanting our attention Paycock clumsily knocked Mel's gun over. Instantly Bruno jumped up on the stairs and knocked over that basket of apples so the apples covered Mel's gun. *Algernon, I just can't forget that image!* Do you believe it was coincidental?"

"Apples?! Covering the gun?"

Slowly this image did hit me as it had hit Laburnum, and she said. "Yes, fruit smothering his gun."

"You mean Paycock knocked over Mel's gun, then Bruno covered the gun with apples from that basket, Laburnum?? Hmm! Were they up to more of that closed-eyed funny business?"

"No, both dogs just stood there pleased with themselves, wagging their tails."

"You're thinking *fruit over guns?*"

"Our problem might be, is that what the *dogs* were thinking?"

"Hmm, I'd better be with you when you have this planned good talk with Paycock, my amorist, with Bruno too."

"Yes, my collaborative consort, I think you had better be with me."

THE END

CPSIA information can be obtained
at www.ICGtesting.com
Printed in the USA
BVHW041825180220
572705BV00006B/80

9 781788 785693